I0699290

WHAT YOU WILL

The SEEDER Series

HOWARD LIBES

HAPPY MISTAKE PUBLISHING
Eugene, Oregon

Happy Mistake Publishing
PO Box 42197
Eugene, OR 97404
www.howardlibes.com

LCCN: 2024913973
ISBN: 979-8-218-45574-3

Living is easy with eyes closed
Misunderstanding all you see

"Strawberry Fields Forever"
John Lennon & Paul McCartney

MADO

Before stepping across the threshold into the alien spacecraft, Mado stopped and peered inside, but he only saw darkness. He was having second thoughts about coming here.

A voice inside Mado's head said in Prevorian, "Please come inside, Mado of Prevor."

Mado was surprised to hear this voice speaking his own language inside his mind.

"Would you rather we converse in Kodan?" the voice said.

Mado thought, "Are you reading my mind?"

"Yes, that's one way of defining how we communicate. Please come in."

Mado glanced over his shoulder at the outpost and the WAEF parked beside it.

"No harm will come to Yor Vanderlord or the spaceship."

"If you know Prevorian, why not broadcast it over your speaker system?"

"You're an intelligent creature. You already know the answer."

Mado chuckled. He had to be in close proximity for them to communicate in a language familiar to him, he thought.

"Correct," the voice said. "Please enter. We will do you no harm."

Mado stepped across the threshold and a door slid closed behind him from the ceiling to the floor. There was absolutely no light in the room. He could see nothing. He thought about turning on his helmet's lights, then a dim glow materialized over his head. He couldn't locate a source.

The room was circular.

A small rectangle appeared on the curved wall, displaying a poor-quality vid. Mado walked closer and realized that he was looking at the slope of the crater on B-452 where he and Yorlik had discovered the alien spacecraft. The scene kept cutting out to static and back in again. This place had been in Mado's thoughts ever since Yor told him about observing the aliens during his spacewalk.

In the vid, two figures in spacesuits descended the slope. It was Yorlik and himself.

Mado chuckled.

"Yes, you were correct," the voice said. "This moment was captured by a device on the outside of the craft."

The rectangle disappeared and the entire room became an immersive holographic reenactment of himself and Yorlik in their spacesuits at the bottom of the crater. Mado was shocked by the realism. It was as if he was standing on B-452. He kicked at the surface and dirt flew forward in concert with the planetoid's gravity.

The two figures approached until they were standing on either side of him. They were talking. Mado couldn't hear them, but he recalled the conversation. He had been hesitant to go any further. Yorlik was excited to forge ahead. The sight of Yorlik alive made him emotional.

"Your tech is impressive," Mado thought. "But is there a point to all this?"

"Patience."

The holographic image of the planet's surface changed in a blink of an eye to a scene inside the spacecraft where Yorlik and Mado were observing the dead aliens at the helm.

"This is a revered moment in the history of our people," the voice said. "It altered our view of life in the universe. We debated for centuries about whether other life-forms were worthy of contact, considering how they treat others. Your act of leaving the bodies undisturbed and Yorlik Vanderlord's emotional reaction at the loss of life changed our outlook, giving our species purpose."

"That's why you hailed me to your craft?"

"Yes, and that's why we've been watching you and the Kodan people."

"The Kodan people?"

"Yes, we've been watching from afar. We have our reservations about them, but we are intrigued by why a Prevorian would be inclined to care about them."

There was a flash of light and Mado was standing on a Prevorian beach. The ocean was washing up on the shore. In contrast to the silence of the previous hologram, Mado could hear each wave crashing on the sand, then drawing back with a hiss for another to follow. He could hear the flying sea creatures squawking overhead and even smell the salty ocean air. Memories flooded his mind, of evening meals around the table with his parents as a child, of swimming in the ocean, of his coming-of-age ritual surrounded by his entire clan—mother, father, siblings, aunts, uncles, cousins, grandparents, great-grandparents, great-great grandparents—at the deepest trench on the planet.

The voice said, "For all intents and purposes, you're on Prevor now."

"How is that possible?" Mado thought.

"You will understand this science in the near future, but please satisfy our curiosity now. Why do you care so much about the Kodan people? They're not of your kind and their worthiness is questionable," the voice said. "We are all listening."

"Who are 'we'?"

"We are we."

"We are we?"

"We are individuals of the same planet and the same race, and we are of one consciousness."

Mado thought, "If you're in my mind, then you know why I dedicated myself to the Kodan people."

"Although we are surfing your conscious mind, we're not allowed to access another's deepest thoughts, emotions, or memories, unless you release them yourself."

"Seems arbitrary," Mado thought reflexively, then wished he'd practiced more self-control.

"Many of us believe as you do, but the rule has been in place for as long as we have possessed this ability."

Mado said out loud in Prevorian, "I'm going to speak now. This is getting weird for me."

"Whatever makes you comfortable," said the voice inside Mado's head. "You are our honored guest."

"That's good to know," Mado said. "The answer is simple. I believe in the sanctity of life. I shared this value with Yorlik Vanderlord. I find it ironic that you should place me on Prevor, because this philosophy is one of the foundations of Prevorian civilization."

"That is debatable given our knowledge of Prevorian history, and your Protectorate would not look kindly on you helping the Kodans by sharing your tech. It is against their code."

"That may be so, but they've never been in my position and met someone like Yorlik."

"The value you shared with Yorlik doesn't appear to be prevalent among Kodans. Yorlik was atypical in that way."

"I can't argue that fact, but why would Prevorian code or Kodan ethical standards stop Yorlik and myself from preserving life, respecting life? One hopes a species might be led in the right direction by example and evolve. All species should be afforded that opportunity. They should be given the benefit of the doubt."

"Is that why you did not disturb our life-forms in that craft?"

"One of the reasons."

All at once, a multitude of voices inside Mado's head erupted in simultaneous rapid-fire conversations, speaking over one another. Mado focused to isolate individual voices and noted that they were express-ing themselves in something similar to an ancient Prevorian dialect. He thought this might be in defer-ence to him. Some of the voices believed what he'd said. Others were skeptical of his intentions. They debated whether to move forward with the reason they'd exposed themselves to him, why they'd risked bringing him onboard. This continued for an indeterminate amount of time, then all at once, like a switch was thrown, the discussion stopped and there was silence. Mado's head hurt.

He waited for a voice to engage him, then called out, "Anyone there?"

The original voice in his head said, "Yes, and we apologize if we caused any discomfort."

"You want to tell me what that was about?"

"We can show you what we've decided."

The Prevorian landscape faded away and the room was plunged into darkness. Mado felt a sense of loss. In all his years on Koda, focused on saving the humanoids there, he had forgotten on an emotional level how much he missed his home.

Suddenly, a part of the wall in front of him became a window into outer space like the one in the WAEF's control room. The spacecraft appeared to be approaching a planet. Mado recognized it as the habitable world that Yorlik discovered.

Mado said, "Is that...?"

"It is," said the voice in his head.

"A projection?"

"No, we've just arrived."

"Why have you brought me here? For that matter, how did we get here so quickly?"

"We will show you the answer to the first question. The second is beyond your comprehension."

Mado didn't appreciate the condescension although he was amazed that this spacecraft had traversed the distance from Koda's solar system to the habitable planet in what felt like a few moments. He hadn't felt any acceleration or physical effects from whatever means of propulsion they were utilizing, and the journey would've taken the WAEF over twenty-five years at close to light-speed.

The voice said, "Sorry to rankle your self-esteem. Ego is an interesting quality in the under-evolved. We do have great admiration for your people's scientific achievements—limited though they may be—and how you applied them to save the Kodan people from disaster."

"Thank you, I think," Mado said. "I'm curious. Where I come from, it's rude to communicate with someone from another room, especially a complete stranger."

"In this case, you are communicating with a collective of minds, so we cannot all be there physically. We've also evolved to a point where our physical beings are sensitive to unknown viruses, so we shy away from interacting with outsiders."

"Sure, that makes sense," Mado said. "So why are we here?"

While they'd been chatting, the craft had moved closer to the planet until the blue orb filled the window.

"Keep your eyes on the screen. You will experience dizziness and a sensation of discomfort."

The clouds over the planet had been moving at a normal pace, but now they began to accelerate in one direction until they were a blur, as if an unseen force was causing the planet to spin on its axis at an extraordinary velocity. Mado felt woozy. When the planet's spin slowed to normal, Mado's legs were rubbery. There was nothing in sight to prop himself up with and keep him from falling, but thankfully, he regained his equilibrium before that happened.

"That was interesting," Mado said, then took a long look at the planet. It reminded him of Koda before he and Yor left. The continents had shrunk, overtaken by the oceans. He also noted dozens and dozens of satellites. On the dark side, except for small spots of light, the planet was pitch-black. "What am I looking at?"

"This is the planet in the future, approximately three thousand Kodan years. The Kodan people settled here—that part of your plan worked—then they gradually destroyed it like they did Koda. At this point in time, they are a species on the brink of extinction."

"How is that possible?"

"They never learned from their mistakes. They never followed your example."

"I meant, how am I seeing the planet's future and why should I believe you?"

"In the simplest terms that you'll be able to understand—and again, no disrespect—"

"Of course."

"We have found a way to use technology to view the future through a dimensional shift. You are still in your time of existence."

"So we're not physically in the future?"

"Our minds are in the future. Our bodies are in the past."

"But I can see my body." Mado attempted to touch his arm, but his hand passed through it, then through his torso. "Oh—so my mind is separated from my body?"

"Yes—in a sense, the body you see is an illusion created by your mind."

"So I'm seeing this planet? It's real? It isn't just a depiction of what might happen?"

"Correct."

"I'm still skeptical."

"We thought you'd need convincing," the voice said. "First, you must understand this is all history for us."

"History? So you're communicating from the future?"

"Yes and no. We exist in the present, but we have knowledge from our future selves of events that haven't yet occurred in your time."

"So you've culled your technology from the future. That's why it's so advanced."

"Advanced? That's all relative, isn't it? The easiest way to explain our technological leap from what you saw on what you call 'B-452' is that it's partially due to our communication with the future."

"That does answer a few of my other questions," Mado said. "So what I'm perceiving is something one of your spacecraft in the future is seeing, or has seen, or will see?"

"Yes, that explains it within your range of comprehension, but we understand you still need more evidence," the voice said. "We imagine that your most vivid memory of this planet is the oceans filled with life."

The craft accelerated toward the planet, entered the atmosphere, and broke through cloud cover. It headed for the ocean below and rapidly decelerated before diving into the water. On the WAEF, Mado would have been strapped into the control-room chair to prevent him from being thrown about the room. Here, he was standing the entire time and didn't feel any effects of the maneuvers.

The craft descended into the ocean's depths, leveled off, and moved forward.

The voice said, "You can see for yourself."

The ocean was lifeless. When he and Yorlik had explored here, the water was teeming with aquatic creatures in symbiotic coexistence, and the plant life on the ocean floor was luxuriant. Sadness washed over Mado. He thought again of how much he missed Prevor.

"Do not despair. You will be home soon."

The wall went blank and Mado felt woozy once again. When he regained some semblance of balance, he reached with his hand to pat his arm and this time, he struck himself.

The voice said, "After frequent encounters with the dimensional shift, it gets easier. You're back in your own time now."

A portion of the room's curved wall faded and six aliens stood before him. They were unclothed with smooth grey skin. No genitalia. Their faces appeared just as Mado recalled from the spacecraft on B-452. One of the aliens stepped forward.

The voice said, "To foster trust, this is the captain of the spacecraft and part of his crew. An energy field separates them from you for viral protection."

"I appreciate the gesture," Mado said. "So I guess you know my next question."

"Why are we showing you this now?"

"Yes, it kind of feels like you're rubbing my face in my failure."

"We've revealed the truth about the outcome of your work on Koda as a token of gratitude for honoring our sacred site and gifting our existences with new meaning," the voice said. "Since you're returning to Prevor."

Mado sighed. That was his plan, but maybe he could still do something to save the Kodans.

"And no," the voice said. "Our consensus is that nothing can be done to prevent the future from unfolding the way you've seen. It has been written. It is inevitable."

"I can't believe that."

"Yes, we know."

A doorway opened behind him.

The voice said, "We have returned you to the time and place you came aboard."

Mado approached the aliens. One of them stepped forward while the rest retreated, disappearing behind the missing portion of the room's curved wall, which rematerialized in front of them. The lone alien was a meter shorter than Mado.

"So that's it?" Mado said to the alien. "I know you've revealed all this in good faith, but it's depressing news."

"There is a theory among a minority of our people based on ancient texts." The alien's mouth never moved, but Mado somehow knew that it was this alien alone expressing itself now. "They say the future is malleable and can be altered by behaving differently in the past. The text says, 'The future is yours. Make of it what you will.'"

TWENTY-TWO YEARS LATER...

ORN

"What are *you* doing here?" Flomina said, approaching Orn with a look of disgust on her face.

Orn was walking down the hallway of the Plemso estate's guest wing. Over the years, he hadn't spent much time here and now he'd slowed his pace to gaze at the paintings by Koda's greatest artists hung on the walls. The few people who knew him would be surprised by his admiration for such things. In the days when the Global Assembly forces controlled Nor and he was under Major Plemso's command, he would steal the keys to the regional art gallery from the major's desk, slip into a soldier's uniform, and spend hours roaming the museum by himself, immersed in the beauty captured on canvas.

In the mansion's hallway, he was shocked when he came across a Rostham landscape. He stopped to study the depiction of the coastal Norian mountain range where he grew up. Orn was struck with nostalgia for his carefree youth, meandering those forests and hills.

Flomina halted a few meters away. "You know you're not welcome here."

As she aged, Flomina never lost her looks. She had access to the planet's finest plastic surgeons and never needed them.

"The Leader requested me," Orn said. "He ordered me to come to his bedroom."

"I find that hard to believe."

"You know I haven't been here for years."

"Because I forbade it."

"Then why would I be here now unless I'd been invited?"

"Don't patronize me, you lowlife." Flomina pushed past Orn, entered the Leader's room, and left the door open. Orn stood at the threshold as Flomina approached the Leader's bed, turning on the nightstand light.

The Leader's trophy room had been converted into a place for his convalescence. All along the walls were plaques, medals, and commendations for his military service. There were fotos from the three occasions when Vidor Plemso had been sworn in as President. There was the framed flag from the final battle of the Separatist Revolts. A display case held athletic trophies and medals from secondary school and military college, and fotos of Vidor running obstacle courses as a young man.

Flomina pointed at Orn and said to the Leader, "Did you invite him here?"

"Uh…" the Leader said and stared blankly at Orn. It was clear he couldn't recall, then he glared at Flomina. "Did he say I invited him?

"He did."

"Then that's why he's here," the Leader said, sounding annoyed and more like himself as he struggled to push pillows behind his back and work to a sitting position. Flomina tried to help, but the Leader shunned her assistance, then continued to falter in his task.

Orn was appalled to see the Leader of Koda having difficulty with something a child could do, but he pushed those feelings aside. Even if Vidor Plemso was now beaten down by time, he was the man who had helped him out of the gutter and he still respected him.

Finally, fed up with his performance, the Leader peered over at Orn and said, "There's something wrong with these damn pillows. For Powers-That-Be sake, don't just stand there gawking like an idiot. Get over here and lend me a hand."

Orn began to walk toward the bed, but Flomina put her hand up for him to stop.

"I'll take care of it," she said, then organized the pillows behind the Leader and settled him into a sitting position. "I'll leave you two to whatever you need to discuss, then I want him out of my house."

"Need I remind you that this is my house, too?" the Leader said and sighed. "But yes, I'll have Davik escort him out when we're done with our business."

Flomina looked over at Orn forlornly. Davik had passed away years ago and had stopped working for the Leader more than a decade earlier.

"All right, darling," Flomina said, kissing the Leader on the cheek. "You have a nice meeting."

"Why wouldn't we?" the Leader said.

As Flomina passed Orn, she said, "Don't wear him out," then left the room.

The Leader said, "How are you, son?" He had never addressed Orn that way before. "Everything all right with you and Roneh?"

Orn realized the Leader thought he was Carz who was married to Roneh Rayush. He was even more surprised because Carz was at least thirty years younger than him. He didn't know how to respond without insulting the Leader.

Orn said, "Yes, sir. I'm fine, sir."

"Don't stand all the way over there," the Leader said with annoyance in his voice. "Get over here."

As Orn approached the bed, he noticed how frail and thin the Leader had become.

"Now, why are you here?"

"I don't know," Orn said. "Your Chief of Affairs said you requested me."

"That imbecile Davik. I should have sacked him long ago."

Minok, the Leader's son, had succeeded Davik as Chief of Affairs. Orn said, "Was Minok mistaken?"

"Minok…Right…No, I have an important assignment for you. I wanted…" the Leader said, then fell silent. He couldn't remember why he'd summoned anybody here and was searching for a reason. "Yes. Yes, I wanted to talk to you about Yorlik Vanderlord."

"What about him, sir?"

"You need to keep an eye on him. Maybe have the GSS call him in for questioning."

Orn knew better than to contradict this command that had no basis in reality. "Yes, of course. Anything else, sir?"

"Anything else? Isn't that enough? I gave you an order."

"Yes, sir. I just assumed there was more since you summoned me here. You could just have commed me."

"I'm the Leader, aren't I?"

"Yes, sir."

"You have something more important to do?"

"Absolutely not, sir."

"Then you're dismissed."

Orn reflexively saluted and turned on his heels before marching toward the door.

"Orn?" the Leader said.

Orn halted and returned to the Leader's bedside. He immediately noted a lucidity in the Leader's eyes that was missing before.

"Orn?"

"Yes, sir."

"It is you. This ailment is horrific. One moment I can recall every officer under my command during the Revolts and the next I don't recognize who is standing right in front of me," the Leader said with despair, then he gazed off into the corner of the room for a few moments before looking back at Orn. The lucidity in his eyes was gone. "Why are you here? You're dismissed…soldier."

Orn saluted, then marched toward the door. Before he exited the room, he looked behind him. The Leader was sliding down from his seated position until he was lying on his back, then pulled the covers up to his chin. He reminded Orn of a scared child.

Orn closed the door halfway and when he turned around in the hallway, Flomina was leaning against the opposite wall, waiting for him. She said, "He isn't well."

"No, he isn't. Reminds me of my mother. She had Rejuvium, and in the final years she had the same sort of dementia. It's not pretty."

"The med says there's nothing we can do and this could go on for years. Eventually, he won't remember any of us."

"Unfortunately, it's true," Orn said, thinking this was their longest conversation in decades. "Yes, well—"

"I don't think he's happy," Flomina said and sighed. "Maybe you can come back soon and pay him another visit. Put him out of his misery. If you know what I mean."

"I understand," Orn said. "I'll take care of it."

Flomina's eyes welled with tears.

Although it had happened so many years ago with his mother, Orn knew what Flomina was feeling. *Time only dulls these moments around the edges*, Orn thought. *She'll never truly get rid of the sadness.* Then he was repulsed by his empathy. He found it disheartening, but he was becoming sentimental as he got older. "Just make sure security is out of the way tomorrow night."

Orn turned from Flomina and headed down the hallway. He didn't even notice the paintings now. Flomina was correct. It was time to put the Leader out of his misery, and he scolded himself for not thinking of it sooner. At the moment, there was nobody at the helm of the Global Assembly, so it was his duty to end Vidor Plemso's rule for the next Leader to take power. He wouldn't be doing a favor for Flomina. His loyalty to the Global Assembly compelled him to act. As he headed downstairs, he began plotting how he would handle this assignment.

ORN RETURNED THE NEXT DAY. HE WALKED DOWN the hall illuminating his path with a flashlight. The only resident in this wing was the Leader so Orn wasn't worried about disturbing anyone out of their sleep. The surveillance cams inside the house had been disabled and the guards for the wing were gone. Orn didn't know how Flomina pulled it off, but he had learned long ago not to underestimate her.

When he reached the Leader's room, he turned off and pocketed the flashlight, then slid the door open, entered, and closed the door leaving it slightly ajar. He hadn't noticed yesterday, but now he was immediately struck by the scent of medicated lotions and cleanser. The odors took him back to the days spent caring for his mother. He imagined if he turned on the overhead light he would be transported to the Norian cabin where he had tended her day and night. He took a deep breath and stood still. He waited for his eyes to adjust to the low light leaking beneath the window shades from the estate's compound and the energy shield's glow.

"Who's there?" the Leader said. "Flomina?"

"No, it's Orn," he said and approached the bed. "I've got something for you to sign."

"It's late. Can't it wait until tomorrow?"

"No," Orn said, removing a digi-tablet from inside his coat and placing it along with a digi-pen on the bed beside the prone Leader.

"I need light," the Leader said, squinting up at Orn as he attempted to prop himself up on an elbow.

"It'll be fine." Orn handed the pen to the Leader and placed the point on the signature line. "Just sign on the bottom line."

The Leader took hold of the digi-pen and signed. "Can I sleep now?"

"Very soon." Orn picked up the tablet, then removed the power source from the intercom on the nightstand and turned on the light.

The Leader shielded his eyes as they adjusted to the sudden glare, then said, "Orn, what's the meaning of this?"

"I came to say farewell."

"Farewell? Where are you going?"

"I'm not going anywhere."

"Then what on Koda are you talking about?"

"I'm here to help you abdicate your position." Orn immediately saw the comprehension of what was about to happen in the Leader's eyes.

"You ingrate," the Leader said. "Who were you before you met me? You were nothing. You were less than nothing when they dragged you into my tent with that damn bloody brick."

"That's true. You gave me a life—"

"I could have ended you right then and there, and who would've cared, who would've missed your vile soul, who would've known the difference?"

"That's the irony of the current situation."

"You think so?"

"I know so."

"You're deluded. Do you forget who I am?" Vidor said. "I'm the Leader, dammit. Leave here now and I'll just have you shipped off to a lookout post in the Mlimoan mountains instead of executing you."

The Leader attempted to sit up and push the pillows behind himself for leverage, but he failed again and again, each time sliding down into a prone position.

"If this all wasn't so sad, I would laugh," Orn said. "You're pathetic."

The Leader looked up at Orn with outrage in his eyes and said, "How dare you speak to me in such an insolent manner!"

"I'll speak to you however I damn well please. For years, I put up with you belittling my ideas even when you knew I was right, and now you'll listen to me," Orn said. "You're just a husk of a man. You can't even recognize a person standing right in front of you who you've known for fifty years. You're worthless, and it's time for you to go. You won't relinquish your power and the planet needs a strong Leader. It's time for Carz to take his rightful place."

"You think Carz is the answer?"

"With a little guidance and what you just signed, I'll help establish his rule." Orn waved the digi-tablet at the Leader, snatched the pen from him, and placed them back inside his coat.

"What did I sign?"

"An order to begin the purge."

"As I recall, you said to wait for the right time."

"Correct, then you set it aside and it was your downfall," Orn said. "The right time will be when Carz takes power."

"Now this all makes sense. This is about you taking power beside my son."

"You of all people know that I have no interest in power," Orn said. "No, it's for the good of the globe."

"The good of the globe?" the Leader said. "I invented that mindless drivel for the morons on the street. You know better than that."

"I do know that you haven't been up to the job for years, and there's been a power vacuum at—"

"I know you thought I should've eliminated Mar Jeps and purged the Movement, but how would those spaceships have been built?"

"What does that matter? We're still here and the domes continue collapsing around us."

"You wouldn't understand. You've never been able to think outside of your maliciousness. You never had the brains for command."

"Maybe so, but you lost the ability to command when you kowtowed to that woman," Orn said. "You're just buying time now and I'm finding this act of yours tiresome."

The Leader reached out, pressed the button on the intercom, and said, "Help! Guards, come quick—there's an intruder!" He held the button down harder. "Come quick." When he realized the intercom wasn't working, he picked it up and clutched it to his chest like a life preserver, then called out, "Flomina! Flomina! Help!"

"You can yell all you want—"

"Flomina!"

"But no one is coming to save you, not even Flomina."

"That whore!" the Leader said, then he threw the intercom box in Orn's direction, but it didn't go far, falling to the floor with a crash and breaking into pieces. "She put you up to this, didn't she?"

Orn said, "There's no reason to drag this out."

"Are you going to afford me some dignity or smother me with a pillow?"

"Which would you prefer?"

"Neither."

"At least you haven't lost your sense of humor. And whatever you might think of me, I appreciate everything you've done for me."

"Well, that makes me feel *so much* better," the Leader said sarcastically and knocked the light off the nightstand.

"How's that going to help?" Orn bent down to pick up the light and gathered the pieces of the intercom as well. He placed it all on the nightstand and when he looked at the Leader again, there was confusion in his eyes.

The Leader said, "Who are you and why are you here? Guards!"

Orn sighed, then stared at Vidor. He was hoping the Leader would recognize him in the moment when he acted to end his life. He felt like the Leader deserved that small concession from him, but the longer Orn stood there in silence and watched Vidor searching for his identity, he understood the necessity of doing what he'd come here to do.

Orn hit the button on the side of his ring and a needle emerged from the underside, then he stabbed the Leader in the leg.

The Leader flinched and threw his blankets aside, rolling up the leg of his pajamas. There was neither blood nor mark.

The Leader said, "What have you done?"

"What needed to be done. You're an old man with extensive health problems. Your heart will stop and they'll call it natural causes. Flomina will make sure there won't be an autopsy."

The Leader's eyes were lucid again. The prick of the needle had brought him back. "Orn. You magnificent bastard. You've thought of every angle, haven't you?"

"You taught me well."

"For better or worse, I enabled a killing machine to reach its potential."

"And I truly thank you for it."

"I know we had our differences, but you were like a son to me," the Leader said, reaching out and gripping Orn's forearm. Tears were welling in his eyes.

At first, Orn felt an odd emotion rising inside him, something he hadn't felt since he was a child, then he was repulsed by it. He pulled out of the Leader's grasp and pressed the button on the ring to retract the needle. "The poison is painless and won't take long. Would you like me to wait?"

"So the last person I'll ever see is you?" the Leader said, wiping at his eyes. "No, thank you."

"Goodbye then." Orn turned off the light, then took a few steps back from the bed. He wasn't going to miss his greatest achievement.

"This isn't a peep show," the Leader said. "Get out!"

"Sorry, sir. Goodbye." Orn took a few more steps back.

Then the Leader began having difficulty breathing. His throat was closing up and his nasal passages constricting.

Orn closed his eyes and listened. He relished the moment, feeling a surge of pride as the Leader began gasping for air with a shrill wheezing. Orn focused, waiting for the death rattle, but suddenly, the Leader's breathing normalized.

Orn's heart raced. Maybe he'd failed and the Leader had overcome the toxin with the sheer will to live. Orn opened his eyes.

The Leader sat up with ease and the dim light of the room caught his eyes. He looked directly at Orn, holding his gaze, and said matter-of-factly, "Always the best." Then the Leader's pupils fogged over and he fell back onto the bed.

Vidor Plemso, the Leader, was dead.

Orn thought, *To take from a man the only thing of real value in his existence. I love it so.* It dawned on Orn that he had snuffed out the lives of both his fathers, the biological one and the one who had given him a life worth living, and if he died now, he would be truly satisfied.

FLOMINA

Flomina lay in bed, staring at the ceiling, wondering if Orn had done the deed. She turned onto her side, peering at the pillow where Vidor had rested his head beside hers for over three decades.

Originally, Vidor had been moved into his trophy room so he could convalesce and recuperate from heart surgery. Since then, Vidor had suffered a massive stroke and other complications, and with the rapid onset of dementia, Flomina had imagined him waking up beside her and not recognizing her. That would have devastated her, so she decided it was best for him to stay in his own room. That was over two years ago.

She loved Vidor. She never regretted relinquishing a great deal of her freedom and her former identity to partner with him. As First Lady, she was personally fulfilled as a mother and the savior of Kodan art that would have been lost in the crisis. Vidor wasn't the easiest partner on the planet, but neither was she, for that matter. Maybe that's why their life together had lasted, and it was hard to imagine life without him.

Before Vidor and Flomina met, they traveled in different circles. Vidor was dedicated to the military, then politics. Flomina made her fortune in the fashion industry as a model and designer.

In her late teens, Flomina was the most in-demand model on the planet with her own best-selling clothing

    Howard Libes

line. She posed half-naked in digi-media foto spreads. Her image was plastered on billboards around the globe, and it was once estimated that every thirty minutes she appeared in at least four viewing-channel ads. The people of Koda were transfixed by her. She dated and slept with the most beautiful women and handsome men. Women wanted to possess her beauty and style, and both men and women just wanted to possess her.

By her late twenties, her career reached a turning point. She was still beautiful. Nobody would argue anything different, but she was no longer the highest paid or the most sought after. The fashion industry focused on younger models and she was considered yesterday's news. She hired an acting coach and began appearing on dramatic viewing-channel shows, but the parts were small and inconsequential, and she never dedicated herself to it. Her clothing line was still flying off the shelves, but with too much time on her hands and all the money she would ever need, she became a regular on the high-society party circuit. Gossip about which actor or model she was dating or what outlandish exploit she had perpetrated at a nightclub filled the digi-tabloids.

Seeing any publicity as good publicity, Flomina decided to take control and produce a nonstop party that the tabloids couldn't ignore. At the time, she had residences in Maua and Capitol City, but her Norian coastal estate in Hampinor became the center of this bacchanalia. The home became infamous for celebrities coming and going, a pulsing beat emanating from within, strobing lights in the windows, naked people dancing around the outdoor pool, and orgies from dusk till dawn. Flomina gained a reputation for promiscuity and being high on Flopsy, a designer drug producing euphoria.

Her plan worked. The majority of Kodans couldn't wait for the newest digi-tabloid gossip about Flomina's den of sin, but Gruger Plemso had heard enough. His friendship with Flomina's father, Nomeer, went back decades. Nomeer's corporation, Folt Innovations, was the premiere construction firm on the planet and Gruger was a major stockholder. As CEO of Capitol Weapons Dynamics, Gruger enriched himself by ensuring that contracts for building Kodan military installations were laid at the feet of Folt Innovations. With Vidor as President, Nomeer's corporation had been paid billions in research and development funds for the DOME project and was a shoo-in for the hundred-trillion-unit contract to lay the foundations for all nine domes.

Flomina's outlandish behavior was about to cost Gruger a fortune. There was a portion of the Kodan population who saw Flomina's activities as indicative of society's loosening morals, and Flomina as a bad influence on Kodan youth. A wealthy religio-conservative group was pressuring Global Assembly reps to cut Folt Innovations from the DOME project contracts because they were rewarding sin.

Gruger couldn't let that happen and hatched a plot to bring Vidor and Flomina together. He would hire a promotional firm to frame their romance so that Vidor's love appeared to be reforming Flomina, but Vidor needed assistance as well. He was currently running for a second

Presidential term and the polls were close between him and his opponent, who was campaigning on clearing out the corruption within the Global Assembly. Vidor was doing his best to combat these accusations, but evidence of graft under his administration kept emerging. Gruger imagined that the nuptials would divert the average citizen from darker political realities onto more uplifting themes—a love story and a fairy-tale wedding—and ensure Vidor's victory in the upcoming election, end the controversy around Flomina, and—most importantly— fortify Gruger's stock portfolio.

Gruger approached Nomeer with his idea, and when Nomeer was reticent, Gruger couched it in a threat. If Nomeer didn't convince his daughter what was best for her family, then it would only be prudent for Gruger to sell off his Folt Innovations shares, producing a general panic around the stock, destroying Nomeer financially. Nomeer took this challenge to heart and flew to Nor in his private cruiser for an intervention with his daughter.

He and Flomina met in the living room of her Norian estate. The four walls of the three-hundred-square-meter room were lime-green with two pictures hanging from them. One was a three-meter-square painting by the enigmatic muralist Stint with off-white brushstrokes and a magenta dot in the middle. If one stepped close and examined the dot, they'd discover it was a tiny depiction of a Kimid, a rare Mauan flower. The artwork was entitled *Flo*. She and Stint were a couple for a short time and when they broke up, he presented her with this work. The other installation was probably the most famous foto of Flomina, taken when she was sixteen and at the height of her modeling career. She was wearing a yellow sundress and lying on her side in a vast green field.

The living room's old-growth wood floor, which had been salvaged from a razed royal mansion, was partially covered by antique hand-woven Msituan rugs. Remnants of the ongoing party also littered the floor with shirts, pants and skirts, bathing trunks, bikini tops and bottoms, bras, male underwear, panties and thongs in a rainbow of colors. The room reeked of smoke and sex.

Flomina sat beside her father on the magenta couch in the middle of the room. The low table in front of them was strewn with empty condom packages and the used contents, a small mirror with lines of Flopsy, a thousand-unit note rolled up into a tube beside it, and half-full high-priced bottles of Malrap with cigaro butts in them.

Flomina's father regaled his daughter regarding the reason for his visit, then stared at her, awaiting an answer.

"It's wonderful to see you, Papa, but you've wasted your time if you've come all this way and brought your guards to tell me what that blowhard Gruger had to say," Flomina said, pointing at the two-meter-tall man with broad shoulders dressed in a black suit with white shirt and black tie at the entranceway and a man of similar appearance and dress standing at the door leading to the sun deck and pool.

Flomina's father stared at her in silence. She knew he was furious with her and disturbed by his surroundings. His right eyelid quivered.

Flomina said, "What did you think was going to happen?"

"I wasn't sure, but I wanted to see this place to confirm what I've read," Flomina's father said. "Look at this mess." He pointed at the low table, the floor, and the purple stain on a wall where someone had shattered a glass of Eglew juice. The shards lay below the stain.

"It's morning," Flomina said. "The maid arrives later."

"And who is that? Your newest boy toy?" Flomina's father pointed at the transparent Active Glass wall facing the ocean. On the other side was a young man with six-pack abs lying on a chaise lounge sunning himself. He was wearing an orange thong that barely covered his genitals. At her father's arrival, Flomina had sent the young man to answer the front door in his current attire.

"I met him last night and had him this morning. It was mildly satisfying. I think he has potential."

"It's wonderful to see you, Bugsy," Flomina's father said, using the nickname he'd given her as a little girl. "I just didn't want to see this much."

Flomina chuckled. She was wearing a skimpy yellow bikini that did little to conceal her breasts and nether regions. "You said you were coming today and didn't state a time," she said. "But do tell, how's Mama?"

"Luckily, I can earn money faster than she can spend it."

"Well, at least you don't have to worry about me being dependent on you."

"Your independence makes me proud, Bugsy," Flomina's father said. "But all of Gruger's thoughts aside, I am concerned about you."

"I'm a little concerned about myself, Papa, but this is just a phase. I'm already tiring of it," Flomina said, then pointed to the young man on the deck. "But I'll never grow tired of that if you know what I mean."

Flomina's father rolled his eyes. "So what are your plans for the future, then?"

"Sun myself a little more, help myself to some more of that hunk, and then have lunch."

Flomina's father sighed. "You know what I mean, Bugsy."

"Yes, I know," Flomina said, reaching out and putting her hand on his arm. Flomina was aware that her father always had a soft spot for his little girl. "My fashion line is still doing quite well and I'm hoping to build on it."

"But when are you going to settle down?"

"There it is," Flomina said, throwing up her arms.

"Is that such an unreasonable thing to ask? Your mother worries about you. I worry about you."

"Are your worries truly about me or are you worried about how my current lifestyle reflects on your hoity-toity friends?"

"Well, your lifestyle may cost me the biggest payday in planetary history."

"You know how I like to make history."

"Seriously. Do you have any idea what they're saying about you out there?"

"Publicity is good for sales. And I stopped caring about what the digi-tabloids have to say a long time ago."

"I don't think you're being straight with me, Bugsy. I can't see my daughter living this lifestyle and being truly happy."

The door leading to the sun deck slid open and the barefoot young man stepped into the living room. "Am I interrupting?" he said to Flomina as the door slid closed. His blond hair was slicked back and his tanned body was covered in sweat.

Flomina stood up. "No, come here." The young man glanced over at the guard posted by the sun deck's door who was sneering at him. "Don't concern yourself with him. Come now."

The young man walked cautiously across the living room floor to avoid stepping on anything sharp or squishy in his bare feet. He stopped beside Flomina and said, "Sorry, I didn't mean to interrupt. It's unbearably hot out there. I could feel myself burning even though I bought the highest-rated sun blocker."

Flomina reached out and ran her fingertips down the young man's cheek, neck, chest, and belly to the top of his thong, stopping before she touched his penis through the fabric. "Yes, you're burning up, baby. Go to the shower in my bedroom and I'll join you soon."

Flomina's father said, "For Powers-That-Be sake, can't you cover that?"

The young man had a massive erection. Flomina chuckled.

"Sorry, sir," the young man said, looking down at the ground and picking up a flower-print shirt to cover his genitals.

"Don't be embarrassed, baby. Your body is beautiful. Now, go upstairs. I'll be right there," Flomina said, kissing him on the lips, then pointing to his crotch. "And we'll deal with that."

The young man's face turned red. He forced a smile toward Flomina's father, then made his way carefully across the living room to the staircase, where he dropped the shirt and sprinted up the stairs. Flomina had her eyes on the young man's ass during his entire journey. When he was gone, she turned to her father, sighed, and grinned, then said, "So nice."

Her father shook his head in derision. "So this is your life?

"Don't be such a prude," Flomina said. "Mama told me about your life before she met you. I've heard the tales."

"Yes, I did have fun as a bachelor. Nothing like this, though, and I knew when enough was enough."

Flomina looked over at the staircase. "I haven't had enough yet, I guess."

"From what I can tell," Flomina's father said, scrutinizing the room, "you've had enough for a few lifetimes, Bugsy."

"What can I tell you? I have large appetites."

"But are you happy?"

"I will be soon," Flomina said, looking over at the staircase again.

"Come on, you know what I mean—are you happy? *Truly* happy?"

Flomina stared at her father. He loved her and was concerned for her. She could hear the sincerity in his voice. She knew this question wasn't about manipulating her for his business. She searched for an answer, then said, "What do you want me to say?"

"A simple yes or no would suffice."

"I understand your question, but—"

"But nothing. All I see is you attempting to fill the emptiness in your life."

Flomina felt a twinge of sadness. Her father was right. She couldn't keep up this façade any longer. "What am I supposed to do? My modeling career is down the shitter. Acting is a dead end. I wake up every morning with a hangover, feeling like crap with some boy lying next to me whose name I don't even know. Happy? I don't know what that is anymore."

"Now, you're being honest," Flomina's father said. "You were right. My initial reason for coming here was the fear of losing the DOME project contract and the backlash on our family finances, but now that I'm here, seeing your life, seeing you, I see my Bugsy in trouble and I want to help you do something about it."

"Papa," Flomina said, and she began to weep. Her father embraced. When the tears subsided, she said, "What am I gonna do?"

Flomina's father released her, then peered down at the floor and picked up a white button-down shirt with two fingers. He inspected it for stains, smelled it, then handed it to Flomina. "Dry your eyes."

She laughed, wiped her eyes with the shirt, and threw it beside the couch.

Flomina's father said, "I support whatever you want to do besides what you're doing now."

Flomina said, "What do you really know about this soldier-boy President other than what we read in the news…which is obviously PR generated by his father?"

"Vidor has flaws and won't be easy as a partner. Only a strong woman like yourself will be able to handle him and make a life with him."

"Sounds like a project."

"He may not be your type, but meet him and see what you think. Don't do it because of what Gruger says or me. Do it for yourself. Whatever happens, I'm here for you, and maybe putting yourself out there will help you escape this rut."

Now, Flomina peered over at the pillow where Vidor's head had rested for years. Their life together was never easy, and they both learned early on that's the way they both liked it. Flomina thought, *I wouldn't have had it any other way.*

CARZ

Carz assumed that being summoned to his father's room before morning meal had something to do with his work as Communications Liaison. He was the intermediary between his father and his cabinet, the Global Assembly, the GSS, and the Supreme Commander of Global Forces. This had been Carz's job for years.

These early morning visitations had become more frequent as his father's dementia worsened. The Leader ranted about Yorlik the Great, Mar Jeps, Mado Prevor, or Yor Vanderlord, or about Commander Warver and finishing the domes. Carz would stand there and listen, then say that he'd take care of it. He respected his father and was sad to see this man he admired losing touch with reality.

As he approached his father's room, the guard by the doorway clicked his heels together, stood at attention, and put his hand up to salute. Carz stopped in his tracks as it dawned upon him what must have happened. His body went cold.

His father was dead. All guards were told on their first day that if anything happened to his father that Carz was the presumptive Leader. Every cabinet member and everyone else in the Global Assembly was aware of it, too.

Carz returned the salute and as he passed through the doorway, he understood that his life had changed forever. His mother stood beside the bed, dressed in a yellow robe, staring down at his father's lifeless body, and his brother Minok sat in a chair behind her wearing purple pajamas. He was weeping. When Minok saw Carz, he ran to him, wailing in grief. Tears flowed down his cheeks. He grabbed Carz in a tight embrace and planted his face in Carz's chest, then his hysteria seemed to increase. Minok's body heaved with emotion. Carz could feel his brother's tears soaking through his button-down shirt. He thought now he'd have to change it.

Carz said, "For Powers-That-Be sake, Minok, get ahold of yourself."

"Our father," Minok said. "Our father…he's gone."

"I can see that," Carz said. "Now, act like a man." Carz heard his father in his tone and his words, and he was disconcerted. He took a deep breath, then grabbed Minok's forearms and pried him off.

Minok said, "How can you be so cold?" His face contorted as he attempted to hold back more tears.

"I apologize. That was out of line. I guess I'm emotional, too." Carz looked over at his mother who was observing the scene. Her eyes were red. She'd also been crying. "I'd like to talk to Mother."

Minok stepped aside, then put his face in his hands and began weeping again. Minok wore his feelings on his sleeve. Carz loved his brother, but he found it grating on his nerves.

Carz approached his mother and hugged her. "Were you here when it happened?"

"No, it happened in the night, we presume."

"How was he before you went to bed?'

"He was fine, the same."

"I guess it's for the best. He wasn't really living."

Throwing up his hands in exasperation, Minok said, "How can you say that?"

"You know exactly what I mean, Minok. Stop being such a baby. You're no longer his Chief of Affairs. You're mine. Go inform the majority leader of the Global Assembly and the Supreme Commander what has happened."

Minok threw his hands up again and yelled, "I can't believe you. You want me to work…now?"

"Yes," Carz said and pointed at his brother. "Now!"

Minok pointed back at Carz, screamed and stormed out of the room.

Carz's mother said, "You need to be more sensitive to your brother's feelings. He just lost his father."

"He's such a drama queen," Carz said, staring down at his father's lifeless face. His eyelids had been closed.

"You two are different people. Always have been, always will be." Carz's mother walked up to the bed, grabbed the end of the sheet covering her partner's body, and drew it up to his shoulders before glancing at Carz. "Do you mind?"

"No, go right ahead."

"I just can't anymore," Carz's mother said as she pulled the sheet over her partner's head. "I know you're unmoved, but I can't." Tears began to well in her eyes.

"I didn't say I wasn't moved."

"You are your father's son," Carz's mother said and she kissed him on the cheek.

"I think I'm different, but for now, I'll take it as a compliment." Carz removed his father's lighter from his pocket and recalled the day his father had given it to him.

He was in his final term at the Royal Military College when his father commed and requested that Carz meet him. At the time, Carz was no longer residing in the dorms. He was officially living back at the estate, but his father rarely called him into the study, so Carz was concerned. Recently, there had been fotos and gossip in the digi-media about Carz playing around behind Roneh's—his public girlfriend and future fiancée's—back. It had been agreed by all parties including Roneh that this activity was fine as long as it remained discreet. Carz had been careful, but his latest mistress was a wild one and she'd taken the digi-tabloid payday rather than keeping Carz's confidences.

So when he opened the door to the study and his father was sitting behind his desk, the fear instilled in him when he was growing up returned.

"Sit," his father said, pointing at the armchairs that he'd inherited from Carz's grandfather. Then he bolted down the Malrap in his glass and slammed the glass on the desktop. "So good. Would you like some of the Great man's Malrap?"

His father had never offered him Yorlik the Great's Malrap before. Carz had snuck a sip as a teenager with his friends, so he was aware of the smoothness and taste compared to even the high-end Malrap at local bars. Over the years, the cases bought from Yorlik the Great's estate had dwindled, and his father reserved the bottles for special occasions. That made Carz even more curious about why his father had summoned him.

"I'd love some," Carz said, his fear showing in his shaky voice.

His father cocked his head at hearing the warble in Carz's answer. "Sit," he said again. "I'll pour you one. Is everything all right?" He walked over to the liquor cabinet, removing two glasses and one of Yorlik the Great's Malrap bottles with three-quarters remaining.

Carz seated himself.

His father sat in the chair across from Carz. He placed the glasses in his lap, popped open the bottle and poured the glasses half-full, then placed the bottle and the cork on the low table next to him. "Before we partake, you want to tell me why you're so nervous?"

"I'm sorry," Carz said. "I couldn't stop her from running to the digi-tabloids."

"Oh, that," his father said. "My people have already chatted with the young lady and she'll be retracting the story tomorrow and saying the fotos were doctored."

"You didn't send Orn, did you?"

"Nothing for you to worry about, but you know how he loves being of service."

"That's what concerns me," Carz said. "I'm careful, Father. I swear."

"I know. You've been playing around for three years. It's been seventeen women, I believe, and it's all been kept under wraps, so to speak, but this one got away. It was bound to happen."

"You've been spying on me?"

"Don't act so surprised. It's beneath you. It's something I'd expect from your brother."

"Why am I here, then?"

His father picked up the glasses and handed one to Carz. "We haven't talked man-to-man in a while, and I thought now would be a good opportunity to catch up since you're about to graduate in the top of your class. You've done a commendable job, and it's time to discuss your future." His father raised his glass. "To your future as the next Leader of Koda."

Carz took a big gulp of his Malrap. "Are you stepping down?"

His father guffawed and drank from his glass. "Of course not. If you listened to my toast, I was referring to the future."

"Right," Carz said. "I've been meaning to discuss this arrangement with Roneh."

"What about it?"

"I don't know if I'm really into it."

"Into it?" Carz's father said. "What does that mean? You'll partner with Roneh and you'll become Leader when the times comes."

"What about what I want?"

His father took a swig of Malrap, then paused for a moment to clear his throat. "This is not up for discussion. You know the plan and you'll stick to it."

"Can't Minok become Leader?"

"You're kidding, right?"

"Sorry," Carz said. "As soon as the words came out of my mouth, I realized how stupid it sounded."

"Can you imagine? It'd be a disaster," Carz's father said. "But what's with the desperate tone? The change of heart?"

"I've felt like this for a while. I just couldn't find the right time to tell you," Carz said and sipped at his Malrap. "I just don't think I'm the man for the enormous work ahead. Being out in the world, at college, I've gotten a new perspective on Koda, on the citizens and keeping the peace as the domes fall apart, especially as the situation worsens outside the domes instead of getting better."

"Where'd you get that idea?"

"Come on," Carz said. "You don't need to be an enviro scientist to figure it out. Even the average citizen disbelieves the 'Koda will cure itself while we're inside the domes' crap that you've been slinging all these years. You might be a little out of touch."

"Is that so? Maybe we need to beef up the disinformation campaign."

"So it's true?"

"Between us?"

"Of course."

"You can't mention a word of what I'm about to tell you outside of this room." That's when his father told him the truth—planetary conditions would continue to worsen, the domes were deteriorating ever faster due to shoddy workmanship, and spaceships were only being built for the most loyal Kodans. "The spaceships were finished a few years ago. I haven't launched because I don't have the coordinates to Yorlik's planet, so—"

"Wait! So he did find a planet?"

"Oh yes, but he refused to share the coordinates."

"That's unbelievable."

"Crazy, right? His great-grandson and Mado attempted to trip me up, but I got the situation under control and I've kept it there," his father said. "That'll be your job someday, too."

"See, that's exactly it," Carz said, finishing off his Malrap in one gulp. He breathed in deeply as he felt himself getting high. "This stuff packs a wallop." Carz stared at his glass, contemplating how little of the good stuff it took to achieve this state, compared to the large quantities he and his schoolmates consumed of rotgut to get anywhere near it.

"It's something else," his father said and slugged down the remains of his Malrap, too. "You were saying?"

Carz searched his mind for his previous line of thinking, but the Malrap had wiped it away. "I lost it."

His father laughed and poured himself another half-glass. "I'd offer you more but seems like you've had enough. I've built up a tolerance," he said. "We were talking about how I've kept everything secret. Well, that's just surrounding yourself with the right people. Orn is a good place to start. He scares the shit out of everybody, and he has an instinct about people and knows how to handle the ones who get out of line."

"I remember now. I was going to say, I don't know how I can lie to the people about something that will impact their lives so profoundly."

"You're smart. You'll figure it out. It's best not to tell the masses what will panic them, and we have spaceships so Kodans won't go extinct."

"How many spaceships?"

"Enough," his father said. "So the Plemso dynasty will have plenty of loyal followers on the new planet."

"What planet? You just said we don't have coordinates."

"I convinced Prevor Industries to send up a few satellites with high-powered telescopes to spot viable planets and scientists are analyzing the data daily. We'll find a suitable landing spot before it's too late," his father said. "And when the time comes, I'll show you the most recent report on the state of the domes."

"Yes, I'd like that."

"After graduation and serving a short stint in the military, you'll come work for me as Communications Liaison. It'll be a graduate school on governing the Plemso way."

"Communications Liaison?"

"Yes, we'll make you a major in the Armed Forces just like I was out of school. You'll be given a position with the Supreme Commander and that'll give you security clearance. Then after a short while, you'll come work for me. I'll teach you the ropes. You know I like to give Davik a hard time, but you can learn lots from him, too. When I'm gone, you'll be more than ready."

"I'm not sure," Carz said. "I'm not you."

"I'm not asking you to be me. You just need to know how to deal with your subordinates and keep the citizens blissfully unaware. The rest is up to you. I won't be around to tell you how to rule, but I'll definitely lay a foundation for it."

"I guess that's what I need."

"Of course it is. Nobody expects you to know everything. It'll come with time and experience."

"You'll be a hard act to follow."

"Don't I know it," his father said. "But you'll have plenty of time to prepare and I have faith in you."

"That means a lot."

"Of course, I know," his father said. "Your mother tells me I didn't pat you on the back enough when you were growing up, but that's not my style." He removed his lighter from his pocket.

Carz was well aware that this was one of his father's most prized possessions. When Carz was a child, he attempted to play with it and his father had beaten him. Since then, every time Carz had seen it, he'd thought about that thrashing.

His father popped open the lighter, flicked the wheel, and sparks flew from it. Frustrated, he flicked faster until a flame appeared. "As you know, your grandfather wasn't the most affectionate man, but if it not for him, I wouldn't have become the man I am," his father said, closing the lighter's lid. "He gave this to me as an expression of his… pride in me when I graduated first in my class. I know you won't be the first in your class like me, but I want you to have it."

He handed the lighter to Carz, then raised his glass again. "To my son, to your glorious future as the Leader of Koda and the flame bearer for this family."

Now, sixteen years later, Carz flipped open the lighter and ignited it.

His mother said, "What are you doing?"

"I always carry this around."

"I meant why are you lighting it now."

"Just something Father said when he gave it to me."

"What was that?"

"That's between us."

"You're so like your father."

"I guess we'll see about that," Carz said, closing the lighter and placing it back in his pocket. "I assume you're dealing with the arrangements."

"Yes, I've got it covered," his mother said and hugged Carz. "You know he loved you." Then she released her embrace.

"Yes, of course," Carz said. "I have to comm Roneh. I'll be back soon."

When Carz walked into the hallway and the guard saluted him again, the realization dawned on him that he was now the Leader on a planet hurtling closer every day toward becoming uninhabitable. He'd never disclosed it to his father, but he always told himself that when he took over, he would become responsible for every Kodan life, not just the ones pledging fealty to the Leader. As he headed down the hallway, that burden was already weighing on him.

RONEH

oneh arrived at her Global Assembly office early so
she could finish her budget proposal without inter-
ruption, which included the funding of the Allegiance
Watch Program.

Roneh had become the Director of Allegiance
fourteen years ago. Her crowning achievement up to
this point was increasing her budget every year and
extending the Allegiance Program into preschool. That
had taken some persuasion. When she was promoted to
director, the Allegiance Program was already in secondary school and universities, but the Leader balked at
the idea of deluging preschoolers with politics. Roneh
never backed down. She argued that it was best to
embed the idea in the citizens' minds that the good of
the globe was their duty before they had an independent thought. It took a handful of years, but she finally
convinced the Leader to sign off on it.

The Leader never bought into the Watch Program.
He believed that recruiting citizens to spy on each other
would further fracture Kodan society, driving people
into the arms of the Movement, and that policing the
population was the job of the GSS. After the Leader
told the Global Assembly Allegiance Committee his
feelings about the Watch Program it would never be
approved, but that didn't stop Roneh submitting the

 Howard Libes

proposal year after year. She was obsessed with making it happen and this year was no different.

Roneh's intercom buzzed. It was her assistant telling her that her partner Carz was on the line. Roneh said she'd call back and hung up, but her assistant buzzed again and told her that it was urgent news.

"All right," Roneh said, irritated. "Put him on."

"I'm putting the Leader through now," the assistant said.

"I thought you said it was Carz," Roneh said, but the call was already in the process of being transferred.

"Roneh," Carz said. "My father is dead."

At first, she couldn't believe it or begin to wrap her head around it. Carz had finally succeeded his father as Leader. He would begin the Plemso dynasty, and Roneh would be standing by Carz's side with their child next in line to the seat of power. This had been a long time coming, and she remembered how it all came to pass.

When she was twenty-eight years old, Roneh was in her fourth year of promoting the Global Assembly to young people for the Allegiance Program. She coveted the Director of Allegiance position, but Director Klovach had been running the program for years. She had proposed updating the program's educational content and creating new methods to increase outreach, but Klovach was out of touch and had no idea how to relate to young people under the domes. Roneh conveyed her frustration to the Leader who commended her initiative and told her to be patient.

Then one day, Roneh received a comm from Davik Atmar saying the Leader was inviting her to dinner at the Plemso estate. Roneh was honored by the request and thought this might be the moment when the Leader would appoint her as director.

The night of the dinner she rode a rail car to the station nearest the Plemso estate where a Global Assembly vehicle picked her up. She said nothing to the driver but stared up at the dome, which glowed red with the light of the setting the sun. She had never visited the estate before and she was nervous.

The vehicle turned down the three-kilometer road that led to the estate's gate. On either side, running the entire length of the road, was a metal mesh fence with razor wire on top. Behind the fence were acres of open fields used for military training, and the buildings at the far end of the fields were army barracks so there was an armed presence constantly maintained outside the Leader's residence.

As the vehicle approached the gatehouse, Roneh could hear the hum of the energy-field generators through the rolled-up windows. She observed how the fence line shimmered at the top where the energy generator was emitting the field that engulfed the estate. The vehicle pulled up to the gate and the driver lowered his window.

The soldier in the gatehouse said, "Who you got?" He was a fresh-faced young man no more than twenty years old.

"The Breeze Celebration heroine, Roneh Rayush."

The soldier's face lit up. He exited the gatehouse and walked over to the back window where Roneh was peering out.

"I'm a big fan," he said.

Roneh rolled down her window. "Thank you."

"I heard you speak when I was a teen. You inspired me to join the Global Assembly forces," the soldier said, clicking his heels together as he stiffened to attention. "For the good of the globe."

"Yes, for the good of the globe," Roneh said. "What's your name, soldier?"

"Private Klim Frok, ma'am."

"Well, Klim, I'm honored to meet you. It must be thrilling to protect the Leader and keep him safe from the terrorists who want to harm him. For the good of the globe."

"For the good of the globe," Klim said, reflexively clicking his heels together and standing at attention again. "You don't want to keep the Leader waiting." He reached inside the gatehouse and threw a switch.

A large man in an officer's uniform emerged from the shadows behind the private. "What in Powers-That-Be sake are you doing, Private? This is the final straw. I'm assigning you to latrine duty."

The gate was fully open now.

"Move on, driver," Roneh said and rolled up her window as the vehicle entered the estate grounds.

Before her window closed, Roneh heard Klim plead to the officer, "But I was talking to the heroine of…"

When the vehicle halted in the parking lot, the driver climbed out and opened Roneh's door. He said, "Walk up to the mansion and Davik Atmar will meet you there."

She followed the path through the wooded area, and the scent of the forest and the sounds of the winged creatures thrilled her. She imagined this was what Koda would be like when the citizens were released from the domes in one hundred years, a planetary paradise greeting them and the promise of the Leader fulfilled.

When she emerged from the forest, she was struck by the sight of the Leader's mansion in the distance. The poor girl from the factory district had come a long way. Her parents never would have dreamed up this scenario for their daughter.

Roneh often wondered why her parents weren't selected to live in the domes. It might have been her mother's disability even though she was a true loyalist, and it never made sense that her father was sent away, either, since he was a skilled worker and a loyalist, too. Now, as she walked along the flower-lined path, Roneh thought about how her parents had complained all the time about their lack of units and could never see a better future for their daughter. She realized that it was their shortsightedness in misunderstanding the power of the Global Assembly to uplift citizens to better lives that led to them living outside the domes, and they deserved it.

A smiling Davik Atmar stood waiting for her at the foot of the stairs that climbed to the terrace. As Roneh approached, Davik said, "Hello, young lady. I haven't seen you in a while."

She couldn't recall when she'd last seen Atmar. Less than a year ago, she thought, but in that time he'd become an old man. His grey hair was thin. Lines covered his face and his entire frame bent forward as if he'd been carrying a weight on his shoulders for far too long. From his ashen complexion and weak demeanor, he appeared to be in poor health, too.

"Yes," Roneh said. "Do you know why the Leader asked me here?"

"I'm positive the Leader would rather tell you himself, and the First Lady and Carz Plemso will be joining you as well."

"I thought we'd be talking business."

"Again, I'm positive—" Atmar broke out into a cough that bent him over as it persisted, and he covered his mouth with both hands.

Roneh approached him and said, "Can I…?"

Atmar removed one hand from his mouth and waved her back. As the cough subsided, he straightened, removed a handkerchief from his back pocket, and wiped his mouth. Roneh thought she saw blood on the cloth.

"Nothing an early death won't cure," Atmar said, releasing a nervous chuckle. "Now, we don't want to keep the Leader waiting."

A voice called from above. "What's going on down there, Davik?"

Roneh looked up to see the Leader leaning over the terrace railing. "Show her up this instant," he said, then stepped back.

Atmar released a long sigh and said to Roneh, "After you."

On the terrace, the Leader awaited her with a smile on his face. He was dressed in a Global-Assembly blue suit, his usual outfit, but the top button of his collar was undone. Standing beside him was Flomina Folt. Roneh had never met her in person. Like every Kodan, she'd seen Flomina in ads for clothing lines she could never afford, or on viewing-channel talk shows. She wore a green, form-fitting, strapless dress that only went down to mid-thigh. Her black hair draped her bare shoulders. She was stunning.

The Leader said, "Is everything all right, Roneh?"

Roneh realized that she was staring with her mouth open at the spectacle of this couple who led the planet.

"No, I'm fine," Roneh said. "I'm honored to be here."

"As well you should be," the Leader said and chuckled.

Flomina chuckled, too.

Davik stood beside her now, winded from the climb up the stairs.

The Leader said, "Nice of you to join us, Davik."

"Yes, sir,' Davik said, attempting to catch his breath.

"Davik, would you please tell my son that our guest has arrived," Flomina said. "Then you may go home."

The Leader gave Flomina a stern look and they stared at one another as if they were about to argue.

Atmar didn't budge from his spot.

The Leader broke off his gaze from Flomina and said, "Yes, Davik. Do what Flomina says."

Atmar headed toward a door where a guard was posted. His legs carried him at a slow pace and the Leader observed his passage. Atmar opened the door and entered the mansion.

The Leader said, "Got to put him out to pasture soon or shoot him. I haven't decided which yet."

"You should've stopped torturing him long ago," Flomina said.

The Leader stepped forward and placed his hand on Roneh's shoulder. "As you get to know us," he said, "you'll see my partner believes she's the Leader."

"Well, somebody has to be," Flomina said.

The Leader laughed derisively as he led Roneh to a round table covered by a blue cloth and set for a meal. "I thought we'd dine out here. Much less formal. Better for getting acquainted."

"Oh," Roneh said as the Leader released his hold on her. "I thought this meeting was about Global Assembly business."

"It is, dear," Flomina said. "It is."

"I'm honored to be here."

"You said that already, dear." Flomina glanced over at the Leader. "No reason to keep kissing Vidor's ever-expanding ass."

The Leader smiled at Flomina and stuck out his tongue, then he pulled out a chair. "Please sit, Roneh. My lovely partner and I always banter like this. You'll get used to it. Would you like a drink? Some Malrap or—"

"I don't drink," Roneh said as she seated herself.

Flomina said, "That's good to hear. Enough of that goes on around here. By the way, who dresses you and does your makeup?" She sat across from Roneh, then gathered up her hair and pinned it in a loose bun at her nape. Roneh caught the scent of Flomina's iconic perfume.

"I do it myself unless I have a viewing-channel or public appearance."

"If this all works out, we'll need to find a person to handle those details daily."

"I believe we're getting ahead of ourselves, dear," the Leader said as he filled a goblet to the brim with Malrap. "We haven't told her why she's here yet."

Flomina said, "Where's Carz?"

"If we're waiting for Davik to reach him, we could be here all night," the Leader said, then called to the guard standing by the door, "Head off Davik. Find Carz and tell him to get down here immediately or there will be repercussions."

"Yes, sir," the guard said and ran into the house.

"That should get him here soon enough," the Leader said, seating himself next to the First Lady and drinking down half his glass of Malrap.

"While we're waiting, why don't we tell her why she's here," Flomina said. "Carz already knows, and I've informed you of my thoughts on the subject."

"Yes, dear. Ad nauseam," the Leader said, leaning toward Flomina and attempting to kiss her on the cheek, but she pulled away before he could land it.

"Just proceed, Vidor," Flomina said in an annoyed tone.

The Leader sighed and said to Roneh, "Do you have a boyfriend?"

"No. I'm too busy working for the good of the globe, sir." Roneh was surprised at this inquiry, but she'd never question the Leader's intentions.

"Perfect," Flomina said in a sarcastic tone. "You like men, don't you?"

The Leader gave Flomina a look of displeasure, then said, "Please answer the question, Roneh."

"Yes, I've had boyfriends in the past. Nothing serious. I've never been attracted to women."

"How boring," Flomina said.

"May I ask what you mean, First Lady?"

"One should experience life in its fullest to know what it has in store for you."

Roneh said, "I'm not sure—"

"This is utterly irrelevant to why we're here," the Leader said. "As you know, my son is about to turn twenty. He's attending the Royal Military College and when he graduates he will become an officer, but more importantly he will formally be next in line to become the Leader after my passing."

"I'm sorry, sir. I didn't know you were ill. May I ask what's wrong?"

"Oh, there's plenty wrong with him," Flomina said. "But nothing fatal."

"There's nothing wrong. I'm fine. I probably have a good twenty to forty years left," the Leader said, finishing off his glass of Malrap.

"Not if you keep that up," Flomina said.

The Leader ignored her. "But I'm formalizing my succession now so that if anything should happen, there will be no question who the next Leader will be.'

"That's smart," Roneh said.

"I think so, but there are people out there who may not like it. They may think Carz isn't strong enough to hold together the ideals of the Global Assembly, and that's where you come in."

"How so?"

Flomina said, "She's a little slow, isn't she?"

"Flo, will you please let me finish?"

Flomina motioned with her right hand as if she were swatting away a bug. "Go on."

"I think you're the perfect mate for the next Leader. I want you to partner with Carz. Your loyalty to the Global Assembly is unquestionable so nobody can deny that you and Carz can lead the Kodan people into the future."

Roneh didn't know how to respond.

The Leader said, "Do you understand what I'm saying?"

"I think so."

"So what do you think of my proposition?"

"An arranged partnership?" Roneh said. "I will do my duty for the Global Assembly, sir, but I've never met your son. He's eight years younger than me."

The Leader said, "Your engagement will be years in the making and there's over a decade between myself and Flomina."

"Seventeen years, dear."

At that moment, the door to the mansion slid open and the guard exited the building with Carz behind him. He was dressed casually in a grey button-down shirt with a few buttons undone at the top, tan slacks, and military boots. He was taller than the Leader with broad shoulders and a head of curly dark hair. Roneh assumed Carz got his good looks from his mother's side of the family. He was magnetic and out of her league.

The Leader pushed back his chair and stood. "Nice of you to join us."

"Sorry, Father. I was—"

"That's irrelevant. I told you to be here at a specific time. We'll talk about this later," the Leader said. "Carz, this is Roneh Rayush."

Roneh rose from her seat and the reality of what was happening dawned on her.

Carz said, "Pleased to meet you, Roneh."

"The pleasure is all mine."

Flomina murmured, "It sure is."

"Tell the chef that we're ready to start," the Leader said to the guard. "Now then, let's get to know one another."

The rest of the evening wasn't particularly memorable. They discussed Roneh's family and her humble roots. Carz told her that he was excited to become acquainted with her although his tone suggested otherwise. The table was served exotic meats that Roneh had read about but never eaten, having grown up on protein meals. She found the food hard to digest but did her best to make everyone think she enjoyed it.

After dinner, the Leader told Roneh that her secret engagement and public courtship with Carz would begin immediately. She and Carz would be allowed private sexual indiscretions. After Carz finished military college, their formal public engagement would be announced. A PR campaign would begin to increase the couple's popularity, and when their partnership reached maximum planetary approval, the ceremony would occur. It would be a lavish affair befitting the next Kodan Leader. Afterward, Roneh would live at the estate with her new extended family.

Now, they'd been partnered for thirteen years. It had been a relatively happy and politically effective arrangement. They both knew that their union was one of convenience rather than love, although when Carz was finished with his affairs, he returned to their marital bed physically and sometimes sexually. In Roneh's eyes, Carz became more attractive as he aged.

On the comm with Carz, she dreamed of the power she'd be afforded in her place beside the new Leader. She could put her agenda forward to guarantee that the majority of Kodans were loyal.

Carz said, "Roneh, are you there?"

"Yes, sorry. I was thinking about your father and how this is a great loss for the Kodan people, your mother and brother, our son and you."

Roneh was well aware that Carz and his father had their differences, but Carz also loved and admired him.

"We need you at the estate," Carz said.

"I'm headed right over."

"I've sent a cruiser. It should be waiting for you on the roof of the Global Assembly building," Carz said. "I love you." Then the comm disconnected. She was surprised at his final statement. She couldn't remember the last time he'd said it. She didn't believe he meant it. He was grieving.

Roneh gathered a few important documents and shoved them in her briefcase with her digi-pad. Her assistant stood up when Roneh exited her office and said, "Can I do anything for you?"

"Cancel all my appointments for the next few days. I may comm you later."

Roneh was met at the lift by two of the Leader's guards. When they reached the roof, two more guards standing on either side of the doorway clicked their heels together and stood at attention. An executive cruiser was idling on the landing pad, engines humming. Another guard opened the cruiser's door for her as she approached. She climbed in and the pilot said, "So sorry for your loss, First Lady."

Two guards took the seats in front of her.

As the cruiser lifted off, Roneh thought about the pilot's words. She was surprised at hearing her new title spoken out loud for the first time, but she would get used to it with pleasure.

MAR

T*ime has a way of slipping past us when we're not looking,* Mar thought as she watched the news of Vidor Plemso's death.

When Rajer was executed, the Leader had been so cocksure of himself. Over the years, Vidor had called her complaining the Rejuv Treatment wasn't working. Mar pled ignorance and gave him more topsoil. There were moments when Mar felt guilty, but most of the time, she had to admit that she felt glee in Vidor not knowing Mar had tricked him.

Of course, Mar was taking the Rejuv Treatment herself and as time passed, she told people that the only explanation for her lack of aging was good genetics. During the era of Rejuv Serum, when a majority of the population were indulging in chemically extending their life-spans, it must've seemed normal to everybody. Your family members, your friends, coworkers, and neighbors stopped aging; a few people refused, getting old. In Mar's case, she observed from her timeless bubble as everyone that she remotely cared about paraded toward the reality of their mortality. Their hair greyed. They went bald. Their skin wrinkled. They had age-related health issues, then died.

Gols had been the hardest for her. He developed joint inflammation and discomfort. It became painful for him to type into this viewer. His sharp memory began slipping and he set a date for retirement. Her first impulse was to

 Howard Libes

provide him with the Treatment, but that was a slippery slope. If she gave it to him, then what about Suron, and what about the next person she cared for? So she stood by and watched as Gols' health declined, and she attended his funeral where all of her peers were elderly or infirm.

This was her lot in life. At times, she was lonely and depressed by it. She thought about stopping the Treatment, but she couldn't deny that her life had a higher purpose.

Suron had first brought the news of Vidor's death and now he stood next to her in her office watching the viewing channel launch into a breakdown of Vidor Plemso's life, inflating his importance as one of the greatest rulers in Kodan history. Suron had grown old as well. He was younger than Mar. He hadn't lost his hair, which was now grey, and he kept himself fit, avoiding a middle-aged paunch. Mar had given him less stressful work as her security consultant, putting him in charge of supervising Prevor Industries' global security, although he refused to give up the day-to-day job of protecting her.

"So," Mar said, "what now?"

"I'm not sure what you mean."

"I'm not sure, either. I thought as my security consultant you might have some insight on where we go from here."

"It's kind of late and I was going to call it a day."

"I meant in the political sense."

"I know—I was making a joke."

"You keep working on that," Mar said, and they both laughed.

"Seriously," Suron said, "when Vidor became ill, the rumor was that Carz would be the next Leader."

"Yes, Vidor always wanted a dynasty."

Almost on cue, a "Breaking News" banner slid across the bottom of the screen announcing that Carz Plemso would be ordained the next Leader.

Suron said, "Rumor has it that the Movement has been preparing for this eventuality and they aren't going to take it well."

"Maybe it's time to batten down the hatches, as Yorlik would say."

"Agreed," Suron said. "I'll set everything in motion on my way home. Let's talk in the morning." Suron marched out of the office.

Mar could always count on him. She walked up to her office doorway as the lift doors were closing with Suron inside. Lek Valsted's daughter, Ara, sat at the reception desk reading something on her viewer.

Since Gols' retirement, Mar had gone through a long line of assistants who couldn't live up to Gols' efficiency. At the outset of her employment, Ara was insecure. She was aware she'd been given the job as a result of Mar's fondness for her father, and it was true that Ara's presence kept Rajer's memory alive due to her father's close friendship with Mar's deceased partner, but she was smart and competent. She had come to the position with a University education and no real experience, so Mar molded her into the assistant she wanted, and Ara had been up to the challenge. Mar was pleased with the assistant that Ara had become. She also understood that it was unfair to ask anyone to live up to Gols' standards.

Ara was a red-headed beauty who looked like her mother Linara. Many of Mar's male employees made it up here accidentally-on-purpose to flirt with Ara and ask her out on a date. Ara was always embarrassed and apologized profusely as if Mar would fire her for these incidents. Mar remembered what it was like being young and driven by her hormones.

Now, Ara noticed Mar staring at her. "What?" Ara said and giggled. "You have that distant look on your face."

"With the news today, I'm thinking about your father and Rajer more than usual."

"My father wasn't exactly a fan of the Leader."

"Well, the Leader did attempt to kill him."

"Yes, there's that," Ara said. "I wonder if he's celebrating."

"That's not like your father, although I doubt he's mourning," Mar said. "By the way, why're you still here past the end of the workday? Don't you have a date or something?"

"I wanted to catch up on the digi-mail after all the meetings today, and it's just the viewing screen and a protein drink for me tonight."

"Sounds like my plans. Care to join me?" Mar said. "Come along. I may even have some Eglew juice."

WHEN MAR AND ARA FINISHED THEIR EVENING meal, they sat in the antique chairs on the terrace, enjoying their tumblers of Eglew juice. Mar was aware this was decadent when Kodans were struggling for survival outside the domes, but it wasn't as if this was a daily indulgence so she tried to not feel too guilty.

She took a sip of her juice and stared out at Capitol City. The population had grown significantly even with the one-child mandate. Her unimpeded view of Global Plaza was now blocked in a few places by high-rises, but the city was still stupendous from this vantage point and sitting on this terrace after a day's work was a moment she always cherished.

In the distance, Mar could see the latest collapsed portion of the dome. Over the past six years, the collapses had happened at greater frequency in larger sections of all the domes, and they'd become so normalized that nobody was surprised by them anymore. The horrifying part was the considerable loss of life.

Mar's agreement with Vidor had held and the dome dwellers knew that these numbing disasters were caused by design flaws and not terrorists. The Global Assembly still fed disinformation to the viewing channels about how the domes would hold long enough for the environment to heal and how future generations would live outside the domes.

The Movement had transformed itself into advocating for outer-Kodans. A faction still pushed for settling on a habitable planet and debunked the viewing-channel lies, and every so often a more radical spinoff called the ADM, attacked a government installation, calling for democratic reform. The GSS was less of a daily threat to free expression, although those who persisted in stepping out of line were still arrested, tortured, and put to death.

Ara placed her tumbler on the low table between the chairs and said, "This is nice."

"Yes," Mar said, taking another sip. "This is my retreat."

Ara had been Mar's assistant for over a year, and Mar had been thinking about bringing Ara out here, but since Ara was working for her "aunt," Mar wanted to avoid any hint of favoritism. Vidor's death felt like the right occasion.

"It's nice," Ara said, picking up her tumbler and swishing the Eglew juice around in it.

"You all right? You haven't drunk much."

"Oh, I'm intoxicated already. I'm not much of a drinker. You know how my mother was when I was growing up."

"Sorry, I forgot."

When Linara thought Lek had been executed, she'd fallen into depression and become a Malrap addict. After her recovery, she blamed her alcoholism on Lek's betrayal and his choosing the Movement and sedition over the security of his family. She became a staunch Global Assembly loyalist.

"Not a problem, Auntie Mar. Oops, sorry. I know I'm not supposed to call you that at work. It's the juice."

Mar drank down her remaining Eglew juice and placed the empty glass on the low table. "It's fine. Nobody else is here," she said. "How is your mother these days?"

"I still talk to her every morning before work. She's all right. Her health has stabilized. Good days and bad. She loves the assisted-living condo you helped her get into."

"My pleasure. The least I can do. I know she blames me and Rajer for what happened with your father."

Ara said, "We both know that's misdirected."

"How is your father? I haven't chatted with him in a while." When Ara moved from Mlimoa, where her mother lived, to attend Royal University, Mar had told her that her father was alive and put them in touch. Of course, Linara could never know.

"We still talk pretty regularly through those vids on memory wafer carried by your courier. He is—"

Flashes of light emanated from the Global Plaza, then the sound of explosions rocked the terrace, one after another. Ara placed her tumbler on the low table, leapt out of her chair, and dashed to the railing. By the time Mar reached her, there were more flashes of light and more blasts reaching them.

Mar said, "That's big. We're eight kilometers away."

Ara turned around and entered Mar's apartment, then activated the viewing screen. Mar continued watching the flashes in the distance and listening to the blasts. She had a bad feeling. The peace had been maintained for years, but with Vidor's death, she should have foreseen some sort of upheaval. A military coup might be underway, but it was more likely the radical elements in the Movement. Maybe she had wanted to believe that everything would be all right after Vidor's death, that the transition to Carz would be accepted and everything would go on like normal. She chastised herself for her complacency.

Explosions continued in the Plaza, but they were also occurring now in different parts of the city closer to the Plemso estate. Mar needed to stay on top of these events because the consequences could be devastating. She'd placated Vidor and held off his purge by following through with the spaceships and even launching satellites with telescopes so Vidor could locate a habitable planet. Carz didn't seem the vengeful type, but he did have people like Orn and Roneh by his side.

Mar walked into her apartment and stood beside Ara. The viewing-channel news was reporting the blasts and the military response. No deaths so far. The curfew would cut down on injuries.

Ara said, "Scary."

"Do you want to stay here tonight? I don't think it's safe out there. You can use my spare room."

"If that's all right."

"No problem," Mar said, squeezing Ara's arm. "Make yourself at home. I need to attend to something. I'll be back shortly."

Mar headed into the lift and passed through the hidden doorway into her office. The lights were activated by her presence. The office hadn't changed much in the past twenty years. There were newer framed promotional posters on the walls for the Prevorian Relief Foundation's efforts. Mar had spearheaded food drives and supplied Prevor Industries' medical advances to outer-Kodans for free.

Mar commed the direct line to Vidor's study, using the viewing screen behind her desk.

Minok appeared. "Mar Jeps. You call to gloat?"

"No, I called to offer my condolences."

"I'm sure you're all broken up over my father's death."

"I also called to say I hope you don't think I'm behind this mayhem."

"We know who it is. They've already stated their demands."

"Can you tell me? I might be able to broker a deal."

"We're taking steps to deal with the situation. You're not being bombed so mind your own business."

"I'd like to talk to Carz."

"The Leader is with his son, who is frightened."

"That's too bad," Mar said. "Again, sorry for your loss."

"No, you're not."

The viewing screen went dark. Mar thought about attempting to reach Carz through a different channel or comming Flomina, but that felt desperate and too soon.

Mar sat down in her desk chair and wished she had someone to bounce her thoughts off. She'd need to evaluate the idea, but maybe this turn of events meant the foreseeable future was finally here.

YOR

When Yor heard about Vidor's death, he'd been living at the Terminus A-1 way station alone for three years. He missed his friends and family, but Mado's absence left the biggest hole in his life. Every day, Yor woke up thinking about Mado and wishing Mado was there with him, but Yor understood that Mado had dedicated more than seventy years to Yorlik's crusade and it was time for him to return home.

Before departing for his planet, Mado had insisted on refitting the WAEF with his Prevorian spacecraft's engines and field generators so traveling round trip from Terminus A-1 to Prevor and back again would only take approximately twelve years at near light-speed—nineteen years in real time.

In the initial stages of the overhaul, Yor worked on persuading Mado to ferry him back to Koda, offering Mado the WAEF for his voyage home. Mado argued against the idea. He said that it would be years before it would be safe for Yor to return home, and his mother was more than competent in dealing with the preparations for the Kodan exodus. More importantly, Yor's round-trip voyage would give him the opportunity to develop invaluable skills.

The Prevorian tech being installed on the WAEF was designed into the spaceships at the Shamban facility.

The engineers and pilots there were schooled in this tech, but they only knew simulations. Mado wanted to ensure that Yor could not only maintain the Prevorian tech but also understand how each part worked within the whole, and how that applied to the functioning of the vessel in outer space. By the time Yor returned from Prevor, he'd have more space-travel experience than anyone on Koda. That invaluable knowledge would enable Yor to teach the nuances of these skills to the generation of Kodans preparing to journey among the stars to their new home.

When Yor ended his campaign to return home, Mado wanted him to grasp the difficulty of living for years in space by himself. Yor would be alone for at least six years on his return voyage.

Mado said, "Your great-grandfather was a brilliant individual, but there were times when being alone was too much for him. He'd become depressed about whether he'd ever find a habitable world. He'd go on a Malrap bender, then seriously consider opening the ship up to the vacuum of space and ending his life. Only his feeling of responsibility for the continuance of the Kodan people kept him going. I saw these bouts in our first years of traveling together. He was jealous of my ability to hibernate and pass time that way."

"You told me about that," Yor said. "That's how he came up with the idea for what would become the Holographic Gaming Device."

"Exactly," Mado said. "Like your great-grandfather, you'll have to maintain the ship, but you have Yorlik's biography to write, too. On our journey, I'd also like to tell you about my life on Prevor before I met your great-grandfather, so that when the time is right, you can tell the Kodan people my story. It'll be an additional project to occupy you on the way back from Prevor and your stay on Terminus A-1."

"Almost twenty years will have passed by the time I reenter Koda's solar system. I'll be able to return home by then."

"Wishful thinking. It's more constructive to plan for the worst. If the best occurs, then it's gravy, as your people say. This philosophy has served me well over the centuries. You need to fight your impulses and not head back to Koda too soon. You'll know when the time is right."

"I'll keep that in mind."

"So, you have the maintenance of the ship, your work, and no taste for Malrap, but I've also been planning to refurbish your great-grandfather's HGD and add programs that will fit your life. That'll be of assistance on your way home, too."

"I was wondering why you loaded it onboard."

"It'll serve you well. I saw how it helped your great-grandfather, and what he designed is much more advanced than the version I sold to Kodans. Your great-grandfather's device accessed his memories, so it was personally satisfying. And I'm sure you miss Insol."

"Mado!"

"What? Prevorians hardly ever lose the drive to procreate even as we age. That's one of the reasons I want to return to my home world."

"I've never thought of you that way, not even when I believed you were Kodan."

"Probably best."

"Yes. Now I can't get it out of my head."

"It's quite different from the way humanoids do it. Much more of a biological imperative than a casual liaison."

"Is this the beginning of your plan to increase my understanding of Prevorians for your biography?"

"That wasn't my intention," Mado said. "I was just following the course of the conversation."

"I know. I was joking."

Mado laughed in his way. "You had me there. Very good," he said. "Now, let's get to work on Yorlik's HGD. Like everything else on this ship, I want to take it apart piece by piece in front of you so you understand how its parts interact, and if it malfunctions, you can repair it. And you'll also better understand your great-grandfather's genius."

"Here I am in outer space with you," Yor said. "His genius has come to life for me and never ceases to amaze me."

THE JOURNEY FROM TERMINUS A-1 TO THE OUTER rim of the Prevor planetary system lasted less than six years at just below light-speed. During the final year of travel, Mado focused on upgrading his reentry pod. After being haunted by his hiber-dream, he reinforced the pod's outer shell to reduce the chance of burning up in the atmosphere. He also upgraded the pod's communication capabilities by installing a new transmitter and backup system.

As they neared the system, Mado became even more obsessed about guaranteeing the hiber-dream wouldn't come true, disappearing for days in the loading dock where the pod was stored. Mado even began missing his evening meal with Yor, which was one of the rituals they'd arranged at the start of their voyage. At this get-together, they'd discuss any ship-related problems that required immediate attention, run through the perpetual maintenance list, and just ask how each other's day was faring. At one point, Yor realized he hadn't conversed with Mado in eighteen days. He noted the empty drink cups by the replicator and the crumbs and water on the counter, so he assumed Mado was taking care of himself. They were simply on different schedules. To make sure Mado was all right, Yor began checking up on him. When he peeked into the loading dock, Mado was always in the midst of working so Yor left him alone.

Then there was a day when Yor looked into the dock and found Mado motionless, seated on a crate with his eyes closed. He was hibernating. Yor went inside and pulled up an empty crate to sit on, then leaned back against the hull to observe him. After all the years of traveling with Mado, it wasn't odd to see him in his true form, but there was an indescribable solitude as the blue-and-silver scales on Mado's torso shimmered in the glare of the work lights as he breathed rhythmically.

As a young man, Yor had fashioned himself after the Prevor Industries Mado who was frenetic and perpetually in motion, focused on saving the people of a dying planet. Mado didn't do it for acclaim or fortune. There was no personal agenda. His reasons were selfless. Mado sacrificed years of his existence because he valued life. It dawned on Yor how much that beauty was reflected in Mado's true form and how deeply he loved this Prevorian.

Mado said, "You know…"

Yor was startled.

Mado's eyes were still closed. "…you could come over here and hold my hand like you've done before as you ponder my beauty. I won't be offended."

Yor broke out laughing. "How did you know what I was thinking?"

"Prevorians are renowned for their beauty," Mado said. "Don't make me open my eyes. Come over here."

"Sorry," Yor said through his laughter.

"No need to apologize. I know I'm beautiful."

"Yes, you are. You won't get an argument from me."

Mado opened one set of eyelids, then the other. "That's disappointing. You know how much I like a good debate." Mado attempted a smile.

"I didn't mean to wake you."

"I hadn't fallen into hibernation. I was just taking a nap."

"How's the work going?"

"Every time I believe I'm done, I feel the compulsion to recheck the systems."

"Still concerned about your hiber-dream?"

"Not so much, but I see no reason to push my luck, as you Kodans say."

"I get it. We are coming up on the launch date."

"Yes, that and other things are weighing on my mind."

"Right now, what's your major concern?"

"You."

"Me?" Yor said. "No need."

"Hard for me to stop. That's been my task for almost eighteen years," Mado said. "But my concern is less for you as an individual than for the Kodan people as a whole."

"Do you know something that I don't?"

"I'm not sure how to put it," Mado said, picking up a spanner at his feet and tapping the end of it in the palm of his hand. "It's a notion that different factors could escalate and create a cascading set of problems that end up in catastrophe. I don't have anything specific in mind. We both know the trouble spots—the domes, the political leadership. My best advice is trusting your instincts and remaining vigilant."

"I can do that."

Mado stopped tapping the spanner, stood up, and approached Yor. "I know you can. I know you care about your people, and you are as ready as you'll ever be to join your mother in leading them…when the time is right."

Mado stopped in front of Yor and placed his right hand on Yor's shoulder. A surge of confidence filled Yor as Mado expressed how he felt about Yor's abilities.

"I love you and I'll miss you," Mado said, placing his left hand on Yor's other shoulder.

Yor was overwhelmed by emotion.

"Too much," Mado said, releasing Yor's shoulders.

"No, not at all. Words couldn't communicate what you just expressed. I'm humbled. You know I feel the same. I never knew my father as an adult, and I couldn't have wished for anyone better to fill that place in my life." Yor's emotions flooded over him again and tears filled his eyes.

Mado stood with his hands by his sides. "I was trying to avoid a scene like this."

"I'm glad you didn't."

After that date, Mado's obsession with the pod didn't wane. He seemed more focused. Yor couldn't even coax him out for a meal because Mado began fasting. When he was rescued by the Prevorian Protectorate, he'd tell them the pod was his life raft and that he'd run out of rations many days before, so he wanted to appear malnourished.

A DAY BEFORE MADO WAS SET TO LEAVE THE WAEF, Yor went to the control room to see if he'd left a circuit board there and noted that his great-grandfather's foto was missing from its frame on the wall above the control panel.

Yor checked the frame. After the theft of the foto, the screws had been tightened and the frame secured on the wall. Of course, Mado was the thief. Considering the importance of the coordinates hidden in the photo, Yor tried to imagine why Mado would take it. Maybe to spend some time with his friend before he left. Maybe he wanted to recalibrate the coordinates from Prevorian to Kodan and save Yor the trouble of integrating them into the navigation system himself. Before they left the way station, Mado had balked at revealing the coordinates to Yor's mother. He told Yor that they were safer in their hands. Yor contemplated more sinister reasons for stealing the photo. Maybe Mado never wanted Koda to have the coordinates all along, or he'd given them to the Leader so they could escape Breeze Celebration, but Yor knew this was preposterous overthinking.

As the time for Mado's departure approached, Yor had convinced him to get-together for a final repast to discuss any pressing issues regarding the ship. This would be his opportunity to confront Mado about the missing foto. When mealtime rolled around, Yor arrived early in the living chamber and started eating. Since discovering the theft, Yor had become increasingly worked up about it. He kept telling himself there was a reasonable explanation. He promised himself he'd wait until they were finished with their final briefing before bringing up the foto.

Mado entered the room and talked business as if everything were normal while he nonchalantly pro-grammed the replicator. Yor listened, but his anger built and he couldn't control himself.

Mado was saying, "Yes, I'd recheck that intake valve, there's—"

"So where's the foto?" Yor blurted out.

"What?"

"You heard me," Yor said. "My great-grandfather's foto is missing."

"That's odd," Mado said as the replicator beeped, signaling his meal was ready. Mado removed a small por-tion of Gleckos, their scent filling the room as he placed them on a tray. Mado had programmed a few variations of Prevorian cuisine into the replicator, but Gleckos were still his favorite. He picked up utensils and a cloth napkin from the compartment where they were stored and added them to the tray. He said, "Don't forget to do the laundry. These napkins are piling up."

"It isn't going to be that easy to change the subject."

"What subject?" Mado picked up the tray and approached Yor.

"The missing foto."

"Maybe it fell off the wall. The ride has been bumpy lately." Mado placed the tray on the table and seated himself across from Yor, then picked up a chunk of Glecko and popped it in his mouth, moaning in pleasure.

"You've never been good at this."

"At what?"

"Deceit."

"To my credit, if I got good at it, you never would've discovered my subterfuge."

"So you admit it!" Yor said. "That's a start. Why did you take the foto off the wall? Did you make a deal with the Leader?"

"Absolutely not. I would never make a deal with that vile blowhard," Mado said. "I can't believe you'd think such a thing after everything we've been through."

"Then don't make me guess. I don't want to be angry with you, Mado. I don't want to think the worst, but this is inexcusable. As you would say, there's a high probability I will never see you again. I was hoping we could celebrate our friendship before you left. Spend some quality time together, reminiscing and taking the night off from work… and now this happens. What do you want me to think? It's hurtful. I thought we were friends. It's baffling."

"It wouldn't be if you'd spent time with those aliens."

"The aliens?" Yor said. Mado hadn't talked about them since they'd left the way station. "What do they have to do with this?"

Mado tossed a few more chunks of Glecko into his mouth, chewed, swallowed, then cleared his throat. "I left out a few details about my visit with them," Mado said. "I need some water. You want some?"

"Yes," Yor said, then realized what Mado was doing. "No. Sit right there and tell me about the aliens."

"It wasn't just a first-contact experience," Mado said, licking his fingers.

"So you lied when I asked what happened?

"I've been avoiding this moment," Mado said in a somber tone. "I should've done a better job." He sighed.

"So you're regretting that you got caught?"

"I know that you're not going to like my answer, but yes," Mado said. "I calculated the risk of telling you and I concluded it was better if you didn't know the truth, but here it is…" Mado sighed again, then launched into a detailed account of his interaction with the aliens.

Yor listened closely to see if he could detect Mado lying. At first, it sounded like a tall tale of time travel and some sort of dimensional shift that wasn't scientifically possible, but the details of the story and the tone of Mado's voice convinced Yor that it was true. It reminded him of Mado's recollection of the voyage with his great-grandfather.

When Mado was done, Yor was dumbfounded. He'd just been told that everything he'd worked toward had no impact on changing the future of his people. He didn't know what to say.

Mado said, "That's exactly how I felt about it."

Yor shot out of his chair and said, "You want that cup of water now?"

"Yes, please."

At the water dispenser, Yor turned to Mado and said, "So this is why you made up that excuse about it being dangerous to leave the coordinates with my mother? And you planned on stealing the coordinates this entire trip?"

"Stealing is a strong word."

"Then how would you put it?"

As Yor filled two cups with water, Mado ate some more food and said, "I took a shot at making them go away."

"Let's say the aliens are correct on how the future will turn out," Yor said, carrying the cups back to the table and placing one in front of Mado. "That raises the question of whether the future is inevitable, no matter how hard we try to change it."

"Exactly."

"Then how is stealing the coordinates going to change anything?"

"I'm not sure," Mado said, "but the probability of your people reaching the habitable planet would diminish, and maybe if they spend more time searching they might value their discovery more and take better care of it when they get there."

"Possibly," Yor said, seating himself and taking a sip of water. "Or you give the foto to me and I tell my mother what the aliens said, and we put measures in place that will stop us from destroying the planet's environment so we don't repeat our mistakes."

"Have you met your people?" Mado said in a sarcastic tone. "Seriously, maybe this conversation we're having is an inflection point in history, and whatever we decide at this table in the living chamber on the WAEF will determine the fate of your people and the future of the habitable planet and all the beings who reside there, both organic and inorganic. Perhaps your people will learn from their mistakes on Koda and not repeat them. But it's just as likely that centuries after you, your mother, and I are gone that your people will forget overcoming how divided they were and the monumental effort to leave their home world and they'll revert to their true nature and the behavior patterns that led to the destruction of their planet in the first place."

"So you're saying Kodans can't change?"

"No. Maybe. I don't know," Mado said, drinking down half the cup of water and pouring some over his head.

Yor laughed. "I'm never sure whether you do that to lighten the moment or because you enjoy it."

Mado attempted to smile. "A little of both," he said. "There was a curious thing that one of the aliens said to me. Part of me saw it as a hint at how to change things, but it was vague."

"What was it?"

"The alien made a point of saying to me, 'The future is yours. Make of it what you will.'"

"That is vague."

"I've thought about it over and over for years and I'm still not sure what it means," Mado said. "I regret this conversation because the ramifications might be forming the future, but as a gesture of our friendship and the good faith between us, I will put the foto back in the frame after we eat and we'll forget it ever happened."

Then Mado said something in Prevorian. It was a series of open-throated sounds combined with popping of puckered lips in a variety of tones.

"What was that?"

"A Prevorian prayer for the water to guide us."

ON THE POD'S LAUNCH DATE, YOR WAS IN THE CONtrol room. The WAEF skirted the edge of the Prevorian solar system so the spaceship was not within range of the Prevorian Protectorate's automated probes for detecting objects entering their territory.

Yor turned as the door slid open behind him. Mado had put on his Prevorian spacesuit, which had been stored at the way station. It was the same light blue as the Prevorian Industries spherical logo and was skintight, unlike Kodan spacesuits. Mado had explained how the Prevorian suit breathed oxygen into the Space Traveler's skin as the individual required. Visually, it highlighted the musculature of the Prevorian physique, and the suit was designed for the wearer to have full flexibility, which for the Prevorian was quite extensive.

Mado said, "How do I look?"

"Magnificent!"

"I always liked these suits. The rush of oxygen is exhilarating."

"I can only imagine."

"When you can breathe through your skin, I'll let you try it on."

"I'd say please wait around until I evolve, but I know you have plans."

"Yes, I must be going," Mado said, approaching Yor and looking around the control room. "You take good care of her. Keep an eye on the energy-field emitter on the port bow."

"Got it."

"And don't take any shortcuts. Remember that asteroid field."

"I understand."

"Come here," Mado said, stepping up to Yor and hugging him. Mado's embrace was strong and firm.

Yor hugged him back. "I don't recall having done this with you before."

"An embrace is the human equivalent of the Prevorian ability to communicate emotion through touch, and as you've said, there's the high likelihood this will be the last time we see each other so I thought it appropriate to finally experience it between us. The only other humanoid I've hugged is your great-grandfather, but it happened unexpectedly when he was drunk."

"Sounds like him."

Mado released Yor and stepped back. "I don't want to leave you with the impression that every time he expressed himself emotionally that your great-grandfather was drunk."

"I don't think that," Yor said, "but it does seem to have been a high percentage of times."

"I'm not sure I could argue that point, although I appreciated the sincere sober moments the most."

"Understandable," Yor said. "You should get going."

"I should," Mado said, but remained in place.

"Now's the time if you have anything else to remind me of," Yor said. "After you've gone, I'll remain radio silent. I know to wait out of range until you signal the pod is being retrieved by a Prevorian spacecraft or until you enter the atmosphere. You've only told me fifty-two times."

There was sadness in Mado's eyes.

Yor said, "Get out of here."

Mado spoke in Prevorian.

"What does that mean?"

"We are destined to meet again in the eternal waters. Good life, my dear friend." Then Mado turned and walked out of the room.

A few moments later, an alarm went off along with a light on the control panel, signaling the opening of the loading dock. Yor flipped a switch to turn off the warnings, then watched the pod pass the ship. Mado was staring out the pod window and waved goodbye, then the pod rocketed into the vastness of space. Mado was gone.

The hum of the WAEF's idling engines filled Yor's ears. He sat down in the pilot's chair and looked up at the foto of his great-grandfather. At that precise moment, he understood that his great-grandfather's vision had been achieved. The baton had been passed. When All Else Fails was his spaceship now. He would need to survive a six-year journey home by himself. Then he thought about how Mado had prepared him. *That crazy Prevorian.* Then he went to suit up so he could check the energy-field emitter on the port bow and begin his journey back to the way station.

IN THE NINETEENTH YEAR OF HIS VOYAGE, YOR entered the Kodan system. He had trouble wrapping his head around the idea that so many years had passed in Kodan time. He missed his mother. He missed Insol. He thought frequently about Rajer, and almost two decades later still couldn't get it out of his mind that Rajer had been executed for protecting him.

When he was within listening distance of Koda, Yor was sorely disappointed. Although he had held out hope all those years in transit, as if he wished long enough it would come true, the planet's political dynamics hadn't changed. Later, he spoke with his mother who confirmed that he wouldn't be headed home anytime soon.

Over the next three years, the only thing that kept him from completely losing his mind was overhauling the WAEF, which was in dire need of repairs, his writing, the HGD, and obsessively watching the viewing channels. When he heard the news of Vidor Plemso's death, he felt like a weight had been lifted. Finally, he saw hope for his return and looked forward to taking the next step on his journey, helping the Kodan people reach the habitable planet and survive.

MADO

Mado emerged from the warm waters of the Axikut Ocean and seated himself on the beach's purple sand. He lay on his back, basking in the sun's rays, closed his eyes, and fell asleep.

Then he awoke with a jolt when something heavy landed on his chest. Mado cried out in mock pain as he opened his eyes to his eight-year-old son Pino on his chest squealing in high-pitched Prevorian laughter.

Still on his back, Mado lifted Pino so his son was looking down on him and said in Kodan, "How many times do I have to tell you? That's not funny. You'll hurt someone someday."

Pino stared down at this father. He said in Prevorian, "You're speaking that language again."

Mado was alarmed. Pino's surprise attack had caused him to blurt out words in Kodan. In moments of distress, he returned to the dialect that had dominated his life for close to a century.

"Pino," Mado said, standing up with his son in his arms and kissing him on the cheek. "Don't do that again." He lifted Pino over his head and tossed him. Pino flew thirty meters through the air, squealing in delight the entire way, arms flailing, before he splashed into the ocean and disappeared under the waves.

His mate Alba and his children were aware of his

proclivity to speak this alien language, but neither his family nor anybody else on Prevor was aware of his time on Koda. Mado had explained to Alba that he'd learned Kodan as a distraction, listening to Kodan broadcasts that he picked up on his transmitter while he made his way back to Prevor in his pod. Alba had a brilliant mind, which was one of the reasons he fell in love with her. At first, she accepted the story, but she had grown suspicious over the years.

Pino's head bobbed above the water and he yelled, "Again, again!"

"Let's go home—it's mealtime," Mado said, "and your mother is making your favorite."

Pino rode a wave onto the beach, then sprinted toward Mado and leapt onto his shoulders.

"Hurry, Father. Hurry. The stew is best when it's hot."

"Of course," Mado said. "Hold on to my fins." Mado sprinted up the beach and halted at the walk leading to their dwelling, which was multi-leveled and circular, carved out of the rock formations along the shore.

Pino jumped off Mado's shoulders and ran down the walk, stopping at the threshold of the open doorway. When he turned and noticed that his father was still standing where he'd leapt off him, he said, "Aren't you coming?"

"You go ahead. Tell your mother to start without me. I'll be there in a moment."

Pino disappeared inside the family dwelling, which had been gifted to Mado by the Prevorian Protectorate upon his retirement as a Space Traveler. After his long absence from Prevor, he was deemed more valuable

as a consultant and instructor at the Space Academy.
That worked out well because that's where he met Alba.
Mado's new career path also kept him at home, which
he preferred when they decided to have a family. If he
yearned for outer space, he still had the privilege of bor-
rowing a spacecraft for a training session or maintaining
his pilot rating.

"Father!" said his nine-year-old daughter Jana from
the doorway of the dwelling. "Mother says to get your
gills in here."

"Is that so?" Mado said, walking toward the entrance.
"Doesn't sound like your mother. Sounds more like you."

Jana appeared to be thinking of something smart to
say in response, then said, "No. She just said to hurry.
She won't start without you."

"That's what I thought," Mado said, reaching the door
and kissing Jana on the cheek. "Your mother is always right."

"If you say so." Jana rolled her eyes, then ran ahead of
Mado into the house.

"Get back here," Mado said, chasing her.

When they reached the dining room, Jana ran around
the crystal table where Alba was seated with Pino and his
six-year-old sister Clo. Bowls lay in front of every seat and
a pot of stew sat in the middle of the table.

Jana leapt into the chair between Pino and her mother.

Alba said, "Jana, what have I told you about running
in the house?"

Jana pointed at Mado and said, "He started it."

"*He* is your father."

"Sorry. Father started it."

"Of that, I have no doubt, but you should know better," Alba said, then she winked at Mado. "Your father's behavior seems to regress as you children get older. Now let's eat. Seat yourself, dear. Or is a spanking in order?"

"Spank him!" Clo blurted.

Alba burst out laughing with her two other children.

"Would you listen to that," Mado said as he seated himself beside Alba. "If Clo wants it to happen, I suppose we must."

Alba said, "We'll discuss it later. Now, let's join hands."

Before dinner commenced, Prevorian tradition dictated that family members held hands so their feelings could be shared and communicated with the individuals who loved them the most. Then discussions might occur during the meal to resolve any individual or interpersonal problems. Clo's empathic skills were not developed yet, while Pino had just become capable of interpreting the feelings of others. Of course, Alba and Mado's emotions would be more complex and that was why they sat beside one another. Mado took Alba's hand and kissed it, then reached to his left and took Clo's hand. Alba took Jana's hand. Jana and Clo grasped Pino's hands, and the circle was complete.

Alba said, "Begin."

Everyone bowed their heads and closed their eyes. Mado opened one eye and spotted Pino with one eye open leering at the stew. When Pino saw his father watching him, he closed his eye. Through the circle of sharing, Pino's agitation exposed that he had been reprimanded at school for insolence, while Jana's elation revealed that she had been praised by her teachers. Clo was hungry.

As they began eating, Jana said to her mother, "Why are you worried about Father?"

"That's between us, but I appreciate you asking."

After the meal, the children went off to finish their schoolwork. Alba read to Clo. Mado cleaned up, then climbed a ladder to the roof of the dwelling and watched the sun set, the sky darken, and the stars come out. He noted a green flash of light high up in the atmosphere, which was a Space Traveler amplifying their spacecraft's engines as they accelerated to sub-light-speed. Mado had trained this particular cadet. He took pride in the newest Traveler and felt a twinge of envy, too.

Whenever a pupil left on a mission, he also found himself thinking about his own space travel and obsessing about Koda's future. It had happened over twenty-two years ago, but he was still haunted by the revelation on the alien spacecraft. Something deep in his core told him it was the truth and that gnawed at him.

"Clo wants to say good night," Alba called from the top of the ladder. "What're you doing up here?"

"Watching Cron's departure."

"Nothing else?"

"What else would there be?"

"Your children are waiting for you."

"Tell them I'll be right there."

"Hurry."

"I know. I heard."

Alba groaned and said, "Sometimes you're as bad as them."

"That shouldn't be news to you."

Alba shook her head and climbed down the ladder.

Mado looked back up at the stars. He couldn't help but be concerned that his effort to assist his friend and save the Kodan people would end in disaster, and he couldn't do anything about it.

Alba called out from the bottom of the ladder, "Come on, Mado."

"I'm coming. I'm coming," Mado said and climbed down.

When Mado entered the room that Clo shared with Pino, Clo was already under the blankets with her eyes closed. Mado kissed her on the head.

Clo said, "Can you tell me a story tomorrow night, Father?

"Yes, Clo. I promise."

Clo said, "You do that lots."

"I guess so. I'm sorry," Mado said, kissing her again. "You go to sleep now."

"She waited for you, but she couldn't keep her eyes open," Pino said. He was lying on his bed holding a neuro-display screen.

"Shouldn't you be getting ready for bed yourself?"

"I'm finishing up this stupid assignment about respecting your elders that my idiotic teacher gave me for speaking out of turn in her lame class."

"Obviously, the assignment is teaching you nothing since you're speaking so disparagingly of her," Mado said. "Learning respect for your elders is part of your schooling and you need to take it to heart."

"I suppose," Pino said, placing the screen on the shelf beside his bed and climbing under his blankets. "Can I ask you something?"

Mado walked over to Pino's bed. "Anything."

"Before dinner, on the beach, before I jumped on you—and sorry I did that—"

"Maybe that assignment did teach you something."

"Possibly," Pino said, glancing over at his screen on the shelf. "Before I jumped on you, you were speaking that alien language."

"Really? I must've been dreaming."

"I've heard you speak it before."

"Yes, I'm aware. I told you how I picked it up."

"I've begun to understand the language a little."

"That's fantastic, Pino. You haven't heard it much. You may have the makings of a linguist," Mado said. "Now go to sleep."

"I haven't asked you the question yet," Pino said. "You kept repeating the word Yorlik and—"

"That means friend."

"From what I've extrapolated, that's a name."

"You're mistaken."

"I don't think I am."

"I said, you're mistaken," Mado said, raising his voice in anger.

"I don't think so."

"What makes you so positive?"

Alba said, "The way you're behaving, for a start." She was standing in the bedroom doorway. She was not pleased by Mado's outburst.

"So I'm not trusted by my own family in my own home." Mado stormed out of the bedroom, past Alba, and exited the house.

He didn't stop walking until he stood on the shoreline, listening to each wave crashing onto the sand, then receding with a hiss before another one rolled in. He wasn't expecting his eight year old to figure him out so easily and his tantrum would only bring more questions. When he returned to Prevor, Mado figured his existence on Koda and his guilt about failing the Kodan people would fade with time, but as he built a life around himself and he was happy here, all of those past memories and emotions were resurfacing more and more. How long before his lie was revealed to his family and the Protectorate?

In his pod heading back to Prevor, he had streamlined his backstory. He would tell the Protectorate that he had crash-landed on a planet which he was scouting for mineral deposits and lost all comms. He'd been able to repair his craft enough to escape the planet's gravity, but then his reactor core, which had been damaged in the crash, had started to go critical. He'd built an escape pod, abandoned ship before the core exploded, and made his way home. He kept the story simple to leave little leeway for repeating it differently. Once a spacecraft retrieved his pod from Prevorian orbit, he was fully committed to the lie, and it worked like a charm. He was hailed as a planetary hero and the Protectorate showered him with all the back pay and benefits of a Space Traveler stranded in space. But lying was a behavior so abhorrent in Prevorian civilization that it was considered a high crime.

Being found out would be catastrophic.

CARZ

Carz stood in the Leader's office, staring out the window, observing the protestors packing the Plaza streets below. After the announcement of his father's death, the violence in the Plaza perpetrated by Movement radicals had been squashed by the military, but days later, when the Global Assembly formally declared Carz the new Leader, thousands upon thousands began marching in the streets of every dome.

They demanded that the martial law enacted by Carz's father cease and for a return to an elected Presidency. These protests had persisted for eleven days and Carz had been briefed by the GSS that the demonstrators were given strict instructions by the Movement to remain nonviolent.

Carz crossed his arms and sighed. The intercom buzzed. Kel said that Orn Shiv was here to see him. His father had told him many times to keep Kel in her position after he was gone. She was middle-aged, still had enthusiasm for the job, and as his father would say, "She knows where the bodies are buried." Probably literally.

Carz told Kel to send in Orn.

The door slid open. Orn entered and stopped just past the threshold. Minok entered behind him and headed for the couches in the middle of the room. The door slid closed. Orn clicked his heels together, stood at attention, and saluted.

   Howard Libes

"Please, Orn," Carz said, returning the salute. "There's no need for that from you. At ease."

"Of course there is," Orn said. "May I enter?"

"From what I can see, you're already inside," Carz said. "And I meant, I'm not my father."

Orn approached and stopped in front of the desk. He wore black shoes, black pants, and a white button-down shirt with the top button open. His uniform was the same as when Carz was growing up and Orn was still in prime physical condition. The streaks of grey at the temples of his coiffed hair and the wrinkles in his face were the only real indicators of his senior status.

Orn said, "You may not be your father, but you now hold his position so you should never shirk from being treated with deference by anyone. That's exactly what those protestors want."

"You're right. I'm just not used to it."

"No time like the present."

Carz said to Minok, "What are you doing here?"

"I just arrived and saw Orn entering the office. I know he wasn't on the schedule, but Father always had Davik and myself in his meetings with Orn."

"Davik? Not always," Carz said. "And did he really allow you to attend his meetings with Agent Shiv?"

Minok hesitated, then sheepishly said, "No. Not really."

"Then why would I?"

"I thought—"

"That's never been your strong suit," Carz said. "Why don't you find out what's on the menu for midday meal and get back to me? I'll talk to Orn alone."

"I don't know why I even try," Minok said, then pressed the button beside the door to open it and exited.

Orn said, "I would've been fine with him staying."

The door slid closed.

"I'm not in the mood for him saying something moronic," Carz said. "What brings you here, Orn?"

"I was wondering how I could best serve you, sir."

"Would you care to sit?" Carz walked over to one of the couches and seated himself. "Please." He pointed toward the couch across from him.

Orn stood in the same spot, looking around the room for something. Carz realized Orn was searching for the Global Monarchy torture chair. When Carz took this office as his own, one of his first acts was removing the chair and sending it to the Royal Museum. "That chair's gone, Orn. Please sit on the couch. I'm not my father and I don't intend to treat my subordinates like him or rule like him."

Orn seated himself on the couch, squirming in the cushions as if he wasn't at ease with comfort.

Carz said, "Before we begin, I want to apologize. I had no idea my mother banned you from the funeral. She did it without telling me. You were one of my father's oldest friends and you should've been there."

"I appreciate the concern, but your mother made the correct call. I'm more effective out of the public eye," Orn said. "And not being there doesn't change my admiration for your father."

"I'm sorry for your loss."

"Life goes on and I'm past it," Orn said. "So, what can I do for you, sir?"

"Now that you're here, I'm wondering how you'd counsel me on this situation with the protestors," Carz said. "I've read the intelligence and I'm not surprised this was organized by the Movement. I know my father thought they'd just gone away."

"There was a softening of his stance toward the opposition after his so-called treaty with Mar Jeps."

"True," Carz said. "Sounds like you didn't agree with him. Is that correct?"

"I'd rather not dwell on the past. I'd rather move forward and deal with the current situation."

"It's kind of you to protect my father's memory."

"Being kind is simply not in my nature, sir."

"Perfect, then. I need to know your unvarnished thoughts about how my father governed both right and wrong and how we might secure our rule," Carz said, edging forward on the couch.

A smile stretched across Orn's face. He chuckled, which sounded awkward like he hadn't practiced much.

"Did I say something funny, Orn?"

"No, sir. Sorry, sir. I was laughing because I heard your father in your words. I was relieved to hear his wisdom coming from you."

"He valued your judgment so tell me how you felt about his rule for the past twenty years."

"Yes, sir," Orn said, leaning back into the couch cushions, taking his measure of Carz.

"Speak up. I don't have all day." His father had always told him that Orn responded best to an authoritative tone.

"In short," Orn said, "when your father agreed to Mar Jeps' terms, that was the day he lost his spine. Don't get me wrong—your father was still clearly ruling the planet, but he was never the same afterward. The man I met on the battlefield took calculated risks. He trusted his advisors and not his yes-men. He marched forward with conviction. I watched that man vanish before my eyes into a cloud of doubt."

"Well said, Orn."

"He allowed the Movement to metastasize in Kodan society. They've been organizing, growing in numbers, and waiting patiently for your father to die so they could get their way, so the citizens could rule and not the Leader."

"Well, we're not going to let that happen, but there has to be a happy medium," Carz said. "How do we move forward? I suppose I call Mar Jeps?"

"No, sir," Orn said, jumping forward on the couch until he was on the edge of the cushions. "We don't negotiate with terrorists."

"She is far from a terrorist. She called the estate to offer her condolences when my father died. I see her as an entrepreneur, a businessperson who believes she's doing what's best for the Kodan people."

"What's the Movement?"

"Are you patronizing me?"

"No, sir. I would never. Please just go along with me."

"Ostensibly a group of concerned citizens."

"On the surface, yes, but if the goal is overthrowing your government, then they're terrorists," Orn said. "And

Mar Jeps has been their unspoken leader for the past twenty years. She has been waging a war of attrition, waiting for your father to die, playing the long game. And she conned him into believing that Rejuv Treatment would work, too."

"First of all, she gave him the Treatment to save her partner, then—"

"Who was a convicted terrorist—"

"Don't ever interrupt me again," Carz said, raising his voice. "I'm fine with disagreement, but don't do that again."

"Sorry, sir," Orn said, shifting his position on the couch. "But I just wanted to make clear—"

"Yes, I've heard the argument, but my father duped her."

"Was the Rejuv Treatment ever viable?"

"That's another conversation," Carz said. "Since the treaty, my father was working with her. He wanted the spaceships built. He needed pilots trained to fly them and techs to understand the systems. That took twelve years. Then my father didn't want to leave the planet without knowing where he was going, so he had her build those satellites with observatory-quality telescopes, which took another seven years. Then, while he was looking for viable planets, my father got sick and now he's dead. She was providing him with what he wanted. That's not terrorism."

"One could argue that she played on his weaknesses."

"You give her too much credit," Carz said. "My father had his own flaws that helped create the entire scenario."

"I can't argue with that."

"Now we've settled that point, if you don't think I should negotiate with the Movement or Mar Jeps, then how would you suggest we resolve this uprising?"

"Do what your father failed to do twenty-two years ago—purge the Movement. Remove the leadership and their families across Koda. The Movement will fall flat on its face and Mar Jeps' power will be cut off at the knees."

"I'm not a fan of the purge," Carz said. "And Mar Jeps can always refuse to reenergize the domes, cut off the air circulators."

"That was your father's biggest mistake, thinking she was as ruthless as him."

"Good point," Carz said. "But I need an option other than the purge."

"You don't seem to understand," Orn said, appearing confused that Carz didn't agree with him. "You need to make a strong opening statement and permanently silence the mob. The purge says, 'This is what happens if you stand against me.'"

"Did I stutter?" Carz said. "I want options that don't rely on killing entire families. That would be a horrible precedent to begin my rule."

"I truly believe it's your best option."

Carz stood up. "Come back tomorrow with other options or maybe it's time for you to retire."

Orn struggled to free himself from the cushions, but finally achieved a standing position. "I would ask you to reconsider, sir. Don't make the same mistakes as your father."

"Dismissed," Carz said, pushing a button on his desk to open the door.

"Yes, sir," Orn said, then turned on his heels, marched out of the room, and the door slid closed behind him.

Carz walked over to the windows and peered down on the protestors below. One thing was clear that Orn failed to mention. The Movement had flourished, and their animosity had only grown with his father bullying and torturing the citizenry. Carz would start his changes there. He wanted to be different from his father.

ORN

The door slid closed behind Orn and he took a deep breath. He'd held it together in the Leader's office, but now he was livid. When he looked over at the Leader's receptionist, he saw fear on her face.

He strode into the hallway, jumped on a lift, and pressed a button for the thirty-eighth floor. A man in an expensive suit dashed toward the closing lift doors, hoping to catch it. Orn howled, "Take the next one!" and the man skidded to a halt in the hallway as the lift doors shut.

Orn looked at himself in the shiny silver lift walls and punched his face's reflection with all his might. The pain in his hand was exquisite and just what he needed to focus.

The door opened on the floor where the Department of Education and Well-Being offices were housed. At the front desk, the smiling male receptionist in his early twenties said, "Hello, sir. How can I help you?"

Orn stomped past him and the people sitting in the waiting room. He could hear the receptionist calling to him, "Sir...sir..." as he marched past rows of desks occupied by workers talking on comms or focusing on their viewers. He turned left, entering the lobby of the Allegiance Program offices and stopped at the desk of Roneh Rayush's assistant.

Orn said, "Tell her I'm here."

The assistant said, "Who shall I say—"

  Howard Libes

"Don't bother," Orn said, passing the assistant and throwing open the door to Roneh's office. She was standing at her desk, placing a digi-pad into a viewer case. Orn walked up to her with Roneh's assistant right behind him.

"Sorry," the assistant said. "He just barged in."

"It's fine," Roneh said. "I'll handle it."

The assistant appeared confused but backed out of the doorway.

A security guard entered the office. He was typical ex-Global Forces personnel. He had brawn, tactical know-how, and the ability to take whatever orders were given. He looked like he was about to burst through the seams of his ill-fitting suit.

The guard grabbed Orn's right arm, saying, "I'm sorry. You can't—"

Orn punched the guard in the ribs and he gasped, releasing his hold on Orn's arm, then Orn took hold of the guard's arm and twisted it until he screamed.

Orn said, "Would you like to lose the use of your arm?" With his free hand, he reached into his pocket, removed his ID, and held it in front of the guard's eyes. "You need to leave."

"Sorry, sir," the guard said, the agony clear in his voice. "I was just following protocol." Orn released his hold and the guard scurried out of the office.

Roneh called out to her assistant, "Shut the door, please."

When the door was closed, Roneh said, "Orn Shiv, you do know how to make an entrance. To what do I owe this honor? Please have a seat."

Orn took a few steps toward Roneh and said, "I prefer to stand."

"All right. I hope you don't mind if I do," Roneh said, seating herself in her desk chair. "So what's got you all fired up?"

Framed Allegiance Camp and Club posters hung on the walls. They dated back to the Allegiance Program's inception in President Plemso's second term. The camps and clubs had prospered under Roneh's directorship, but she'd made them controversial, too.

On one occasion, she had attempted to recruit camp participants from families who didn't want their children indoctrinated, and when the parents expressed their outrage, she gave them a choice. Their child could attend, or their entire family could leave their dome. In this instance, the Leader disagreed with the policy and cancelled the idea. Roneh argued her stance vehemently with the Leader, but he wouldn't back down.

At the time, Roneh had cornered Orn and fumed about her frustration. Orn was close to the Leader so she assumed he could change Vidor Plemso's mind for her, and there were a few times when Orn had helped push the Leader into Roneh's camp on a policy matter or two. When that happened, he'd made sure she knew he was the deciding factor in her getting her way, and she owed him. That's why he was here.

Orn said, "We need to talk about the new Leader."

"I'm intrigued," Roneh said, taking her viewer case from the desk and placing it on the floor. "Proceed."

"I don't want to get into the details of my conversation, but I won't let him make the same mistakes as his father. I truly believe that now is the time for the purge. It would mark a new beginning for Koda with a new ruler, but the Leader is against it."

"So how does this involve me?"

"I want you to convince him that it's the right thing to do."

"I've heard him go on and on about how he doesn't want to rule like his father."

"Yes, he said that to me, too, but nobody is asking him to be Vidor Plemso. There'll never be another like him," Orn said, feeling rage rising in him. "The Leader needs to comprehend the danger the Movement poses to the Global Assembly. He needs to understand the demonstrations in the streets could end what's been built over the past four decades. He needs to understand that now is the time to eliminate the threat for good before it erases the Plemso legacy from history." Orn was yelling by the end of his tirade.

"I can see you feel strongly about this," Roneh said. "I just can't believe that Carz of all people got you so riled up."

"You mean the Leader…Are you going to help me or not?" Orn said, lowering his voice. "Between you and me, before Vidor died, I had him sign off on the purge, then got the old GSS director to approve it. I've placed it in the system with like-minded people and it will happen in a handful of days."

"You bad boy," Roneh said with glee in her voice.

"There's no turning back, and I don't want to be left holding the bag."

"So you *really* need the Leader to agree with it, don't you?"

"I need him to accept it so he'll embrace it when it happens,."

"So you won't get blamed for instituting a major policy without the Leader's permission. I get it," Roneh said. "So you've come to me for help? You must be losing your edge."

Orn stared at Roneh. He thought about the satisfaction he'd get from torturing her. She was self-assured and cocky. Those were always the best subjects. He was losing his temper again, and he noted fear appearing on Roneh's face in the glare of his rage.

"You are in a lather, aren't you?" Roneh said. Her was voice shaky. "I can help. I know Carz. I know what makes him tick. We can push him into approving the purge, but there needs to be an incident, something personal, a threat to his family that produces a desire for revenge. I have an idea."

"And what would this incident entail?"

"Before I tell you any more, I want something in return."

"This is for the good of the globe and you're blackmailing me?"

"No, this is not blackmail. This is an exchange of services. You get what you want, and I get what I want, and both will be for the good of the globe."

"What do you want?"

"I have a policy agenda stuck at the committee level. I need you to convince the committee reps that not passing it will be bad for their health."

"You'll need to persuade the Leader to sign the policy into law, too."

"Let me deal with that."

"I'm going to need a list of names."

"Done," Roneh said. "And you may even enjoy yourself."

"Quite possibly," Orn said, stepping toward the desk until he stood directly in front of it. "Now tell me your idea."

"I'm surprised you haven't thought of it yourself," Roneh said. "For all of his bluster, the Leader is a mama's boy. What if we find a pawn who has a history of violence, of hating the Global Assembly, and they endanger her life. We make sure they die before they can be interrogated, and we create a fiction around their association with the Movement leadership. The Leader will be furious at the Movement and will see the purge as revenge."

Orn immediately thought of a few disgruntled GSS agents who could be encouraged to put together that sort of operation. "What if we do this and the Leader decides not to purge?"

"You said it's already set in motion?

"Yes."

"We'll just time it so he can't stop it, so even if the incident doesn't cause him to approve it, then the purge will happen anyway," Roneh said. "And if he blames you for it, he'll look weak."

"Blames me?" In that moment, Orn realized that coming to Roneh might have been a mistake. She wouldn't hesitate to blame him to gain an advantage for herself.

"You know what I mean," Roneh said. "If he accuses anyone of acting without his permission, he'll look weak."

Orn thought her attempt to cover her tracks was lame, but he liked her idea. "I think it could work."

"Of course it will, and I have the perfect inside man to help," Roneh said. "It's a win-win situation for everybody."

Orn could see how much Roneh wanted this to happen. She had the tendency to push her advantage, which could be dangerous for both of them, but at this point in his career, Orn had nothing to lose. He said, "Let's do it."

FLOMINA

Flomina wandered the Great Hall of the Plemso mansion, examining the Kodan antiquities. There was a distinct delineation between the displays that Flomina curated—the clothing of the first emperor and empress on mannequins, the priceless jewels of the Second Kodan Dynasty in glass cases, the vases with miniature paintings of Kodan life thousands of years ago on pedestals—and Vidor's items, which were more in the line of Leen the Magnificent's sword or paintings depicting coronations and historic battles. Flomina cherished the relics that she and Vidor had collected in their life together. They symbolized the start of their relationship, their differences as people, and how they came together to create something meaningful.

When she looked back on her time working as a fashion model and mogul, a smile spread across her face. The days were full of wheeling, dealing, and creativity. The nights were a potpourri of sex and drugs. That life brought her fame and a never-ending fortune, but as she got older, the entire scene became tedious. When her father suggested the idea of meeting Vidor, she was reluctant, but she was aware that her life needed to change. Like any businessperson, she decided to take a meeting that could lead to a promising new venture.

Gruger had convinced Nomeer that subterfuge was necessary for the first date between Vidor and Flomina.

Vidor was President of the Global Assembly and Flomina one of the most recognized faces on the planet, so their fame and notoriety made it difficult for them to meet in public. Viewing-channel news followed Vidor's every move. A phalanx of digi-tabloid freelance foto journalists were constantly on Flomina's tail. She didn't mind foto ops and happily posed with her dates—it was good for business. But her recent partying with the seedier element of the leisure class wasn't a good association for the bachelor President. If their meeting didn't go well, it was best to keep it out of the media. On the surface, Flomina was insulted that her father and Gruger felt her public image had sunk so low that this date required sneaking around. Deep down, she understood and giggled at what she'd brought on herself.

It was settled that Flomina would meet Vidor for a late-evening meal after business hours at the Royal Palace, which was a museum. The President would arrive earlier by vehicle to meet with schoolchildren. After the museum staff left, the President's vehicle would leave the palace without him and return to the Presidential mansion. Nobody would know he was still at the Palace.

A cruiser that wasn't owned by Flomina ferried her from the roof of her Capitol City high-rise apartment on Oedor Drive to the manicured lawn of the Palace gardens. She observed that the magnificent four-story twenty-eight-room building was unlit except for a row of windows on the first floor, which she assumed was the dining room. Presidential guards jogged down a cobblestone path toward her cruiser as it was descending. Her escort, she presumed.

For the evening, Flomina had chosen one of her signature evening dresses with a plunging neckline. She'd applied the most intoxicating perfume and wore her hair up to display her neck, which was considered one of her most sensual features. She figured that even if the date didn't lead to anything, she'd get a literal rise out of the most powerful man on Koda.

Flomina buttoned up her Ashtecki overcoat and eased its hood over her head. If she was playing into this charade, then she'd do it fully. She exited the cruiser and walked across the lawn, relishing the multitude of scents from the famed Royal blossoms. When she reached the cobblestone path, she continued toward the palace flanked by the two guards.

She said to the guard she considered the most handsome—tall, broad-shouldered, coiffed hair, winning smile—"Do you like working for President Plemso?"

The guard was surprised by the question and said, "It's my job."

Flomina chuckled and asked the other guard, "And you?"

The guard continued looking straight ahead and said, "It's an honor to serve."

"That all sounds like a barrel of laughs," Flomina said.

The guards looked at each other and shrugged.

Before they reached the building, the handsome guard to her right jogged ahead, opened the ornately carved wooden door, and said, "Just head down the hall toward the light. The President will meet you there."

She walked through the doorway, but the guards weren't following. "You're not coming?"

"No, we'll be standing guard out here," the handsome one said. "Enjoy your meal."

As Flomina headed down a half-lit hallway toward the bright light at the end of it, she heard the door shut behind her. She gently removed her hood without disturbing her hair, then unbuttoned and removed her overcoat, draping it over her arm. This hallway was an entry from the gardens. It was no wider than two people, but in the dim illumination she could see the portraits of Royal family members and landscape paintings of forested mountain ranges with lakes below them, a winged creature flying overhead. The cabinets and chairs pushed against the walls were constructed of antique wood from forests that were probably portrayed in the landscapes and no longer existed. She was transfixed by this setting and felt as if she'd stepped into the past.

Then she walked into a fully lit corridor ten times wider than her current one, running perpendicular to it, and was startled by a male voice saying, "May I take your coat, Flomina Folt?"

"Davik, you scared her, you oaf," said President Plemso. He wore a blue military dress uniform, towering over a man with thinning hair, wearing a cheap suit with a paunch hanging over his belt.

Davik said, "I apologize, Flomina Folt. May I take your coat?"

"Davik is a good man," the President said. "Does his job competently…most of the time."

"Thank you, sir," Davik said.

"He just lacks grace and a few other things," the President said and chuckled.

"He seems fine to me," Flomina said, "just enthusiastic, which isn't a bad thing." She handed her coat to Davik.

"Take care of that coat, Davik," the President said. "Probably cost more than ten of your paychecks."

"I'll guard it with my life, sir," Davik said, walking off down the hallway.

"That'll probably do," the President said, chuckling at Davik's expense. He thought he'd get a laugh out of Flomina and he was visibly disappointed when he didn't.

Flomina was put off by Vidor's treatment of Davik. It reminded her of the frat boys at her college. In their misguided machismo, they thought being unkind to someone they believed weaker was a show of strength and attractive to a woman.

The President approached Flomina, pointing in the opposite direction than Davik had fled. "Evening meal awaits."

"Yes, let's," Flomina said. "I'm famished."

They started down the corridor, walking side by side. The hallway had ten-meter-high ceilings and the walls were covered with floor-to-ceiling paintings of hunting scenes from hundreds of years ago in intricately carved wooden frames. They depicted large, antlered animals slung over the backs of furry hunting beasts. There were paintings of feasts where peasants in simple dress served royal women wearing bejeweled dresses and noblemen in elaborate multicolored robes.

Flomina was so taken by a painting of a lavish Royal Court dinner with a juggling jester that she stopped to examine it. "Must've been something to be alive in those days," she said. "With those resources at hand, must've been debauchery day and night."

The President placed himself between Flomina and the painting so he was standing face-to-face with her and said, "Does that turn you on?"

Flomina leaned forward so they were nose-to-nose. "You're full of yourself, aren't you?" Then she took a step back. "What do you expect from this date?"

"I have no expectations."

"Men like you always have expectations."

"Men like me?" the President said, stepping toward Flomina again.

"You know what I mean."

"I don't—please enlighten me."

Flomina said, "You're a politically powerful man and you obviously think you're powerful in other ways, too." Flomina stepped back again and stared at Vidor's crotch.

"There's only one way to find out," the President said, stepping toward Flomina a third time, but she held out her hand and stopped him from coming any closer.

She said, "Let's get one thing straight. I'm here for dinner and conversation. From my first impression, I'm repulsed by you and I have zero desire to have sex. I don't know what your father told you, but you're not my messiah."

Vidor turned toward the painting and pointed at the jester in the scene. "I suppose I'm the fool in our scenario."

"You're definitely making a run for it."

"I don't date much," the President said. "As you might imagine."

"I suppose," Flomina said. "I don't know a whole lot about you other than what I've heard through the social grapevine. You're seventeen years older than me so maybe you're more desperate for a partner than our fathers let on."

"I've no idea what you've been told, but this get-together wasn't our fathers' idea. It was mine."

"I bet."

"Not in that way."

"In what way, then?"

"My father came to me concerned that I was well into my forties and hadn't started a family yet. He told me that I hadn't considered my legacy, a family to carry on what I'd attained. I explained that it wasn't easy dating someone as President. We talked about women I'd dated in the past, but the ones I'd have any interest in were already partnered. So he asked me if there was anybody available that I'd like to date. I told him I recalled meeting you as a young girl and even then, you exhibited wit and strength of character far beyond your years. I've followed your career and the incredible life you've created for yourself. You're the type of woman I see as partner, a strong woman with ideas of her own, and a woman whose children will attain greatness in their own right."

"So you see me as some sort of breeding animal?"

"That's not what I meant."

"Sounds like it."

"Of course, there'd be some breeding involved."

"That's what this is all about. I should've known."

"No!" the President said.

He was upset that he couldn't express what he meant to say. The great Vidor Plemso, the leader of armies and the planet, was shy and tongue-tied. He had been so focused on his career that he lacked the practice and skills to speak with a woman. Flomina was attracted and turned off at the same time.

The President walked down the hallway, raised his hand and said, "Follow me."

Flomina stayed in place and sighed. She didn't know what to do. Part of her wanted to leave, but another part was curious and wanted to follow.

The President halted and turned around. He was about six meters away. "Are you coming?" he said, clearly still upset. "You're welcome to leave at any time."

"Lead on," Flomina said.

The President began walking forward again.

Flomina hurried until she was keeping pace by his side. She said, "Please continue your story about how this date was your idea."

Vidor turned to her and smiled. She liked his smile. It was genuine. He was happy that she was still here.

"My father told me that you'd been in the media lately for all the wrong reasons. Multiple sex partners. Drugs and partying. He attempted to dissuade me from my interest in you. I told him I had no idea about any tabloid nonsense. I was running a planet in crisis, but from what I read in the business sections of a few digi-media outlets, your corporation was continuing to do well. And there's no way an ex-military commander who ran a corporation dealing in weapons like my father could understand your lifestyle, which said nothing about you as a human being. I told him that I'd like to meet you, get to know you, but we exist in two different worlds and it didn't seem destined to happen. He reminded me that I was President of the planet, and I could command anyone to join me for dinner and have them be my partner. So that's my father. The same man who put a restraining order on my mother and would never let me see her because she didn't like him beating me with a meter stick."

"Sounds like a real charmer."

"You don't know the half of it. If we get to know each other better, I'll tell you more, but it's not pretty," he said, then pointed to the right down a hallway similar to the one they'd been traversing. "This way. You do look beautiful this evening, by the way."

Flomina felt herself blushing. It'd been a long time since that had happened. "Thank you. So how did you convince your father to arrange this evening?"

"I actually told my father to forget about it, but he said that any woman would want to meet the President of the planet and would be flattered to be courted by him. I reminded him that my position as President wasn't impressive to someone like you and that's not the reason I want anyone to be my partner."

That's kind of sweet, Flomina thought.

Vidor continued, "But during their monthly get-together to plan how they'll make more money and consolidate their power further, my father said something to your father about us having a date."

"Your father actually threatened my father financially to make the date happen, making it seem like it was his idea."

"Sounds like him. I know both of them get off on outmaneuvering one another," Vidor said. "I assume you're aware of their meetings."

"Oh yes," Flomina said. "My father would never miss them. My mother resents it. My father told me about those get-togethers in the form of a bedtime story when I was a child as a way to put me to sleep at night."

"That's peculiar."

"That's my father. Nothing drives him more than earning units beyond his wildest imagination, and nothing drives my mother more than spending as much of his earnings as possible to make him crazy. Fortunately, she can't spend the quantities he earns these days."

"Sounds like quite a match."

"People find happiness in strange ways."

Vidor turned left through an open archway that could fit maybe four people walking side by side and they entered the palace's ballroom.

Flomina had seen fotos of this room, but they hadn't come close to capturing the sheer size, about thirty-five meters from end to end and twenty-five meters wide. The vaulted ceiling was twenty meters high with three colossal half-lit lead glass chandeliers hanging from it. The walls were plastered with the forms of intricate blossoms painted in dynamic colors. The floor was pink marbled stone.

Flomina stopped in her tracks while Vidor headed to the large round table in the middle of the room where a lit candelabra and Msituan blossoms in a vase sat between a setting for two—plates, utensils, napkins, and drinking glasses.

"This room takes your breath away," Flomina said, surveying the entirety of the interior design.

Vidor halted near the table and turned around, observing Flomina's fascination. "It's really something, isn't it?"

"Yes, they can't make anything like this anymore...ever."

"Sad, but true," Vidor said. "As a people, we can preserve this as a remnant of our triumphs. I hope to have a room in my home one day that emulates this majestic chamber."

"That would be an achievement."

Vidor approached Flomina and took hold of her forearm. "I'd have to find the right woman first."

Flomina yanked her arm from Vidor's grasp. "You could simply hire an interior decorator."

Vidor stepped closer again. "Now, that wouldn't be much fun, would it?" He leaned forward and kissed her on the lips.

Flomina stepped back and slapped Vidor's face as hard as she could.

He hardly moved, then a smile spread across his face as he rubbed his cheek. He leaned forward and whispered in Flomina's ear, "You have fight in you. I like that."

Flomina swung her arm again, but Vidor caught it in mid-flight. Flomina fought to finish her strike, but he was too strong for her, so she tore her arm from his grasp.

"Is this the reason you invited me here? Charm me with the story of the lonely President who has no way to find a partner?" Flomina said. "That all sounded like poppycock."

"Don't play little Miss Innocent with me. You know you're enjoying yourself. I could've shut down any restaurant in the city to meet you for a date, but I did my research. I knew you'd love this place and I thought it'd be like a dream for us to meet here. Something we could bond over forever. We both have an understanding of grandeur and—"

"I think the reason we're here is because this is the only room in Koda that your ego will fit into," Flomina said. "I'm out of here."

"Are you seriously leaving? You can feel the energy between us. Don't try and deny it!"

Flomina chuckled. "At least now I know why you're so good at politics—you're full of crap."

"I'm sorry you feel that way," Vidor said. There was either genuine sadness in his voice or he was a better actor than she'd thought.

Flomina turned on her heels and headed back the way she'd come.

"Please," Vidor said. "Don't leave."

Flomina thought he sounded like a child who'd had something taken away from him. She didn't know if she should be insulted or flattered.

On the cruiser ride back to her place, in the lift down to her apartment, and drinking a half-bottle of Eglew juice while lounging on her couch, she couldn't stop thinking about the President. She thought about how handsome he looked in his uniform. She recalled how he sounded like a vulnerable little boy when he mentioned the way his father treated his mother. She pondered his story about meeting with her being his idea. He seemed sincere, but then he acted like any other rich and powerful man who figured that he could simply take whatever he wanted by applying a dollop of charm. But she had to admit she was turned on by their tussle.

She was packing the next day to head back to Nor when there was a knock on the door. She thought it might be building maintenance to repair the plumbing in her kitchen. When she peered through the peephole, she saw it was the President. He was wearing a suit and tie with a Global Assembly pin on the lapel.

Flomina said loud enough for him to hear through the door, "How did you get past the doorman?"

"Being President has its privileges."

"What do you want?"

"I came to return your coat. You left it at the palace, and I wanted to apologize for last night and explain myself. I thought it was the least I could do for wasting your time."

Flomina put her forehead against the door and laughed. She hesitated for a moment, then opened it.

Vidor entered with a sheepish grin on his face and her Ashtecki overcoat draped over his arm. To the guards behind him, he said, "You two wait outside," then he turned to Flomina as she closed the door and they were alone.

Vidor said, "You do have a mean right cross. I won't need them, will I?"

"That's up to you," Flomina said.

"I promise to be on my best behavior."

"All right, then."

"So," Vidor said. "Here's your coat." He handed it to her and she tossed it on the couch. In Vidor's hand, formerly hidden beneath the coat, was a plain white box about a meter long and a quarter-meter wide. He held it out to Flomina.

"What's this?" she said.

"A peace offering."

"You could simply say you're sorry for acting like an ass."

"I am. I'm truly sorry. I just—"

"Please. No more excuses. It's such a turnoff." Flomina took the box, opened it, and removed wrapping paper from around a painted vase. It was a museum piece, an invaluable relic. The vase was decorated with two paintings of the same woman with shoulder-length black hair, wearing a stunning yellow-and-green full-length dress with a plunging neckline.

Vidor said, "It's Third Kodan Dynasty. She was a Msituan princess."

Then they both said at the same time, "Princess Myla." And they both laughed.

Vidor pointed at the vase. "I saw it awhile back, before my conversation with my father, and it reminded me of you."

"It must've cost a fortune," Flomina said.

"I may have a military and civil service background, but I'm not poor."

"I can't take it." She held it out to Vidor. "It's too much."

"No. It's yours. I was going to give it to you last night, but things didn't turn out…Well, you know how it turned out. I'm an idiot."

"Yes, you are."

Vidor said in a sincere tone, "I came here to apologize and now I've done it…I should get going."

Flomina placed the vase on a table. "No need to rush off."

"I've got the business of running the planet, but I can probably stick around for a few more moments if you want."

"I hope you can last longer than a few moments."

"I don't understand."

Flomina sighed. "You really are clueless, aren't you?" She unbuttoned Vidor's suit jacket, then pulled his shirt out of his pants. "Why don't you show me what you've got?"

That was the first time they had sex. She never left Capitol City that day and shortly thereafter she took up residence there.

Now, Flomina walked over to a pedestal in the Plemso mansion's Great Hall and picked up the Princess Myla vase. With Vidor's passing, she cherished this piece more than any other. It was part of her history, given to her by the man she loved.

She thought about how in the later years of their relationship, she and Vidor would spend time on the terrace at sunset. They'd get a breath of fresh air and lie on a chaise lounge in each other's arms, speaking of their wondrous life together while observing the dome turning red and the winged creatures flying over the estate.

So she rode the escalator up to the terrace door. She noticed there were no guards inside or outside the doorway. She exited onto the terrace and approached the railing, breathing in the sweet smell of the blossoms below. She and Vidor had made a good team and like any relationship there had been bumps in the road.

Then there was a bright flash in the distance by the fence line, the sound of an explosion, and a bizarre static storm above her head. She reflexively turned to ask the guard what was happening, then recalled he wasn't there. She heard stun-weapon fire from the area of the explosion, then a shrieking sound, and spotted a projectile heading over the estate's forest toward the terrace. She turned to run for the doorway, but it was too late. An explosion blew her into the air and she fell through the collapsing terrace.

CARZ

Carz thanked the Global Assembly Corps of Engineer's Director for his sobering and honest assessment, then the Director departed, leaving behind a memory wafer containing the seventy-eight-page GACE report on the condition of the domes.

The Director had told Carz that the fatal breakdown of all nine domes would occur in twelve to eighteen years. This was due to the degradation of the poor-quality metallic alloys in the pane frames and their rapid rate of failure with the ever-increasing planetary temperatures and the violent storms outside. It was structurally impossible to make any repairs now. The Director explained that if Carz's father had taken GACE's advice twenty years ago and replaced the faulty panes, this calamity could have been averted.

Carz didn't wonder what his father had been thinking. He knew full well. His father thought that any renovation of the domes represented a capitulation to the anti-DOME movement. It had never crossed his mind that the survival of the Kodan people should come before his ego and reputation. Also, he'd never have publicly admitted to the shoddy workmanship because it would've discredited his wealthy backers who benefited from the dome construction. There would've been an outcry for accountability and charges of willful malpractice. In his father's mind, there was no reason for any of that drama when he was building spaceships so he could escape unscathed to a new planet. He didn't care about the lives that would be lost because those Kodans didn't express the degree of loyalty he expected for his future dynasty. Carz cursed the legacy he'd inherited from his father.

Now, the sun was setting and the dome was blood-red. It had been seventeen days since Carz's ascension was announced. Demonstrators were still marching in the streets below, and dealing with the discontent of the citizens regarding the transition of power was an ongoing issue. His father's remaining staff advised that the military should simply clear the streets of the rabble. If the citizens were injured or killed, then it was their fault for protesting in the first place. Carz listened, then told them to hand in their resignations. The Majority Whip of the Global Assembly—an empty title since there was essentially only one party—lectured him on Kodan political history. He spoke about how the masses required strong leadership from one person and how the theories about the masses needing a voice in governance was a delusion left over from the failure of democracy. The masses didn't know what they desired and that produced unwanted chaos. Carz lost his temper over the condescension and audacity of the myth that citizens were like children who yearned for the divine direction of a ruler. He chased the Majority Whip out of his office.

Carz wanted to appease the demonstrators. Give them some powers without losing his own. Maybe the planet was in such a mess because the government's agenda was rooted in greed and authoritarian domination. He reasoned that voices from outside that dynamic might be enlightening, but until he found a solution, he decided that the demonstrators were being peaceful enough, and that his utmost priority was dealing with the overall survival of the Kodan people.

Time wasn't on their side. The Director's assessment reinforced that conclusion. Carz had already been working on that supposition based on a GACE report from the latter days of his father's rule. A few days ago, he'd met with the person in charge of financing the Global Assembly spaceships. Her existence was known to only a handful of individuals. Carz discovered the funds available for more spaceships had been depleted by the construction and launch of the satellites. If they cut corners, there were enough units left to build one more spaceship. He told the financial person that he wanted options on funding more than ten ships even if it meant extracting back taxes from wealthy Kodans.

This was all wrapped in an overarching plan that Carz was formulating. First, he would come clean with the citizens by revealing the truth about their dire circumstances and in that manner, mobilize them to build more spaceships for their survival while promising to institute democratic reforms going forward. For the moment, he figured it was best to avoid throwing the planetary population into panic about their dim future until he heard back from the financial person and had an idea of how to salvage the situation. He might even have to call Mar Jeps about working out a payment arrangement on the spaceships.

Carz had just begun reading the GACE report when his personal comm buzzed.

"Leader?" a male voice on the other end of the comm said. Carz didn't recognize the voice and his comm didn't identify him. He did notice by the integers that this person was calling from a Global Assembly comm.

"Who is this?"

"Sorry, sir. This is Reis Venit. I work security at the estate. I regret to inform you that the estate has been bombed. The Head of Security isn't calling because he's been injured as well as your mother. Your brother and son are fine."

"My mother?"

"Yes, sir. She's in critical but stable condition, getting the best care."

"Where is she?"

"Since the hospital bed, gear, and med inventory were still in your father's room, she's at the estate. We thought it best not to move her. One of our guards was an Armed Forces med so he stabilized her and a formal med is on the way."

"I'll be right there," Carz said and disconnected the call.

He commed Roneh and said, "There's been an attack on the estate and my mother has been injured. Meet me at the cruiser pad on the roof."

"Is Filo all right?"

"Yes."

"Then I'll meet you back at the estate," Roneh said. "I have a few things to take care of."

"No," Carz said. "Get to the roof now."

Roneh hung up. Other than asking about their son, Carz was struck by Roneh's dismissiveness. She didn't sound shocked about the incident or concerned over his mother's condition. Roneh wasn't the best of friends with his mother and she wasn't an emotional individual, but her reaction felt off.

Carz activated the intercom. "Kel, could you please alert security that I need to leave right away for the estate?"

Kel said, "Yes, sir. They've actually just arrived to increase your protection and told me what happened. I will relay that you're ready to leave."

Carz placed the GACE memory wafer in his desk drawer and slid his viewer into its case, then stood, hung the case's strap over his shoulder, and headed toward the exit. The door slid open to reveal two guards standing on either side of the threshold.

Kel got to her feet as he approached her desk. "I hope your mother will be all right, sir. This is a terrible tragedy."

Carz said, "Thank you, Kel."

Two more guards were standing in the hallway outside the waiting room. Carz walked down the corridor flanked by the four guards. As they approached the lift, two guards stepped in front of Carz while the two in back went ahead to summon the lift.

One of the guards in front of him said, "Security has been sent to the First Lady's office as well."

"Any news on how my mother sustained her injuries?"

"She was injured as the result of a fall."

"A fall?"

"Yes, sir. The mansion's terrace was blown out from under her."

Carz was angry and baffled how the estate's security could have failed so badly.

The lift doors opened. The two guards standing by the lift entered and called out, "Clear." The guard who had been talking to Carz said, "Please proceed, sir." Once Carz was inside the lift, the other two guards entered and one of them pressed the button for the roof. The doors closed and the lift headed up.

"How did something like this happen?" Carz asked the guard he'd been conversing with before.

"As far as we know right now, four armed men attacked the energy shield's main power station. They killed the guards there, destroyed the station with explosives, knocking out the shield, then fired a rocket at the mansion."

"How did four men get inside the estate's gates in the first place?"

"The GSS is investigating, sir."

"Anything known about the attackers?

"The GSS is looking into the identity of one of the attackers killed at the relay station."

"I want updates."

"The GSS will be on-site."

"Stinks of an inside job," Carz said as the lift doors slid open. Guards with rocket launchers were posted at the four corners of the roof. A cruiser circled overhead in the night sky. The executive cruiser hummed on the pad, surrounded by more guards. There was no sign of Roneh.

Carz said, "Comm the First Lady and tell her we're leaving—now."

"Will do, sir."

Carz strode to the cruiser and climbed inside, keeping the door open. He waited an interminable amount of time for Roneh. At one point, he noticed the guard who spoke with him in the lift, huddled with the other guards, talking to them while they listened intently. The guard from the lift wore a round, solid blue pin that denoted he was a supervising officer. Carz hadn't noticed before. He looked familiar, too. As the guard passed by the open cruiser doorway, Carz called out, "What's your name?"

The guard stopped in his tracks and approached the cruiser, leaning in. "Glym Atmar, sir."

"Atmar? You're Davik's oldest son?"

"Yes, sir. We met once or twice when we were children."

"Are you in charge of this contingent?"

"Yes, sir."

"I want you to send two more men down to the First Lady and have her dragged up here if she won't come right away."

"Let me check her status." Glym took a step from the cruiser and spoke on his audio implant, then returned to the doorway. "They're on their way up."

"Appreciate it," Carz said. "Ride with me to the estate. Place your second-in-command in charge here."

"Yes, sir," Glym said and hurried over to speak with another guard.

While this was happening, the roof's lift doors opened and four guards emerged flanking Roneh who carried a viewer case. She appeared annoyed. Carz was angered that she had kept him waiting and that she was upset about being summoned.

Carz scooted over on the seat and Roneh slid in beside him. A guard shut the cruiser door. Carz decided that he'd wait to speak with her. Glym finished briefing the other guard, then climbed into the backseat of the cruiser and closed his door.

Carz leaned forward and said to the pilot, "Let's go."

As the cruiser lifted off and cleared the rooftop, Roneh peered out the window and said, "Look at the scum down there. They should be wiped off the face of the planet. For the good of the globe."

"That's the first thing you have to say after keeping me waiting?" Carz said, noting the anger in his raised voice.

"I was in the middle of something."

"I bet you were."

"What does that mean?"

"You haven't asked about my mother's condition."

"You told me about your mother, didn't you?"

"I just told you she was injured, but I know more now," Carz said. "This is my mother and the grandmother of your child, but you don't seem to care one bit."

"You need to control yourself. You're the Leader, not some sensitive schoolgirl."

Carz took a deep breath. He didn't like Roneh getting the upper hand, but he didn't want to quarrel anymore.

When the cruiser was nearing the estate grounds, the pilot said, "The landing pad and the estate lawn are jammed with emergency vehicles and first responders so we're going to set down in the parking lot. Security has been alerted to our approach."

Carz said, "Do what you need to do, but can you circle the estate first so I can get a look at the damage?"

"Yes, sir."

The cruiser flew over the estate. There were emergency vehicles everywhere. The property was crawling with personnel. There was a tent on the lawn by the forest. Carz assumed this was being utilized as a command post to coordinate the emergency operations and investigate the crime scene.

The terrace was a smoking pile of timber. Floodlights had been stationed around it, providing the area with illumination for the workers. A truck was spraying water from the estate's resources on the smoldering wreckage. Pipes, electrical lines, and beams were exposed where the façade of the mansion that faced the terrace had collapsed. The cruiser continued to circle and Carz got one more look at the damage on their way back to the parking lot. It seemed worse the second time around. His home had been attacked. He felt violated.

The pilot said, "It'll be a moment before we land."

An ambulance with flashing lights and siren blaring shot through the lot and out the entrance.

Carz said to the pilot, "You have any idea what that was about?"

The pilot said something inaudible into the microphone attached to his headphones, then responded, "The terrace collapsed on a guard who was on the staircase at the time of the attack. They just dug him out. He's barely alive so they rushed him to the nearest clinic."

The cruiser began descending.

Roneh said, "Damn terrorists."

Carz shot her an angry look. "Just keep your opinions to yourself until we have proof."

"You know I'm right."

"Until we have conclusive evidence, do as I say."

When the cruiser touched down, Carz noted an estate security guard standing at attention in the lot, waiting for him. The guard stepped forward and slid open the door. Carz exited and Roneh followed.

Glym Atmar exited from the backseat and said, "Can I take your cases?" Carz handed his case to Glym, and Roneh waved him off.

The estate guard said, "I'm Reis Venit, sir. We talked earlier."

"Yes, Reis. What's the status here?"

"The med is attending to your mother. Your son and brother are shaken up, but fine. We've lost the two guards at the relay station, the Head of Security is in critical condition, and another guard was just rushed to a clinic. His prognosis on departure was not good."

"Who's in charge here?"

"With all the losses, I'm the highest ranking on duty, sir. The GSS is set up on the lawn, collecting evidence and questioning the staff and the guards on duty at the time of the incident. Head Director Bolonar is waiting for you."

Carz said, "How long have you worked here, Reis? I don't recognize you."

"I used to be the lead guard at the gate, but I got moved onto the grounds today."

"Lucky you," Carz said. "Why were you reassigned?"

"I replaced a guard who stopped coming to work."

"That's curious," Carz said. "I'd like to meet with Bolonar now. Take me to him."

Glym said, "What would you like me to do, sir?"

"You come with me, and you'll see why I brought you here."

Reis walked ahead of Carz and Roneh while Glym fell in behind them. As Carz passed the landing pad, emergency workers who were packing up their cruisers and vehicles stopped and stood at attention.

Passing through the forest, it was clear that vehicle tires had flattened the foliage on the edges of the path to reach the terrace. Carz was struck by the forest's silence. No winged creatures were singing or shrieking. No small woodland creatures shifted under the flora at their approach. Carz had spent his childhood playing in this forest and he'd never experienced anything like it. He wondered with the energy field down if the winged creatures had flown off and the land creatures had dispersed, or if they were frightened by the explosion and the flurry of activity and were hiding. The smell of the smoldering rubble intensified as they neared the mansion.

Before they reached the GSS tent, Carz reached out and grabbed Reis's shoulder.

Reis turned to Carz and said, "Yes, sir."

"You wait here with Glym and the First Lady. I'd like to speak to the Head Director by myself."

Reis and Glym snapped to attention. "Yes, sir."

Roneh said, "I'll head to the house."

"No," Carz said in a stern tone. "You stay here."

As Carz entered the tent, the dozen GSS officers gathered around tables with viewers or comm devices snapped to attention. Carz said, "At ease."

Tarq Bolonar, Head Director of the GSS, approached Carz. "Sorry to see you under these circumstances, sir."

"What do we have on the attackers?"

"We've ID'd the one who was killed. We know his current Movement affiliation and he has a history of violence against the Global Assembly. The attackers who got away were wearing masks and didn't leave any prints. I've given all the information on the attacker, the guards on duty at the time, and a breakdown of the attack from start to finish to Agent Shiv."

"Really?"

"Yes, sir. He asked and he gets what he wants. At least, that's the protocol set in place by your father."

"I'm not my father, am I?"

"Sorry, sir. I just—"

"No need. I never revoked that order. From now on, make sure I approve any intel that Agent Shiv requests. If he has a problem with that, then tell him to talk to me," Carz said. "I want all the information you've given Shiv on my desk in the mansion by the time you leave here."

"Yes, sir," Bolonar said.

"By the way, are you looking into the guard who left his job unexpectedly?"

"Yes, sir. We have agents heading to his residence as we speak."

"Keep up the good work."

"Sir, before you leave, I have a question. I mean no disrespect, but I was wondering why you'd let the purge of the Movement go forward without telling me."

"What're you talking about?" Carz was shocked.

"You don't know? The purge," Bolonar said. "I was in the dark until this evening when it went into motion planetwide. Right before the bombing, matter of fact, so I've had no time to contact you about it. It seems your father signed off on it and orders were filed with my predecessor. It was planned need-to-know and you're the only one who can stop it."

Carz didn't know what to say, but Orn came to mind. "Right. Please contact Agent Shiv and order him to meet me at my office here immediately. I'll attempt to countermand the purge. I may comm you later. If not, we'll talk tomorrow." Carz turned and exited the tent. Reis and Glym were standing where Carz had left them. Roneh was gone.

Reis said, "The First Lady went on ahead."

"Really, Reis? I thought she'd become invisible!" Carz said, then sighed. "Sorry. That was uncalled for."

Glym said, "We all understand, sir. This is a trying situation."

"Good way of putting it, Atmar. I knew I'd brought you here for a reason."

"Yes, sir."

"Now, let's go see how my mother is doing."

Carz headed down the path toward the mansion ahead of Reis and Glym. As he got closer to the smoldering wreckage of the terrace, the air stung his eyes and it became difficult to breathe. He broke out coughing. The firefighters wore oxygen masks and were spraying fire-retardant foam on the entire charred area. The estate's water resources must've been depleted.

The lawn had been ruined by the heavy machinery driving on it. Carz thought about the price in units required to repair the estate, but that was the least of the cost. More importantly, there was the damage to the reputation of the estate's security. The investigation would need to go deeper than what Bolonar had done today. Millions of units were spent on security here so how could four men strike at the Leader's home and cause such destruction?

Carz noticed that the Vanderlord estate cart had been crushed under the collapsed terrace. In their childhood, he and Minok had raced around the estate in it, with Davik Atmar yelling at them to slow down. Carz had pictured his own son driving the cart. He pondered fixing the antique, but it might be beyond restoration.

Carz slowed so he was walking beside Glym, then pointed to the cart. "So many memories of your father driving that thing."

"He hated it," Glym said. Carz heard resentment in Glym's voice. "That thing was your father's way of infantilizing mine. He felt demeaned by it like he was a clown at an amusement park."

"I had no idea," Carz said. "But he'd never say anything to my father."

"You got that right. Those two had a bizarre relationship."

"Takes two," Carz said as they followed the path around the house to the workers' entrance. He wondered why he was defending his father who he'd watched bully Davik for years. "You're right, though. Bizarre indeed. Your father was a good man. He was like a second father to me. He was the only one around here with a genuine sense of humor. He made me laugh. I miss him."

"I miss him, too."

"Don't ever repeat that second-father thing. It's between you and me."

"Copy that," Glym said.

Two Global Guards holding stun rifles stood on either side of the mansion's service entrance. It was odd seeing them here. They only appeared on special occasions when his father wanted to create an atmosphere of fear and intimidate his guests. He guessed there must be a standing order for them to be here as a show of force after an attack. Carz bet there were others guarding the main entrance and patrolling the perimeter of the estate, and he had to admit that their intimidating presence made him feel safer.

As Carz approached, the Global Guards snapped to attention and saluted. Carz returned the salute and stopped short of the doorway. He said to Reis, "Take my case from Glym and put it in my office, then head to my mother's room and station yourself outside. I'll be right up."

"Yes, sir," Reis said, then took the case from Glym and entered the building.

When the door closed, Carz faced Glym and said, "I'd like you to take over as Head of Security around here. It'll be a while before this place gets back to normal, whatever that is, but you'd be a welcome addition."

"I'm honored, sir, but there are many in the security corps who are ahead of me in seniority."

"I have a feeling you won't disappoint, and it'll be good having an Atmar around here. I need someone I can trust and you're like family."

"That's nice to hear, sir."

"Let your supervisor know and Reis can get you up to speed. I'll have my people handle the paperwork and we'll run a security check on you."

"Thank you, sir. It'll mean a lot to my family."

Carz patted Glym's arm. "Glad to do it. Now let's see how my mother is doing."

Carz turned toward the entrance and one of the Global Guards opened the door. Glym entered first.

Carz smelled evening meal cooking in the kitchen ahead of him. He could see people in white aprons moving around. He heard the clank of a lid covering a pot. A knife cutting something.

"To the right," Carz said to Glym, who was still ahead of him. "Take the stairs to the third floor, then left."

Reis and another guard were standing on either side of the doorway leading into his father's trophy room. Carz tapped Glym on the shoulder and scooted by him.

Reis said to Carz, "The med just left and said he'd be back shortly. He gave me his comm info in case you have any questions, or if he's needed urgently. There's a nurse attending to your mother as well."

"Have you seen the First Lady?"

"No, sir, but you have a visitor from another planet," Reis said. "At least, that's what he said."

"Oh, do I?" Carz said. "You two stay here. Glym, come with me. I'll need protection from this extraterrestrial." Glym looked confused.

When Carz entered the room, he stopped in his tracks, shocked at the sight of his mother who was laid out in bed. Both her legs were elevated in casts, along with one of her arms.

Then seven-year-old Filo burst out from behind a dresser. He was wearing a yellow T-shirt and cream color shorts, and he was barefoot. He screeched "Woop! Woop!" and dashed over to Carz who lifted Filo up in his arms until he was face-to-face with him. Filo's cheeks were red and his blond hair unkempt.

Carz said, "What is this creature, Glym? I believe he is a danger to our planet."

Filo giggled.

Glym said, "What shall be done, sir?"

"The only thing that can be done. Their only weakness is kisses and hugs."

"No!" Filo yelled, then screeched in a high-pitched tone.

Carz kissed Filo rapidly on his cheeks and forehead, then hugged him.

"No!" Filo said. "No! Stop!"

"You see," Carz said, "it's working." Then he carried Filo toward his grandmother.

"Put me down," Filo screamed. "Let me go!"

Carz held Filo at arm's length, then kissed him with a farting noise on his neck.

"No, Papa. No."

Carz hugged Filo one more time, then held him at arm's length again. "I love you."

"I love you, too, Papa. Now, please put me down."

Carz lowered Filo and as soon as his feet hit the floor, he raced around the room in circles.

"Where is his nanny?" Carz said to the nurse, who was a Msituan woman in her twenties wearing a white uniform. "Why is he here? This isn't a proper place for him right now,"

The nurse said, "No idea, sir. Your brother dropped him off here."

Filo began strutting around the room with his arms straight out squawking like one of the winged creatures in the estate's forest.

As Carz approached his mother's left side, he noticed that the drawer of the night table where his father had stashed his favorite candy was open and filled with empty wrappers. Filo's frenetic behavior made sense now. His mother's eyes were closed. She was semiconscious and moaning. A bandage had been wrapped around her head and part of her left cheek was covered with a dressing that was stained red. An IV ran into her arm and a hi-tech monitor left over from his father's convalescence kept track of her heart and brain functions.

"Mother," Carz said, taking her hand, which was covered in scrapes. "I'm so sorry." Carz fought back tears. He needed to keep up a brave face. He was the head of the family now.

"Carz," his mother said, opening her eyes like she was coming out of a deep sleep. "I'm glad you're all right. You can cry if you want to."

"I'm fine."

"Your father trained you well. Minok was here a short time ago. He was hysterical. I couldn't get him to stop crying. I asked him to leave."

"He'll be all right."

"Yes," his mother said and flinched in pain.

The nurse pressed a button on the IV.

His mother sighed with relief. "I've been told that he and Filo were on the other side of the house when the attack happened."

Filo was still circling the room, squawking.

"Reis!" Carz called out. "Where is the First Lady? Go find her."

A moment later, Roneh entered the room. "I'm right here."

"About time," Carz said. "Deal with your son."

"Momma," Filo said, running up to Roneh who embraced him.

"My baby boy," Roneh said. "I'm so happy you're all right."

Filo continued squawking in Roneh's arms.

Carz said, "He ate all of my father's candy and needs a time out."

"Why haven't you dealt with him?"

"I'm talking to my mother," Carz said.

Roneh lifted Filo off the ground and carried him toward the bed. Filo nestled his head into the crook of Roneh's neck, then said, "I love you, Momma."

"We're all so glad that you made it out alive, Flomina. It could've been so much worse," Roneh said in a somber tone. "I think we should find some real food for your grandson and get him ready for bed."

Filo twisted in Roneh's arms and reached out for Carz, screaming, "No! Papa. No! I wanna stay."

Carz said, "You go with your mother and I'll be there to tuck you in."

Filo's cries continued, but faded as Roneh carried him out the door and down the hallway.

Carz's mother said, "I never liked that girl."

"Yet you and Father demanded that I partner with her."

Soon after his graduation from Military College, Carz had gone to his mother to see if she could change the plans his father had laid out for him. He'd met a young woman who he loved and preferred over Roneh.

Carz recalled being upset and saying to his mother, "I've known Roneh for three years. I have nothing in common with her. She's rude and abrasive. I'm not attracted to her—in fact, she repulses me."

His mother had put her finger to Carz's lips, then pointed in the direction of the study where his father was dealing with another dome collapse. "We should go for a walk in the garden. We don't want to disturb him."

When they exited the house, they descended the terrace stairs and turned down the path toward the forest, leaving behind the security guard stationed at the bottom of the stairs. The air was strong with the scent of freshly cut lawn.

Carz's mother said, "Your father wants you to partner with Roneh so you will."

"I don't want—"

"It doesn't matter what you want if your father thinks otherwise," she said. "I understand that like everyone else your age, you think your life choices come from your desires, but you'll understand soon enough that everyone makes choices, consciously or unconsciously, based on some outside influence. In your case, it's just more blatant."

"Blatant? It's robbery."

"Yes, well, this is the life you've been born into. One day, you'll be the most powerful person on Koda, so this is a small sacrifice."

"Easy for you to say. You went from massive wealth and fame to partnering with the President of the planet."

"Yes, but I compromised, too," Carz's mother said. "You know full well your father isn't the easiest person to be partnered with. He is a daily challenge. I've learned to live with it. And it's given me an incredible life."

"From what I've heard, your life was pretty awesome before you met Father."

"Yes," his mother said. A smile spread across her face and she seemed to drift off to someplace else, then giggled. "It was pretty damned good."

"So why did you leave it all behind to partner with Father?"

"It was time to enter a new phase of my existence," she said as they continued down the path through the forest. "But this isn't about me. How did we end up talking about me?"

"Because I'm being commanded to partner with this horrid person and you're comparing her to Father to make the point that you've been through the same thing," Carz said. "I just don't see it."

His mother stopped walking and said, "Shall we?" Then she headed off the paved path and onto a narrow dirt trail winding between the trees and other flora.

Carz followed. He heard creatures skittering away and winged creatures taking off above them. His mother reached a wooden bench in the midst of the forest and sat down, then beckoned Carz to sit beside her.

His mother threw her head back, breathed in deeply, and sighed loudly. "This is one of my favorite places on the estate."

"Yes, I know."

"And do you know why?"

"You've told me before," Carz said. "Because this place is away from the constant static of Father and his governance."

A small, furry four-legged creature about the size of the palm of a hand emerged from the underbrush, stood on its hind legs, and chittered. His mother reached into her pocket, removed a karanga—an edible nut—and placed it on her knee.

Carz said, "What're you doing?"

"Wait for it," his mother said, then patted her knee beside the nut. "Come on, Karanga."

The creature climbed up his mother's pant leg. It picked up the nut in its mouth, then jumped to the ground. Facing the bench, it dropped the nut, stood up on its hind legs, and chittered again.

Carz's mother said, "You're welcome, Karanga." Then the creature picked up the nut in its mouth and disappeared into the underbrush.

Carz said, "Friend of yours?"

"Yes, that's Karanga, maybe Karanga the twenty-first. I've been coming here a long time."

"You visited this place a lot when I was growing up, but this is the first time I've seen Karanga."

"Yes, well, if you or Minok hunted me down here, it was usually because you were upset. Karanga would stay away from your raised voice or your brother's crying," Carz's mother said. "Where was I before I was interrupted?"

"You were talking about this place."

"Yes. I love this bench. The solitude here gives me the strength to deal with your father. His shortcomings are evident. We don't need to get into it. He's not as vile as Roneh, but my point is that I found a way to cope with him, otherwise he would've sucked all the life out of me and I would've turned into someone I didn't like. I wasn't going to become a victim like your grandmother. As far as your situation is concerned, it's clear that Roneh isn't fond of you, either."

"I wouldn't say that."

"Don't kid yourself. She didn't agree to this partnership out of attraction to you. She accepted it because by the time your father dies and you take over, she'll have accrued enough power to capitalize on the influence that the position of First Lady will give her," his mother said. "You think your father doesn't knows what he's doing. This match isn't about you two loving each other. He knows by the time he passes away Roneh's popularity will be immense. Her being by your side will help ease you into the position of Leader and that'll start this dynasty your father has been obsessing over for years."

"He always has been forward thinking."

"I know you're a catch and I'm saying that objectively—although as your mother, I'm certainly biased. Roneh doesn't care about you. She's all about the good of the globe, which I find boring, but to each his own."

"Right. So if this match is written in stone, then my life going forward will be miserable. Is that what you want for me? What you're saying is she will never grow to love me, and I can't see feeling the same for her so—"

"So you continue having relationships with women who enjoy your company in and out of the bedroom, women who know that they'll never be your partner. You're good-looking and charming. You'll be a powerful man even before your father passes. Women will be waiting in line, fighting for your attention. You'll have your pick. And if they get out of line and want to tell the viewing channels or digi-media about your affair, you just threaten to bring the GSS down on them like your father has done in the past," his mother said, patting Carz on the thigh. "Roneh will not care one iota. I guarantee it. And I'll give you my high-rise apartment on Oedor Drive so you can live this alternative life. I never got rid of it. You'll need to redecorate, make it more of a man's pad, but it'll be like your bench in the forest."

"I don't know what to say," Carz said. "That's generous of you, and I hope you're right about Roneh not caring."

"I'd bet on it."

His mother was right. The engagement lasted another four years and it took another five years for Filo to be born. Artificial insemination rather than physical contact made their son possible.

Now, his father had passed, and his mother was lying in bed with broken limbs.

Carz's mother said, "Sometimes I regretted letting you go forward with that arrangement, but your father had his mind set and your life hasn't been too bad." She winked at Carz who chuckled.

"Yes, I made it work. Thanks to you." Carz squeezed his mother's hand.

Her gaze shifted from Carz and over to Glym. "Good to see you, Davik. You're looking well."

Carz said, "That's not Davik, Mother."

"I know Davik when I see him."

"Davik passed away years ago, remember?" Carz said, walking over to Glym and placing a hand on his shoulder. "This is his son, Glym. He will be our new Head of Security."

"Don't be silly. Glym is a little boy. That's Davik."

Carz gazed over at the nurse who was observing the interaction. "She's not right at the moment," the nurse said. "She has a severe concussion and she's pumped full of pain meds."

Roneh entered the room and said, "I just wanted to make sure you have everything you need, Flomina, and Filo wants to see you, Carz."

"I never liked you," Carz's mother said to Roneh. "I don't trust you and I wouldn't be surprised if this attack was all your doing."

Roneh appeared to be caught off guard by her mother-in-law's statement. "That's the most ridiculous thing I've ever heard. I would never," she said, then turned on her heels and exited the room.

ORN

Orn knocked on the door of the Leader's study.

From the other side, he heard Carz call out, "Come!"

Orn entered and closed the door behind him. Carz was sitting at the desk, clutching half a glass of Malrap as he watched the floor-mounted viewing screen. Orn heard the news reporter saying, "…a terrorist in the Movement perpetrated this horrific bombing at—"

Carz deactivated the viewing screen and it descended into the floor. "Come in," Carz said, waving Orn closer. He appeared tired.

Orn approached the desk, halted a few meters from it, then snapped to attention.

"At ease."

Orn said, "How's your mother?"

"Broken and in bed, but feisty as ever."

"That's a good sign."

"She asked about you." Carz swigged down the rest of his Malrap.

"Really?"

Carz chuckled. "No, she still hates your guts."

"She's no worse for the wear, then."

"No worse for the wear?" Carz said, raising his voice and banging the bottom of the glass on the desktop. "Broken limbs and a severe concussion. She may never be the same. The incident tonight was deplorable."

"Yes, sir. You'll get no argument from me."

Carz said in a sarcastic tone, "I'm so glad to hear that."

"Sorry, sir."

"Cut the crap, Orn. You know why I asked you here."

"I would imagine to hear my advice on the next course of action."

"Well, then. Tell me what you think."

"I would—"

"No, let me guess. The attack was perpetrated by a radical element within the Movement who've gained sway over the organization," Carz said. "That's what they're spouting on all the viewing channels. They know about the dead bomber and the injury to my mother, too."

"I didn't—"

"Doesn't it strike you as odd that the viewing channels—which are the mouthpieces of the Global Assembly—all of a sudden have an investigative arm of their own? Why do you think they're saying these things?"

"I don't—"

"Me neither," Carz said, throwing up his hands. "It's news to me and I'm the Leader, aren't I?"

"Yes, sir."

"Well, I'm glad we agree on that," Carz said. "I want to know who told them to say these things. I want the news editors of all the channels interviewed, and I want the vidcam footage of those interrogations. I'm certain that'll lead us to Roneh, who has a working relationship with those editors, and that should get us to the bottom of this conspiracy."

Orn felt something he hadn't felt in a long time. Fear. His own need to make the purge happen, in the best interests of the Leader, had gotten in the way of executing it properly. He should've waited to file the orders until he'd convinced Carz. Roneh had overplayed their hand by contacting the viewing channels. He should've heeded his instincts before he concocted this plan with her. He shouldn't have trusted her.

"Nothing to add?" Carz said. "Roneh was behind this bombing. You know why, don't you?"

Orn was aware that Roneh was a force to be reckoned with. He'd hired her decades ago to charm information out of Rajer Jeps, but her rise to prominence had been a brilliant maneuver by Vidor Plemso, who had wielded her powerful propaganda skills to keep the Kodan population in line. He knew how to control her, and he assumed that his son, being his progeny, would know as well. That was where he'd miscalculated. Roneh was now a loose cannon.

"Come on, Orn," Carz said. "My father always said that you were a few steps ahead of him."

"I'm not sure—"

"Power," Carz said. "That's all she's ever wanted. This will give her the cachet she needs with the Global Assembly reps to approve her Watch Program, and I just learned from Head Director Bolonar that somehow my father signed off on the purge before he died and it's happening as we speak. I'm positive Roneh was behind that, too."

"Maybe this would best be discussed in the morning, sir. After a good night's sleep."

"How am I going to get a good night's sleep after this revelation? My partner and mother of my child being so duplicitous."

"It's a tough pill to swallow," Orn said. "The bright side is you can always blame your father, because as you say, his signature is on the orders. After this bombing by the Movement, you'll have no choice. You'll have to let the purge proceed otherwise you'll look weak. The bottom line is that the purge has already been set in motion and can't be stopped."

"I do have a choice," Carz said. "Once you leave this room, I'm going to get on the comm and do my best to stop it. All those people and their families. Innocent lives lost. It's barbaric."

"Your father was a field commander in an unforgiving war, sir. His job was defeating the enemy. If he saw a path to victory, then he took it. The purge will be a brilliant—"

"When I think of the unethical nature of this purge and its magnitude, it makes me see my father in a different light. I have no intention of allowing it to continue. I won't discuss it any further. My priority is Roneh now. We can't let her know that we're on to her. I want you to weed out whoever might have collaborated with her. I want to know how she perpetrated this attack and how she got my father to sign off on the purge. Can you do that for me?"

"Of course," Orn said.

"Good to hear," Carz said, wiping at his eyes. "I'm tired and I still have work to do. Let me know as soon as you have any new intel."

Orn walked out the door, closed it behind him, then stood in the silence of the hallway. He took a deep breath and exhaled. He had lied to the Leader. He'd never lied to Vidor Plemso. Clearly, Carz trusted him and didn't think he was involved in the bombing. Orn had somehow avoided retribution, but now he was supposed to investigate the bombing he had been complicit in causing.

He could reenter the study and confess, but he didn't feel guilty. He felt solace in the knowledge that the purge was happening across the planet. The Leader could attempt to halt it, but the majority of the action had already taken place, and whether the Leader understood or not, it was for the good of the Global Assembly. Orn had executed Vidor's final order and he was certain that it was the right thing to do.

INSOL

Insol sat at her desk in her office, grading term papers. She'd taken over as the SEEDER-program studies department chair seven years ago when Harmin had an emotional breakdown and never returned.

A framed digi-foto of her, Mel, Ador, and Yor hung on the wall across the room. It had been taken on the campus green when she was hired as a professor. That felt like yesterday, but so much had changed since then. Ador had been assassinated. Mel had retired from academia and now worked for the Prevor Relief Foundation. She hadn't heard from Yor in years, except for messages relayed through Mar. Insol wasn't much for nostalgia, but the recent change in government and all the demonstrations made her look back on her life.

She gave the student paper in front of her a passing grade, then closed her viewer and thought about calling it a day. She'd been so focused on grading papers she hadn't realized that night had descended and she was sitting in a dark room, except for her desk lamp. She hadn't eaten evening meal, either. She stood up and stretched, then packed her briefcase with the memory wafer containing the backup for her grade book and her viewer.

Her comm buzzed. Her first impulse was not to answer. She figured it was a student who wanted her to

     Howard Libes

accept a late paper, then she noticed from the digits that the call was from the Shamban region, so she picked up.

"Insol, this is Lek Valsted. I'm so glad to hear your voice." He was noticeably concerned about something.

"Lek, is my mother all right?"

"Yes," Lek said. "But we've been worried sick. The GSS is coming for you."

"What else is new?"

"No, it's more serious than bringing you in for questioning. You recall Vidor Plemso's purge idea?"

"Of course."

"It's underway. Thousands have already been impacted," Lek said. "I've been notified by my inside man that they're coming for you."

Insol turned off her desk light, plunging the room into darkness, then gazed out the window onto the campus green. The lampposts lining the paths that criss-crossed the campus were off, which was odd, and in the dim light emanating from the surrounding buildings, she noticed figures carrying stun rifles moving across the green side by side, toward her building.

Lek said, "You still there?"

"Yes."

"Hide in the office shelter, then run to Prevor Industries when the coast is clear."

The comm deactivated.

Outside her office, Insol heard boots stomping down the hallway, then a fist banged on the door.

A male voice said, "Insol Renta, by order of the Global Assembly, we're here to arrest you."

Insol was silent. She panicked. She looked outside. Soldiers were standing at the foot of the building, weapons drawn, peering up at her windows. Insol turned her back to them.

"We know you're there. We have infrared on you. If you come out with your hands up, it'll go easier."

Insol thought, *I don't think there's anything easy about being executed.*

"We're preparing to knock down the door. You've been warned."

Lek had told her to hide in the shelter, but she didn't know what he was talking about.

A battering ram banged up against the door, which was a reinforced high-tech security model installed during Yor's tenure as department chair. *Thank the Powers-That-Be for Mado*, Insol thought.

She had a memory of Mado's people hammering away inside the office after the door installation. Later, when she asked Yor what they'd been doing, he'd pointed to the new lounge area and said, "A little insurance."

Her eyes now fully adjusted to the dim light, she grabbed her briefcase and walked over to the lounge. She'd always thought it was odd that the lounge's floor appeared to slide underneath the main floor, that it sounded hollow underneath when she walked over it, and that the armchairs were mounted to the floor. She'd just taken it for granted as part of the design.

Insol pushed against the back of a chair. Nothing happened. She did it again harder, leaning into it, and still nothing. Then she walked around to the other side of the lounge, grabbed the arms of a chair from behind, and pulled with all her might. The floor and all the chairs on that side slid back slightly.

The battering ram continued slamming against the door.

She pulled again and again, and the mounted chairs and floor moved back on a track, revealing a square hole in the floor.

The battering continued.

Insol grabbed a memory wafer taped on the underside of her middle desk drawer that contained the latest Movement meeting notes and passwords and tossed it in her briefcase. Since the GSS could track her comm, she crushed it under the heel of her shoe and left it on her desk, then she dropped her briefcase into the hole in the floor. She thought about bringing a light, but even if she had one, the beam might radiate through cracks in the floor and give away her location. She wasn't fond of dark, enclosed places and was a bit claustrophobic, but this cramped space seemed like her only choice between life and death.

With each hit of the battering ram, she could hear the doorframe cracking.

Insol sat down on the floor and lowered herself into the space until she was seated cross-legged on the bottom. There were two glow-in-the-dark green arrows on one wall which were sequentially numbered. She felt along the wall below the first arrow and discovered a latch. She pulled down on it and the floor above slid closed. The second arrow pointed to the right of the latch, so she turned it laterally right and a lock clicked above her. She presumed that sealed the floor.

She settled in, scooting herself back against one of the space's walls. The side walls were about an arm's length away. Her briefcase was beside her.

The battering ram smashed open the door and she heard bootsteps above her. Insol slowed her breathing.

The commanding officer who had been speaking to her through the door said, "Where in blazes is she? Go check the infrared. She has to be in here somewhere."

"Yes, sir."

Bootsteps scrambled above her.

"The rest of you—tear this place apart!"

There was the sound of bookshelves hurled over. The storage closet was opened and items thrown onto the floor. There was banging on the walls.

Bootsteps came running into the office. "Nothing on the infrared, sir, and the sergeant wants you to know that the men are maintaining a perimeter and searching the other offices."

The commanding officer said, "Tell the sergeant to have the men sweep the campus. Comm the GSS and tell them to put out an APB and place her image on all facial recog software for all the surrounding vidcams."

"Yes, sir." Bootsteps ran out of the office.

Insol could hear people pulling on the chairs above her.

Someone said, "That's odd. The chairs are bolted to the floor. They don't look valuable."

The commanding officer said, "Are you an expert on office furniture? Keep searching."

The ruckus in the office above lasted for an indeterminate amount of time until the commanding officer said, "There's nothing here. She can't have gone far. We'll find her. She's an academic not an escape artist. Move out."

Bootsteps exited the office.

The commanding officer said, "Where is she?"

There was a moment of silence, then a boot came down on the floor above her, but it sounded solid. Insol was startled. She placed her hand on the latch. Then she heard the commanding officer marched out of the office.

Insol waited to make sure the office above her was vacant, then took a deep breath and exhaled. She'd been limiting her breathing the entire time the soldiers were above her. She wondered why she hadn't appeared on their infrared scanners, which were probably on a cruiser hovering over the campus. It had to be Mado. He probably lined this space with a metal that shielded her.

I might as well get comfortable, Insol thought. She stretched her legs out, then scooted back again and positioned her feet against the opposite wall. She wasn't sure how long she should wait in the hole, but assumed she should hold out as long as possible.

Although it was different in size and scope, this hole in the floor made her think about her father's bomb shelter in Shamba. It was on the family farm, which had belonged to Insol's grandparents on her father's side. Along with six of her aunts and uncles, her grandfather had died in the Revolts, but her grandmother survived. She was never a soldier but contributed to the Shamban effort by manufacturing improvised explosives for the guerillas. Also, many fighters injured both physically and mentally had taken refuge at the farm. Insol's grandmother cared for them, and she was respected for her service. Insol recalled strange men and women appearing at the farm from time to time to thank her for her kindness.

Her grandmother told her about her grandfather, who had been a smart, resourceful man. She swore that her only surviving son, Insol's father Lart, was like him, but Lart struggled to find his way in the world. He came up with one oddball scheme after another to earn units for his family, but every venture ended in debt and he'd fall into depression, binge-drinking Malrap from his makeshift still.

Insol's mother Rika was the real earner. After the Revolts, she managed a local mining company that extracted metal ore that eventually went into building the Shamban dome. When Insol's father had exhausted all his business ideas and none of his friends would lend him any more investment capital, Rika got him a job in the deep pit mine. A few of Insol's older brothers, who already had families of their own, worked there as well. Laboring in the mine gave Insol's father the idea of building a bomb shelter.

Insol recalled her father announcing his shelter idea at evening meal with the entire family present.

Insol's grandmother cried, "Oh, Lart," then shook her head and rolled her eyes. She had grown intolerant of her son's shenanigans. She looked over at Insol's mother, then took her dentures from her mouth and began cleaning them with her napkin, waiting for her daughter-in-law to put her son in his place.

Insol's mother said, "And why do we need a bomb shelter, Lart?"

"Doesn't the name answer the question?"

"Why would anyone want to bomb us?"

Insol and her siblings giggled.

Insol's mother said, "I don't need any input from the gallery."

Insol and her siblings peered down at their plates or began eating again. Insol's grandmother continued polishing her dentures with a toothless smirk.

Insol's mother leaned across the table toward her partner and pointed around the room. "Look at this house. Windows are broken. All the rooms could use a coat of paint. The porch is rotted out. The roof needs replacing. I don't see any reason to spend our hard-earned units on a hole in the ground that we'll never use."

"Seriously, it'll come in handy against the environmental crisis," Insol's father said. "And I'll make it happen."

"I'll believe it when I see it," Insol's mother said and chuckled, which was the cue for everyone at the table, including Insol's grandmother, to begin laughing again.

"And," Insol's father said, standing up from his seat and pointing at Insol's mother, "*and* I will take care of all the repairs, too. You make a list."

"Oh! I *will* make a list," Insol's mother said and stood too.

"It's a deal, then," Insol's father said and strode around the table to kiss her to seal the deal.

Shortly thereafter, Lart and Insol's older brothers were employed full time to work construction on high-rises in Kuu City.

The high-rises were being built there because of the uproar from the planet's citizens when Kuu City was designated the site of the Shamban dome. It was the smallest city in the region, and President Vidor Plemso was accused of choosing it out of vindictiveness. It was public knowledge that he held animosity toward Shamba over their violent and unending resistance against his forces in the Separatist Revolts. The citizens thought he was punishing the Shambans, wanting to save fewer of them than other Kodans from the crisis. If the planet was supposed to move forward in peace, then something needed to be done about this poor decision. As President, Vidor Plemso was still subject to the ballot box and feeling the weight of public opinion against him, he ordered a series of high-rise housing projects to be built in Kuu City, increasing the number of Shambans who could live within the dome.

That created plenty of construction jobs. The pay was much better than the mines, and Insol's father and her older brothers jumped on the opportunity. One disadvantage was Kuu City's distance from the farm. It was a half-day's drive so instead of coming home every evening, it was more cost-efficient for them to stay in the city. Still, Insol's father kept his promise. On his days off, Lart chipped away at Rika's home-repair list and when that was completed, he began working on the bomb shelter.

Now, hiding under the office's floor, Insol rolled onto her side, pulling her legs into a fetal position. While she was lying there, she felt a slight breeze on her face and reached out her hands. She felt a metal panel with slots installed in one of the walls. Mado had built in ventilation, probably tied into the building's air-circulation system.

Insol lay so her face was an arm's length from the vent and breathed in the air. She closed her eyes and attempted to sleep. She thought about how her father had rented digging machinery to excavate a fallow field on the farm, then built his shelter in the hole that he'd created, using discarded metal from the construction site in Kuu City. Her father recruited her younger brothers, who lived at home, to help him.

Insol remembered her mother, sitting in a folding chair with an umbrella shading her from the sun, reading a book. Every once in a while, she'd take a break to sip a cold drink and observe her partner laboring away at his project. As a young girl, Insol would lounge on a large towel beside her mother, under the shade of the umbrella, reading books as well.

When Insol's father finished the shell of the shelter, he furnished the interior with beds, shelves, a dining table with chairs, and kitchen appliances. He hooked up a comm transmitter, stocked the shelves with dry goods, and filled the water tank. After he tested the AID generator, ventilation system, water purification device, and composting toilet, he filled in the hole.

With the shelter now complete, Insol's mother asked her partner, "Now what?"

"We wait," Insol's father said.

Seven years passed, and although its systems and devices were tested regularly, the unused bomb shelter became a running joke on the farm.

Then one day, Insol was walking home from school with her younger sister when they heard air-raid sirens, long-silent relics from the Separatist Revolts. Insol and her sister raced home where their mother met them at the front door. She told them and Insol's brothers to gather books and a change of clothes and join her at the bomb shelter's hatch. Insol's grandmother had died a few years earlier so Rika was the matriarch of the family now.

The family gathered at the bomb shelter hatch with the exception of Insol's father who was working in Kuu City on the dome. Air-raid sirens were still blaring in the distance, then the rumble of Global Assembly air-battle cruiser engines could be heard approaching. Insol's mother hurried her children through the hatch and down the ladder into the shelter. She was on the ladder sealing the hatch when the first explosions shook the ground. Her feet slipped off the rung and she fell, but her hands caught the ladder and she hung there. Insol and her siblings gasped as their mother pulled herself up to reset her feet on the rung and climb down.

The ground was rocked by explosions for an extended period. The bombs landed in the distance, but every detonation was powerful enough to shock everyone in the shelter. Silent lapses between explosions brought hope that the bombing might be over, but then another barrage occurred. Nerves began to fray. Insol's youngest brother yelled for it to stop. Her youngest sister wept.

Insol's mother activated the transmitter and there was news about carpet bombing along the roads leading to Kuu City. Everyone knew about the migration of people who were hoping to get ahead of the selection process for the domes, and the traffic jams extending hundreds of kilometers. Due to their history as guerillas in the Revolts, the Rentas were never considered eligible for the domed city, but many of Insol's schoolfriends, her parents' friends, and even her extended family had headed to the city. Insol and her family feared for these lives, but when they heard about the DOME riots, they fretted for their father and brothers, too.

Days passed. Insol's mother thought it best that the family stay in the shelter until the violence had ended or Insol's father returned. Personal recollections had been exhausted and conversation felt trite. Books were read and passed from person to person. Insol and her siblings' bunks became their sanctuary. The ventilation in the shelter was horrible and Insol's mother opened the hatch from time to time for fresh air until the outside air turned putrid.

Insol's mother spent part of the days with headphones on, sitting at the transmitter, turning its dial. When she finally landed on an active channel, Insol heard the murmur of a voice leaking out from the headphones, and her mother's face froze in horror. At one point, her mother removed the headphones, and Insol asked whether she could listen. Her mother's eyes filled with tears, and she hugged Insol tightly. She whispered into Insol's ear, "We'll talk about it later. I don't want to frighten your brothers and sister." Insol was eventually told that her mother was listening to descriptions of the devastation, the rising number of casualties, and the lists of the dead.

Nine days into the confinement, there was a knock at the hatch. Insol's mother picked up a shotgun and handed a crowbar to Insol. She told all the children to stand in the corner of the shelter farthest from the ladder. At the foot of the ladder, she turned and stared at her children as if this might be the last time she'd see them. A couple of Insol's siblings were shaking and crying. Insol weighed the crowbar in her hand, telling her younger siblings that everything would be all right.

There was another knock on the hatch.

Insol's mother said to her children, "You need to stay quiet. I love you all."

A voice outside, muffled by the thick metal of the hatch, said, "Open up. I'm friendly and unarmed."

Insol's mother cocked the shotgun, climbed up the ladder, unlocked the hatch, and aimed the weapon toward it.

The hatch creaked as it opened and a rush of putrid air flowed into the shelter.

A familiar voice said, "Whoa! Careful with that shotgun, Rika."

"Kubwa, you frightened everyone," Insol's mother said, lowering her weapon.

"It's good to see you alive and well, too," Kubwa said. "Are the children with you and all right?"

Insol was relieved to hear Kubwa's voice. She and her siblings rushed to the bottom of the ladder.

"Yes," Insol's mother said. "All here and as well as can be expected. You have the mtunga shida with you?"

"Yes, I'm here, Rika," Uncle Gnviri said.

Insol experienced a rush of joy hearing her uncle's voice. She loved him dearly.

Insol's mother said, "Any word from Lart and the boys?"

Uncle Gnviri said, "Yes, the comms are back up. He wanted me to check on you and the children, and he knew you'd be worried, but he and the boys are fine. We're all lucky. The death and destruction are like nothing I've ever seen and we've seen some horrors in our day."

"Sad," Insol's mother said.

"Indeed," Uncle Gnviri said. "Now, you and the children should come up. We brought fresh food. Better than that canned, pickled crap that Lart stored down there. By the way, they should be home soon, but it'll be a while before the roads are cleared."

In the days that followed, the reports regarding the deaths of loved ones, family, and friends who had died in the bombings or been massacred on the city streets were overwhelming in their magnitude. Insol's father returned to a teary family reunion and when the younger children had gone to sleep, he told horrific tales of what he'd witnessed.

Now, hiding in the hole in the office floor, Insol attempted to push the images of the devastation on the roadway to Kuu City out of her mind. She took a deep breath and exhaled. She reminded herself that her path in life—becoming a SEEDER scholar, working for the Movement—was inspired by the horrors of the DOME riots and making certain it could never happen again.

Eventually, Insol slipped off to sleep.

INSOL WOKE TO BOOTSTEPS ABOVE HER AND A voice saying, "Man, they trashed this place. What're we looking for?"

There was knock on the floor above and she recognized Suron's voice saying, "Insol, open up."

Insol unlocked and reversed the latch. The floor slid open, and her eyes were stung by the light.

Suron and two Prevor Industries guards were staring down at her.

Suron dropped to one knee and reached with both hands to help her out of the hole. "You don't look any worse for wear."

Insol grabbed Suron's hands and he lifted her up and into one of the lounge's chairs. She couldn't stand until the circulation returned to her legs. It was light outside, but the shadows indicated it was close to sunset.

Insol said, "How long was I down there?"

"Almost an entire day," Suron said, handing her a water container. "You must be dehydrated."

Insol took a few sips, then a larger gulp. "Thanks."

Insol looked around at the shattered doorframe, holes in the walls, bookshelves on their sides, and objects strewn all over the floor.

Suron said, "Could've been worse."

"How's that?"

"They could've found you."

She picked up the cracked digi-foto of herself, Ador, Mel, and Yor from the floor and took a long look at it. This experience hiding in a hole reminded her that their goals had never been achieved. She placed the foto on the desk and said, "I guess I'm back to fight another day."

MAR

When Suron commed saying he'd recovered Insol and they were heading back to the Complex, Mar was elated.

Insol was the daughter Mar never had. There were rough edges to her personality—quick to temper, a propensity to hold grudges, hardheaded—but she had a big heart. She was dear to Mar before Yor left the planet, but in the decades since Yor's departure, they'd grown even closer. For the past day, Mar had been thinking the worst had happened. If any harm had come to Insol, Mar didn't think she'd be able to forgive herself.

Now, Mar peered out the shatterproof plate-glass door of the building that housed her penthouse and her office. The sun had set, and in the distance she could see the approaching headlamps of a cruiser. Her heart soared as the cruiser touched down and the lights activated in the passenger compartment and she saw Insol. Of course, Rika was concerned as well and Mar thought about calling her now that Insol was in sight, but she decided to wait until she assessed how Insol was doing.

Mar heard the engines power down and attempted to open the door, but it was locked. When they received word that the purge was in progress, Suron had placed the Complex on Level One Lockdown. Employees were required to travel the underground walkway between buildings. Nobody was allowed to enter from the outside or stay on the Complex grounds without a Level One security pass. If someone left the Complex with a Level One pass, then they couldn't come back until the lockdown was over. It also meant all the outer doors in the Complex were secured.

Mar knocked on the door to attract the attention of the two guards standing outside.

"Open up, please," she said, loud enough for them to hear her. She had Priority Access and could've used the DNA scanner to open the door, but she knew that the guards were under orders to keep it locked, and she didn't think it wise to undermine Suron's authority.

Both of the guards looked at each other.

"Open the door, please."

One of them reached behind his ear, activated his audio implant, and spoke. Mar couldn't make out what he was saying but assumed he was checking with Suron. Although she understood procedure, in a moment like this, Mar felt frustrated by the rules.

After listening to a reply, the guard turned, unlocked the door, and opened it. The dome's circulated air rushed in. It was distinct from the air in the Prevor Industries buildings. The metallic scent from the dome's air circulators had become more pronounced over the years while the Prevor Industries air was still fresh.

The guard said, "Sorry, boss. We have orders. You're free to go."

Yet when she hurried outside, the guards escorted her to the cruiser. It wasn't like she didn't understand Suron's strict protocols. She knew he had her best interests at heart. Over the years, there had been attempts on her life by people ginned up by Roneh Rayush's "for the good of the globe" disinformation campaigns. One was caused by Roneh's rantings on loyalist viewing channels about how Mar and Prevor Industries were funding outer-Kodan "terrorists." Each time the violence was thwarted, Vidor would comm, concerned for Mar's well-being, but she could hear the amusement in his voice. She wondered if he had concocted the lies Roneh spouted to get back at her. The man was a spiteful little boy.

As Insol stepped out of the cruiser with her viewer case in hand, Mar wrapped Insol in her arms. Insol embraced Mar in return, but when Insol loosened her grip, Mar didn't let go. She had lost too many people close to her and she wanted to express her love for those still alive.

Mar released Insol and stepped back to examine her. Other than looking exhausted and giving off a ripe odor, Insol appeared unharmed. She still had scars on her face from the attack years ago and her prosthetic eye didn't look any worse for the wear. While Insol was here, Mar would upgrade her to the latest Prevor Industries model.

"How are you?" Mar said. "I was worried."

"I'm all right," Insol said, "thanks to Mado and Lek. I used Suron's comm on the way over and reached somebody in the Movement. Dozens of my dearest friends and their families have been hauled off by the GSS. We can only assume they're all in mass graves by now." There was anger in Insol's voice and tears in her eyes.

"I've heard similar news. It's horrible. I'm sorry for your loss."

"How could you let this happen?

"I had no—"

"You're one of the most powerful people on the planet, and you couldn't do anything to stop it?"

"By the time I heard about it, the arrests were already in progress. I've tried calling the Leader, but nobody in the Global Assembly will return my calls," Mar said. "I'm heartbroken—I didn't see it coming and I will regret my inaction for the rest of my days."

Suron now stood behind Insol, observing the interaction.

Insol pointed at Mar and yelled, "So what are you going to do about it now?"

"I'm still hoping to put a halt to this massacre, but—"

"I meant, when are we going to strike back?"

Mar glanced at Suron who shrugged.

Insol noticed the exchange, peered over her shoulder at Suron, and said, "Don't look at him. Why are you looking at him? You're his boss, aren't you?"

Mar said, "He's the security expert."

"He's doing a shitty job, then," Insol said, her voice even louder.

"I'm as frustrated as you are."

"Doubtful."

"You're tired, hungry, and upset," Mar said. "Maybe after you rest we can have a reasonable conversation about what's happened."

"Reasonable? The only thing reasonable to do is really hurt them, then the people will see they're not powerless and rise up, and we can execute the butchers at the top."

"We can't just lash out without thinking it through," Mar said. "Why don't you go to your usual room? I got you a change of clothes. I ordered the food you like. It's on the way. Then take a nap and we can continue this discussion later."

Insol released a loud groan. "You're infuriating," she said. "All right. I could use a shower…but I want to hear what you're going to do. I want action now!"

"I promise we'll talk," Mar said, stepping toward Insol and kissing her on the cheek. "I'm happy you're safe. We're on lockdown at the moment, so guards will escort you to your room."

Insol sighed. "I don't mean to sound ungrateful, but we—"

"I know you've been through a lot and what's happened to your friends is unconscionable," Mar said, then turned to the guards who had accompanied her to the cruiser. "You two—please show her to her room."

They looked over at Suron who said, "Go ahead. I'll secure things here."

Mar patted Insol on the arm and Insol forced a smile, then left with the guards. Mar waited for Insol to enter the building, then said to Suron, "What do you think?"

Suron began walking side by side with Mar across the tarmac. "Hard to tell. I think she'll be all right. She's always been volatile. I don't see her going back to the University any time soon. The GSS will be looking for her. While she's here, we'll keep an eye on her, and you might encourage her to see a corporate psych med for evaluation."

"You think that's necessary?"

They reached the building and Suron held the door open for Mar. When they were both inside, he used the DNA scanner to lock the door. "Considering her past history? Absolutely."

Mar pressed the button to summon the lift and said, "I'll consider it." Then the lift arrived, and they both stepped in and headed up in silence. When the doors opened into her penthouse, they exited through the door at the back of the lift and stepped into the office.

Ara was waiting for her in front of the office doorway. She said, "We've received no replies from anyone in the Global Assembly yet."

"Thanks," Mar said. "How are you?"

"Not great. I just heard about some friends. I suppose they're gone."

"So sorry," Mar said. "Please hold all my comms unless it's the Leader or anyone from the Global Assembly. If you need to take some time and leave early today, let me know."

Ara went back into the reception area and Mar sat down in her desk chair. Suron stood in front of Mar's desk, deep in thought.

Mar said, "Are you going to close the door?"

Suron snapped out of his state of reflection, then shut the door and stood in front of the desk again.

Mar said, "What're your thoughts?"

"I was just thinking about what Ara said and from what I've heard about this purge so far, nobody will be untouched by it."

"Unfortunately, I think you're right," Mar said, pushing her chair closer to the desk. "Maybe I could have done something to stop it. When Vidor died, I should have contacted Carz and made clear I wouldn't stand for his father's heinous plan, but I really didn't see it in him."

"I wouldn't eat yourself up about it. You certainly have no control over other people's actions."

"Doesn't make me feel less guilty."

"We don't know all the variables that went into Carz's decision. Part of it probably was the bombing of the estate. I'm aware you've known Carz since he was a child," Suron said, taking a step closer to the desk. "But he was thrust into being the Leader because he's his father's son. That's it. I don't think he has the self-esteem or experience to stand up to the officials in the Global Assembly that want the Movement wiped out."

"Maybe you're right."

"It's definitely a setback for the Movement," Suron said. "That's for certain, although it may have paved the way for the radical element to become stronger."

"Yes, you might be right. That concerns me," Mar said, pushing her chair back from the desk. "I need to make a move. This morning, I read the recent GACE report provided by your person on the inside. It's a dire situation. There's nothing Carz can do to rectify the problem, and maybe I'm reading him incorrectly again, but other intel shows him looking into building more spaceships. That makes me believe that he cares about the Kodan people. That he wants to save more lives than his father's spaceships can fit…which is another reason why this purge makes no sense."

"That stands to logic."

"It might be time to unveil Foreseeable Future to the public. The pretext would be reaching an agreement with Carz to allow its implementation. It might be our best opportunity to save every Kodan before it's too late."

"Risky."

"Of course," Mar said. "But we need to build more ships and faster. I wouldn't tell him about the Shamban facility at first. I'd posit the idea of building spaceships for the entire populace and see where it goes from there."

"That could work."

"I need to make a trip to Shamba, though. I haven't visited in a few years and evaluating things there could be instructive on how to deal with Carz."

"Commercial flights are sparse these days," Suron said. "They probably run every thirty to forty-eight days, depending on the atmospheric conditions."

"We need to move quicker."

"We could take one of our cruisers equipped for the conditions, and if it comes out that you made the trip, you can say it was for the Foundation."

Mar stood up. "Great. You handle the logistics. I'll coordinate with Rika and Lek and work the trip into my schedule, then we'll concoct the cover story," she said, walking over to the door and opening it. "I'll bring Ara with me and consider asking Insol. It'd be good for her to see her family."

MAR WOKE TO A HAND GRIPPING HER SHOULDER and Ara saying, "Mar, rise and shine. We're preparing to land."

Mar was buckled into her seat behind the cruiser's pilot and copilot. She wiped the drool from her chin and hoped no one had seen it. She turned to her right and said to Ara, "I don't think I've slept that well in a while."

"Yes, we all noticed," Ara said and giggled.

"Getting away from your busy life at the Complex probably helps," Insol said. She was seated to Mar's left.

"I think it's the pressurization of the cabin," Mar said. "How much longer before we land?"

"Soon," Ara said. "The pilot said we're descending."

Outside the cockpit window, the brown landscape appeared rocky and desolate yet there were outcroppings of greenery. Mar assumed the roots of the plants snaked underground until they could feed from the same source that supplied water to the cavern where the spaceships were constructed. *Life always finds a way to survive*, Mar thought.

Insol was staring out the window.

"How are you, Insol?" Mar said, squeezing Insol's forearm, but she didn't reply.

During Insol's sixteen-day stay at the Complex, Mar hadn't seen her much. A few days into Insol's visit, Suron delivered the news to her that Uncle Gnviri and her brother Islo had been killed in the purge. He said that Insol broke down crying and slammed the apartment door in his face. Mar decided to give Insol space and expected Insol would come to her when she wanted to talk. Days passed and that didn't happen so Mar scheduled a time for her to visit the office.

When Insol arrived, she stopped in front of Ara's desk. Mar had gotten up from her desk and was standing in her office doorway.

Ara said, "How are you today, Insol?"

Insol screamed at her, "If you're asking, you must be a complete and utter idiot. I was rotting in a hole while my friends, their families, and my own family members were slaughtered, you primped-up twat!"

Mar told Insol to never speak that way to Ara and to leave the office immediately.

After the incident, Mar scheduled an appointment for Insol with the Prevor Industries psych med. She told Insol that there was the possibility of going to Shamba with her, but Insol needed to take the psych-med session seriously. Insol went to the appointment, then booked a few more by herself. After each session, Insol seemed in better spirits and made stops at Mar's office. She brought gifts for Ara like flowers or candy, apologizing for her outburst, and she acknowledged her gratitude to Mar for caring about her. She promised she'd work toward change. This behavior seemed suspect to Mar, but she thought Insol might be on the right path so decided to bring her on the trip. Mar understood that it would take more than a couple of appointments for Insol to deal with her issues, but hoped the Shamba trip would help the healing.

As the cruiser descended, Mar's ears popped. She repeated her question to Insol, "How are you?"

Still staring out the window, Insol said, "Excited to see my family."

"I am, too," Mar said. "They're wonderful. You're lucky to have them."

"The ones that're left."

Mar squeezed Insol's forearm again. In the distance, Mar observed four men in brown Shamban clothing, wearing wide-brimmed hats and cloth masks over their mouths and noses.

Insol said, "I'm happy to be here. Thanks again for inviting me." She leaned over and hugged Mar. "You know that I love you."

"I love you, too."

The cruiser touched down on uneven ground and the landing stanchions leveled off the craft in a whir of hydraulics.

Suron had remained at the Complex. The security guard in charge was seated behind Insol, Mar, and Ara. He unbuckled, leaned forward, and said, "Please wait here until we signal all's safe."

Mar said, "And what would that signal be? You hopping up and down on one leg?"

"No, ma'am," the guard said. "I'll simply wave and you can prepare to disembark."

"I was kidding."

"Yes, ma'am."

Mar said to Insol, "Been around these guys for years and none of them has a sense of humor."

A few moments later, the guard in charge and two others exited the cruiser from the backseat, the doors closing behind them. They were outfitted in enviro-suits from head to toe to keep themselves cool. They drew their stun rifles as they headed toward the Shambans who lowered their dust masks. The two groups spoke.

One of the Shambans was Kubwa and another was Insol's brother Nabo. Insol undid her harness and attempted to open the door beside her, pulling at the handle.

Mar said, "We'll get out in a minute."

The pilot was flipping switches and the cruiser's engines were powering down.

Mar removed her viewer case from under the seat. "Let's activate our enviro-suits and wait for the guards."

She reached up and opened the ceiling compartment, removing her enviro-suit headgear. Like Insol and Ara, Mar was already wearing the rest of the suit. They dressed up before boarding the cruiser, because it would've been difficult to put on the cumbersome suit in a crowded space during the flight.

Mar handed headgear to Ara and Insol, who placed them over their heads, secured them, then turned on their suits. Mar did the same. The heat from the guards opening the door had been overwhelming, but Mar felt better as the suit cooled her and she took deep breaths of the suit's oxygen.

The guard waved to Mar.

Mar said, "Let's go."

The door opened and Insol rushed into Kubwa's arms.

A few of the guards had already taken a brown tarp from the cruiser's rear cargo hold and were unfolding it as the pilot and copilot disembarked. Nabo and the other Shambans unloaded boxes of tech supplies and clothing bags from the cruiser, stacking them about ten meters away. The pilot placed covers over the engines' exhaust ports so dirt wouldn't blow into them.

Mar strolled to where the boxes were stacked. Ara walked beside her.

The guard in charge approached Mar and said, "Why don't you go ahead to the cave entrance with the cargo and we'll catch up when the camouflage is in place? These

Shamban gentlemen should be competent enough to get you there safely."

Kubwa said, "More than capable." He was offended by the guard's statement.

"We're all in this together," Mar said. "Isn't that correct, gentlemen?"

"Yes," they both said.

"All right. I just wanted to make sure that we're on the same page. Now is not the time to get regional on each other. Don't you agree?"

"Yes," they both said.

The other two Shambans and Nabo finished unloading the baggage. Ara was still by Mar's side. Insol was a few meters away by herself, staring at the mountains.

Kubwa said, "Let's move out."

"I'll get Insol," Nabo said and approached his sister.

Mar strolled over to Kubwa and patted him on the shoulder. "It's good to see you."

"You too, Kuvutia."

Kubwa picked up a stack of boxes with baggage on top and the other Shambans followed suit. The Prevor Industries guards and pilots were securing the camouflage over the cruiser.

As Mar walked over to Insol and Nabo to get them moving, she heard them arguing.

Nabo began yelling at Insol. "Don't blame me. He was a mean, stubborn old man. He treated everybody like garbage. Nobody wanted to be around him."

Insol said, "So you're saying what happened to Uncle was his fault?"

"Absolutely," Nabo said. "He was a horrible person."

"It was your job to protect him."

"Are you listening to me? I relinquished my duty to him years ago."

"Just admit it was your fault."

"Whatever," Nabo said, throwing a hand in the air, dismissing her. "You aren't here and you have no idea what goes on so don't put this on me. Uncle Gnviri got what he deserved."

Insol launched herself at Nabo, shoving him to the ground and jumping on top of him. She began pummeling him with her fists while she screamed, "He didn't deserve it! It's your fault! It's your fault!"

Kubwa dropped his load and dashed over to the scuffle. Mar yelled, "Insol, stop!"

Insol continued swinging at Nabo who covered his face with his arms, but a blow to his neck caused him to choke and when he dropped his guard, Insol struck him in the face over and over.

Kubwa grabbed Insol by the back of her enviro-suit and lifted her off Nabo. As he carried her away, she was screaming, "Let me go! It's his fault!" When Kubwa placed Insol on her feet, she attempted to race over to Nabo, but Kubwa caught her and held her in place.

One of the other Shambans helped Nabo to stand. Nabo's nose and mouth were bleeding and one of his eye sockets was swelling up.

Mar approached Nabo and said, "Let me take a look." She held Nabo's head in her hands and assessed his injuries. His nose was broken. His eye would require further examination. He'd need stitches for a cut under his lower lip and one of the Shambans gave Nabo a handkerchief to stem the bleeding. His knee was gashed open, too.

"You'll live," Mar said. "We'll patch you up at the facility." She patted Nabo on the cheek. "You're in shock."

Mar turned her attention to Kubwa, who was still holding the struggling Insol. "Kubwa, how's it going over here?"

"She's strong, but I've got her."

Mar said. "Insol, are you going to calm down?"

"I'll kill that imbecile." Insol tested Kubwa's grip again.

"I'd guess that's a no."

The guard in charge came up behind Mar and said, "The camouflage is all set and we shouldn't linger much longer."

Mar said, "We need to move, Insol. Do we have to restrain you?"

Insol grunted, her eyes darting wildly, and made another unsuccessful attempt to escape from Kubwa's grip.

"You have restraints on you?" Mar asked the guard in charge.

"Always."

"Restrain her," Mar said. "We'll keep Kubwa on her and put one of your men on her, too. With Kubwa otherwise engaged, your men are going to have to help carry the boxes. If she gets further out of control, I give you permission to stun her."

The guard waved one of his men over and spoke with him.

Insol said to Mar, "I thought we were friends."

"We are. I love you, dear, but you don't seem to be listening, and we need to keep moving. I'm sorry we can't wait for you to calm down."

"You want me to calm down?" Insol said, getting agitated again. "You know what that moron did." She began fighting Kubwa's hold once again. "Let go of me, you big lout."

The Prevor Industries guard assigned to help Kubwa removed a set of restraints from his belt.

Mar said, "You two do what you need to do."

Insol fought Kubwa as he moved her arms behind her back. The guard stationed himself beside her and clamped the restraints on one of her wrists and grabbed her other arm. Kubwa stepped aside. Insol fought the guard, so he tripped her face down into the dirt and put his knee on her back. Insol squirmed under the guard's weight, so he applied more pressure to keep her in place while he clamped her wrists together. Then the guard stood and helped Insol up. She continued thrashing to escape his grip, so Kubwa took one of her arms and the guard held the other.

Insol said to Mar, "I hope this makes you happy."

"Not in the slightest," Mar said, wiping dirt from the transparent facing of Insol's enviro-suit. "But you've given me no choice."

"My mother won't be happy about any of this."

"You can be sure of that, but not for the reasons you're thinking." To Kubwa and the guard holding Insol, Mar said, "You two lead the way with Insol. We'll see you at the mouth of the cave."

Mar walked back over to Nabo and said, "What caused that?"

"She asked me what happened to Uncle Gnviri. She said I was supposed to be watching him, but she never dealt with him. He was impossible. I did what I could. I drove him around and made sure he got where he wanted to go. Every seventh day, I dropped him off at a café where he met his old war buddies. Islo went there, too. He liked to listen to their stories. I never hung around, but when I went to pick them up, the streets were blocked by armored Global Assembly vehicles. Global Guards were everywhere. I couldn't get close to the café. There was nothing I could do. Later, I heard there was a raid and Uncle Gnviri and his buddies and Islo were arrested by the GSS. Someone told me they were coming for me so I made my way here. When word of the purge spread, we assumed that's what happened to them, then we got news of their deaths." Nabo began weeping. "I shouldn't of said what I said, but it's not my fault."

Turning to Ara, Mar said, "Keep an eye on him. Make sure he remains conscious." Then she addressed everyone else who was grouped together observing the scene—pilot, copilot, the other guards, the Shambans. "Let's move out. Rika and Lek will be getting concerned."

LEK

Lek removed the glasses he wore so he could read an endless array of documents—staffing and daily security memos, threat assessments, requests for repairs to cams and door locks, upgrade ideas—and placed them on his desk, then he stood in front of a mirror observing himself. He smoothed out the creases in his white button-down shirt, leaving the top button undone, and hitched up his brown pants, tightening the belt. He ran his hands over his grey hair and checked if anything was stuck in his teeth. He inspected the rings under his eyes.

He was more nervous than he'd been in decades. In a few moments, he'd see his daughter in person for the first time since that day he exited the dome. Ara was in her late twenties now. When she started working at Prevor Industries, Lek had begun talking with her on a viewer screen. She was a delightful young woman. She was kind to him, but he wouldn't blame her for hating him. With his decision to betray the Global Assembly, he had turned her childhood upside down.

Twenty-two years ago, when Lek was carried onto the cruiser outside the Capitol City dome, he had been treated for exposure to the toxic environment, then ferried through a network of Movement safe houses to Shamba. He spent those days constantly questioning his decision

    Howard Libes

to alienate himself from Kodan society and abandon his family. Then he was told about Rajer's execution.

By the time he reached the Shamban facility, he'd fallen into depression. His caretaker had provided him with a room and given him a tour of the facility. After that, Lek was free to roam around by himself, but instead, he spent his days sleeping, bringing food from the nearest cafeteria back to his room, then lying on his bunk, staring at the ceiling and wallowing in sadness. His caretaker told Lek that the Movement and the workers in the facility considered him a hero for stopping the purge, but Lek could only think of the family he'd lost, and Rajer. If someone spoke to him outside his room, he didn't respond. For all intents and purposes, he was a ghost haunting his corner of the facility.

Finally, Lek told the caretaker that he wanted to speak with someone in authority. The caretaker smiled and said, "That I can do." Then he disappeared, never to return.

With the caretaker's absence, Lek started to feel lonely, so he began strolling the floors of the facility and learning his way around. He counted four cafeterias. He discovered the dorms where workers from all the regions could be found socializing with one another as regional music emanated from open doorways. One floor was dedicated to conference rooms and offices. A wing of another floor contained tech labs where Lek was passed in the hall by enthusiastic scientists discussing their work.

Lek ended his strolls staring out at the shipyard. He was thrilled by the sleek spaceships housed in the massive cave with the water flowing down the walls to the lake below.

Executing this daily routine, Lek lost track of time. He wasn't sure how long it'd been since he arrived at the facility. Then one day while he was engrossed by the view of the shipyard, a person walked up behind him and said, "It's magnificent, isn't it? The future of the Kodan people."

Lek recognized the voice, and he turned around to face Mar Jeps and another woman dressed in a Shamban brown T-shirt, short pants, and army boots. She exuded strength and beauty, and her long, dark hair hung down to her shoulders.

Lek threw his arms around Mar and began weeping.

"Mar," Lek said through his crying. "I'm so sorry about Rajer. You know how much I loved him." Then he held her tighter and cried uncontrollably and Mar embraced him back.

"I know," Mar said. "I know. He loved you, too."

Lek's bawling came in waves. Mar's presence exposed the gaping hole in his existence left by Rajer's death and the loss of his family. Mar patted Lek on the back and continued to hold him tight. At one point, Lek noticed tears welling in the Shamban woman's eyes, and when their gazes met, she struggled to smile, then turned to look at the shipyard.

When Lek was cried out, he released his hold on Mar and stepped back, wiping his eyes. "Sorry," Lek said. "That was a long time coming."

"You have absolutely nothing to be sorry about," Mar said. "Rajer is gone, but your actions saved thousands of lives."

"Yes," the Shamban woman said. "Many are eternally grateful and in your debt."

"Nobody owes me anything," Lek said. "I only did what I thought was right after years of doing things for the GSS that I'm ashamed of."

"Change for the better is one of the hardest things we can ever achieve in our lives," the Shamban woman said. "And it's often extremely painful."

"I'm sorry," Mar said. "You two haven't been properly introduced. This is Rika Renta, Chief Administrator of the Facility."

"Renta?" Lek said. "Are you related to Insol?"

"She's my daughter. Do you know her?"

"Not personally. I met her once with Yor, but I'm familiar with her GSS file," Lek said, lowering his eyes. "I'm sorry."

"Everyone knows you worked for the GSS, and many here have done things they're not proud of, myself included," Rika said. "But all the people here look at this place as a fresh start for them and a fresh start for Koda."

"Absolutely," Mar said, then placed an arm around Lek's shoulders and turned him to face the view of the shipyard. "That's why I'm here. The latest report said you might be ready to get back to work."

"Work?"

"You haven't forgotten work, have you?" Mar said.

"Well, my work wasn't exactly on the side of the people who reside here."

"True," Rika said, "but we desperately need someone to head up security and your experience would be invaluable."

Lek said, "I'm not the right person to head up anything right now."

Rika said, "You've been roaming around the facility. You must have a few ideas about our security needs."

"Sure…" Lek hesitated to speak. The facility had major security problems, but he didn't want to be disrespectful to his host.

"Like?"

"You really want to know?"

"I do."

"Well, I can think of a few things off the top of my head," Lek said, turning to face Rika. "You have no surveillance cams in the most sensitive areas like the labs. An amateur forger could reproduce your so-called security passes and the locking systems on your doors could be violated with a good kick from a child. And that's just to start."

"You see," Mar said, "that's why we need you."

Rika said, "The person currently in charge of security is well meaning, but as the project grows so does theft, and the job is beyond his grasp. With Mado Prevor off-planet, nobody here has a clue how to apply modern security techniques. It's clear you do."

"Mado's off-planet?"

"Yes, and we can discuss that later," Mar said. "But you're here, and since you can't leave this place, because the Global Assembly considers you dead, you can concentrate on making your new home more secure."

"I was never told this would be the end of the line."

"'End of the line' sounds so final. You just can't leave here, and you still have plenty to offer," Mar said. "By saving all those people, you showed your willingness to serve Koda beyond the amoral ethics of the Global Assembly and we need you to continue that work here."

"I don't know if I want that kind of responsibility again." Lek turned to the view and took a few steps forward, peering out at a welder atop a ship under construction, sparks raining down into the lake below.

Mar and Rika stood behind him, whispering to one another. The tone of Rika's voice was emotional. She was excited about Lek's input on the facility's needs but annoyed by his apathetic response to their job offer. Mar countered with Lek's skills, work ethic, and how he'd come around.

Lek turned to them and said, "I didn't mean to cause any tension between you two."

Mar said, "Rika is just passionate about this place."

"What else are you going to do around here?" Rika said. "You'll need to pay for your keep. If you'd prefer, I have an opening for a janitor."

Lek chuckled and said, "I am considering your offer. I just need some time."

"See," Mar said, smiling and patting Rika on the arm. "That's what I said."

Rika said, "I don't have time for people who've lost their balls. At some point, you might consider growing a new pair."

"I assure you," Lek said, "my balls are firmly attached."

"That's not what I'm hearing," Rika said.

Mar said, "The state of your genitalia aside, you need to face facts, Lek, and until things change politically, you can't go anywhere. The moment you arrive at a city with GSS surveillance and facial recog software, you'll be arrested. If you got as far as Linara and attempted to reconcile with her, from all reports she would turn you in to the GSS. Obviously, neither of those scenarios would turn out well for you, and if the Leader finds out you survived, let's just say he won't be pleased that I stole a portion of his victory in our negotiations. The repercussions would not be pretty."

"So I'm screwed," Lek said.

"Not entirely," Mar said. "Time is on your side. When Ara is grown, she may feel differently about you than her mother does. And I promise I will facilitate a reunion between you two, but in the meantime the Kodan people need you."

"I've heard that before." Lek noticed that Rika was observing him with a critical look on her face. He found her extraordinarily sexy.

"So?" Rika said. "Do you want the janitorial position?"

Mar chuckled nervously. "I don't think it'd be a bad thing to give Lek more time."

"No, getting back to work might be just what I need, and I'm not crazy about cleaning toilets so I'll take the security position," Lek said. "First, I'll require a viewer or a digi-pad to make a report on my initial observations and how best to deal with the shortcomings around here. I'll need a list of all personnel, their IDs and photos. And I mean all of them. I can hack into the GSS mainframe to check whether spies or potential criminals are among your ranks, and I'll need an office to interview suspicious individuals. Also, we'll have to talk about a budget so we can install the necessary equipment to tighten the gaping holes in security around here. It won't be cheap."

Mar said, "Does that work for you, Rika?"

"Definitely."

"I'll also need bigger living quarters than where I'm currently residing."

Rika said, "We converted a janitor's closet into that room for you…just in case you wanted the job."

"That's funny, and it explains the ever-present smell of cleanser, but even the GSS gives their prisoners bigger cells," Lek said. "Frankly, my accommodations here suck."

Rika smiled. "Looks like your balls have begun to drop."

Mar said, "I'm beginning to feel uncomfortable with this conversation. I'll try to provide you with fotos of Ara, too."

Now, Lek forced a smile at his reflection in the mirror. He got emotional thinking about seeing Ara in person.

There was a knock at the door.

Lek said, "Come in."

The door opened and Rika stood there, wearing her uniform and looking as stunning as she had the first day he'd laid eyes on her. For over a decade now, she and Lek had shared an intimate relationship.

Rika closed the door, strode up to Lek, and kissed him on the lips. "Are you excited?"

"Excited. Nervous."

"It'll be wonderful."

"I know," Lek said. " I just want everything to be all right between us. Ara told me again over the viewer that she's proud of what I did and has never blamed me for abandoning her and her mother. But I still can't help wondering whether Linara poisoned the well."

"Ara didn't have to come here with Mar."

"True," Lek said, "although she is Mar's assistant. I assume you saw them arriving on the exterior surveillance cams. Something happened out there. Your son looks like he was in a fight."

"We'll know soon enough. I called a few extra guards to the entrance."

"I was going to do that."

"It's not like I need your permission. I am your boss and don't you forget it."

There was a moment of silence, then they both laughed, which made Lek feel less nervous. He leaned forward and kissed Rika on the cheek.

Lek said, "That's a down payment."

"I can't wait to receive the balance," Rika said, kissing him on the cheek, too.

Lek gave himself one last glance in the mirror.

"You look great, my dear," Rika said. "We need to get going."

Lek removed his blazer from the back of his desk chair and put it on, then stopped in front of the door.

"You have everything you need," Rika said. "You ready?"

"As I'll ever be," Lek said, then he kissed Rika on the lips before they exited into the corridor. Lek always attempted to keep their relationship professional in public.

When they reached the tunnel, the lights had been activated and four guards were already there, standing shoulder-to-shoulder in front of the entrance. Travel bags and boxes from Prevor Industries had accumulated at the end of the conveyor belt, and five men in brown coveralls arrived to remove the items and carry them to their final destinations. Najubo showed up as well and stood smiling at Lek and Rika from a distance.

Rika whispered in Lek's ear, "Take a deep breath. This will be a joyful moment for both of you."

Lek drew in a breath and exhaled. He and Rika stood behind the guards, peering over their shoulders. The first person to appear was Nabo, walking at a fast pace and limping. His left pants leg was torn open and his knee was lacerated. His right eye was swollen shut and his nose appeared broken. He was dabbing at his bottom lip with a bloody handkerchief.

Lek said, "Let him through."

The guards parted, then returned to formation.

"What happened?" Rika said to Nabo with concern in her voice. "Is anyone else hurt?"

"No," Nabo said, then began crying and pointed at his face. "Insol did this to me. She's out of control. Mar Jeps thought it best for me to come down the tunnel first and tell you that Insol is on her way with Kubwa. She's restrained."

"What? Why?" Rika said.

"You'll see."

Rika hugged Nabo. "It'll be all right. Now go see a med. Najubo, please accompany him to the clinic."

Nabo put his arm around Najubo's shoulders and they headed down the corridor.

Lek heard shrieking in the tunnel. Kubwa appeared, grasping Insol's right arm. An enviro-suited Prevor Industries guard was holding her left arm. Insol was thrashing to escape from them.

Insol began screaming, "Mother! Mother! I know you're there. Tell these imbeciles to let me go. Now!"

Staring down the tunnel, Rika was transfixed by what she saw and reached out for Lek, who took her hand.

"Mother! I know you're there."

Lek said, "Let them through." Still holding Rika's hand, Lek guided her back and to the side of the tunnel.

Kubwa stopped in front of the facility guards and positioned himself directly behind Insol, taking hold of both her arms as the Prevor Industries guard let go of her. Then Kubwa led Insol between the facility guards and approached Rika.

Insol was furious.

Rika said, "Kubwa, what is the meaning of this?"

Kubwa said, "You saw what she did to Nabo. She wouldn't stop behaving like a madwoman, so we restrained her."

Insol yelled at Rika, "You're going to listen to this moron? Look at how they're treating me."

Rika released Lek's hand then took a step forward and observed her daughter as if she'd never seen her before. She said, "I'm understandably concerned to see my daughter screaming like a wild animal."

"What about my side of the story?"

Rika said, "And why would you treat your brother that way?"

"He let Uncle Gnviri and Islo die on purpose."

"That's nonsense," Rika said.

"Oh, I get it," Insol said. "You don't care that they're dead, either."

Rika slapped Insol's cheek so hard that the smack resounded down the tunnel.

Insol became hysterical, wailing loudly.

"Take her to the med bay," Rika said. "Have her sedated and kept her away from her brother. I'll talk to both of them later and get to the bottom of this."

Kubwa and the Prevor Industries guard took hold of Insol's arms again and escorted her down the corridor while she continued weeping.

Lek said, "That was awful. I'm so sorry."

"Me too," Rika said. "Me too." It was clear she was stunned by what she'd experienced.

Then Mar approached with Ara beside her, holding their enviro-suit helmets in one hand. Lek felt his heart racing. Flanking them were Mar's security detail, while the rest of the Shambans sent to retrieve them and the pilot and copilot followed on behind. Mar turned and waved the Shambans and the pilots past her.

"Part formation, gentlemen," Lek said to the facility guards. "Let everyone through. After everyone is clear of the tunnel, secure the entrance. The mop-up crews are already outside normalizing the trail."

The Shamban guards who had arrived with Mar halted in front of Lek and one of them stepped forward.

"Gleer," Lek said.

"Lek," the guard said. He was twenty years younger than Lek, a head taller, and twice as wide. Gleer held a position of authority over all the facility guards with the exception of Lek and Kubwa. He had been mentored by Kubwa and was considered Kubwa's successor as commander of the guards.

Lek said, "Looks like things went less than normal out there."

"Yes, sir," Gleer said. "Less than normal, indeed."

"I'll expect a report from you and Kubwa. You and your men are dismissed."

"Let's move out," Gleer said, and his men headed down the corridor, the heavy clopping of their boots fading in the distance.

Ara had been standing a few meters away. Tears were streaming down her cheeks. Lek began to cry. It was like a dream. They strode toward one another and embraced. Lek squeezed her tight for reassurance that this moment was truly happening. He kept his eyes shut, because he wanted to feel her arms around him and his around her. When Lek loosened his hold on her, they both took a step back. Lek drank in the vision of her. She looked like her mother.

Ara said, "You left the door open a crack, Papa."

"Always my beautiful blossom."

They chuckled and embraced again. When they separated, Lek kissed Ara on the cheek and put his arm around her. They walked together toward Mar and Rika who had both been crying, too.

Wiping tears from her eyes, Rika said, "You see? Joyful."

"You were right, my dear," Lek said. "Mar, I can't thank you enough."

"It took me twenty-two years," Mar said, "but I like to keep my word."

CARZ

Carz was drunk again. He sat in the study by himself, leaning back in an armchair and staring up at the ceiling. He cradled a half-full glass of Malrap on his belly. Prior to being officially declared Leader, he barely drank, but since then, every evening he'd been drunk on Malrap.

When he was a young man, Carz had often observed his father returning home from a long day at his Global Assembly office in a vile mood. He'd get into an argument with Carz's mother, then disappear into this study to drink Malrap. Sometimes he'd emerge sedated. Sometimes his mood worsened, and he'd take it out on Carz or Minok. Whenever Vidor beat Carz's behind with a meter stick, he lamented beating his son but believed it was the best way to turn Carz into a man, as Vidor's father had done for him.

Carz wondered if Vidor had used this reason for his bad behavior as an excuse for drinking and venting his rage at a job that he hated, and that scared Carz.

He never wanted to be like his father as a person or Leader, bur his mother always said she saw Carz's father in him, and in the eyes of the Kodan people, there was no difference between them, either. He'd failed to halt the purge and now everyone believed he had signed off on it. The demonstrations on the streets were now a howl of hatred aimed at him. The military wanted to bring their full might to bear and clear out the protestors, but Carz had told his officers to stand down and let the people vent their anger.

They had every right. He'd read a report on the purge and was horrified by the number of victims sent to corpse-disposal sites. Living with those results wasn't easy. He carried around a feeling of disgust. Drinking Malrap numbed him, but it didn't make the self-loathing go away. When he drank and thought about the purge, what had been done in his name, he felt rage rise in him and he avoided any interaction with his son.

In order to be truly accountable, Carz decided that he needed to face the consequences of the purge, so this past morning, he'd scheduled an inspection of the corpse-disposal site outside Capitol City.

While he was preparing to board the cruiser to take him out of the dome, Kel intercommed that Roneh was in the waiting room. Carz told Kel to give him a thirty count before opening the door, then seated himself behind his desk and opened his viewer.

Carz stared at his viewer screen and skimmed a disappointing digi-mail on the lack of funds available for building more spaceships. Carz digi-mailed the financial person back to find a solution. He went as far as telling her to look into the prospect of cutting the budgets of the GSS, the military, and the Allegiance Program by thirty percent, and dig further into the idea of a new tax on the ultra-wealthy. Carz was aware this would cause a fuss in the Assembly, but from now on, he was going to do what he thought was right as Leader and damn the reactions from the wealthy or the Global Assembly reps in their pockets. Then he opened a report on the increasing energy consumption of the domes' air-circulation fans as the outside temperature increased.

The door slid open and Roneh marched into the office, stopping in front of Carz's desk. He continued reading the report, which concluded that the solution was reenergizing the generators more frequently with Prevor Industries' approval, otherwise extended blackouts would create unhealthy temperatures inside the domes.

Roneh said, "Hello, dear." When Carz looked up to see her smiling, he second-guessed his decision to rid the office of his father's Global Monarchy torture chair.

A few days after the bombing, he and Roneh had a nasty argument in the study after she had made the rounds of the viewing channels and spoken about how the purge was a political expediency resulting from the bombing at the estate. She told him that she was doing him a favor by explaining the necessity of the purge. Carz was drunk. He vented his frustration. He yelled at her about how she shouldn't speak for him without his permission, how it was ludicrous to rationalize a purge, and her saying he was responsible for the purge made his political predicament worse. Carz began sleeping in one of the mansion's guest rooms. He couldn't stand seeing her, much less sleeping beside her. Since then, they hadn't spoken more than a few words to each other, and now here she was in front of him.

Roneh cleared her throat, then smiled at Carz again.

"Wipe that smile off your face," Carz said. "I know why you're here."

"Enlighten me. Why am I here?"

"Because I allow you to be," Carz said, raising his voice.

Orn had commed earlier to stop his visit to the disposal site. Carz told him to focus on investigating the viewing channels, Roneh, and the bombing. It was evident that when Orn couldn't convince Carz to stay in Capitol City he'd sent Roneh to succeed where he had failed. The two of them working together was problematic, but when it came to the big picture, they had no idea what Carz was doing and that's the way he wanted it.

Carz said, "I'm not in the mood for squabbling. State your business or get out."

"Our son is fine, by the way," Roneh said. "He's been asking about you."

"Is that why you're here?"

"No," Roneh said. "Is it true you're going to one of the mass grave sites?"

"Yes, but it's none of your business."

"Why are you working yourself up over the deaths of terrorists? It's not worth it and it's not going to change anything."

"If you say so."

"You need to embrace what your administration has done."

"Get it through your head," Carz said. "My administration didn't do it."

"You could've fooled me."

Carz said, "I do want to talk to you about Orn, actually."

"What about him?"

"You know anything about him setting up the purge?"

"I don't," Roneh said. "But it makes sense now that I think about it. Some time ago he came to my office and made quite a scene. He was upset you wouldn't agree to your father's purge."

"What did you tell him?"

"I told him that you were the Leader and it was your decision."

"I appreciate that," Carz said.

"I've been wondering whether he may have been behind the bombing, too."

"Why would you think that?"

"Simple," Roneh said. "The bombing was cover for the purge."

"That sounds far-fetched."

"No, that's what I would've done," Roneh said. "Now, I feel ridiculous going on the viewing channels and upsetting you. He knew I'd play right into his hands."

"Don't blame yourself. My father always said Orn was a diabolical genius. I have people investigating and I'll tell them what you said, but if you hear anything implicating him, get back to me. Maybe you can check with your sources."

"Of course—and let me know what your investigation uncovers. I'm happy to help and I'd like to be in the loop."

"Will do."

"And I beg you not to visit the site. Nothing good can come of it."

"Your concern is duly noted."

"And please come to see your son tonight. He's upset that you haven't been around."

"I'll do my best, but I know he adores you and he's in good hands. Now I've got work to do." Carz went back to reading the report. Roneh stood her ground in front of the desk. He peered up from his screen. "Anything else?"

"I've been meaning to ask you about Minok. He seems to have disappeared."

"Yes, I know. After the bombing, he decided to take time off from work, and in his absence I have to say it's been much more pleasant around here."

"If you speak to him, tell him to comm me. I'm concerned about him."

"Since when are you pals?"

"He's family, and Filo has been asking about him," Roneh said. "Just please let me know if you hear anything from him."

"Sure."

"I'll keep an ear out for anything about Orn. You're on the right track there," Roneh said. "I have to go now or I'll be late for a meeting."

Carz watched as Roneh exited the room and the door slid closed behind her. He couldn't believe her gall. He hated her. Rage filled him and he thought about throwing the intercom across the room, but if he wasn't going to act like his father, then he should control himself.

Later, Carz was on a cruiser, speeding toward the roof of the dome. He was wearing an enviro-suit with the helmet at his feet. The pilot punched a code into his security console and up ahead a panel in the dome's roof slid open.

Carz raised his voice to be heard over the cruiser's straining engines. "So what should I expect out there?"

Nobody answered. Two of his security detail were seated on either side of him and two more in back. He caught the guards sneaking concerned looks at one another.

Carz said, "I didn't mean the grave site. I meant outside the dome. Believe it or not, this is the first time I've been out there."

One of the guards sitting behind Carz said, "It can get kind of hairy."

"What do you mean?" Carz leaned his head back so he could hear better.

"Winds get anywhere from two hundred to three hundred kilometers per hour so turbulence can be pretty bad. This cruiser is outfitted for those conditions so it shouldn't be too rocky. We shouldn't feel the intense heat, either."

The dome panel was completely open by the time the cruiser approached the point of passing through it. Outward-bound flights were timed this way so the outside heat didn't affect the moderate temperatures inside the dome and place a strain on the air circulators. The cruiser slowed, engaged the engines for hovering, and accelerated straight up toward the open space in the dome.

The guard behind Carz said, "This maneuver makes the cruiser less vulnerable as it leaves the dome. When the cruiser is horizontal, it's the most stable against high winds. If we flew outside at an angle, the winds might hit the cruiser and flip us."

Carz said, "I recall when those incidents started happening. They were deadly. The commercial cruisers learned that lesson the hard way, but the pilots caught on quickly."

The guard said, "I guess we're fortunate to live inside the domes."

Carz didn't say anything in response. Only a few were privy to the knowledge that the day was coming soon when the domes would no longer be a safe haven. In his spare time, Carz had been writing a speech for planetwide broadcast that not only took responsibility for the failings of his government and the purge but also informed the Kodans about the impending doom under the domes and how he intended to unify the planetary population in the spaceship-building effort that would be necessary to save them. The people deserved to know the truth and it was his job as Leader to tell them.

The cruiser shot up and outside the dome, where high winds began tossing it around. The pilot strained to keep control, shouting orders to the copilot. When the cruiser was stabilized, it accelerated and climbed through the clouds. Turbulence caused the cruiser to lose lift, fall downward a few hundred meters, then recover to ascend again. This pattern of climbing and dropping happened over and over, making Carz nauseous. Eventually, the cruiser broke through the clouds into clear skies.

Carz took a few deep breaths, leaned forward as far as he could against his harness, and said to the pilot, "How long before we arrive at our destination?"

"It's not far," the pilot said. "Just enjoy the smooth sailing while you can, but don't look directly at the sun—it can blind you. Another perk of the crisis."

"Aren't these windows tinted?"

"Yes, sir," the pilot said, "but up here, it's become ineffective. If you want goggles, I have a spare for you." The pilot held up tinted goggles and put them on. Carz noticed that the copilot was already wearing them.

"I appreciate the offer, but I'm fine."

Through the windows, Carz scanned the horizon one-hundred-eighty degrees. The blue sky was beautiful. He didn't see it all that often. The storm clouds below them were a light brown and stretched as far as the eye could see.

Carz said to the pilot, "When is this storm supposed to clear?"

"This one's been going for twenty-nine days," the pilot said.

"Forecasters aren't sure," the copilot said. "Nobody expected this one to last so long and there's always another close behind."

"Understood."

Carz was glad he'd come on this trip. Reading about the environment was one thing, but the danger lurking out here was much worse than he'd ever imagined.

The cruiser began increasing altitude.

Carz said to the pilot, "Why are we climbing?"

"You'll see in a moment."

Carz saw a flash of light on the horizon, then another and another as they jumped around the clouds. When the pyrotechnic show was directly below them, Carz had a bird's-eye view of the lightning generated inside the clouds.

The pilot said, "More than a few cruisers have gotten too close. We'll circle our landing site until it passes."

Over the years, Carz had observed these storms at night from the mansion's terrace. They were a spectacular show for the dome's residents. Fortunately, the designers of the domes had the foresight to install lightning rods that kept the structures safe from the strikes.

On its descent, the cruiser bounced around again, but Carz knew what to expect now so he wasn't as unnerved by the experience as before. When they were below the clouds, he saw the plains littered with thousands of abandoned vehicles from the DOME riots, rusting and decomposing along the roadway heading toward Capitol City. As the cruiser flew low over the windowless vehicles, the bleached bones of the dead were clearly visible inside them. Carz had never seen the aftermath of the DOME riots this close, and the wreckage brought home the disastrous nature of his father's decision. He was sickened by it.

In the distance, he spotted a makeshift blue-tarp tent and a line of soldiers in enviro-suits unloading body bags from the back of cargo cruisers.

"Time to get suited up, sir," the lead guard said. "If you need any assistance, please let me know."

The cruiser landed beside the cargo vehicles. As the engines powered down, Carz picked up his helmet, placed it over his head, and secured it to his suit, then activated the temperature and oxygen output controls. The monitor on his forearm confirmed that the suit was sealed and the oxygen was flowing at 99% capacity. The atmosphere inside the suit was room temperature. Wearing this suit had been part of his military training so prepping it was second nature.

Carz gave a thumbs-up to the lead guard who called out to the pilot, "Ready to disembark."

Carz heard the thud of the door locks disengaging and when the doors slid open, he followed the guards outside.

The lead guard and his three men took up position around Carz as they walked toward the tent. Tarq Bolonar met them at the entrance. He was also suited up.

Tarq said, "Can we speak in private, sir?"

Carz said to the lead guard, "Give us a few moments alone."

The lead guard and his men walked away.

"What is it, Tarq?"

"Sir, I know you want to do this, but I don't think it's a good idea."

"I've made my decision, Tarq. I expect you to support it. I'm not turning back. Didn't I put you in your position personally?"

"Yes, sir."

"Then don't make me regret that decision."

"Yes, sir. This way, sir." He turned and entered the tent. Carz followed with the guards behind him. On either side of them were body bags piled five high and three deep. By the time they passed through the tent and reached the mine shaft, Carz approximated that he'd walked past almost two hundred bodies.

Tarq pressed a red button mounted on a metal post outside the mine shaft's gate. A siren went off and a mechanism began clanking, bringing up the elevator.

Carz said, "I read this mine was stripped of all usable resources about twenty-four years ago."

"That's correct," Tarq said. "Folt Innovations declared their mining subsidiary bankrupt and released their claim to the mine, so the property was forfeited back to the Global Assembly."

"Yes, my grandfather was an expert in that sort of maneuver."

"I didn't mean—"

"It was common practice by the DOME project corporations. Their way of maximizing profit. My grandfather wasn't the only one."

The clanking turned to rattling as the elevator moved upward into view and halted behind the gate.

Tarq said, "We'll be dropping down far and fast so your ears will probably pop during the descent. We've also had security and engineering experts reinspect the elevator's workings to ensure your safety on your visit, sir."

"Considerate," Carz said. "By the way, why are you the only person up here? I saw soldiers on our approach."

"I sent the men down to a lower level with bodies and they're sorting them out now," Tarq said. "I thought it best that your arrival and departure be conducted with as little ceremony as possible considering what's happening here."

The lead guard raised the elevator's gate and walked inside, inspecting the space. He told his guards to enter first to make sure it would hold their weight, then he said, "All set, sir."

"One moment." Carz turned his back to the lead guard and said to Tarq, "Why did you want to avoid any ceremony on my arrival?"

"With all due respect, sir," Tarq said, "that was what I wanted to discuss at the tent. I'm concerned your arrival here might be misconstrued by the soldiers and the GSS agents."

"How so?"

"The men take pride in their duty to the Global Assembly, sir. They eliminate your enemies and die on your command," Tarq said. "A ceremonious arrival might be perceived as a sign of respect to the Global Assembly's enemies, sending mixed signals and causing discontent within the ranks."

"Good thinking, Tarq."

"Thank you, sir."

"Now I remember why I appointed you. Sorry about my earlier remarks. Please keep giving your advice."

"Yes, sir." Tarq gestured toward the awaiting elevator. "Shall we, sir?"

Carz walked onto the elevator platform.

Tarq followed, lowered the gate, and said, "You might want to hang on to the railing. The vertical drop is rapid and can be jarring."

Carz and all the other men grabbed the waist-high railing that ran along three sides of the platform, then Tarq pressed one of the red buttons mounted on a panel, which was attached to the railing beside him.

When the mechanism holding the elevator in place released the platform, there was an immediate feeling of free fall. Had Carz and the guards not been holding the railing, they'd all have been knocked off their feet. Tarq appeared unfazed by the drop. He'd probably taken this ride countless times.

The elevator dropped fast. Carz continued to hold tight. The trip downward lasted longer than Carz expected. The guards were talking among themselves the entire time.

Raising his voice to be heard over the loud clanking

of the elevator's mechanism, Carz said to Tarq, "How deep is this mine?"

"About five kilometers and we're going close to four," Tarq said, turning to face Carz. "We've filled the lower levels. All in all, this is much easier than shipping equipment outside the dome to dig mass graves, considering the environment."

"Understood."

"How's your family since the incident at the estate?"

"Working through it," Carz said. "My mother is antsy to get her casts off and begin rehab. She refuses to let anything slow her down. Spending lots of time with her grandson."

"Good to hear."

Tarq turned around and faced the elevator's gate again which made Carz think they were nearing their destination, but the platform continued downward.

Carz thought about how Tarq had ensured that his appearance here was low profile. Carz had been too wrapped up in his own concerns to perceive the consequences of his visit. If not for Tarq, who was a friend from Military College, then his arrival would have created more problems. Carz needed to be careful. There was always the danger of the GSS attempting a power grab with the Global Guards as their military branch. If Carz wanted to produce more spaceships, then he couldn't forget the optics of his decisions within his own government, especially when he was a Leader who had only come to power because of his lineage. He needed to build allies within the government. That would be another priority when he returned to Capitol City and Tarq could help.

Tarq said, "We're about to reach our destination. There'll be a jolt at the stop, so I'd recommend holding tight to the railing again." Carz and the guards did what they were told.

The clanking of the elevator's mechanism slowed and the platform halted abruptly. Carz lost his balance and almost fell, but the lead guard took hold of his shoulders and righted him. Carz noticed that Tarq had bent his knees to absorb the shock of the impact, then stood straight as if nothing had happened.

Carz said, "Been down here a few times before, huh?"

"More than I care to count," Tarq said while raising the elevator's gate. "You might want to activate the lights on your helmets for this initial tunnel. We've set up lamps up ahead."

Carz did as Tarq suggested. He found it ironic that the enviro-suits were adapted from the SEEDER program spacesuits, and here they were kilometers under the planet's surface instead of kilometers above it. The suit's control panel on Carz's forearm noted that it was fifty degrees cooler than when they were on the surface.

"This way," Tarq said.

Carz didn't see any need for his guards to be here except for protocol, but as he stepped into the tunnel, he waited for them to take up their positions around him. Their helmet lights helped illuminate the way ahead.

When they reached the entrance to the well-lit chamber at the end of the tunnel, Carz told the guards to wait there. Inside the chamber, the bodies of men, women, and children were piled to the ceiling on either side. They were no longer in body bags and were fully clothed. Carz walked by the corpses, examining them. The number of children in short pants and knee-high socks was sickening. He thought of Filo. The corpses had dark blood around their mouths and under their noses or a bullet hole in their forehead. Their eyes had been closed.

Carz felt himself go cold inside and thought, *What have I done?*

He continued through the chamber. When he finally reached the other side and turned around, he realized that he'd walked twenty-five meters in a daze past a cave stacked with corpses. Tarq had trailed behind him. Carz waved him closer.

Carz said, "How many bodies on this level?"

"There are twelve chambers on this level. I'd estimate about six thousand bodies."

"Are all the levels the exact same dimensions?"

"Yes, sir."

"And how many levels are full of bodies and sealed off?"

"Nine including this one, which is about to be sealed."

"How many more bodies still need to be processed?"

"This mine has been dealing with overflow from mines in other regions that couldn't accommodate all their bodies. There's at least another three cruiser loads en route from Mlimoa. That's supposedly the final region to send us their bodies. Then we'll have two more levels to seal off."

"I've seen enough," Carz said. With similar mines utilized in the other regions, Carz calculated over half a million dead.

"Yes, sir."

Carz turned away from the guards in the distance and lowered his voice. "What do you think about all of this?" Noticing the uncomfortable expression on Tarq's face, he added, "Please speak freely."

"With all due respect, sir, this should never have happened."

"I agree. I didn't sign the damn order and I will have to live with this atrocity, but the people who made this happen will pay," Carz said. "I've developed a few leads on where to focus the investigation. When this assignment is wrapped up, come and see me. We need to catch up and get our affairs in order."

"Yes, sir. I'm interested to hear what you've found," Tarq said, patting Carz on the shoulder. "I'm with you, Carz."

"I appreciate your support, Tarq. By the way, do me a favor and locate my brother."

"Will do."

When the cruiser left the site and ascended through the clouds, it was nighttime. Carz hardly noticed the turbulence. He was still thinking about what he'd seen in that chamber, about the children, about the men and women eliminated with a stroke of his father's pen. Their existence snuffed out in a disgusting denigration of life's value. This journey made him see his father in a truly different light.

When the cruiser emerged from the clouds, Carz leaned forward and peered out the front window. He was stunned by the number of stars in the sky. After a lifetime spent living within Capitol City's dome, he'd never seen so many.

One of those stars was the new home for the Kodan people. If this trip confirmed anything, it was his commitment to construct as many spaceships as necessary to save as many Kodans as possible. That's what a true Leader would do.

He'd need to swallow his pride and communicate with Mar Jeps. Minok had told him that she'd called when his father died. She'd called again after the bombing at the estate and then about the purge. The first time, he didn't feel like talking. The other two times, he was embarrassed and ashamed of what had happened. Now, he needed to talk to her about the air circulators and it felt necessary to create a partnership between the Global Assembly and Prevor Industries to finance the Kodans' survival. He'd known Mar Jeps for a great deal of his life and although his father reviled her, he was sure that she was a caring person who wanted the best for the Kodan people.

Now, in his father's study, he poured the Malrap in his glass back into a bottle and corked it. He wouldn't drink a drop again until the final Kodan boarded the final spaceship and the journey began to a habitable planet. Until then, he would be haunted by the images of that chamber. He would bottle up his anger toward the perpetrators of this outrage and vowed to gain retribution for the victims, but at that moment, he wanted to hug his son and begin his redemption.

MADO

Mado built a platform on the roof of his home and out-fitted it with a table and enough chairs for the family to eat dinner there. When the children fell asleep, Mado and Alba would climb back up, listen to the waves crashing on the shore, discuss their day and future plans, then make love.

But those activities weren't the real reasons for the construction. Mado borrowed a high-powered telescope from the Space Academy, and night after night, after Alba went to bed, he inspected the cosmos. He hoped to catch a glimpse of Yor and When All Else Fails or the spaceships streaming from Koda on their exodus to the habitable planet. Maybe if he was lucky, he'd come across the aliens. Eventually, Mado became frustrated with the fruitless results of his astronomical observations and decided to rebuild the telescope. He absconded with a more powerful lens from the Academy. As time passed, he became more obsessed with his stargazing. He began heading to the roof earlier by himself, putting an end to the picnics and private time with Alba.

Then one evening, Mado was transfixed, peering through the lens of the telescope, when he was startled by Alba saying, "Were our romantic evenings and dinners with the children just a ploy so you could lose yourself up here?" She had climbed the ladder and stepped onto the platform without him noticing.

Mado didn't move his eye from the lens as he increased the telescope's magnification, zooming in on B-452.

Alba continued, "I heard through a coworker that you spoke that language again when a meeting got heated, discussing which quadrants of space to inspect on future missions. I was told you were anxious about one quadrant in particular."

Mado closed both his eyes. He needed to be careful about what he said next. In the meeting, he had told his colleagues he'd done a cursory inspection of the quadrant on one of his last voyages and that it wasn't worthy of closer examination. When his colleagues checked the Protectorate archives to confirm Mado's conclusion and came up empty, they asked Mado for corroboration of his assessment and he deflected the conversation to another subject. He didn't want exploration in that area because the next quadrant over was the Kodan system and roaming any further in that direction might uncover his secrets. They pressed the issue, so he acted insulted that they'd doubt his expertise. When they told him that wasn't an answer to their question, Mado panicked, racking his brain for a lie. He reminded himself that lying on Prevor led to consequences that were much greater than suspension from his job. So he blurted out in Kodan, "You have no idea what you'd be stumbling across, you ignoramuses." His colleagues stared at him, dumbfounded at what they'd just witnessed. Mado apologized for his gibberish. He offered to provide them with a detailed breakdown of his thinking about the quadrant at a later date, gathered his things, and hurried out of the conference room.

"I've heard of at least four other occasions recently where these outbursts happened," Alba said. "There's a rumor that the Academy is thinking about ordering a checkup to find a physiological reason for your behavior."

"I'm not concerned," Mado said. The tone of his voice belied the fact that he was anxious, and he knew Alba could hear it, too.

Alba's footsteps approached and Mado felt her hand on his back. "I'm concerned about you. I'm concerned how your behavior effects this family."

Mado opened his eyes and took a few steps beyond her reach. He didn't want her sensing his feelings. "Everyone's making a big deal out of nothing."

"I don't think it's nothing," Alba said. "I've spent more time with you than anyone, and I see how you're acting. The children see it and they're concerned, too."

"So much concern. Humor me. What do you think is the basis of this behavior?" Mado hoped that if they talked it out, then the desire to discuss the matter further would stop for a while, and in the meantime, he might be able to alter his behavior and end this line of inquiry. "Do you think I've been cheating on you?"

"Knowing you, that's hilarious."

"Let's have it, then," Mado said. "What do you think is troubling me?"

"I didn't say anything about something troubling you, so that's interesting," Alba said. "I was talking to Zev about—"

"So you're talking to my closest friend behind my back?"

"We're both worried about you," Alba said. "Let me finish."

"Fine, go on."

"Zev and I were wondering what this is all about," Alba said, walking over to the telescope and pointing up to the sky. "We both agreed that it has to do with your final journey. Your story about being lost was similar to the experiences of other Space Travelers—"

"Only a handful."

"That's true," Alba said. "Few were lost as long as you, but Zev doesn't buy that your ship was destroyed the way you described. He said there are too many backup systems, but it was likely the ship was damaged beyond repair. He didn't think you'd scuttle the ship intentionally."

Mado said with sarcasm, "Well, good to know the best man at my mating ceremony holds me in such high regard."

"He did say that the Protectorate sent out a spacecraft to recover the wreckage at the coordinates where you reported the spacecraft detonated but found nothing."

"I was close to the gravity well of a black hole and the debris was probably pulled into it."

"So you said in your report, and the Protectorate signed off on it even though there were skeptics."

"It's science. There are always skeptics," Mado said. "So now that you've laid out the case, counselor, what is this far-flung theory about my behavior that you've concocted with Zev?"

"Our far-flung theory, as you call it, is that you laid out a fictional tale about your accident and your voyage home," Alba said. "What really happened? After your mishap, you were rescued by another interstellar species, which isn't against regulations, but maybe you became fond of them, learned their language, and stayed with them. You traveled with them until you had the longing to return home."

"That's ridiculous." Mado was amazed at how easily they'd reconstructed the truth.

"We're close, though, aren't we?" Alba walked toward Mado until she was face-to-face with him. "I know you, Mado. I know you're scared. You violated a sacrosanct Traveler rule. You established a relationship with an interstellar species for reasons beyond survival, and you learned their language. Now the language is hardwired in your brain. You probably cared about them because that's the kind of Prevorian you are. That's what all this obsessive stargazing is about, isn't it?"

Mado didn't know what to say.

"Tell me I'm wrong. Go on—tell me," Alba said. "And that's another thing. I know you don't want to lie to me. That would be against our sacred vows and that's why you've danced around the subject. That's why you've begun acting like a cornered animal as you run out of ways to avoid telling the truth. Tell me—am I wrong?" Alba yelled the final question.

Mado stared at her face as it quivered with fear and rage. He hated himself for what he'd done to the woman he loved. After returning to Prevor, he'd gone on many dates, but Alba was the only female with whom he felt a connection. He enjoyed spending time with her. She was an intellectual equal and practically finished his thoughts. She made him laugh. He was attracted to her with every fiber of his being, and he felt lucky to have ever met her. Now look what he'd done to her.

"Tell me!" Alba yelled. "Tell me!"

He loved her even more for caring so much about what was tearing him apart.

"Tell me!"

"What's wrong, Mother?" Clo was clinging to the top of the ladder. She'd never climbed up by herself before. Mado usually carried her because her legs weren't long enough to reach the platform from the ladder.

Clo moved herself to one side of the ladder, took one hand off a rung, and swung her body and one of her legs toward the platform, but that maneuver was unsuccessful.

Both Mado and Alba called out, "Clo, wait!"

They rushed to help her, but before they could get to her, Clo extended her body so far off the ladder that the tiny fingers of her one anchoring hand slipped off the rung she was clutching. There was shock on her face and she seemed to hang in the air, then she plummeted out of sight, screaming. There was a sickening thud when her body struck the ground.

Mado peered over the side of the roof. Clo was lying on her back on the ground, unmoving, illuminated by the light from the kitchen window. A pool of blood spread beneath her head. Mado wailed in grief. Alba jumped onto the ladder, grabbed the rails on either side of the rungs with her hands and placed her feet on the rails instead of the rungs, then slid down to the ground.

IN THE HOSPITAL WAITING ROOM, MADO SAT IN silence with Alba, holding her hand. They both rose from their chairs when the physician emerged from Clo's room and approached them. He was younger than Mado and Alba, wearing a light-green lab coat.

Before the physician could speak, Mado said, "How is she?" as if questioning the physician first might cushion the blow of bad news.

"She's fine," the physician said. "She has a concussion, which isn't good for someone her age, but a brain scan showed zero damage. We'll know more about her condition when she wakes up and we can do cognitive tests. We'd like to keep her overnight to monitor brain functions."

Alba said, "I thought you said there was no damage."

"The scan is insightful, but only one aspect of our examination. You can take her home in the morning."

Alba said, "What about blood loss?"

"The compress you applied stemmed it. We've stitched up the wound and don't see any need to give her blood."

Alba said, "It was a lot of blood—are you sure?"

"Bleeding is always traumatic to see, especially when it's a child, but in this case, she's fine."

Mado said in Kodan, "Thank the Powers-That-Be."

"What was that?" the physician said.

"Nothing," Alba said. "My partner sometimes speaks nonsense when he's upset."

"Has anyone looked into it?" The physician was clearly concerned.

"I was a Space Traveler, and I developed the condition as a result of being alone for too long."

"Oh, yes—I thought I recognized you," the physician said. "You were lost for decades."

"Yes, but all's well that ends well," Mado said and kissed Alba on the cheek.

"That's what they say," the physician said. "Your daughter is sedated and sleeping, but you're welcome to sit with her and encouraged to bond with her. There's also some administrative forms to fill out at the front desk."

Alba said to Mado. "I'll take care of the paperwork. You go see her."

"This way," the physician said to Alba, and they walked off together toward the front desk.

Mado entered Clo's room and when the door swung closed, he slumped against the doorframe and cried. Clo was unconscious, lying on her back in the bed with a blanket covering her up to her shoulders. Her head was wrapped in a bandage. On the wall above and behind the bed was a holographic monitoring device, tracking Clo's vital signs. The readings were normal. Clo was in a deep sleep.

Mado approached the bed and stared down at his child. He blamed himself for what had happened. His behavior had provoked Alba into hollering at him and brought Clo to the roof. For his entire lifetime, Prevorian lore had taught him that lying led to disaster, and here those teachings had come to fruition. On Koda, he'd used lies to get his way, creating a positive result using a negative attribute. That had been a cornerstone of Yorlik's plan. He thought he could bring what he'd learned on Koda to

Prevor and live a normal life. He should have assumed in a society grounded in transparency that his lies would fail under the weight of attempting to hide them.

Here was his beautiful child damaged by his toxic behavior. He couldn't continue this conduct. He needed to find a way of being truthful again. That would be his challenge going forward. The first step would be the most difficult. That would be coming clean with Alba.

He bent down and kissed Clo on the cheek, then stood watching the blanket rise and fall with her breathing. He pulled up a chair and sat beside her. He reached out, placed his hand on her arm, which was outside of the blanket, then closed his eyes.

He conjured the memory of footraces along the beach where Clo was convinced that she could outrun her father. They'd stand at a starting line, and Mado would yell, "Go," then he'd wait while Clo dashed down the beach with her little legs pumping. As she moved further away, she would peek over her shoulder, giggling in anticipation of her father running to overtake her. Mado reveled in the joy Clo was experiencing for as long as possible, then raced after her. When she looked over her shoulder and observed Mado closing the distance between them, she giggled louder and attempted to sprint faster toward the finish line that her brother had drawn in the sand with his foot. Before Clo reached the line, Mado caught up with her, scooped her into his arms, then carried her over the line and collapsed onto the sand.

Clo would lie beside him, shrieking in delight, then holler, "I won. I won."

Mado would say, "I think we both won," pulling her close and kissing her on the cheek.

In that moment, Mado was overwhelmed by how much he loved Clo.

All that happiness could have been darkened by sadness because he was concealing the truth about the past and obsessing over the aliens' prediction of failure.

Mado thought, *I refuse to fail as a father.*

Clo said, "Who are those creatures with the big eyes, Father?"

Mado opened his own eyes to see Clo looking at him, then he heard the door shut and Alba said, "Yes, Mado. Tell us about them."

INSOL

"There was absolutely no reason to lock me up for the entire evening after my arrival," Insol said as she walked down a corridor of the facility with her mother beside her. Kubwa sauntered behind them.

Insol's mother said in an exasperated tone, "There was after what you did to your brother."

"He deserved it."

"I talked to him," Insol's mother said. "He shouldn't have said those things about your uncle, but you were out of line."

"He's a crybaby. He'll be fine."

"Sure, after his retina is reattached. His nose had to be reset, and his face is so swollen I hardly recognize him, and I'm his mother."

"You always exaggerate," Insol said. "I'd like to see for myself."

A group of workers strolled toward them, acknowledging Rika and giving Insol dirty looks as they passed.

Insol's mother said, "You're the last person he wants to see."

Insol stopped, turned to the workers, and yelled, "You have a problem with me? Come over here, you bunch of bitches."

The workers halted and turned toward Insol, glaring at her. Kubwa blocked Insol's path.

"No offense," Insol's mother said to the workers. "Sorry. Have a great day."

The workers exchanged words with each other and walked away.

"That kind of behavior is not helping."

"Sorry. You're right, mother" Insol said. "And what's Kubwa doing here?"

"Keeping you out of trouble."

Insol patted Kubwa on the chest and said to him as if he were a pet, "Good boy. That's a good boy."

"Let's keep moving," Insol's mother said. "You must be hungry."

"Yes, I'm famished."

Kubwa gave Insol a stern look. "Get going before I carry you back to your room."

Insol said, "Did everyone lose their sense of humor around here?"

"I love you, Insol, but you're not right." Rika pointed at her daughter's head. "Until we determine you're not a danger to anyone in this facility, including yourself, you can only roam around under guard, and again, your brother is off-limits until he says so. That's the deal, and you will adhere to those ground rules until I say otherwise."

Insol had already begun thinking of ways to shake the guards. Kubwa wouldn't be around all the time. He had other responsibilities. She assumed he was only here now because her mother wanted him to assess Insol's state of mind. Insol took a deep breath and exhaled. She'd played Mar just right to get here, and if this mission was going to be a success, she needed to control herself. It was too important.

"All right," Insol said, hooking her arm with her mother's. "I'll be a good girl now."

"I'm not falling for the I'll-be-good-girl-now act."

"I don't know what you're talking about."

"Don't forget I raised you," Insol's mother said, and they proceeded down the corridor.

As they approached the cafeteria, Insol caught the scent of cooked food and realized how hungry she was. She hadn't eaten since she left Capitol City over a day ago.

Yesterday evening, a young guard had brought a tray of food to her room, balancing it on one hand as he locked the door behind him. Through the fog of a sedative, she watched him put the tray on the table beside her bed. The guard was about eighteen years old, the same age as her students. She figured this might be a good time to escape, so she waited until he was almost back to the door and marshaled her strength. She yelled, "Hey, asshole!" then pushed herself into a sitting position on the bed with her legs hanging over the side of the mattress. The guard turned and Insol threw the tray at him. She was more disoriented than she'd estimated because the tray missed the guard by a wide margin to his right and splattered food against the wall before the metallic tray crashed to the ground. With her initial idea for escape gone wrong, she decided to just rush the guard. She'd knock him aside, snatch his keys, and make it out the door before he caught up with her, but when her feet hit the ground, her legs had no strength in them, and she collapsed to the cold cement floor.

The guard laughed and pointed at her. "Nice try. Looks like you're not eating unless you want to lick the wall." He turned and unlocked the door.

When he was halfway out the doorway, Insol said, "Aren't you going to help me up?"

The guard looked at her and said, "Nope." Then he closed the door and she heard the lock engage.

Now, Insol stood in front of the cafeteria entrance with her mother beside her. The room was relatively empty, maybe ten to fifteen people in total either in groups or scattered around a room that could hold two hundred workers. It wasn't the current shift's mealtime. Her mother had brought her here now so Insol couldn't make a big public scene.

Insol's mother said, "Take a seat. I'll bring you some food."

"You don't have to coddle me. I know you're busy. Why don't you let Kubwa watch me and you can go on your way?"

"Because you're my daughter and I want to spend time with you. When was the last time we saw one another?"

"It's been a while."

"It's been three years and four hundred and seven days," Insol's mother said, wrapping her arms around Insol. "No matter what's happening with you, I'm thrilled to see you in person. I love you."

Insol hugged her mother so tightly that she heard her mother grunt from the exertion. She buried her face in her mother's chest and held herself there. When Insol released her hold, her mother did the same, adding a kiss on Insol's nose.

"I'm your mother. You know I'm always here for you. No matter what you're going through."

"I'm sorry," Insol said. "I'm not in a good place."

"I want us to spend quality time together," Insol's mother said. "Now take a seat and I'll get you some food." She kissed Insol on the forehead.

"Where should I sit?"

"Wherever you like," Insol's mother said, then went to the cafeteria counter.

Insol turned to Kubwa. "I assume you're following me?"

"Absolutely."

Insol headed for an empty table in the far corner of the room. A few of the diners stared at her. She restrained the compulsion to yell at them, but instead forced a smile. That stopped them from gawking. She sat with her back to a wall at the end of a bench that ran the length of a two-meter table. Another bench the same length was on the opposite side. Kubwa stood with his back to the wall at the opposite end of her bench. Insol couldn't leave the cafeteria without attempting to pass him.

Insol said, "You gonna sit? I'm not gonna bite."

"Could've fooled me."

"Suit yourself."

In the distance, Insol observed her mother holding a tray and ordering food from a cafeteria worker on the other side of a counter. Nobody was paying attention to Insol now. She reasoned that she shouldn't be angry at these workers. She'd put one of their own in the clinic, and she respected their effort to secure the survival of the Kodan people. They were doing their part to beat the Global Assembly at their game, but after the horror of the purge, Insol believed that direct action against the government was required to end their bad behavior, and that was one of the reasons why she was here.

A man rose from his seat and walked over to a garbage can beside a waist-high metal table holding a tub. He dumped the waste from his plate into the garbage and placed his utensils, cup, plate, and cloth napkin in the tub. Then he looked around the room until his eyes landed on Insol and his mouth gaped in surprise. He pointed at her and said, "Hey!" then ambled toward her. She didn't recognize him. He was Shamban, wearing grease-stained brown coveralls in a style that hadn't been made in years and were too small for him. He was clean-shaven, but as he moved closer, he reeked.

Kubwa had taken notice and stepped forward. He eyeballed the man, who waved at him. Kubwa didn't show any signs of recognition, either. The man stopped when he was directly across the table from Insol.

"Hello, Insol," he said. "Been a while."

Insol decided to play along, and she might remember his name. She remained seated and said, "Hello."

The man walked around the end of the table until he was standing only a meter away from Insol. "You don't recognize me, do you?"

"I'm not great at remembering faces."

"Makes sense you wouldn't remember me. We met once and that was thirty years ago."

"Refresh my memory," Insol said. She noted he hadn't introduced himself by name although his security ID read "Dex Murt."

"We met at college before you left for Capitol City. I'll never forget. You stood up at a meeting and spoke eloquently about the future of the Kodan people. You suggested that we proceed through rebellion not protest. Of course, your ideas were too radical, so they fell on deaf ears."

"A meeting" was code for an anti-DOME movement gathering and the phrase "rebellion not protest" indicated the more radical element of the Movement, the ADM. This man was her contact and the reason why she'd come to the facility.

Dex continued, "After you spoke, I told you how much I agreed with you."

"I gave a bunch of those lectures back then," Insol said. "I'm flattered you remember."

"I've followed your career ever since."

Dex touched behind his ear and began paying attention to something he was hearing on an audio implant, which was unusual gear for workers here. He glanced over his shoulder at Insol's mother who was approaching with a tray full of food. He turned back to Insol and said, "I have to go. It's wonderful to see you." He put his hand in his pants pocket, then reached out and shook Insol's hand. He passed her something cold and hard. It was the size of Insol's palm and she closed her fist around it so Kubwa couldn't see it.

Dex turned around when Insol's mother was a few meters behind him. He said, "Madame Administrator," then he strode away with his head down past Kubwa and into the hallway.

"Who was that?" Insol's mother said, sliding the tray onto the table.

Insol slipped the man's gift into her pocket then grabbed the tray, unwrapped eating utensils from a napkin, and began devouring the food. Insol couldn't recall the last time she'd eaten freshly grown food, but that was the fare here. The facility was outfitted with massive greenhouses for transfer to the hydroponic bays on the ships when it was time to leave.

"Insol? Who was that?"

"I have no idea," Insol said with her mouth full. "Some strange little man who said he knew me from college."

Insol's mother said to Kubwa, "You get his name?"

"He tried to hide his ID when he walked by, which was suspicious, but I got it."

"That's odd," Insol's mother said. "I'll have Lek look into it." She sat down on the bench across from Insol.

"Please don't harass the poor man. He's just a fan of my work."

"You should take advantage of it. There are lots of lonely men around here, and you're new on the market. Might be good to get some before you leave."

"I'll pass," Insol said. "What's the situation these days with you and Lek Valsted?"

"Eat and I'll tell you about it."

LEK

As Lek was unlocking his office door, he heard his desk comm buzzing. He closed the door behind him and turned on the lights. According to the facility comm-number ID, it was Rika calling. He sat down behind the desk, activated the comm, and put her on speaker.

"Hello, boss," Lek said.

"Lek," Rika said. "How was your midday meal with Ara?"

"Fantastic."

"Sorry I couldn't make it. Yesterday and today have been tumultuous with Mar visiting and Insol's breakdown. How has your time with Ara been?"

"I don't know if I have the words," Lek said. "We've had many conversations over our viewers, but being with her in person and getting to know her again after twenty-two years is more than I could've wished for."

"Well," Rika said in mock outrage. "Good to know who's the number one woman in your life."

"What I feel for you is different."

"I'm just kidding, Lek."

"Of course," Lek said, chuckling nervously. "How was your time with Insol?"

"Had its moments both good and bad," Rika said. "I'm glad Kubwa came along. I don't know what's gotten into her."

"According to Mar, the Complex's psych med con-cluded that the shock of the purge may have reignited her post-traumatic stress from that incident twenty years ago."

"Just kills me that she's so broken," Rika said. Her voice was shaky with emotion.

"Mar said she'll get the best people on it."

"It isn't easy seeing her this way and I trust Mar will do her part, but that's not why I'm calling," Rika said. "At the cafeteria, a man spoke with Insol. Both Kubwa and I thought he was peculiar. His ID appeared out of date and read Dex Murt. I recognize that name from somewhere. I was hoping you could look into it. Make it a priority. Their interaction gave me a bad feeling."

"First rule of security is trust your instincts so I'll get right on it—and the name sounds familiar to me, too." Lek picked up the receiver and took Rika off speaker. "Me and Ara are planning on getting together at evening meal. You care to join us?"

"Aside from my other duties, I have a slew of meetings with Mar and the division heads today, so I'll let you know. In the meantime, look into that man."

"Will do," Lek said. "Hope to see you later."

"If you're lucky," Rika said and chuckled.

"Right now, I feel like the luckiest man on Koda."

"If you look at the women in your life, it appears that you are," Rika said. "A meeting is about to start. Gotta go. See you soon."

The comm disconnected. Lek opened his viewer and read the digi-mail that had accumulated since yesterday. Most of it was from department heads regarding repairs on surveillance cams and the DNA and retina scanners for locks. He forwarded the requests to the security's maintenance crew. They were a reliable handpicked team. Protocol dictated that he receive these messages first so he might catch any patterns indicating criminal activity.

There was a digi-mail reporting the theft of an ID belonging to someone who no longer worked in the facility. It was from Mira Murt. She apologized for breaking the rules and not handing the expired ID to security for shredding. She couldn't bring herself to do it because the ID was the last surviving foto of her father Dex Murt who had died at the facility.

Rika and Kubwa were correct about the individual who approached Insol. Lek sent a digi-mail to Mira and requested that she meet with him. He needed to know who had access to her possessions.

Lek checked the facility's med database for deaths reported in the past five years. There were a handful of work-related accidents, but the majority of deaths were due to old age. There was no Dex Murt. He searched back ten years and still found nothing. Lek was astonished at the small number of deaths due to illness. Maybe it was the uncontaminated environment with organically grown food and an exercise period every day that resulted in the healthiness of the workers. Also, all workers were required to take a yearly medical to ensure early detection of ailments and the clinic was free to the workers.

Then Lek went back eighteen years in the med database and discovered that Dex Murt had died in a construction mishap. According to the date-stamp on the coroner's report, Lek had been here for four years at the time. He stared at the foto of Dex's corpse at the death scene. Lek was annoyed at himself for not remembering this incident. He searched the security database and located Dex's ID photo and the accident report. Dex had been a Separatist Revolt vet who built skyscrapers in Shamba after the war. At the Shamban facility, he'd walked the beams of the spaceships in their initial stages of construction, welding the frames together.

One day, Dex fell to his death. An interview with his supervisor disclosed that Dex loved his job. He came to work every day with a smile on his face. He was liked by his colleagues and never had an unkind word for them. He often forgot to wear his safety harness and his supervisor reprimanded him, but Dex did it out of habit. He wasn't shirking the rules on purpose. That's how he worked on skyscrapers. He was wearing a safety harness on the day of the accident, though. He was on the late shift, so it was just him and one other person on duty. The rule was that no beam walkers should be left alone, but Dex told his coworker to go on break and he'd catch up to him. His fall was surprising to everyone who worked with him. His balance was renowned. When they were ahead of schedule and the supervisor wasn't watching, he'd do balancing tricks and cartwheels on the beams. The reason for the incident was a faulty harness with a slight cut that tore with stress. Harnesses were inspected before every shift, and since Dex never relied on a harness sufficiently to put stress on it, the accident was considered tragic and baffling. His daughter had arranged for him to be cremated at the facility. In the forensic report, the med found no toxins or mood-altering drugs in Dex's system, and there was no sign of foul play. He died of a broken neck. Lek had filed it away as an accident.

Now, Lek felt a sense of urgency and his old GSS training came to bear. First question: Who was this man wearing a stolen security ID previously owned by someone who died eighteen years ago in a questionable accident? The ID had been taken from the owner's daughter. By reporting the theft, she risked censure for not handing the ID in to the authorities, so either she knew the thief and was suspicious of his motives, or maybe she thought whoever had stolen it was planning to use it for nefarious reasons. If the man had stolen the ID, then he had done so for a purpose, and that wasn't to work at the facility.

Lek activated his desk comm and contacted the facility's security headquarters, which was down the corridor. He told the senior officer to bring Mira Murt to him right away. If she wasn't at her residence, then he was to check her ID info and track her down. The action was priority one. In his twenty-two years as security chief, he had only used the highest alert a handful of times so his men understood the urgency.

When he deactivated his comm, he checked the vidcam archive for the cafeteria closest to Insol's room. He observed a man wearing outdated construction coveralls speaking to Insol, and when he shook her hand, it was clear to someone with Lek's training that the man was passing her something. He stood at a specific angle so the cam didn't pick up a facial image. Lek tracked him out of the cafeteria and he avoided showing his face to every vidcam along the way. He was clearly well versed in dodging surveillance. Then he entered a lift with an inoperable cam. Lek found the floor where the man got off, but he had put on a hat that he'd been carrying in his back pocket and Lek lost him in a crowd of workers wearing the same hat. Lek rewound the lift's cam footage until he found the point where the man originally entered the lift on his way to the cafeteria. He'd walked into the lift with his back to the cam, then reached behind himself and sprayed something into the cam's lens, blacking it out.

This was a professional job. The man had stolen an ID to traverse the facility freely and then deftly dodged the surveillance layout. All of this to clandestinely contact Insol. What were they up to? Lek doubted they were working alone, and that worried him even more. He activated his comm and told the senior security officer that he wanted Insol brought to him priority one as well.

Lek had an idea. There was a hidden vidcam in the temperature gauge over the freezers in all the cafeteria kitchens. Lek had installed them himself so nobody else was aware of them. Many outer-Kodans were so accustomed to stealing food to survive that this habit didn't end when they began working here. By placing these cams over the freezers, Lek had retrieved almost a hundred percent of the stolen goods and discouraged such thefts going forward.

Lek found the freezer-cam feed for the cafeteria where the meeting took place. The cam looked out into the kitchen. In the distance was the server's station and the interior of the cafeteria itself. Lek had requisitioned high-resolution cams for the entire facility and that would come in handy here. He zoomed out of the kitchen. He went to the time frame when Rika had taken Insol to the cafeteria and scanned the footage until he caught Rika at the counter, ordering food. Slowly moving the footage forward, he observed the blurry image of a man in outdated construction coveralls touching the back of his ear as if he were listening to an audio implant. When the man glanced back at Rika, Lek froze the image. He zoomed in further and focused on the culprit's face until he had a perfect image.

"I've got you!" Lek said.

The man's short-cropped hair revealed a Shamban prison-gang tattoo on his neck. It was a knife with a curved blade and a handle branded with an "S." The man had rolled up his sleeves, and Lek saw something familiar on the man's arm. Zooming in, he noted that the veins on the man's left arm were not purple but black from being injected during torture by the GSS. There was no way Lek would have given this man clearance to enter the facility and not known about his history. Lek panned back up to the face. There was a distinct resemblance to Dex Murt so if someone compared the man's face to the ID, then it'd be a match and he could pass through checkpoints.

Lek ran a facial recog program comparing the man's face with anybody who had ever worked in the facility since he took over security and set up his own ID system. He hacked into the GSS arrest database through a back-door and ran the same program.

His desk comm buzzed. It was security headquarters. The officer reported that Insol had escaped her room. Lek said he was digi-mailing an image of Insol and the suspect. An all-points bulletin should be put out for both of them. Lek asked how Insol got out of her room. The officer didn't have a clue but it was being investigated, and Mira Murt was on her way to Lek's office. Lek asked to be notified the moment that Insol or the man were apprehended, and he told the officer to comm Rika about her daughter's status. Lek didn't want to say anything to Rika yet, but the subterfuge involved in Insol's escape plus the presence of an infiltrator utilizing an audio implant had convinced Lek that this security breach might involve other workers or even some of his guards.

Lek deactivated his comm. His viewer was still working to find the suspect's identity. He sighed. He'd dealt with domestic issues, fights in the facility's Malrap bars, and theft. There was a murder every couple of years, but the perpetrator was always evident. He didn't miss this sort of investigation, but it was energizing to use his old skills again and take full advantage of the security features he'd put in place.

The facility's community board had debated over the need for security measures like surveillance cams. Mar convinced them that it wasn't to intrude on the workers' privacy like the Global Assembly had done, but it would come in handy when facility security and the safety of the workers and their accomplishments were endangered.

There was a knock on the door.

Lek said, "Come in."

Two tall, well-built Shamban security guards in brown uniforms entered flanking and towering over a five-foot-tall Mira Murt who appeared confused and scared. She wore blue coveralls designating her as a worker from the facility's greenhouse gardens. The coveralls were soiled from kneeling in the dirt. She was in her mid-to-late 40s and looked nothing like her father. She had the features of an aging attractive Shamban woman with grey hair hanging below her shoulders.

Lek noted the guards had placed restraints on her wrists and said, "The restraints aren't necessary."

One of the guards said, "We were told priority one."

"True," Lek said. "Sorry. You were correct in following protocol. I should've been more specific in my orders. Unlock them, please."

"You have the key?" one guard said to the other who shrugged.

Lek opened the middle drawer of his desk, dug out a key, and tossed it to one of the guards who caught it and unlocked the restraints. Lek noted Mira's dirty hands—some of the hydroponics crew liked to feel the soil as they worked and didn't wear gloves. The guard placed the key on Lek's desk.

"Find your damn keys," Lek said. "You're dismissed, but stand guard outside the door."

As the guards left, one reprimanded the other for making them look stupid. They stood outside the open door, getting into an argument.

Lek yelled, "Shut the door, please." Lek made a mental note that he needed to speak to the senior officer about the unpreparedness and unprofessional behavior of these guards.

The door closed. Lek peered at his viewer, which was still running the facial recog program. Mira was standing in the middle of the office, looking sheepish. "Please sit," Lek said. "Can I offer you some water?"

"No, I'm fine," Mira said, rubbing at her wrists as she sat down in the chair in front of Lek's desk.

"Were they rough with you?"

"No, but the restraints were tight." Her voice was shaky and she clutched at herself.

"Nervous about something?"

"No…well, yes—I've never been arrested before and I know I should've destroyed the ID."

"Yes. Technically, I could toss you out of the facility for keeping your father's ID."

"I know," Mira said, placing her hands on her knees and leaning forward. "I know. It was just the foto. Please have mercy. My life's in danger." She began to cry, covering her face with her hands.

Lek's viewer beeped as the program found a match for a Cerio Murt in the facility database. The foto was from the year before Dex's death, which explained why the program had taken so long. It was obviously a much younger version of the man in the cafeteria, plus the young man in the foto was smiling with no marks of GSS detainment. Then Lek's viewer beeped again and an image appeared from Cerio Murt's GSS prison record. This foto resembled the person who was on the loose in the facility. The look on his face was angry and bitter.

"What's that thing telling you?" Mira said. She had stopped crying and was wiping her eyes with the sleeves of her coveralls.

"One moment," Lek said. He read the prison document. Cerio had been incarcerated for the murder of a Global Assembly rep who Lek recalled from his previous life working for the GSS. The rep had been a hardened loyalist from the Msituan region. He was a supporter of increasing the GSS budget every year by cutting funds for the Shamban region's food relief efforts. He was infamous for racist anti-Shamban speeches on the Global Assembly floor. Lek remembered reading about his gruesome murder. The rep was beaten to death in front of his infant child. The act was caught by a nanny cam in a stuffed animal. That was eleven years ago. Lek was surprised that Cerio had been released from prison so soon, but the prison system was jammed up since no new prisons were being built and some thought being an outer-Kodan was punishment enough.

"So why is your brother here and how did he get into the facility?"

"How did you…? I don't know."

"You don't know the answer to either question?" Lek said. "Why are you in danger?"

"Because I told you Cerio stole the ID. He'll kill me for telling you like he killed my father."

"And why did he kill your father?"

"Cerio was communicating with a radical element of the Movement on the outside. My father wanted Cerio to stop because he was concerned that the facility might be exposed. They argued about it constantly. It got to the point where my father threatened to tell you, so Cerio killed him."

"When your father died, you failed to tell security that he was murdered. Why?"

"I made a deal with my brother. If he left the facility, I wouldn't turn him in."

"So you didn't report a murder, which is a major crime," Lek said. "You realize the implications are termination of employment."

"Yes," Mira said and began crying again.

"Why did you turn him in now?"

"I told him to never come back," Mira said. "And he stole the only foto I had of my father."

"Is he staying with you?"

"No, he's sleeping in one of the old tunnels that were used when they were creating the facility. He worked maintenance when he was here, so he knows them well. I presume he used one of those tunnels to get in, but I'm not sure."

"Why is he here?"

"He said something about having a meeting with serious consequences."

"You seem to know a lot more than you originally stated," Lek said. "Anything else come to mind?"

"No."

Lek stood, walked around his desk, opened the door, and waved the guards into the office.

"Get up," Lek said to Mira, and she rose from the chair. "If you think of anything else or you hear from your brother, I want to know. I'm putting you under house arrest. The guards will escort you back to your room and you'll be confined there. Your violations of protocol will be reported to Employee Resources. It's up to them to decide the outcome. You have two marks against you, and not reporting your father's murder when it happened is a big one. I can't say how things will go."

"Please, I told you my brother snuck in here."

"You only told me because I brought you here. Your digi-mail just says your father's ID was stolen. You should've reported your brother's presence right away," Lek said, feeling himself getting angry. "Now run along."

Lek said to the guards, "Check her room thoroughly for the APB suspects, then remain on guard outside her door until you're relieved."

Mira stood in the middle of the room, quaking.

"Go on!" Lek said. The moment Mira entered the corridor, Lek shut the door.

Alone in his office, Lek found himself feeling angry at Mira, but mostly annoyed at himself. There had been good reason not to investigate Dex Murt's death with greater tenacity at the time. When he first took the job here, Rika had received major blowback for the surveillance cam installation throughout the facility even though the community board had approved it. Lek was suspected of spying for the GSS. There was a rumor that his heroism was a ruse to get into the facility. Lek would have preferred to place locator chips in the IDs, but after the surveillance cam uproar, that was shot down by the board to avoid any more controversy. If he wanted to keep his job, he was told by the community board to tread lightly.

So in the Murt case, he hadn't interrogated anyone to avoid rattling the population's suspicions about him. He knew it was ridiculous to bemoan something left undone nearly twenty years ago, but the Dex Murt case was his responsibility, and he should've known better than to let it slide for political reasons.

He also should've scheduled inspections of those old supply tunnels to ensure that they were sealed off. How many people both good and bad had snuck in over the years? Cerio breaking into the facility undetected was on him. Maybe he was getting too old for this job, losing his edge. He'd recently thought about retiring after a few mistakes that he might not have made when he was younger.

Lek would call for a lockdown of the facility, which would include room-to-room searches for Cerio and Insol. First, he would comm the main conference room where Rika and Mar were meeting the department heads. The lockdown required Rika's approval and she needed to know about Cerio, and that Insol was possibly conspiring with a murderer and an infiltrator of the facility. He'd let her tell Mar and her security team. Then the lockdown would be activated, and Lek would tender his resignation.

INSOL

The three knocks at the door woke Insol from a nightmare. She sat up in bed, then she heard the door's lock disengage and looked around the room to get her bearings. She was groggy.

Earlier today, she'd read the message on the scrap of metal that the man had handed her in the cafeteria. Written on one side was: *In the coming days, someone will knock three times and unlock your door.* On the other side was a location within the facility. If the meeting was happening so soon, she assumed something had gone wrong and she'd need to get moving.

She threw her blankets aside and swung her legs over the side of the bed. She had left her clothes in a pile at the foot of the bed and when she bent down to pick them up, she felt dizzy. Her head didn't feel normal. It dawned on her that her mother had drugged her food so she'd get a good night's sleep, but she'd come all this way for a reason and she wouldn't be deterred. Fighting through her altered state, she dressed sitting down and memorized the location of the meeting.

When she stood, she had trouble with her balance and braced herself with one arm on the wall. She steadied herself and made her way to the sink. She turned on the tap, threw chilly water in her face, and drank a few glasses of water.

Her steps to the door were challenging, and she leaned on the wall adjoining the doorway before reaching out with one hand to slowly slide the door open. When she peeked into the corridor, she saw that the guard was gone. She opened the door just wide enough for her body to fit through the space and noticed a hoodie lying on the ground outside the door. She put it on with the hood as far down over her face as possible while still being able to see.

She was being kept where the workers once lived. When the facility was expanded and more comfortable dorms were constructed, the majority of rooms here had been converted into storage lockers. Consequently there was no foot traffic, and the hoodie would help with the surveillance cams.

She slid the door closed and made her way down the hall, keeping the wall at arm's length in case the dizziness overcame her again. In the distance, she could see where her passage intersected with a main corridor. Surveillance cams and workers would be abundant there.

Her head was beginning to clear, and with a few steps remaining before she entered the corridor, she propped herself up against the wall and gave herself a few moments to prepare. She inhaled and exhaled a couple of times, then stood up straight and entered the corridor, doing her best to act "normal." A few workers passed, but the area was relatively empty. She could see the lift that she needed in the distance.

Insol recalled what she'd been dreaming about now. It was the last time she was summoned to a crucial clandestine meeting, just before the Breeze Celebration when

Yor made his presentation. She received a digi-mail from an anti-DOME movement operative through the proper channels. She didn't recognize the sender, but the mail was about convening in regard to the Celebration. She contacted the people in her circle to find out whether they'd be going. Ador Wint's partner Shika answered his comm and told her that he was ill. Insol couldn't reach Mel, either. Yor was working with Mado on the WAEF so his comm would be deactivated. She tried to call anyway and there was no answer.

The upcoming Breeze Celebration was a pivotal event, and as one of the key planetwide organizers in the Movement it was her duty to attend the meeting. There was always the chance of a GSS raid, so she removed a small, palm-sized stun weapon from a lockbox in her apartment closet. She had purchased it on the black market when she still lived in Shamba. Although she'd only fired the weapon in practice, it carried a wallop and she'd seen vids of attackers knocked unconscious by it. Insol never told Yor that she owned it, thinking it best to keep its existence to herself.

When she left her apartment that evening, she carried a satchel containing her ID, digi-pad, and the weapon. The campus green was usually vacant of pedestrians at this time of night, but a strange man approached. She plunged her hand in the satchel and grabbed ahold of the weapon. When the individual walked under a lamp, Insol saw that it was a student of hers. As they passed one another, he smiled and waved. Insol chuckled at herself for being so petrified.

She walked under the stone arch marking the University's border and into the section of the Royal Quarter that had been transformed into a place for students to shop and interact outside of the classroom. There were digi-book stores, Malrap bars, hairdressers, viewer and digi-pad vendors, and food carts peddling cuisine from every region. All the stores were shut for the night, except for the Malrap bars.

A half-block away, a young man with stylish blond hair stood in front of one of the bars. He was wearing fashionable slacks and a button-down shirt. Insol could smell his cologne when she was meters away, and he gave her a coy smile as she approached. Insol knew the type.

He said to Insol, "Hey baby! Why don't you come inside and I'll buy you a drink? You're hot so I bet you're thirsty."

Insol stopped in front of him and said, "You're disgusting. Go back inside and stop embarrassing yourself."

"You wish you could have a piece of this, you whore."

"What did you say?" Insol yelled and shoved the young man in the chest with both hands. He stumbled backward through the bar's open doorway and smashed into a table with students sitting around it. The students scattered. The table fell over. The young man hit the floor beside it, and full glasses shattered on the floor around him. The students screamed at him, saying he'd need to pay for his clumsiness. The young man pointed to the door. Insol hurried away, laughing.

She reached the end of the student marketplace, then turned right onto the street leading to the Plaza rail-car station. A few policemen were posted on the corner. Insol smiled at them and quickened her pace. The street was well lit for commuters, but when Insol turned onto the cobbled Old Quarter side street, her path was dimly lit by antique gas lamps. During the day, the Old Quarter was known for its historical ambiance, but at night, the tourist shops were shuttered and the gambling and after-hours Malrap joints opened. The streets were inhabited by Flopsy dealers and prostitutes. The authorities stayed away as long as the illegal activity was contained here. It was the perfect place for a covert gathering.

Insol wasn't afraid of her surroundings. These streets were child's play compared to the seedier parts of Shamba's cities, but just to be on the safe side, Insol had dressed down for the occasion in torn pants and an old shirt so she wouldn't look like a mark. Her satchel was the only thing that might be enticing to a thief. She turned left, and after a few blocks took a right.

The building for the meeting was in the middle of a block. A lamp over the door illuminated a handwritten sign on it reading *Enter through* the side with an arrow pointing left. Insol walked over to an alley alongside the building and paused before proceeding. With the exception of the light pollution from the Plaza and the dim glow of the gas lamps from the street, the alley was dark.

She glimpsed the silhouette of a person a short distance down the alley before a man's voice called out, "Over here."

Insol's instincts told her to run, but she convinced herself otherwise. She'd been in less savory locations, she could handle herself, and this Movement meeting was important. She slipped her hand inside her satchel and gripped the stun weapon before heading toward the man. As she approached him, she saw he was wearing a mask over his head with slits for his eyes and mouth. She thought this could be a Movement operative protecting his identity, but she decided to head back the way she'd come and wait for someone familiar to show up and confirm whether the meeting was happening or not.

Then she was struck in the back of the head. As she staggered toward the street, she smelled blood. She didn't have her hand on the weapon anymore and fumbled around the inside of the satchel, but couldn't locate it. She put her other hand to the back of her head and found it wet with blood.

She heard men laughing as something struck the side of her face. Her left eye went dark. She was hit on the side of the head again.

"I can't believe she's still standing," a man said as he stepped in front of her, wearing a mask and wielding a pipe.

"She's a tough one," a man behind her said. "That'll make this more fun."

As Insol continued searching for the weapon, the man behind her grabbed the satchel. Insol pulled back and a tug of war ensued. Insol took another blow to her head and the man yanked the satchel from her hands. She lost her balance, and her legs betrayed her. She couldn't put her hands up to protect her head before it hit the pavement with a sickening pop.

"That's gonna leave a mark," one of the men said.

Both men cackled.

Insol lay on the pavement, barely conscious. The two masked men stood on either side of her, peering down.

The man with the satchel said, "You're quite a mess, young lady." He reached inside the satchel, removed the weapon, and examined it. "Looky here," he said, showing it to his companion. "That's the cutest thing ever. Well, at least she came prepared. I'll give her that. Not that it'll do her any good." He threw the weapon down the alley, and Insol heard it bouncing off the pavement in the distance.

Now, she was in the facility, waiting for the lift to descend to her level. The corridor was becoming crowded. Shifts must've been changing. People walked in front of her and behind her, coming from left and right. She stepped close to the lift doors so nobody could walk in front of her. She was afraid she'd be recognized so she stared down at her shoes. The lift arrived and the doors opened. Insol looked up quickly and the hoodie slipped off her head.

A young man wearing Capitol City attire was standing inside the lift. He said, "I know you." He didn't leave the lift.

Insol said, "I don't think so." She pulled the hoodie back over her head.

"I do."

"Well, I don't know you," Insol said with anger in her voice. "Are you getting out of the lift or do I have to call security, pervert?"

"What?" the man said, stepping out of the lift into the hallway.

Insol hurried inside and pressed the button to go up.

The Capitol City man said, "I do know you. You're a professor at Royal University. You're Rika's dau—"

The lift doors closed. Insol inhaled and exhaled in relief. She thought she smelled blood in her nose. She pinched it and examined her hand.

Her mind immediately went back to the assault in the alley. She recalled lying on her back with the two men standing on either side, staring down at her. When light from the street caught their eyes, she could see their rage. She was certain they weren't through with her. She attempted to stand, but dizziness overcame her and she fell back to the pavement.

One of the men said, "She's still got fight in her."

"That's too bad for her," the other man said. He lifted his military-issued boot so Insol could see what was coming, then stamped it into her ribs over and over again. The man on the other side commenced kicking her in the head. He got in more than a few blows before Insol managed to raise both arms to block him, but the man wasn't deterred. He joined his partner in kicking her in the ribs from his side. Insol was screaming the entire time she was being pummeled, hoping someone would come to her rescue.

Finally, she heard a familiar voice say, "You two idiots need to shut her up and get the job done." The men stopped kicking and Insol lowered one arm slightly, looking over at the lit street. With her less damaged eye, she saw the man with the scarred hands.

One of her attackers pulled something cloth out of his pocket and reached toward Insol's mouth. Insol tried to bite him but was unsuccessful. A kick to her ribs made her gasp in pain, and the cloth was stuffed into her mouth. When she tried to remove the gag, she was kicked in the ribs again.

"I've got an idea," one man said. "You take one end and I'll take the other."

They lifted her by her arms and legs. She attempted to thrash out of their grasp with no success. They carried her to what she assumed was a loading dock she had spotted when she first entered the alley. They dumped her on her back, with the upper half of her body flat on the dock and her legs dangling over the edge.

The man in front of her said, "I go first."

"So I get sloppy seconds," the man behind her said.

"I outrank you," said the other, then he pulled down Insol's pants and underwear.

Insol marshalled her strength and kicked at him, but she missed.

"Did you see that?" he said, then kicked her in the kneecap. The pain was excruciating. She screamed, but it was muffled by the gag.

The man behind her grabbed both sides of her head and slammed it over and over again into the loading dock floor as the man in front of her began raping her.

Before losing consciousness, Insol remembered seeing a GG tattoo on the rapist's neck, and in the distance, a man muttering, "Lovely…lovely…lovely…" It was the man with the scarred hands.

Now, a young Shamban woman in clean brown coveralls was standing in front of the open lift doors. "Getting off here?" she said.

"Yes," Insol said. "I was just…" Her mind went back to the assault.

"Are you all right?"

Insol rushed from the lift and past the woman, noted that she was on the correct floor for the meeting, and turned right down the corridor. She knew her way around the facility. When she was a college student and the facility was under construction, she'd worked as an assistant to her mother.

She approached what the workers called "The Porch," which was the best view of the spaceships under construction. It was on the highest level, jutting out from the corridor to offer a more panoramic vista. This was where you took visitors so they would never forget the scope of the facility's mission. Nowadays, there weren't many visitors, so The Porch was vacant during business hours. That made it an ideal place to meet someone without being noticed.

At the far end of The Porch, she saw the man from the cafeteria nervously scoping out his surroundings. His behavior made him look suspicious.

"Hey!" Insol called out and removed her hood.

The man halted his manic behavior and approached her. "Where have you been?" he said.

They stopped in front of one another. Her contact turned toward the view. He was avoiding the cams mounted on the wall behind them.

"I got here as quick as I could," Insol said. "Your note didn't indicate this would be happening so soon."

The man glanced over his shoulders. "My bitch sister turned me in. Now they're looking for me, and you got yourself locked up which made this meeting all the more difficult—"

"Yes, well, shit happens." Insol observed the man's prison tattoo and that he was behaving like a Flopsy addict, which probably started or intensified in jail.

"You got that right," the man said. "Why does this meeting have to happen at the facility anyway?"

"I couldn't meet with anyone or make a drop-off in Capitol City. The GSS is searching for me, so I'm confined to the Prevor Industries Complex."

"Not bad digs."

"That's beside the point," Insol said. "I couldn't leave the Complex so the opportunity to come on this trip was the only secure way for me to communicate with the higher-ups. Tell them all the pieces are in place to make my suggested operation a reality. I have a reliable inside man. I'll need three more with tactical know-how."

"They want logistical details for the operation detailing its scope and target, otherwise it sounds like a delusion—especially considering your recent behavior."

"Understood," Insol said. "Just pass on to the higher-ups what I just said. When I get back to the University, the heat will have died down, and I'll be in touch over normal channels with the details they'll need. The window of opportunity will be limited so those men must be ready at a moment's notice."

"They'll need that intel to convince them this is the real deal."

"Yes, I understand," Insol said. She was becoming concerned about this man's reliability. "The higher-ups know I'm trustworthy."

"Trust is in short supply these days."

Then the security lockdown siren went off. The man didn't say anything. He just turned tail and ran. He was out of sight when the security guards grabbed her.

MAR

A siren howled. Blue lights were flashing at intervals along the corridor where the ceiling met the walls.

Mar stood with Rika outside a conference room and watched the workers hurrying down the hallway in panic and confusion, questioning each other about the state of emergency.

A Shamban woman about Rika's age approached Mar. Two Prevor Industries guards stepped in front of her while another stood a few steps behind her. The woman yelled over the siren, "What's happening, Mar Jeps?"

Rika leaned toward Mar and said in her ear, "That's Yehta. She's been here for years. She works in Interiors with my ex-partner. She's harmless."

Mar tapped a guard's shoulder and yelled, "Let her pass."

One of the guards moved to the left and the other to the right. The woman cautiously sidestepped between them and said to Mar, "What's happening?"

Before Mar could say anything, Rika said, "Lockdown, Yehta. This is not a drill. You hear the siren and see the lights flashing. You know what that means. Your division is digi-mailed security measures every hundred and twenty days."

Yehta said, "Oh, who reads that?"

"You should, and if you're in the corridor when the siren stops, you'll be detained and lose your employment."

"That would never happen," Yehta said.

"It will. I'll make sure of it," Rika said, stepping closer to Yehta. "Look at my face. Am I joking? Go. Now."

Yehta peered at Rika's face, and the next moment she was running down the hall, then turned a corner and disappeared.

Mar said, "Friend of yours?"

"Not in the slightest. She had an affair with my ex Lart when he was still my partner. When I confronted her, she had no remorse."

"Why did you stay with him so long?"

"Oh, you know, kids…and screaming orgasmic sex," Rika said. "And convincing myself I still loved him. All the wrong reasons."

"How come I've never met this man?"

"You never will if I can help it," Rika said. "We should get back inside the conference room before the siren stops. I have to set a good example."

"I hear you," Mar said and followed Rika into the glass-walled conference room. One of Mar's guards entered as well, closing the glass door behind him and muffling the siren. Two of the guards stationed themselves outside the room in front of the door.

Mar sat down at the head of a long table where her viewer lay closed. She'd been in the middle of a meeting with the Navigational Division when Lek commed and told her that he was declaring the lockdown. The division had been making a presentation on their work with the Astronomy Division. They were plotting courses to star systems with potential habitable planets based on hacked Global Assembly telescopic satellite imagery. The presentation displayed star systems and planets with the greatest likelihood of sustaining life and predicted the time required to reach them, utilizing the spaceships in the caverns.

Now, Rika seated herself to Mar's right. "Your visits are always eventful, Mar. Don't get me wrong, I'm glad to see you, but this one is worthy of a full glass of Malrap."

"And I haven't even gotten to the good stuff yet, I—"

A wall comm near the door buzzed.

Rika began to stand, but the guard said, "Would you like me to get that?"

"Please," Rika said.

The guard picked up the comm and said into the receiver, "Yes…Yes, she's right here." He walked over to the table and handed the comm to Rika, who thanked him, and the guard went back to his station by the door.

Rika put the receiver to her ear. "Hi…Yes, I'm fine… Yes, everyone should be in their rooms by now…That's unfortunate, but glad you got her…I'd like to say I'm surprised, but I've—"

"Is that Lek?" Mar said. "What's going on?"

"They've apprehended Insol. Still searching for the infiltrator."

"Please tell Lek to come here while the search continues," Mar said. "I have a few things to discuss with both of you in private and this seems like an opportune time."

"You heard all that?" Rika said into the comm. "No, your resignation is denied. Get your ass down here." Rika deactivated the comm and placed it on the table, then sighed and slumped in the chair.

Mar said, "You hanging in there?"

"This thing with Insol is weighing on me. Everything about it. I guess it's confirmed. She was caught meeting with the infiltrator so she's definitely conspiring with him. I feel like a bad mother."

The sirens fell silent and the blue lights stopped flashing.

Mar said, "You know how she is. She doesn't listen to anybody."

"She never did. She was born that way." Rika took hold of Mar's hand and gripped it. "You know I appreciate how you've looked after my girl all these years."

"Yes, of course," Mar said, gripping Rika's hand in return.

"I need to clear my head," Rika said. She released her hold on Mar, pushed back her chair, stretched out her legs, and crossed her arms. "I'm going to rest before Lek arrives." She closed her eyes and in a few moments she was softly snoring.

Mar marveled at Rika's ability to sleep on command. She'd been fighting insomnia for years. She activated her viewer and opened a spreadsheet that she'd created before leaving the Complex. It listed each of the facility's divisions working toward the completion of the mission. Her aim was to meet with each one and figure out how many spaceships would be ready for final review within the year.

Her most important meeting today had been the first one, with the Spaceship Storage and Upkeep Division. Their task was ensuring that ships sitting in the depths of the caverns built twenty years ago were ready for launch. The division also upgraded the ships' systems with invaluable tech invented while the ships were in storage. They assured Mar that twenty-seven ships were fully prepared for launch. Mar considered that number an accomplishment, but it meant only two million Kodans could leave the planet.

Before the lockdown, Mar had met with many other divisions—Exterior, Interior, Propulsion, Cryo, Navigation, Artificial Gravity, Energy Shields—and her next meetings would be with Pilot Training, Security, Med, Hydroponics, and Replicator Tech.

From the meetings so far, she estimated that another fifteen ships were nearing completion, which could save another million lives. That put the number of passengers closer to the surviving domed Kodans and outer-Kodans, but it still didn't meet the goal of saving everyone.

There was a knock on the conference room door. Through the windowed walls, Mar saw Lek.

Mar said, "Lek is here."

Rika's eyelids shot open and she sat up straight. "I'm ready."

A guard outside the room opened the door and Lek entered. He looked haggard. His hair wasn't combed. Part of his shirt was untucked from his pants. This wasn't like him. Rajer used to tease him that no matter the circumstance Lek was always buttoned-up and kempt.

Lek glanced around the room and said, "Ara's not here?"

Rika said, "Don't be so excited to see me."

"You know that's not what I meant."

"I was kidding," Rika said. "You're in a state."

Mar said, "I sent her to her quarters when you declared lockdown. My security advised it when I told them I was staying here. Rika sent one of your guards to watch over her."

"Good," Lek said, sounding relieved. He sat at the table across from Rika and to the left of Mar. "I asked because there's a murderer roaming around who is somehow connected to your daughter."

Rika said, "We don't know the extent of her involvement yet."

There was an awkward silence as Lek and Rika stared at one another.

Mar said, "Let's not waste any emotional energy until we capture this man and talk to Insol."

Lek said, "Unfortunately, the odds of capturing him aren't great. He's got a head start. I assume he's heading for the old supply tunnels, and he knows them well. I've sent guards to hunt him down with some of the old-timers who know the tunnels, but they're a labyrinth."

Mar said, "I'm sure your men will do a commendable job."

"I don't know," Lek said. "I may have dropped the ball overseeing new recruitment and training. In this crisis, some of the new guys stand out as substandard."

Rika said, "You're always too critical of yourself, but you can weed them out now."

"I intend to supervise the search myself," Lek said.

Rika said, "So you're not resigning?"

"No, I'll finish the job, and afterward, I'll push for raising the security standards. Hopefully, now the board can see the problems caused by being lax. Plus a review of the entire workforce is necessary to spot the people who are conspiring with Cerio. Then we can discuss my future."

"We're all happy to hear it," Mar said. "And I think Rika and I would like to attend Insol's interrogation."

"That can happen."

Mar said, "Is that all the present business?"

Rika and Lek looked at one another, then nodded to Mar who said to the guard, "You mind stepping outside?"

"No, ma'am," the guard said and exited.

"You're probably wondering why I asked you both here."

Lek said, "To reprimand me for my massive screwup."

Mar said, "Get a grip, Lek."

"May I venture a guess?" Rika said. "You're considering a launch date."

"Is it that obvious?"

Rika said, "I hate to tell you, Mar, but your secret is out. When I went to the cafeteria with Insol, my server said she'd heard a rumor that a launch date is being planned. The meetings gave it away. This is a small community and word spreads fast."

Mar said, "Probably not a bad thing. Be that as it may, I wanted to talk to you about my strategy moving forward."

"Fire away," Lek said, turning his seat towards Mar and sitting up straight.

"Ready when you are," Rika said, also turning toward Mar, placing her right hand on her cheek and leaning her right elbow on the arm of the chair.

"Glad to have a captive audience," Mar said, releasing a nervous laugh. She was jittery about the next statement to come out of her mouth, which might be the most impactful in Kodan history. "Time has come to leave this dying planet for a new one. I was hoping we could wait another ten years before setting a launch date, but a number of factors have led to my current conclusion…"

Mar was distracted by an alert on her viewer. Somebody on a short list of people had sent her a vid message. The file had been received before she left Capitol City, but for some reason it had taken until now to download onto her viewer.

Lek said, "Everything all right?"

"I'll handle it later," Mar said, closing her viewer. "First of all, my materials acquisition personnel have notified me that in a hundred and fifty-six days they'll hit a dead end on acquiring resources for producing more spaceships. Our existing mines are nearly tapped out and the government runs the other mines. The security around their mines is increasing with the resources being seen as critical for the pane-frame repairs for the ever-collapsing domes. Also, the current planetary geological survey shows that due to the location and depth of any untapped deposits it would be unfeasible for us to drill for fresh resources.

"The key word is finite. The resources available for the spaceships and the domes are finite. Koda has returned to the choice we faced more than a century ago. Domes or spaceships. If we're lucky, we've got fifteen years, more like ten, before there will be a sizeable increase in dome collapses. The Global Assembly can continue throwing their remaining resources at the domes, but it doesn't matter. The domes will continue collapsing with hundreds of thousands dying until the resources are gone and the domes reach catastrophic failure. With the domes gone, millions upon millions will be exposed to the chaotic environment and die with no place to run.

"None of us wants to see that happen. But we're up against a capacity problem—not enough ships for the population. If we wait for the domes to collapse, that'll solve our problem as the population thins, but I'd think you'd both agree that's not a solution."

Rika and Lek both nodded.

"As I see it, we have a few choices available to us. One is instituting a selection process to choose the people who will fill the spaceships available in five years. The infirm and the terminally ill will have to be left behind. As a med, that doesn't sit right with me, but even if we did go there, we'd still need to further limit the passengers. The selection process wouldn't be politically based like what the Global Assembly did with the domes, but we'd need to come up with criteria for selection that everyone will agree on, and that is tricky. We could set up a lottery system. Spin the wheel, take your chances on dying a slow death while everyone else takes off for a new planet."

Mar released a nervous chuckle. "The second option is better than the first and I believe it's closer to what Mado and Yorlik were thinking. Unfortunately, the purge makes it problematic. It requires—"

Lek raised his hand. "You're not going to say what I think you're going to say."

Rika said, "Why don't you let her finish and we'll find out, dear?" She smiled at Lek.

"Thank you, Rika." Mar paused and cleared her throat. "It requires convincing Carz to use the resources allocated for patching the domes to build more spaceships instead.

"Now, before you tell me I'm insane, first of all, the government would find out about this place when people started coming here to climb aboard the ships anyway. Yorlik and Mado knew that. They were just hoping that Vidor's ships would have left or that Vidor would've died before it was time for us to launch our ships.

"Vidor's ships are still here, but he has died. Since then, things haven't unfolded in the best way possible, to say the least, but purge aside, Suron's people inside the government and GSS have discovered that Carz might not be like his narcissistic, vindictive father. Intel shows he has marshalled his budgetary expert to figure out how to build more spaceships. Why? It would seem he's attempting to save as many Kodans as possible. He's seen the most recent GACE report. What if he doesn't want to see his people perish while he takes off in his father's spaceships with the Global Assembly sycophants and the jewelry-rattling crowd?"

Lek looked like he was about to say something, but Mar continued, "And before you tell me I've completely lost my mind, my strategy is not to freely open up to Carz about the operation here. I'd feel out his stance on saving Kodans beyond their loyalty to the Global Assembly first."

Rika said, "We can't simply put the purge aside. The Leader did just preside over one of the most murderous acts in modern Kodan history against people who were perceived to be disloyal to his government. How do you expect anyone connected to those slaughtered to trust this monster as their savior?"

"I completely understand," Mar said. "I know Carz well and his instituting the purge makes no sense to me. Maybe there were mitigating circumstances. I say we cross that bridge when we come to it. The initial get-together with Carz will only be a meet-and-greet to feel out his position. Nothing more."

Rika said, "I can see the advantage of teaming up with him, especially given the issues we're facing with dwindling resources, so I support the idea. I trust you, but people here won't take this meeting well. They'll see it as consorting with the enemy. On the other hand, they do hold you in high regard so maybe they'll accept it."

"Lek?" Mar said. "Thoughts?"

"You know I have faith in you. You saved my life."

"I appreciate that," Mar said, "but I also know you have an opinion."

"I agree with Rika. I know you'd tread lightly and would never reveal anything that would place the people here in harm's way. Like Rika, I'm more concerned about the impression this meeting will give."

"I think it's worth the risk and if there's backlash, I will deal with it," Mar said. "One thing is certain: More than at any other time in its existence, this facility needs to be secure. That's why I deny your resignation, too. Now is not the time to lose your spine, especially in the final years of this project when we have so much at stake. We hired you for a reason. Nobody blames you for this breach in security."

"I blame myself," Lek said. "I assumed the old tunnels were properly sealed off years ago. I never considered sending patrols down there to inspect if they were still secure, and that's how this person snuck in."

Mar said, "My question is why did this person want to get in so badly and speak with Insol?"

Lek threw up his hands. "That's something we definitely need to find out."

Mar said, "I need answers, Lek. I need you on the case. I need you sharp. I need you bringing all your expertise to ensure this place is fully secure. I want those old tunnels reinforced so nobody can ever get in through them again. If necessary, collapse them. My final point might be the most important and it deeply concerns me. A meeting occurred here that was clearly set up on the outside by unauthorized people and this facility is supposed to be secret."

CARZ

"What is it, Kel?" Carz said.

When the intercom buzzed, Carz had been standing at his Global Assembly office window looking into the distance at the gaping hole in the dome. The collapse had occurred fifty-two days before his father died. The repair crews hadn't started fixing it yet because the collapse had destroyed buildings in the Capitol City industrial district where dome parts were manufactured. Rebuilding that industrial infrastructure was first priority before fixing the dome. In the meantime, an unrepaired Capitol City dome meant greater strain on the air-circulation system and a drain on energy consumption. He wanted to speak with Mar Jeps about it, but she wasn't returning his calls so he'd asked the GSS to locate her.

Kel said, "Orn Shiv is here."

"What does he want?"

"I already asked and he said, 'He knows what it's about.'"

Carz didn't want to speak with him, but his father always said Orn had a knack for putting his finger on a problem. Maybe it was about his investigation into Roneh. "Send him in."

The door slid open. Orn entered, halted in front of Carz's desk, clicked his heels, and saluted. "Leader, sir," Orn said.

Carz returned the salute, then said, "When I ask you a question, even if it's through my receptionist, you will give an answer. 'He knows what it's about' was not an answer to my question."

"I apologize."

Carz said, raising his voice, "I apologize, what?"

"I apologize, sir."

"That's better. You will show me the respect due to my position or I won't give you the respect of waiting for your resignation letter. I'll simply throw your ass out of the building for good. Do you understand?"

"Yes, sir."

"This is the new normal. I will no longer be treated like Vidor's little boy. I am the Leader of this planet, and I will do what I think is right for the Kodan people."

"Yes, sir!" Orn called out.

"Now we've got that straight, why are you here? Have you interrogated the reporters at the viewing channels? Any new intel on Roneh working behind the scenes to undermine me? I expect you're digging deep." Carz knew the answer. He had Tarq watching Orn.

"No, sir, but—"

"Why not?" Carz said. "Isn't that what I asked you to do?"

"Yes, sir, but you tasked the GSS to find Mar Jeps. The Head Director sent a bulletin to all agents."

"I'm aware, but that wasn't your assignment."

"Well, I found her, sir."

"Does the Director know you're here?"

"No, sir, but—"

Carz pressed the button to activate the intercom. "Kel, can you alert the Head Director of the GSS that I'd like to see him in my office immediately?"

Kel said, "Yes, sir."

"Thank you," Carz said and deactivated the intercom. "Now, Orn, what is it you've discovered?"

"I'm just curious, why—"

"Is this an answer to my question?"

"No, sir," Orn said, "I was just—"

Carz stepped up to Orn and said, "I thought we had this discussion a moment ago about the protocol for answering questions. Maybe you're closer to retirement than you've let on, Agent Shiv. Are you becoming senile?"

"I don't believe so, sir."

"I'm going to order you a comprehensive med and psych exam to evaluate your health. My father would never have forgiven me if I didn't look after you in your old age," Carz said. He could see from the twitch in Orn's cheek that he was controlling his anger. "Do you have anything else to say?"

"I appreciate your concern, sir."

"So, what is the answer to my question?" Carz said, taking a few steps back. "Or are you going to make me repeat myself?"

"No, sir,' Orn said. "As you're well aware, your father commissioned Prevor Industries to launch satellites with telescopes so we might make a list of habitable worlds for our new home. But there is a highly classified secret about those satellites that you might not have been told yet since you haven't been in the job that long."

"And what is that?"

"I came up with the idea to mount telescopic cams on the satellites without Prevor Industries' knowledge so we could spy on any illicit activity outside of the domes."

"How did you get it past Prevor Industries?"

"Only a few people knew about it—your father, myself, the previous Head Director," Orn said. "And we paid a few Prevor Industries techs eighteen years of salary up front, which wasn't cheap since they were high-end employees, to install the cams a day before the rocket was placed on the launchpad. The weight of the cams was calculated as part of the rocket's payload so it didn't affect the launch, and the cams were attached directly to the outside of the satellites, facing the planet most of the time. It wasn't ideal, but nobody was aware of their existence so that gave us an advantage. It never really paid off until now."

"Where did the funding come from?"

"The fund that paid for the spaceships."

"So how does this relate to locating Mar Jeps?"

"When I saw the bulletin, I didn't do a facial recog on Mar Jeps for the surveillance cams inside the domes. I figured that's the first thing anyone else would've done and nobody had found her, so she wasn't in a dome. I thought maybe she went on one of her relief operations outside of the domes where the cams couldn't locate her. I checked the commercial cruiser boarding lists and that was another dead end. Then I had the idea that she might have taken one of her corporate cruisers. As you know, all private passage out of the domes must be granted permission to open the retractable panels," Orn said, appearing more relaxed as he explained himself. "I found one for Prevor Industries, but there was no flight plan. Your father changed that rule for private citizens."

"Yes, a bizarre perk for his donors to more easily cheat on their wives."

"I did have the time when the panel was retracted and using the satellite cams, I tracked the cruiser to a remote mountain range in the eastern Shamban region. On landing, the cruiser was camouflaged and it's still there now. The passengers hiked into the mountain range and vanished. All of this was fairly lucky because there was clear sky the day the cruiser left the dome."

"So your assumption is Mar Jeps was on that cruiser?"

"Yes, sir."

"It's possible," Carz said. "Or she could just be in her penthouse by herself and her people went there."

"That could be the case," Orn said. "But she is still missing, and I believe this flight is worth investigating. As far as we know, there is nothing of value in that remote region of Shamba, so why would a Prevor Industries cruiser—or any cruiser, for that matter—fly halfway across the planet to land there? This wasn't a relief mission."

"I have to agree," Carz said, walking back to the window and peering out at the collapsed section of dome. "It's intriguing. Definitely worth investigating, but I think we should wait for the cruiser to leave and track where it goes, then I'll task the Head Director to deploy men to the area."

"Wouldn't it be more efficient to have a tactical team on standby and arrest the occupants of the cruiser before it takes off?"

"If they're smart, which I assume they are since they've pulled off this clandestine flight and probably not for the first time, they'll send out security with the pilot so the more important passengers are protected from any ambush," Carz said. "I do agree that it's curious, though. What's so worthwhile in that remote area that a cruiser would risk flying through this treacherous environment to go there? We can find out who is on the cruiser by tracking them back to their home. If it is Mar Jeps, then she has some questions to answer, especially when our team discovers what's there."

"Permission to join the team."

"Permission denied," Carz said. "I need you tracking the cruiser. It's best to keep those cams secret. You'll need to report the cruiser's final departure from Shamba to the Head Director so he can activate the team. I'd like stills of the cruiser in the remote area and possibly its return trip, too."

"Yes, sir," Orn said. "But I'd be more valuable in the field."

Carz still had his back to Orn, looking out the window. Not being in the field was eating Orn up inside and he wanted to convince Carz to change his mind. *Can't let him get too comfortable*, Carz thought.

Carz turned around. "Did you not hear what I said? You know, this interaction has been enlightening. I see it now—you do need a checkup." Carz walked to his desk and activated his intercom. "Kel, make an appointment with my personal med for Orn Shiv to have a comprehensive physical including a psych eval and have the time and date of the appointment ready for him before he leaves."

Kel said, "Yes, sir. The Head Director has arrived."

"Tell him I'll be done with Agent Shiv shortly." Carz deactivated the intercom and took a few steps toward Orn, who clicked his heels together and stood at attention. "Make sure you get your appointment on your way out."

"Yes, sir."

"Have you told the Head Director about your findings?"

"No, sir."

"You should've told him first, especially since he is your superior and he needs to know about the cams. Your actions break protocol, but since my being Leader is new to you and you are old and set in your ways, I'll let this mistake pass without repercussions. I'll tell Tarq myself, too."

"Yes, sir."

"Now get to work. I want to see fotos from your investigation by the end of the day," Carz said. "And I want you to take this investigation into Roneh seriously—the viewing channels, the attack on the estate, how she got my father to sign off on the purge. I want answers. You were my father's most trusted friend and advisor. You were his right-hand man. I expect the same from you. We have to put Roneh in her place. What she did was unforgivable. I need answers so we can leave Roneh and this nasty business behind us. She's a serious threat. Wouldn't you agree?"

"Yes, sir."

"I want to know how she got her Allegiance Watch legislation passed, too," Carz said. "I'm counting on you, Orn. If I can't trust you, who can I trust?"

"I appreciate the—"

"We can't let her get away with what she's done. It sets a bad precedent for others. Don't you agree?"

"Yes, sir."

"So you'll get on it?"

"Yes, sir," Orn said, fidgeting. "Anything else, sir?"

"There is something else. I may have you take a trip

with me soon to tie up a loose end, but I'll let you know," Carz said. "Great work finding Mar Jeps, by the way. You're dismissed."

Orn saluted and performed an about-face. He marched through the door as it slid open and exited.

Tarq entered and the door closed behind him. He was wearing a sharp blue suit and his GSS pin.

"How did that go?" Tarq said. "He didn't look happy."

"Yes, sometimes an unruly creature needs reminding who his master is," Carz said. "You got here quickly."

"I was already in the building, talking to the person working on your new budget. She called me here for a meeting about cuts to GSS funding."

"Yes, I told her to contact you. Roneh has no idea so keep whatever you were told between us."

"Yes, the budget manager told me that, too."

"Along with cuts, I'll also need you to seize private corporate records, but I'll explain that later. For now, take a seat," Carz said, pointing to the couches. "Agent Shiv delivered some news, but I want to hear about your investigation into the bombing and the purge first."

Tarq sat down on a couch. "You remember that guard who stopped coming to work at the estate? He was found dead in an Old Quarter dumpster. Somebody did a number on him. Took time to identify his body," Tarq said. "And your theories on the purge and the bombing are bearing fruit. I've got some news there."

"Great to hear it. I've been keeping the suspects biting at each other's heels," Carz said. "Now tell me what you've discovered. You've got my undivided attention."

MAR

Mar said good night to her security detail, then shut the door to her room and locked it. She placed her right palm on the metal door and closed her eyes.

With the lockdown still in force, her walk here from the conference room with her security detail was eerie. Usually the corridors were teeming with vibrant energy; a group walking down the hallway laughing or having a heated discussion; a lone person taking a stroll in deep contemplation; somebody striding along hurriedly, intent on reaching their destination as soon as possible. All that was gone. The corridors were empty, and the only sound was the boots of her guards tramping beside her. The facility felt abandoned, and in Mar's mind, it was an open question whether this breach in security would change the future for better or worse.

Mar opened her eyes. She trusted that Lek would perform his job and capture the intruder. She sat down on the edge of her bed and contemplated sleeping. She hadn't gotten much rest lately. Upon her arrival, she'd chatted with Rika, catching up over evening meal, and when she'd finally reached her room, she lay in bed with her mind racing about the day ahead of her. She contemplated all the meetings and how she'd tell Lek and Rika about her plan to accelerate the Kodan exodus. She assumed they'd argue against her idea to meet with

Carz so she'd stayed awake, staring at the ceiling honing her argument.

Tomorrow would be another long day. Mar thought about taking a shower and going to sleep, but she recalled the vid alert on her viewer. Only a vid from Rika, Lek, Insol, Yor, or Mado triggered an alert. She stood up from the bed and seated herself in the metal desk chair. She removed her viewer from the case, placed it on the desk, and opened it.

First, she listened to a message from the person receiving comms at her office. The Leader's office had commed twice and the Leader wished to speak with her as soon as possible. There was a message from Suron. He said Carz wanted to speak with her and according to Suron's sources, Carz was so agitated by her lack of response that he'd ordered the GSS to locate her. Suron was more than capable of conveying urgency through the tone of his voice. In this case, Suron was telling her that she needed to return and deal with Carz right away. *Add it to the list*, Mar thought.

She tapped on the vid alert and opened a window showing Yor staring at his viewer cam. He appeared bedraggled. Here was her little boy at forty-six years old. Some grey in his hair and beard. He looked like his great-grandfather. Mar activated the vid.

Yor said, "Hello, Mother. I was hoping to have an actual conversation with you. I've been keeping track of the news on Koda. Looks like that bastard finally died, but Carz has taken over as Leader. I haven't commed until now because I thought you'd be busy with the ramifications of this transfer of power.

"I see Carz unleashed a purge, although the viewing channels are calling it a 'justifiable act of self-defense' and 'a preemptive strike at impending future acts of terrorism.' I was sad to see it. I imagine I've lost many friends.

"My greater concern is Insol. I know she was on Vidor Plemso's list. I haven't communicated with her since I returned from Prevor because I'm lame. Knowing her, she probably thinks that I've abandoned the cause, although I know that you've told her a version of what I've been doing.

"There's an important reason for this call. I guess I could comm back, but I'll just put it out there. As you know, Mado told Vidor Plemso that Great-grandfather never gave him the coordinates to the habitable planet. That was sort of the truth. I'll tell you someday how I discovered them, but in short, they've been in my possession all along. Mado wanted to wait until the right time to tell you. I agreed, so you can blame me for withholding them, too.

"I'm feeling kind of desperate, and I know its selfish, but I was hoping you might be able to use the coordinates as leverage to get me home. Not sure about negotiating with Carz, especially now that he's unleashed the purge. I could see how that would dampen the possibility of a relationship between you and him.

"Anyway, now you have this information and I know you'll do what's right. Please comm me when you can. It'd be fantastic to speak with you and hear how Insol is doing, and what you've concluded from what I've just told you. Love you."

Yor forced a smile, waved goodbye, and the screen went dark.

Mar sat staring at the blank screen until the vid rebooted to the beginning and Yor's face reappeared. "You have impeccable timing," Mar said to her son's image.

The coordinates could be a game changer. If she was going to negotiate with Carz, the coordinates might be the perfect bargaining chip to obtain what the facility required, and of course she'd see what she could do for Yor.

Mar closed her eyes and basked in the quiet of her room. She thought about how Mado had withheld the coordinates, and she was reminded of her final conversation with him.

It wasn't long after Rajer had been executed. Maybe a few months had passed. The WAEF was docked at the way station. Gols entered her office in a state of excitement, saying, "I have a surprise for you."

"Do they have my favorite cake in the cafeteria again?"

"No, better than that," Gols said, tinkering with the viewing screen behind her desk. "Something much better than that."

Mar swiveled around on her desk chair to face Gols and said, "Please don't make me guess. It's been a crazy day."

"This will cheer you up."

Mar looked at the screen and there was Yor. She bolted out of her chair. "Yor!"

"Hello, Mother." Yor looked healthy. He was attempting to grow a beard, but there were patchy spots on his cheeks where hair wasn't coming in. He wore green coveralls with a SEEDER program insignia over his right breast, and he was sitting in the control room of the WAEF.

"This is unexpected. Is everything all right?"

"I'm fantastic. I'm in outer space, what could be better…
other than being there with you in person, I mean."

"That's sweet of you to say, but you're having quite an
adventure," Mar said. "Any plans to come home? Maybe
take up residence at the Facility?"

"Mado doesn't think that's safe right now or in the
near future and—"

"I agree," Mar said and sighed. "I just miss you. Some
days are hard here without you or Rajer."

"It's hard to believe Rajer is gone," Yor said, sadness
creeping into his voice. "I can't stop thinking…if it wasn't
for him, I probably wouldn't be alive."

"Well, he loved you," Mar said, feeling emotional and
sitting down.

Yor bowed his head and put his hands over his eyes.
He was attempting to control his emotions.

Mar said, "Let it out, dear."

When Yor looked up, tears were streaming down
his face. He wiped them away. He said with a shaky
voice, "Sorry."

"No need," Mar said, attempting to keep herself
together. "I assume this comm has some purpose other
than catching up, although it's nice to hear from you. We
do have the time limit."

"Yes, of course," he said. "Before we get into it, how
is Insol? And Mel?"

"They're fine. I had evening meal with them a few
days ago. Mel is thinking about taking a sabbatical from
the University."

"That would be good for him."

"Exactly what I was thinking," Mar said. "Insol is Insol. I got her a new prosthetic eye and it looks completely natural."

"That's great," Yor said, then there was the sound of Mado's voice and Yor looked to his right. He said to Mado, "Of course."

Yor turned back to the cam and said, "Mado is reminding me that our time is limited, and we don't want to cause you trouble."

Gols called out from the doorway, "Hello, Mado."

Mar hadn't realized Gols had been standing behind her the entire time. Over the course of their relationship, Mar had come to understand Gols' admiration for Mado, who had offered him the job that gave his life meaning. Gols missed him.

"Hello, Gols," Mado called out from somewhere in the control room.

Yor looked to his right again. He was listening to Mado. "Yes, got it."

Yor turned back to the cam and said, "Gols, Mado said that he can't speak to you right now on screen. He hopes you're doing well, and he needs you to leave the office, close the door behind you, and not oversee the comm when you get to your desk. Do you understand?"

"Yes," Gols said with disappointment in his voice, then turned and left the room, closing the door softly behind him.

Mar said, "That was tough to watch. Gols was excited to speak with Mado."

Mado called out, "I think highly of him, too, Mar. I just can't let him see what I'm about to show you."

"All right then," Yor said and straightened himself in his chair. "What you're about to see will come as a shock… at first. It was for me, but it'll make sense once you have the time to think over your relationship with Mado. You, Great-grandfather, and I are the only Kodans who will ever see this. He's showing you this now because he feels like you should know the truth."

Yor turned to his right and said to Mado, "You ready?"

Mado said in an annoyed tone, "Yes, I have been ready for a while."

"All right," Yor said, "no need to be that way. I just wanted to set it up for you." Then she heard Mado say something but couldn't make it out.

Yor responded, "Yes, I know. How many times do you have to tell me?"

Yor stepped out of the cam's view and adjusted it so that it was looking further into the control room. A moment later, Yor appeared at a distance. He waved to Mar and walked to the left of the cam's picture. He said, "Mother, meet Mado from the planet Prevor. He and Great-grandfather designed prosthetics so he would appear Kodan. This is what he actually looks like."

When the part-humanoid part-aquatic creature stepped into view, Mar was glad she was sitting down.

"Hello, Mar," the creature said. The voice coming out of the creature's mouth was Mado's, but that didn't make this any less unbelievable.

Yor stood in the background, observing his mother's reaction. Mar understood that Mado had positioned Yor so the bizarre nature of this revelation would be set in reality and not look like some sort of foto trickery…but she had to say it. "This is some sort of prank, right?"

Mado said, "I know my history of being a prodigious jokester might make you think that's the case, but it isn't."

No matter how unbelievable, this was Mado. Mar continued observing the viewing screen in disbelief. She thought about all the years of shaking her head at his quirkiness and how it all made sense now. Mado had been attempting to fit into a civilization that probably wasn't even close to the one he'd known from birth.

"How?" Mar said, which was about as much as she could muster in her shock.

"It's a long story," Mado said. "Due to our time constraint, I'll make it as brief as possible. We don't want the Global Assembly to get a glimpse of this beautiful visage."

"Indeed."

Mado told her about crashing on the lava planet, how his entire relationship with Yorlik unfolded, and how Yorlik had asked Mado to return with him to Koda and save his people.

Mar said, "That's quite a tale."

"Yes," Mado said. "There's more to fill in, but Yor can do that at a later date."

"In the foreseeable future," Mar said in a deadpan voice.

Mado laughed in that high-pitched shrieking way that had become so familiar, but his laugh made complete sense now, too. "That's a good one," he said. "There are two reasons for revealing my true self to you now. The first is I'm returning to Prevor. I miss my people and my world, and I want to start a family of my own. That will mean Yor and the WAEF taking me home and being gone for twenty years in your time. We're leaving in a few days and you'll never see me again. The other is I hold you in high regard and I didn't want to leave our relationship based on a lie."

"I know who you are," Mar said. "How you appear doesn't matter that much to me, but I'm honored that you respect me enough to tell me the truth. It would be quite a scandal if the entire planet was aware of it."

"That would be something."

"So, is this the last time we'll speak?"

"Most likely."

Mar didn't know what to say, then she flashed back to the night Yorlik died and how she'd felt like Mado was literally passing his grief to her. That had always stuck with her as one of the strangest interactions in her lifetime. "Well, in that case I have a question."

"If it's quick."

"There was a moment between us that's left a mark on my memory and emotions."

"You're referring to Yorlik's passing from existence."

"Matter of fact, yes," Mar said. Her first reaction was surprise that he was immediately aware of what she was going to say, but again this was Mado.

He said, "Part of the Prevorian death ceremony is sharing emotions. Prevorians have the ability to share their feelings with one another through physical contact. That's what happened back then. I'm conjecturing that my feelings were so strong in that moment that they became part of your emotional memory. Imprinting is a good way of putting it. That doesn't happen much between Prevorians. We're practiced at empathic transference and understand how to handle another's emotions when they're passed to us. Due to a lack of empathic ability, humanoids obviously don't have the same sort of experience to fall back on."

"Yes, well, whenever I think about Yorlik's death, like now, I'm overwhelmed by emotions that I now know were yours."

"I sincerely apologize," Mado said. "And whether it's any consolation, what I experienced of your emotions is still a vivid memory for me as well."

"Please don't apologize," Mar said. "Yorlik was certainly worthy of those emotions and again, I'm honored that you shared them with me."

"I'm glad you and Tetrick were there. I needed to share what I was feeling. As you say, I was overwhelmed."

"And that song was Prevorian?"

"Yes, it was. It's sung on the passing of a loved one."

"It was memorable as well," Mar said, noticing Yor listening closely in the background. "One more thing before you go—I wanted to thank you on behalf of every Kodan. You've done more for the Kodan species than anyone will ever know."

Mado said, "I believe someday the Kodan people will know my story. There's a young man standing behind me who has a thirst for history and facts. Would you like to have a word with him before we depart? This will be the last time you two will have an actual conversation for a while and the one-way messages will become farther between as the years pass. You only have time for a few words, but nonetheless…"

"I understand," Mar said. "Thanks again for everything you've done. You've certainly changed my life in a way I could never have imagined."

"Thank you," Mado said. He closed his eyes and another set of eyelids closed over the first ones, then he uttered something in a language rife with guttural sounds, pops, and whistles. "That is a Prevorian prayer of farewell, thanking you for being so gracious and wishing you good fortune, health, and happiness until the end of your days. Goodbye." Mado stepped to the right and disappeared from sight.

Yor moved closer to the cam, peering to the right and listening to something Mado was saying. He said to Mado, "Yes, I understand. I'll keep it short…the more you tell me the less time I have."

Mar giggled.

"You think this is funny,' Yor said. "I have years of this ahead of me."

"I'm sure you'll work it out."

"I don't have much choice," Yor said. "Well…what do you say to someone, much less your mother, who you won't speak with directly for twenty years?"

"I'd say, I love you more than anyone else in the universe and I'll miss you every day for the next twenty years."

"I'll go with that, then," Yor said. "But seriously, it's a comfort to know because of the Rejuv Treatment you'll likely be here when I return. Goodbye, Mother. I love you." He smiled, but Mar noticed he was controlling himself so he wouldn't cry. He blew her a kiss, then reached out and the screen went blank.

Now, Mar sat in her room at the facility with the image of Yor still on her viewer screen and she thought, *Here we are, in the future.* She recalled that conversation with Mado as one of the strangest she'd ever had in her life. Sure, the revelation that Mado was from another planet and different physiologically from her species made it bizarre. But the fact she was saying goodbye to her son, and that she'd see him in twenty years due to some miraculous treatment Yorlik had concocted, made it unreal.

Mar reflected on Yor's vid about the habitable planet's coordinates. She was annoyed that Mado and Yor had them in their possession but hadn't told her before they left for Prevor. It was reckless. What if something happened on their voyage that deleted those coordinates forever? She'd never thought of asking about them because she assumed they'd been lost with the Leader's destruction of the WAEF's data drives. So why hadn't Mado given her the coordinates before he left the way station? She wanted to believe that he forgot, but that wasn't like Mado. It wasn't as if he didn't trust her with secrets. It just didn't make sense.

She'd have to ask Yor about it when they spoke, but right now she needed to figure out how to utilize the coordinates to her advantage in a conversation with Carz.

CARZ

Carz arrived at the mansion and called out for his son, but Filo didn't answer. He headed for the study. He wasn't thinking about drinking but he was pondering change and putting his own personal touches on the room. First thing to do was remove the painting of his grandfather that always gave him the creeps.

Right before he stepped across the threshold into the study, he smelled cigar smoke.

"Papa!" Filo ran up to Carz. He was wearing his pajamas with hand-drawn depictions of the Global Plaza buildings on them.

Carz picked him up and kissed him on the forehead. "How's my boy?"

Filo hugged him.

Roneh was sitting behind the desk sipping Malrap.

Carz said, "Don't get too comfortable, dear."

"I could get used to this, though."

Carz put Filo down.

Roneh said, "Filo, why don't you get into bed and I'll be there soon to tuck you in?"

"What about Papa?"

Carz said, "I'll wake you in the morning and we'll eat morning meal and play some games before you go to school."

"All right, Papa," Filo said. "Good night."

Carz bent down and kissed Filo on the cheek, then Filo dashed out of the room.

Roneh said, "I don't think I could love him any more."

Caz said, "At least one good thing has come of our relationship."

"Maybe that's the one thing we agree on."

Carz approached Roneh, observing an empty bottle of his father's private brand of Malrap on the desk and a half-glass of the liquor beside it. A half-smoked cigar lay on the edge of an ashtray.

Carz said, "What're you doing here?"

"I wanted to talk and getting an appointment at your office is difficult these days. Feels like you're avoiding me."

"I'm busy running a planet, and you were at my office a few days ago."

"That was twelve days ago, and I haven't seen you since," Roneh said. "When your mother moved back into her room, you began sleeping in your father's trophy room. I get the impression you're not pleased with me."

"That's an understatement," Carz said, stopping in the middle of the room. "You're taking advantage of this relationship in ways I'd never imagined."

"You're Leader," Roneh said. "Why shouldn't I get mine?"

"I suppose you're talking about your Allegiance Program legislation."

"What else would I be talking about?" Roneh said. "Now is the time to put the Watch into action. The purge has swung things in the right direction. The citizens are clamoring for it and the reps have complied with their wishes."

"Save the propaganda for someone else," Carz said. "You've been doing the viewing-channel circuit without consulting me about your talking points again. I should fire you for that infraction alone." Carz stomped toward the desk and halted in front of it, then he jabbed his finger at Roneh. "Now, get out from there."

Roneh stood with the glass of Malrap in her hand, slugged down the contents, and placed the glass back down on the desk. "You can have the rest of this," she said, picking up the cigar from the ashtray. "Half is good enough for me, at least when it comes to cigars." She placed the cigar back in the ashtray and walked around the desk.

Carz passed around the other side of the desk until they'd switched positions. "So you're here to harangue me into signing your legislation into law. The Majority Whip came to my office today to discuss it."

"It's been sitting on your desk for some time."

"There won't be any signing," Carz said, seating himself and pushing the chair closer to the desk. "Don't count on it."

"Oh, I'm counting on it."

"Then you'll be sorely disappointed. I'm going to veto it."

Roneh said, "Do you really want to play this game?"

"What game would that be?"

Roneh walked over to the Malrap cabinet, popped the cork on a bottle, and filled a glass to the brim. She recorked the bottle, placed it back in the cabinet, and plopped down in an armchair facing the desk. "I'll have to get the Assembly to force your hand somehow."

"Good luck. You know as well as I do that my father rewrote the constitution so that the Assembly could never override his vetoes and the loyalists complied."

"Do you know why your father put us together?"

"Other than to torture me?" Carz said. "He thought your popularity as the heroine of Breeze Celebration and executioner of terrorists would solidify my position when I became Leader."

"On a practical level," Roneh said and sipped her Malrap. "But mostly because he knew you were spineless."

Carz thought about throwing her out of the room, but he was curious where the conversation was going. "My father was a great military strategist, but not the best judge of character. Just look at Mado Prevor or Joro Camtur or Mar Jeps or—"

"I get it," Roneh said. "But I wouldn't bet against me."

"Yes, I've heard you've accumulated quite the list of allies—Global Assembly reps, department heads, GSS agents."

Roneh took a bigger swallow of Malrap. "Yes, I know Tarq is keeping you apprised of my doings. No matter. I have nothing to hide."

"If you say so."

"And when are you going to arrest Mar Jeps?"

"On what grounds?"

"Flying to Shamba. Consorting with terrorists and harboring them," Roneh said, gulping down the remaining Malrap in her glass. "Holding back Kodan civilization from its true destiny."

"I guess I shouldn't be surprised you know about that flight, but we have no confirmation that she was onboard, and there's absolutely no evidence of terrorist collaboration," Carz said. "The other accusation is debatable. She's considered a great humanitarian."

Roneh rose from the armchair. "You're so naïve. You haven't done your research like I have."

Carz wasn't going to challenge that statement. It only proved she was focused on the rhetoric of the most extreme loyalists, and for all her bluster, it seemed she wasn't clued in to his plans. He'd continue to push her in the opposite direction. "By the way, you hear anything reliable about Orn's traitorous behavior? I could really use your help, and I might be willing to sign the legislation in return. Tarq has new intel, but I was hoping your allies might corroborate them."

"What has Bolonar uncovered?"

"I can't tell you."

"I won't tell anyone, and knowing what you know might put me on the right track."

"I'd rather not," Carz said. "It hits too close to home."

"What does that mean? Who are you talking about?" Roneh said with concern in her voice.

"Again, I can't discuss it. Probably said too much already."

"Bolonar's sources are morons anyway. You shouldn't rely on them," Roneh said, before hurrying out of the room.

That was fun, Carz thought. He'd touched a nerve, but Roneh's knowledge of the Shamban flight concerned him. There were too many Global Assembly higher-ups who wanted to associate themselves with her increasingly powerful position in the government. Her ability to manipulate people was a boon to her career, but if things went Carz's way, that wouldn't last long.

Carz basked in the quiet for a moment, then thought about his mother. He went to her room where she'd been convalescing. She wasn't in bed and her nurse wasn't there, either. A guard told him that the nurse was eating a late evening meal in the staff dining room and another guard had wheeled his mother outside. The terrace was still under construction, so he knew where the guard was taking her.

He followed the path toward the forest and in the distance, he saw a guard standing beside an unoccupied wheelchair. Carz listened to the familiar chittering of insects and the hoot of nocturnal winged creatures. He'd spent a lifetime lying in bed with their calls singing him to sleep. He was pleased that they'd all stayed when the shield went down in the attack.

As he approached the vacant wheelchair on the path, the guard nearby snapped to attention.

"At ease," Carz said. "What's the situation here?"

"Your mother is over there, sir," the guard said, pointing down the dirt path leading deeper into the forest.

"So let me venture a guess," Carz said. "After the nurse went to eat, she threatened to fire you if you didn't bring her here, then she made you carry her to the bench and told you to leave and not come back until she called you."

"I work at the pleasure of the First Family, sir."

"Yes," Carz said. "I understand." He stepped off the paved path and made his way down the dirt trail that had been worn over the years by his mother's treks to the bench. A few winged creatures squawked in the trees above and took flight. His mother was sitting on the bench staring straight ahead. She made no attempt to acknowledge Carz's approach. Her head was still bandaged and her limbs still in casts; one of her legs was propped up on a log that he assumed she'd had the guard procure for her.

Carz's mother said, not turning toward him, "I know, Carz, and I don't want to hear it."

Carz chuckled and stopped beside the bench. "Yes, you're a big girl. I've got nothing to say, except you may want to fix any damage you've caused along the way."

Carz's mother turned to him. "Why? Did he complain?"

"Nobody said anything, Mother. I just know the med ordered you to spend more time in bed, so I assume arms were twisted on your way here."

Carz's mother said, "I'll smooth things over."

"Any sign of Karanga?"

Carz's mother opened her right hand. She was holding two treats for her animal friend. "Not yet."

"Where did you get those?"

Carz's mother pointed to a rock by the bench. "Under there. I have my hiding places," she said. "Are you going to sit down? You know how I hate when you hover."

"Something you and Father had in common," Carz said, sitting to her left and kissing her on the cheek.

She patted him on the thigh. "Your father and I had many things in common. You were always a good son."

"I appreciate that, but I think you have a selective memory."

"That's a mother's prerogative. Now, what's on your mind?"

"Can't a son come and check up on his mother?"

"Certainly, but I can see more on your face.

Carz released a long sigh.

"I know. Being Leader isn't easy, Carz."

"Yet you and Father foisted it on me."

"Don't blame me. That was your father's doing," Carz's mother said. "I wanted a different life for you, but he couldn't see anyone else following him as Leader. Not Minok, Powers-That-Be bless him."

"That's for sure," Carz said. "It's not being Leader that I despise, it's the people around me."

"Yes, your father excelled at surrounding himself with talented people. He developed that skill during the Revolts. When he got older, he lost a step and there were lots of suck-ups."

"Unfortunately, the problems are closer to home."

"I warned your father about Roneh, but he always thought you could handle her."

"He might have underestimated her."

"Your father tended to do that with women," Carz's mother said. "When he was growing up, there weren't any around and your grandfather was the definition of a sexist bastard."

"You'd think Father would've learned his lesson being partnered to you."

"I believe your father thought I was the exception to the rule, and who was I to dissuade him? I taught him some lessons along the way, but he worshipped his father and never changed much in his disregard for women."

"Yes," Carz said, thinking about his grandfather's portrait in the study. "He definitely wasn't paying close enough attention to Roneh."

"Now that you're Leader, I can see her showing her true stripes. A little power-hungry, I imagine."

"You could say that."

"You've always had a good heart. I tried to instill that in you. I figured it would balance out your father's vindictiveness."

"The jury's out on that one."

"Get to the point, dear. It's lovely spending time with you, but I came out here for a little solitude."

"Right. I'll cut straight to it," Carz said. "I'm compiling evidence that Roneh arranged the bombing and—"

"I'm not surprised," Carz's mother said matter-of-factly. "Not in the slightest."

"I thought you'd be angrier."

"Look at me," Carz's mother said, pointing at her leg in its cast. "I'm an old woman who is broken and healing slowly. I can't do anything about it so why waste the energy? Your father would've taken her out back and shot her."

"I don't think I have that option quite yet."

"Roneh knows it, too," Carz's mother said. "I assume she wants something out of her actions otherwise she wouldn't have gone to all the trouble."

"She's pretty transparent that way."

There was a rustling in the underbrush and Carz's mother made a chirping sound, opened her hand, and placed a treat on the armrest of the bench to her right. Karanga emerged from the underbrush and chirped. Carz's mother chirped back. Karanga scurried toward the bench, then jumped up on the armrest and sat there eating the treat.

His mother leaned toward Carz, kissed him on the cheek, and whispered in his ear, "What're you going to do about your Roneh problem?"

Karanga finished devouring the treat, turned to Carz's mother and chittered. She held the remaining treat between the thumb and forefinger of her right hand and offered it to Karanga, who reached out for it with his two tiny paws. The creature took the treat from her, then jumped off the armrest and disappeared into the underbrush.

"I'm not sure yet," Carz said. "She wants that Allegiance expansion that Father was always against because it would give her too much power. I can refuse to sign it into law, but right now, it doesn't seem worth the fight."

"Give it to her, and while she's reveling in her victory, you get one step ahead of her and cut her legs out from under her," Carz's mother said. "You must have some ideas."

"I have something in the works."

"See, you have it under control."

"Time will tell."

"On a completely different subject, what is going on with your brother?"

"I found out that he's staying at your place in Nor."

"Yes, I knew that."

"Why didn't you tell me?"

"You never asked," Carz's mother said. "I talked to him today and he's acting stranger than usual which is saying something. He wouldn't tell me when he's coming home. What is happening with him?"

"I'm going to visit him soon, and I'll let you know."

MADO

Before Mado could answer Alba's question regarding Clo's vision, a nurse entered the room. She told them that Clo needed her rest, and they should leave and return in the morning.

On their walk home, Mado was expecting Alba to say something, but she was silent, and when they reached their destination, she went straight inside and thanked their neighbor for watching their children, who were still asleep. Mado climbed the ladder to the roof and lay down on his back staring up at the stars. He was overwhelmed by guilt about how his actions had injured his daughter.

A star appeared in the sky where there shouldn't be one, then it vanished and reappeared somewhere else in the sky. This pattern occurred seven times until a spacecraft materialized over the house. It was the aliens. Mado leapt to his feet and yelled with his arms in the air, saying, "What do you want from me, you bastards?" Then the spacecraft disappeared.

"What are you doing?" Alba said from the top of the ladder. "You'll wake the children."

"I didn't hear you coming up."

"I know," Alba said, stepping onto the platform. "You want to tell me why an alien spacecraft was hovering over our home?"

"I have no idea, but it's probably time you know the truth. You should sit down. I'll give you an abbreviated history."

So Mado regaled Alba with the past, beginning when he crashed on the lava planet. He went into more detail in telling his story than he had planned, but Alba deserved it. She sat there the entire time, not saying a word and not asking any questions. When Mado had begun, she'd had a serious look on her face. She wasn't happy that Mado had been lying to her for years, but as Mado continued, she relaxed and even laughed at a few anecdotes of Yorlik and Mado's relationship and grunted at the vile nature of Vidor Plemso.

When the sun was rising on a new day, Mado ended his confession with his pod's return to Prevor and said, "That's why I'm so obsessed with the stars."

Alba stood up and stretched. "What did you think you were going to actually achieve by sitting here night after night examining the cosmos?"

"I'm not sure," Mado said. "A glimpse of spaceships leaving Koda on the way to the habitable world. A sign that the aliens were wrong. I never expected a flyby."

"That leads us back to my original question—why have these aliens shown up here?"

"Maybe it was a gesture to force me into confessing to you."

"So they fly across the universe to mend our relationship?"

"When you put it that way it does sounds silly."

"Then how should I put it?"

"I don't know if they exactly travel across the universe as we understand it—their means of conveyance—"

"That's beside the point, Mado," Alba said. "You said they can see the future. Maybe they're reminding you that you can't do anything about the future so you should stop wasting your time and endangering your family."

"That doesn't seem right."

"You know what isn't right? Breaking a few Space Traveler codes and lying to the Protectorate," Alba said. "What are you going to do about it?"

"At the moment, they believe my story," Mado said. "I'm more concerned that I've made you complicit. That's one of the reasons why I never told you."

"And you couldn't have told me when we first met because we were strangers."

"I knew I loved you from the start and I didn't want to lose our connection," Mado said. "As our lives became intertwined, telling you became more complicated."

"We mated and had children, and now it jeopardizes our family. I get it."

"I could have told you before we were bound together. That being said, I don't regret it."

Alba walked up to Mado and placed her hand on his shoulder. Mado felt a rush of compassion, then a rush of anticipation and excitement like when you're about to be reunited with someone you truly love after not seeing one another for a long time.

Alba said, "I understand. I fully understand. We need to keep this secret between us and protect it, but no more lying to each other." She released her hold on Mado.

"Agreed."

Pino and Jana began calling for them from inside the house.

Mado said, "We should get off this damn roof, but we haven't discussed what Clo did at the hospital. Let's take the day off from work. We need to see if she's one of *them*."

"Our child a telepath," Alba said. "Seems unbelievable, but we need to find out before the authorities do."

"Maybe it's just a symptom of the accident. There's no history of telepaths in either of our families."

Pino called out from the bottom of the ladder and they could hear him beginning to climb up.

Mado walked with Alba to the ladder. He stared down at the dried pool of blood from Clo's head.

Alba said, "Get down, Pino. Go back inside. We'll be with you in a moment."

LATER THAT DAY, WHEN MADO WALKED HAND IN hand with Alba down the road toward the hospital, they were both concerned about the prospect of a catastrophic occurrence for their family.

In the early formation of Prevorian civilization, empathic ability was embraced as a way for Prevorians to carve out a peaceful society. A small percentage of the population possessed telepathic ability and their existence produced chaos. There were many instances of telepaths taking advantage of the unwitting, and a few had gone down in history as infamous criminals, murderers, and tyrants. Upon its inception, the Protectorate marked telepaths as a danger to universal prosperity and devised a solution. Telepaths' genetic lines were sent off-world and settled on a planet that would sustain them, and the Protectorate destroyed all traces of the planet's location.

Peace reigned in the Protectorate's empathic society for hundreds of thousands of years. The birth of a telepath was rare. Maybe one was born in a millennium. Since the occurrences were so few and the Protectorate had erased any knowledge of the telepath's planet, a new protocol was arranged for banishment. The telepath and their entire family line were exiled to the island installation of Lipa. They were provided with food, shelter, and heath care, and the Protectorate sterilized them so their kind would be eliminated within a generation.

Mado had been so shocked by Clo's performance the previous day that he'd forgotten to warn her about displaying the ability in front of the hospital staff. She had no idea what the emergence of this ability would do to her family, and Mado and Alba agreed on removing Clo from the hospital as quickly as possible.

When they reached the reception desk outside Clo's room, the aide told them that a physician wanted to speak to them. He was on his rounds and would be with them shortly. Worry shot through Mado. Still holding hands with Alba, he could tell she felt the same.

The aide said, "Are you all right, sir?"

"I'm fine," Mado said. "Why?"

"I'm trained to spot agitation and I assure you that your daughter is well, and she can leave as soon as the physician meets with you and your mate," the aide said. "You're welcome to visit your daughter. The physician will arrive shortly."

Alba said, "That's great news. Thank you."

Mado and Alba hurried to their daughter's bedside. Clo was asleep, and the readings on her monitors were normal. She lay on her side breathing softly. Mado loved her, and he hated to see her here. Alba stood silently beside him. Even though they weren't in physical contact, he knew her feelings were similar.

Clo said without opening her eyes, "Mother! Father! Don't be sad."

Mado didn't say anything, but thought, *Clo, you're awake.* Then Mado heard Clo's voice inside his head. *Yes, Father, I was faking it so the nurse would leave me alone.*

Mado glanced over at Alba. There was a look on her face as if she were daydreaming. Clo was communicating with her, too. A moment later, Alba gasped and stared at Mado in horror.

Mado said, "Stop that, Clo. Open your eyes this instant."

Clo's eyes opened. Alba bent down and kissed her on the forehead, then adjusted the bed so Clo was sitting up.

Clo said, "Sorry, Father. I was just playing. It's fun. I've been practicing."

Mado panicked. "Who have you been practicing on, Clo? Have you spoken to the nurses or the physician the way you just spoke to me?"

"No, Father. Our conversation was actually my first attempt," Clo said. "I've just seen inside their minds."

Alba said, "You need to stop."

"I'm not sure how," Clo said. "It's like sitting on the beach with your eyes closed, attempting to shut out the sound of the waves crashing ashore. It's a constant barrage. Hearing it all is fun, but confusing."

Mado said, "For now, it's best if only the three of us know about this ability. You can't even tell your brother or your sister."

Clo said, "Why not?"

Alba said, "We'll explain more when we get home."

"Fine," Clo said. "But when did you and Father start being able to do this?"

"Neither of us can do it. Your brother and sister can't do it. You're special," Mado said. "When did this start?"

"When I woke up and you showed me those creatures with the big eyes. Who are they?"

"We'll explain everything when we get home," Alba said again.

The door swung open and the physician entered. He was a different physician from yesterday. He was older and carried himself with confidence. "Hello. How's my favorite patient doing? I assume you're her parents. Your daughter is a lucky young lady. After a fall like that, she only has a bump on her head. We can't find anything else wrong with her."

Mado put his arm around Alba's shoulders. "She comes from good stock."

"Of that I have no doubt," the physician said, moving further into the room and standing on the opposite side of the bed from Alba and Mado. "You're Mado, aren't you? The Space Traveler."

"Yes, that's me."

"I read about your mission and how you survived," the physician said. "I heard you lived in this community. Strange we've never met."

Mado said, "Fortunately, we don't visit the hospital often."

"You probably wouldn't have much need for a brain specialist, either," the physician said. "But your daughter brought us together."

Alba said, "We'd like to take her home now."

"Sure, after we speak," the physician said. "In our examination, we did find an anomaly."

"Her readings look normal to me," Mado said, pointing at the monitor.

The physician chuckled. "That's only displaying basic stuff."

"So what's the problem?" Mado asked.

"I didn't say there's a problem," the physician replied. "I said there's an anomaly."

Alba said, "What's the difference?"

"When Clo was brought in, the physician on call performed a brain scan, which is normal procedure in a case like your daughter's, and he found a small anomaly that he'd never seen before so he called me in."

Mado said, "She seems fine to us."

"Yes, we ran a series of tests. The results were normal for her reflexes, but she was off the charts for a child her age in the cognitive exams," the physician said. "We ran another scan to make sure the first one wasn't a glitch, and the anomaly was more pronounced."

"You keep using the word anomaly, and you say that's not a problem," Mado said. "Does that mean you're not sure what was detected?"

"We have an idea, but we'd rather not say until we can be sure," the physician said. "You could take her home, but it'd be advantageous to keep her here at least one more day so we can perform another scan. We have a tech on the way to ensure our device is properly calibrated."

Alba said, "Is she in danger?"

"Not that we can tell."

Mado said, "Have you told us everything that we need to know?"

"Yes."

"Then we'll be taking her home now," Mado said.

"Aren't you concerned there might be something wrong with your daughter?"

"Are you saying we don't care about our child?" Alba said angrily.

"Certainly not."

Mado said, "All the tests have demonstrated that our daughter is fine. Your device displayed something, but you're not sure what it is. So we're going to take our daughter home, and when you get your machine straightened out, then contact us and we'll make an appointment. How does that sound?"

The physician said, "It would be more convenient if she stayed overnight."

"Convenient for whom?" Mado said. "I'd consider it an inconvenience for us. We're taking our daughter home and that's final."

Alba went to the closet and retrieved Clo's garments, then waved her over. Clo climbed out of bed, scampered to her mother, and stripped off her hospital gown. The holographic monitor shut down as the gown was integrated with the detection circuitry.

The physician observed Clo dressing in disbelief. "I sincerely advise that your daughter stay," he said with agitation in his voice.

When Clo was ready to leave, Alba took her hand and they headed for the door.

Mado followed Clo and Alba and said to the physician, "Good day, sir,"

When they exited the hospital, Mado lifted Clo onto his shoulders, and he and Alba picked up the pace toward home.

Alba said, "What're we going to do?"

"What's wrong, Mother?"

Mado said, "Nothing Clo."

Mado grasped Clo's legs, and he and Alba began to jog.

Clo said, "This is fun, Father. Faster."

"I'm glad you like it, Clo," Mado said. "I have a question for you. Did you cheat on those cognitive tests?"

"What does cheat mean?"

Mado had forgotten for a moment that the concept of cheating didn't exist on Prevor because of the onus on not lying. "Did you get the answers from the person giving the test?"

"Yes, the answers were right there in his mind. It was before you told me not to do it," Clo said. "I couldn't help it. Don't be worried, Mother."

Mado glanced over at Alba who was staring at her child as if she didn't know her. He reflexively attempted to smile like he'd have done on Koda.

"Are you all right, Mado?" Alba said. "You look ill."

"Yes, he's fine, Mother. He's doing something called smiling, which was a practice that people on Koda performed when they were attempting to console someone."

Mado laughed.

Alba said, "You find this amusing?"

Mado said, "I was thinking that I can't keep secrets from you anymore when she's around. It's kind of a relief."

"How is this a relief?" Alba said, throwing her hands in Clo's direction.

"It's not. I'm sorry," Mado said. "Clo, in a moment I'm going to show you why you can't use this ability anymore. You'll read my thoughts."

"All right, Father."

Alba said, "Are you sure that's a good idea?"

"It's the best way to convey the dangers. It'd take too long to explain."

Alba said with displeasure in her voice, "If you think so, go right ahead."

Mado said, "Clo, you'll read my thoughts now, but after this time, you will never do it again."

"Never?"

"At least until we say you can do it again," Mado said. "We'll help you practice to shut it all out when we get home. Do you understand?"

"I'll try, Father, but it won't be easy."

"Ready," Mado said. "Start...now." Mado thought about everything he'd learned regarding the history of Prevorian telepaths. In particular, he recalled images of telepaths who'd been the victims of discrimination and their expulsion from the planet and banishment to Lipa. He couldn't see Clo's face, but through their contact, he sensed her fear and holding her legs, he could feel her body tensing up.

Mado halted, reached back, took hold of Clo's waist, and placed her on the ground in front of him.

Clo was frantic. "Don't let that happen, Father. Please, I'll do as you say. Nobody will know. I promise. Please."

Mado picked her up and embraced her. "Nobody will ever know."

Tears were streaming down Alba's face.

The rest of the day, Clo was agitated. It was difficult explaining her state of mind to her brother and sister. If Clo was fine, then why was she so upset? Alba told Pino and Jana that Clo was recovering from her injuries and the household would need to adapt.

When the children were asleep, Alba wanted time by herself, so Mado went for a walk on the beach to clear his head. He recalled the physician's insistence on another brain scan and he wondered if the physician was aware of what the anomaly signified. Under Prevorian law, the physician would need to report it. The penalty for hiding a telepath was stringent.

Mado couldn't believe this was happening to his family. He stopped walking and peered up at the sky, which was clear of clouds. The moons had already risen. The stars were out. He sat down on the beach and picked up a handful of sand, sifting it through his fingers. He wondered about the alien flyby. Then it dawned on him that it had coincided with his daughter discovering her telepathy.

MAR

The door to Lek's office opened and Insol was escorted inside by two guards. Her hands were in restraints.

Mar sat behind the desk with Lek standing beside her. The security guards deposited Insol in a chair at the front of the desk. Rika stood at the side of the room, peering at her daughter with a pained look on her face.

"Good morning, Insol," Mar said. "I don't think restraints are necessary, do you, Lek?"

"Are you sure?" Insol said in a snide tone, leaning toward Mar. "I could leap out of this chair and strangle you."

Mar said, "I'll take my chances."

"Right. You're a master at taking chances with other people's lives."

Mar gasped.

"You know what?" Lek said. "Lock one hand to the chair. It's bolted to the floor."

The guard did as he asked, then Lek said, "You two can leave. Take post outside. I'll let you know when we're done."

The guards exited and closed the door behind them.

Mar pushed her chair closer to the desk and said to Insol, "What's gotten into you?"

"Maybe you haven't been paying attention."

"You might be right about that."

Rika said, "She's acting out just like she did when she was a child."

"What would you know? You weren't around," Insol said, still facing Mar.

Rika said, "I was working to put food on the table for you, your brothers, and your sisters,"

"And they were the ones who raised me."

"I don't think anyone raised you. They monitored you," Rika said, sounding annoyed. "You've always had it in for the world around you."

"What's left of it," Insol said. "And why not? Some of us have to take a stand."

Lek said, "Is that what you were doing with Cerio yesterday?"

"Cerio?" Insol said.

"The man you met at The Porch."

"Is that his name? I didn't ask."

"Why were you meeting him?"

"I won't say."

"Where is he hiding?"

"You tell me."

Mar said, "I don't understand you. Why would you protect this man? He has endangered this facility."

Insol said, "You're all clueless."

Lek said, "Why don't you educate us half-wits, Madame Professor?"

"You'll find out soon enough, and that man had no desire to endanger what's happening here."

Rika said, "His unauthorized presence does just that."

Lek said, "What will we find out soon enough?"

"I won't say."

"Why were you meeting him?"

"I won't say."

Lek said, "Where is he hiding?"

"I'll say it slow so you can understand," Insol said. "I… don't…know."

Moving herself even closer to the desk, Mar said, "The way you're acting is completely counterproductive. What would Yor say?"

"You mean your son who pulled the curtain aside on the Global Assembly's lies, then disappeared like a coward?" Insol said. "He's counterproductive personified."

"I didn't know you felt that way."

"Just another example of you being out of touch."

"Please tell me what I'm missing, then," Mar said.

"You made a deal with that bastard Vidor Plemso. You let it ride for twenty years as the domes collapsed. Then the purge happened anyway. So in the end, you've done nothing for the Kodan people."

"That's unfair!"

"Unfair?" Insol said and began to laugh.

Rika walked up behind Insol and smacked the side of her head, which immediately stopped the outburst. "That's enough. Show some respect."

"Yes, whatever you say, Mother."

"Respect is a good place to start," Mar said. This entire conversation disturbed her and she needed to find a way to ground it so they could receive a few relevant answers. "I know you're hurting, Insol. I know it's been going on for quite some time and you want to lash out."

"You got that right."

"I've always had the utmost respect for your intelligence and the way that you speak your mind no matter the consequences or who the subject of your wrath might be," Mar said. "But the way you've acted in the past few days has been out of line, and now you've not only disrespected us, but everyone who works in this facility. All we want is an explanation of your actions."

"I have nothing to say."

Mar looked over at Lek who said to Insol, "We're sorry to hear that. You'll be confined to your room and food will be brought to you until the time comes for your departure."

"That's fine by me."

Lek said to Rika, "Tell the guards to come back."

Rika opened the door and motioned to the guards to come in.

Lek said to the guards as they entered, "Take her back to her room. Restrain her until she's inside. Lock her in the room, post yourselves outside, and await further instructions."

One of the guards unfastened Insol's wrist from the arm of the chair, asked her to stand, then locked her wrists behind her back and escorted her out the door.

Rika closed the door, then sat down in the chair that Insol had been occupying. She sighed.

Silence filled the room except for the thrumming of the air-circulation system blowing through the ceiling vent.

Mar felt like she'd failed Insol somehow. While she'd been focused on saving the population, maybe she'd lost track of her personal priorities. She said to Rika, "I don't know what to say."

"Don't take it personally, Mar," Rika said. "That's what she wants. She's always felt misunderstood, and she's proficient at hurting the ones who love her the most."

"That doesn't make it any easier."

Lek said, "I don't want to be insensitive, but I'm still concerned why Cerio was meeting clandestinely with Insol. We still have no answers."

Rika rose from the chair and said, "You'll figure it out. That's your job. Let's end the lockdown. My people need to get back to work."

"Yes," Mar said, standing up from the desk chair. "I need to finish my meetings this morning and return to Capitol City after midday. I'll have Suron look into this Cerio character, too."

MADO

Days went by.

Mado and Alba ignored requests from the hospital to return for another brain scan. They'd heard nothing from the Prevorian authorities, but Mado wasn't assuming the problem would go away.

He understood that his family required a reasonable course of action. He could easily hack into the hospital's database and make Clo's scans disappear, but that wouldn't make the physician forget about it. He and Alba discussed the prospect of running. They'd abandon their house and hide out in a secluded area until Mado could get his hands on a decommissioned spacecraft, make it space-worthy, then find a new home somewhere among the stars. Mado proposed reaching out to Mar so they could return to Koda. Alba had no desire to impose the wearing of prosthetics on her children. They'd have to pretend they were somebody else, especially through their formative years, and base their lives on a lie. She rejected it outright. Mado proposed other planets where they might settle, including Yorlik's planet. He even suggested spending years in space until they discovered the ideal home. Maybe if they traveled from star system to star system, they'd eventually stumble across the aliens' home planet or run across an alien spacecraft. In the end, Alba refused to run from their problem because it wasn't a good example for their children.

 Howard Libes

Alba had the notion that they might be able to reason with the authorities. A telepath hadn't appeared on Koda in nearly a thousand years, and they were mythologized as evil. Nobody could predict who Clo would become as an adult. Nobody could say she'd be a threat when she grew up. If she was raised properly, she might be an asset to Prevorian society. Mado argued that there was no reason to believe the authorities would make an exception for Clo. Prevor was a civilization steeped in rules and regulations, and enforcing edicts was seen as the foundation for millennia of stability. Sticking to them was a tenet bordering on religion. Why would the Protectorate alter the basis of their civilization for Clo? Prevorian regulations preached that a telepath's genetic line must be separated from society for civilization to hum happily along. If the Protectorate had to carve out part of their planetary budget to ensure the safe exile of Alba and Mado's extended family, it would be done. Case closed.

Then one night, Mado was on the roof, sitting in a chair and listening to the waves crashing on the shore. The children had gone to bed. He was waiting for Alba who wanted to catch up on work before she joined Mado for their nightly strategy sessions.

Mado heard a knock on the front door and peered over the side of the house. It was the physician from the hospital who had insisted on another brain scan. He was dressed in street attire. Mado wondered whether Alba would answer the door. He had installed a mini-cam above the entrance so if the authorities arrived they'd have fair warning. The monitor for the cam was in their shared office. Undoubtedly, Alba was looking at it now. Since there was no way for the physician to know Mado was on the roof, he left it up to Alba to engage with the physician or not.

The physician knocked again. The light turned on over the doorway and Alba opened the door.

The physician said, "Sorry to come by so late and unannounced, but I have something to discuss with you and your mate. It's of the utmost importance. May I come in?"

"I don't see why you need to, and you'll wake the children. We can talk right here," Alba said, then called out, "Mado, please come down."

Mado climbed down the ladder and approached the physician while Alba waited inside the doorway.

Mado said, "What can we do for you?"

"You never brought your daughter back for the scan."

Alba said, "As the child's parents, that's our decision."

"In normal circumstances, that's true, but this is far from normal."

"What do you mean?" Mado said.

"Are you going to make me explain what you already know?"

Alba said, "What do we know?"

"It's obvious from your hasty departure from the hospital and the way you're acting that you know."

Mado said, "Why don't we come to your office in the morning?"

"I doubt you'd show up."

Alba said, "Are you questioning my mate's word?"

"Unfortunately, I am," the physician said. "If you don't come in for another scan, then I will be obligated by Regulation 452 of the Medical Code to contact the Planetary Council."

Mado said, "And what does this regulation say?"

The physician sighed. "The regulation reads, 'If any physician becomes aware of a telepath through examination and does not report the discovery to the Protectorate Medical Council, they will forever lose their right to practice medicine.' I don't want to contact the Council, but if you don't come in, then you leave me no choice based on the results of earlier scans."

Mado said, "Can you excuse us for a moment so my mate and I can speak in private?"

"Absolutely," the physician said. "I'll take a stroll and return shortly." He left the stoop, walked the path to the beach, disappearing into the darkness.

Mado took a few steps toward Alba, then checked that the physician was out of hearing range. "What do you think? This might be an opportunity."

"I don't understand," Alba said. "The scan will confirm Clo's abilities. The physician will report her, and we'll all be exiled."

"Hear me out. First of all, we agree on an appointment for the scan," Mado said. "Then you show up with Clo, and you contact me when they wheel her into the scanning room. I'll already be hacked into the hospital system ready to replace the scan with a normal one from a child of Clo's age."

"Part of me is astounded by this devious yet brilliant idea," Alba said. "Another part is appalled by how good you got at thinking underhandedly when you were on Koda."

"You learn lots about yourself both good and bad as a Space Traveler," Mado said. "I'm not proud of this skill but it comes in handy on a planet where nobody expects it."

"That's one way of looking at it."

Mado saw the physician coming their way and said, "So, quickly, tell me. What do you think?"

"As a Prevorian, I don't believe it's the right course of action, but as Clo's mother, I don't see any other option."

The physician halted at a distance and called out, "Are you ready for me?"

Alba whispered to Mado, "Set up the appointment as far in the future as possible. Maybe in the meantime we'll come up with a less heinous option."

Alba waved to the physician and said, "Good night," before entering the house and closing the door behind her.

Mado agreed to a date and time for the scan. Leading up to it, he spent the nights researching what a normal scan should look like for a child of Clo's gender and age, then chose one from a different hospital's database. He practiced the most efficient and clandestine method to exchange Clo's scan for another without anybody noticing. His plan had a distinct advantage. No Prevorian would ever dream of such subterfuge.

The scheme went off without a hitch. Mado was in the system when Alba contacted him that the scan was in progress. He seamlessly swapped the stolen scan for Clo's, which he deleted from existence. When Alba returned from the hospital with Clo, she was ecstatic. Clo was given a clean bill of health.

Life went back to normal in Mado and Alba's household. They continued having discussions with Clo about not revealing her telepathic abilities to anybody including her brother and sister. They promised her that when she was older, they would relocate to a place where she could practice her telepathic skills far from individuals who would be intolerant of it.

Mado began to search in earnest for this future location on Prevor. This place needed to be remote with a small population, where his other children could live a normal life and he and Alba could still earn a living. It wouldn't be exile, but they would have to cut themselves off from a large portion of Prevorian society. As time passed, finding this place superseded his unproductive obsession with Koda. He didn't know what he'd been thinking. From light-years away, he couldn't do anything to save the Kodans from their bad behavior patterns. He felt foolish that he'd lost focus on the life he had created and cherished on Prevor. Mado made a conscious effort to avoid speaking Kodan, too. He forced himself to think before he said anything. With the secret of Clo's telepathy looming, the revelation of his journey with Yorlik or his tampering with Kodan civilization would be even more unwelcome and disastrous.

ONE DAY, MADO WAS RETURNING HOME FROM SWIM-ming. He reached the path leading to the house and spotted Pino on the front stoop, talking to the physician from the hospital. Pino noticed his father and pointed to him.

Since they'd last seen the physician, Mado and Alba had never been happier. Alba was pregnant with their fourth child, which increased the urgency of finding their new home before the baby was born. Mado had scouted and narrowed their choices to two locations.

The physician waved to Mado and they walked toward one another. Before they met, the physician stopped, peered out at the ocean, and closed his eyelids. He was listening to the waves crashing on shore, the tide receding, then another wave crashing. This was a common Prevorian practice of revering the waters that spawned existence in order to give an individual the strength to confront something disconcerting or significant in life.

The physician opened his eyes and looked directly at Mado, who was now standing in front of him. "I have some embarrassing news relating to your daughter's case."

"Embarrassing?"

"Yes, embarrassing for me, but quite serious for your family," the physician said. "I'd like to tell both you and your mate at the same time."

"She's out right now with Clo," Mado said. "They're clothes shopping. Children grow out of their clothes as fast as you can buy them, and she doesn't want her sister's hand-me-downs."

"I would normally ask you to come to my office tomorrow, but it's best we discuss this now," the physician said. "Talking to you without your mate isn't ideal, but it'll have to do."

"Would you care to walk along the shore and tell me your news?"

"Yes," the physician said. "That would ease my emotions."

When they walked the beach, the physician was silent for a long time. Mado noted he was staring down at his feet, and his confidence was now replaced by a downtrodden demeanor.

"Please," Mado said. "You have me concerned. What is it?"

The physician stopped. He turned toward the ocean, breathed in deeply through his gills, and closed his secondary eyelids again. This only increased Mado's concern. He wished Alba was with him to help bear the brunt of whatever the physician was about to say.

Mado wanted to be respectful of the physician's moment of prayer, but he lost his patience. "Please," he said. "With all due respect."

The physician opened his eyes and looked out at the ocean. "Well, as you know, we performed two scans on your daughter. In the first, the scanner wasn't calibrated properly, but there was a hint of an abnormality. I recalibrated the equipment myself before the second scan and I found the results problematic. They indicated the possible genesis of activity in the brain of someone who might become telepathic, but still the results were inconclusive." The physician paused and sighed, digging his feet into the sand. "On the third scan, I had a tech recalibrate the device and it showed definitively that your daughter was normal without telepathic tendencies." The physician closed his eyes and went silent again.

All the stalling was infuriating Mado. "Yes, I'm aware of everything you just said."

The physician opened his eyes. Mado's anger must have been apparent because he reached out and put his hand on Mado's bare shoulder.

Mado received a rush of emotions—frustration, anger, sadness, incompetence.

The physician removed his hand. "I know that was unprofessional, but I wanted you to experience my emotions," he said. "While I was waiting for you and your mate to schedule a third scan, I presented the first two scans to a colleague, and he implored me to send them to the district medical council. I told him that I preferred to wait for the third scan. He reminded me as Prevorian physicians we were bound to report any results revealing a telepath. I told him I didn't agree. After the first two scans, I didn't have a definitive diagnosis. After receiving the third scan, I went to show my colleague that his concern was unwarranted. And that's when he told me he'd already sent the first two scans to the council."

"What?" Mado said. "How could you let that happen?"

"I was infuriated. Since your daughter is my patient, he was completely out of line," the physician said, looking down at his feet in the sand. "I know I shouldn't have shown him the scans in the first place, but your daughter's case is so rare. Showing him the scans was hubris on my part."

"This is my daughter we're talking about," Mado said, "not a virus."

"Yes, I know," the physician said, "and it was unprofessional on my colleague's part as well."

"This is your fault."

"Yes," the physician said, still looking down at his feet. "So I contacted the council. I explained the misunderstanding and sent them the third scan, telling them it should put an end to this unfortunate affair…but that isn't the case…" He closed his eyes again.

"And?"

The physician didn't respond.

Mado shoved him, knocking him down onto the sand. "Stop that!"

The physician opened his eyes and said, "You have every right to be upset."

"Upset doesn't begin to describe my feelings," Mado said, taking a step so he was standing over the physician. "Now finish what you came here to say."

The physician seemed resigned to stay seated on the sand. "So I heard back from the district council and they told me they'd forwarded all the scans to the Protectorate Medical Council, who are in charge of the investigation now."

"Investigation?"

"Yes, I'm so agitated I forgot to mention it. When they received the first two scans, the district launched an investigation, and their conclusion was forwarding the scans to the PMC who have greater resources and would ultimately make the final decision," the physician said. "I've reached out to the PMC a few times, leaving messages telling them this was a misunderstanding, that if they took a look at the third scan the results clearly demonstrated no telepathic proclivity. I finally heard back from them today, saying they'd decided to contact you and your mate so they could further examine your daughter and come to a final conclusion. That's when I rushed over here to speak with you and your mate, and to apologize for my shameful mishandling of your daughter's case."

"I don't know what to say,' Mado said. "You've single-handedly destroyed my family. You know the planetary authorities will put my daughter through test after test after test until they've concluded one way or the other. This could go on for years while they guarantee that their regulations are properly applied. Politics and public scrutiny will come into play and my daughter's life will be ruined. No child should experience such unnecessary mayhem. This is your fault. Isn't there anything you can do to stop this?"

"I plan on having my dissension heard, but the ultimate decision is out of my hands," the physician said. "I'm ashamed and feel responsible for whatever problems your family may experience due to my unprofessional actions."

"If you don't make this right, I'll make sure you lose the privilege to practice medicine."

"That may happen anyway."

"I won't shed a tear." Mado wanted to kick sand in the physician's face, but he might be Clo's only advocate, no matter how pathetic he looked at that moment.

Mado reached out and the physician grasped his hand. Mado hoisted him to his feet and said, "Maybe you can file a complaint against the physician who sent the scans to the district and have the entire investigation nullified because the initial inquiry wasn't submitted by my daughter's physician. You know how it is. One improper bureaucratic step might override the entire affair."

"You're right. It might muddle the process," the physician said, patting sand off his clothes. "It's a long shot, but I'll see what I can do."

"Yes, see what you can do," Mado said. "Now I have to attend to my children. Goodbye."

Mado walked past the physician and headed home, contemplating how he was going to avoid a horrible fate for his daughter and his family.

LEK

"We should get to the entry tunnel," Lek said to Ara, peering at the clock mounted on the cafeteria wall. "You don't want to keep Mar waiting."

Ara wiped her mouth with a cloth napkin and placed it on top of her empty plate. "Aunt Mar knows I'm having morning meal with you so if I'm a little late, she'll understand."

"Nevertheless, being late is rude," Lek said. "I hope you don't call her Aunt Mar at work. You've done it a few times since you've been here and I haven't said anything."

"You don't have to worry. In public, nobody knows I'm your daughter."

"I know your mother legally changed your surname to her family's." Lek stood, piling Ara's tray on top of his own. "I understand why she did it, but I don't like it."

Lek carried the trays to the garbage cans where he dumped the food they hadn't eaten in the compost recycling, then laid the trays, plates, utensils, and cups on the conveyor belt to the cleaning station. He met Ara in the corridor, hugging her tightly and kissing her on the cheek.

Ara said, "You're walking with me to the tunnel, aren't you?"

"Of course," Lek said. "Why do you ask?"

"Just the way you hugged, it felt like you were saying goodbye."

"I've always been an affectionate person," Lek said, noting the cafeteria clock again. "This has been wonderful, my blossom, but we really need to get going."

Ara hooked her arm with Lek's and they headed down the corridor in silence.

Finally, Lek said, "I'm so happy we've been able to spend this time together."

"I wish we could see each other more often."

"I know there's no way to make up for lost time. We just have to make the best of the time we have," Lek said and sighed. "As I get older and look back on my life, all I see is a cavalcade of regrets. My life consists of one failure after another…except for you, my blossom."

"Don't talk that way," Ara said, hooking her arm tighter around Lek's. "That's not true."

"That's nice of you to say," Lek said. He kissed Ara on the cheek again. He was beginning to feel emotional. "But there's truth in it and it's important to embrace it no matter how…Anyway, I don't want to be a downer with you leaving. Let's talk about you."

"That's all we've been doing since I got here," Ara said. "You've evaded personal questions except when Rika was around, and you dodged most of those, too."

"What do you want me to say?"

"Tell me about your regrets," Ara said. "It'd be good to talk about them. Get them out in the open. It'll make you feel better."

Ara stopped walking. Since their arms were hooked together, Lek halted, too.

"Please, Papa. It'll be good for you, and I won't judge."

Ara released Lek's arm and grabbed both his hands.

"You're a lot like your mother. Relentless."

"She does have some good qualities."

"Your mother is a wonderful woman, and I blew up her life and for what…" Lek said, his voice trailing off.

"I know you regret leaving Mother and me."

"Of all my regrets, that's the biggest," Lek said. "But look how you turned out."

Ara said, "When I asked Mother why you left us, she said you made the decision against her wishes to side with terrorists and commit treason, and that you were executed by the Global Assembly."

"Perspective is reality."

"Mar told me that you attempted to prevent your friend from being harmed, you kept her informed of his condition, you gave her the wafer containing intel about the purge, and you stopped the Leader from murdering tens of thousands of people," Ara said. "In my mind, that makes you a hero."

"Some hero," Lek said. "My best friend was executed and twenty years later all those people were killed including their grandchildren. I just paused the inevitable."

"You gave all those people twenty years of life they might not have had," Ara said. "They were able to watch their families flourish and grow."

"Until they were snuffed out…Small consolation," Lek said. "Come, you'll be late."

He attempted to pull out of Ara's grip, but she held on to him. She gazed into his eyes and he knew she saw his sadness.

Lek said, "I don't know how to explain my feelings of regret to a person who has their entire life ahead them."

"Try."

"Like I said, I look back on all those past decisions and I think, 'What if I'd done it differently? What would my life be like now?' Maybe I'd be happier. I would've spent the past twenty years living with you and your mother."

"I know I'm young, but it seems foolish to dwell on the past, to wallow in your regrets. You have plenty of life in front of you and we're back together and you're in a relationship with a fabulous woman—"

"You're right," Lek said. "You're right. You were always smarter than me."

"That goes without saying," Ara said and chuckled.

"I guess at least I did one thing correctly. And now that I have you in my life, the future is bright," Lek said. "Now we should really hurry."

When they approached the tunnel, Rika, Mar, the Prevor Industries guards, the pilot and copilot, Kubwa and his men were chatting and milling around. Insol stood away from the group, staring off into the distance. Baggage was scattered around with enviro-suit helmets placed on top of them.

Rika spotted Lek and Ara, then strode toward them. "Nice of you to join us. Late as usual."

Lek said, "I hate not to live up to my reputation."

Ara said, "It's my fault. I wanted him for myself for as long as I could have him."

Rika leaned forward, kissing Lek on the lips and said, "I can certainly understand that." She extended her arm toward the people waiting at the mouth of the tunnel. "Shall we?"

Mar said, "It's wonderful to see you two together."

"It's pretty great," Lek said. "I'm sorry to see her go."

Ara said to Rika, "You take good care of him."

"I'll do my best." Rika smiled at Lek. "If he lets me."

"Everyone," Mar said. "Let's get going."

The Prevor Industries guards lifted the bags scattered around them and made their way down the tunnel with the pilots and Kubwa and his men behind them.

Insol hadn't moved from her spot.

"Come here, mtunga shida," Rika said to Insol who hesitated, then strode over to her mother. Rika wrapped her arms around Insol, who just stood there with her arms by her sides. "I love you, baby. I only want the best for you." Insol finally lifted her arms and embraced her mother.

Mar said to Ara, "Why don't you say goodbye to your father, then go on ahead?"

Ara said to Lek, "I wish we had more time." She kissed Lek on the cheek and he embraced her.

Mar said, "If all goes as planned, we'll see each other sooner than later and more often."

Lek released his hold on Ara and she headed down the tunnel, waving goodbye.

Mar said, "Insol, let's go."

Insol separated from her mother.

Lek said to Insol, "You stay safe, young lady. I have a feeling you're wading into dangerous waters."

Insol said, "I'll do my best." Then she hurried away down the tunnel.

Mar said to Lek, "Let me know if you come up with any intel on the breach. I'll be in touch."

Rika hugged Mar and said, "Good luck."

Mar hugged her back and said, "I don't know if I'll need it, but it's always good to have it on my side."

"That's one of Rajer's catchphrases," Lek said.

"Yes, it is," Mar said. "We haven't discussed him, but I think about him every day."

"Me, too."

"So in a way he's still with us." There was an awkward silence, then Mar picked up her viewer case and said, "Gotta go."

Lek watched Mar as she went down the tunnel until she disappeared around a bend in the distance. He continued staring at the empty tunnel thinking about his conversation with Ara. He missed her already. He'd never be able to make up for the time they'd lost while she was growing up. If Mar could negotiate her deal with the new Leader, then maybe she could convince Carz to pardon him, and he'd be able to spend more time with his daughter. Talking about his regrets with her did help.

Rika said, "You all right?"

Lek was jarred out of his daydream. "I'm great."

"Your girl is something else."

"Linara did a good job."

Rika chuckled. "You never give yourself any credit. I see lots of you in your daughter, too. I think you laid the foundation for who she's become before you left."

"I'd like to think so."

Lek peered down the corridor and spotted the youngest Shamban member of the facility's security team, a man in his early twenties, sprinting toward them. He slid to a halt in front of Lek and Rika, then bent over and placed his hands on his knees, panting.

"Lek Valsted," the young man gasped, still attempting to catch his breath.

"What's the rush, son?"

The young man continued to gulp down air.

Lek said to Rika, "You don't need to wait around."

"Are you kidding? I want to hear what this is all about."

The young man straightened up and was starting to breathe normally. He towered over Lek and Rika.

Lek said, "Out with it, son. We're waiting."

"They've found where the infiltrator was holed up. The team attempted to comm you, but you weren't answering."

Lek checked his pockets and realized he'd left his comm in his office by accident when he was late to meet Ara. "Let's go, then," Lek said. "Rika, I'll fill you in later."

"Count on it," Rika said and headed off down the corridor.

"Lead the way, son."

"The team said to tell you they're looking for your advice. You don't need to join them."

"I'm going and you're taking me."

"Are you sure?"

"Of course I'm sure," Lek said. "What's the problem?"

"It's not easy to get there."

"What exactly are you saying?"

"Well…"

"Out with it."

"It's one of the old, abandoned tunnels and there's lots of climbing involved getting there and…"

"And what?"

"Well, with all due respect, sir—you're old."

Lek chortled. "Yes, I am, but this is still my job, and I will do it. Now lead the way."

Together they strode through the concrete utility tunnels. They climbed ladders for floors at a time until they were above the main cavern.

At one point, Lek asked, "How much further?" and the young man replied, "Not even close."

The journey got tougher. The old tunnels were drilled into the mountain. They were dirt and rock. Water dripped from the ceiling. Lek was wearing practical walking shoes instead of boots so he couldn't keep his footing on wet rocks. He constantly slipped, tearing up his hands as he grasped at jagged walls to remain standing. Sometimes he couldn't gain a handhold and fell, splashing in rock-filled puddles, banging his knees and tearing his pants. He wouldn't let the young man help him up. His pride was hurt. The young man was correct in his assessment of Lek's ability to reach the destination and that galled him.

The young man finally said, "We're close," and Lek could only think of the difficult return journey and retracing his steps on his weakened legs.

They turned a corner where the tunnel widened and a few of his most distinguished guards awaited him. Lek was soaked and shivering. His pants were ripped up. His knees and his hands were bloody. He was sure he looked a mess.

As Lek approached, it was clear that the guards were surprised to see him.

The guard in charge said, "Are you all right, sir?"

"I made it," Lek said. "Who won the bet?"

"Sorry, sir?"

"One of you must've bet that I wouldn't make it."

The guards looked at each other.

The guard in charge said, "I'm sure we don't know what you're talking about, sir."

"I just hope one of you bet on me," Lek said. "So, what have you found?"

The guards showed Lek a blanket and a towel rolled up for a pillow. Under the blanket, the ground had been scraped clean of rocks. Cerio slept here.

Nearby on a large rock was a makeshift transmitter, connected to a battery and a small speaker. Cerio had even procured a microphone with a cord that plugged into the transmitter. He'd had assistance from somebody or a group of people who could steal parts that were stored in the most secure areas of the facility, alter inventory logs, and had the know-how to build the transmitter. That meant a conspiracy of Movement sympathizers inside the facility who had probably been radicalized by the purge, and they were now willing to break protocols that kept the project secret. Some of Lek's security team had overlooked what was happening or they were in on it, too. Either way, Lek had failed in his duties.

Lek flipped a switch on the side of the transmitter, activating it. Static emitted from the speaker and he turned a knob until the static disappeared. He had found an active channel.

Lek picked up the mic, pressed the switch on the side, and said in Shamban, "This is Cerio. Is anybody there?"

There was no response.

Lek repeated, "Is anybody there?"

"Cerio, what's wrong?" a voice replied in Shamban. "Transport is en route. You should hurry to the rendezvous point. Why are you still there? Is there a problem?"

Lek reached down, turned off the transmitter, and dropped the mic to the ground. "He's gone."

"Yes, sir," the guard in charge said. "We can show you where he got out…and probably in."

Lek followed the guard down the tunnel. The air became warmer the further they went. In the distance, Lek could see blinding light emanating through a vertical break that ran from the ceiling to the ground in the wall at the end of the tunnel. As Lek approached the light, he shielded his eyes. Steam was coming off his drenched pants and in moments they were dry. Lek halted six meters from the breach. The heat was scorching and he was perspiring profusely. He used the back of his sleeve to stop the sweat streaming into his eyes.

The guard walked to the wall and turned around. He was surprised that Lek wasn't right behind him. He said, "The intruder probably squeezed through the gap here. From what we can tell, this entry was made from outside." He pointed to the debris on the ground by the breach. "When the tunnel was sealed off, not sure how many years ago, maybe twenty-five years ago, the mortar used didn't account for the increase in heat and was weakened by it. Actually, the entire wall could be taken down by a few blows of a mallet. I'm assuming this man wanted to camp as close as possible to the exit for escape purposes, so he didn't want to take the entire wall down. That would've severely increased the temperature in the tunnel."

Lek said, "Have you confirmed his escape route?"

"Yes, sir. We sent someone out and she picked up fresh tracks leading away from the tunnel."

Lek turned to move away from the heat and was startled by the young man standing right behind him.

"I've got a job for you," Lek said.

"Yes, sir."

"Hurry back to security headquarters and tell the senior officer I want a forensics team down here right away. I want this entire area and the transmitter checked for fingerprints. I want to know where each transmitter part was stolen from and any evidence that will lead us to whoever helped the intruder. Tell Chief Administrator Renta that work crews need to be organized to reinforce the outer walls of all the abandoned tunnels so they are bombproof, starting with this one. Also let the Chief Administrator know that from this moment on, there will be no communication with the outside and nobody will be allowed out of the facility until I'm satisfied that all of Cerio's conspirators are caught."

The young guard had been listening and nodding his head. He was silent now, staring at Lek.

Lek said, "Any questions?"

"No, sir."

"Then what are you waiting for…go!"

The young guard turned and raced away down the tunnel.

MAR

When the lift doors opened to her penthouse, Mar was happy to be home. The trip from the Facility to the Complex with Insol sitting in the backseat between Mar's guards instead of up front with her had been silent and uncomfortable.

Mar plopped her viewer case and bag down behind the couch, then unlocked the terrace door. She felt like she could breathe again as she stepped out onto the terrace that had become her sanctuary for contemplation and relaxation over the years. She lowered herself into one of the Vanderlord estate antique chairs. She considered them the most comfortable seats in her house but couldn't figure out why that was the case. She had wanted to recruit one of the Prevor Industries engineers to perform a study on the seats, but that would have been an extravagant use of corporate resources so she'd let the idea go. Maybe the answer was simple.

Maybe these chairs gave her comfort because they reminded her of sitting on the patio at the Vanderlord estate, watching six-year-old Yor playing "Travels in Outer Space" with his great-grandfather.

Yor had invented the game, which entailed Yorlik exploring the forest around the estate with his great-grandchild and digging up soil samples as if they were discovering a planet. Tetrick would sit beside Mar in the antique chairs. They'd hold hands, observing Yor's make-believe drama unfold, and every now and then leaned toward one another for a kiss.

Those were simpler times, Mar thought. She was aware she was glorifying the past like an old person, but those moments had been an escape from the stress and aggravation of Tetrick's arrests and the public scrutiny of Yorlik's expedition.

As part of the game, Yor would holler that a dangerous meteor was headed their way. He'd hide under the patio table with his great-grandfather who would look at Mar with a mischievous smile on his face and say to Yor, "What about your parents? They'll need shelter, too."

Yor would say, "Yes, what am I thinking? Mother, Father—quick. The meteor will be here in a matter of seconds. You'll be incinerated. Join us immediately."

Mar would gaze over at Tetrick who had already sprung out of his chair and was making his way under the table. He'd say, "Hurry, Mar," and Mar would squat under the table between Yor and his great-grandfather. There was barely enough room for the four of them, and they were tightly packed together.

Mar would hug Yor and say, "I'm so glad you're here to save us."

"Don't thank me yet, Mother," Yor would say. "This meteor is category nine and if it impacts Koda, it could mean planetary disaster although we'll survive now that we're shielded."

Mar would turn to Yorlik and say, "Category nine?"

"The boy has lots of questions," Yorlik would say, smiling again.

"And let me guess—you're the man with the answers."

"What can I say?" Yorlik would take hold of Mar's forearm and squeeze it.

"Look," Yor would say, moving forward so he was peeking up at the sky. "Here it comes. Look, look…"

Mar would edge forward and stare up at the sky. "I see it. It's a big one."

Yorlik would move forward and peer up. "Yes, it's bigger than we thought."

Yor would say, "Yes, Great-grandfather. I think it might be a category eleven. I don't know if we'll survive. Isn't it too big to burn up in the atmosphere?"

"I'd say so."

"What do we do now?" Tetrick would say to Yor, squatting on the other side of him.

"There's not much we can do but hope and pray the meteor misses the planet."

"Hope and pray?" Mar would say.

"He picks up everything," Yorlik would say. "He's a definitely a Vanderlord."

"Yes, Mother. Great-grandfather says that the Vanderlords' genetics plus yours makes me who I am, but he won't tell me how that happened."

Mar would muss Yor's hair. "Well, thank the Powers-That-Be that your great-grandfather has some discretion."

"Yes, I like to think I have some," Yorlik would say. "But not much."

"Look, everyone. Look, the meteor is going to miss Koda," Yor would say, performing an overexaggerated sigh and acting like he was wiping perspiration from his brow. "That was a close one."

"It certainly was," Mar would say. "What do you think, Great-grandfather?"

"Absolutely! A close one, but we must always keep vigilant for the next crisis on the horizon."

"What do you think about that, Yor?" Tetrick would say.

"I always listen to Great-grandfather." Yor would climb out from under the table and stand in front of the adults, who were still crouching beneath it. "Joro says I should always listen to Great-grandfather. That he's a wise man."

Now, sitting in the antique chair on her penthouse terrace, there was a knock on the doorway leading outside. Mar knew the knock. "Come on out, Suron."

"Your door was open."

"Isn't it always?" Mar said. "Good to see you. How are things around here?"

"Overall status quo, but we have a problem."

"I suspected when you showed up unexpectedly."

"Well, this is bad," Suron said. "I'd tell you to sit down, but you've already got that covered."

Suron's serious tone of voice was familiar, but she hadn't heard it in a long time. "I can tell I'm not gonna like it, but go ahead."

Suron said he'd been commed by his contact about GSS agents and Global Guards being scrambled by cruiser to the Shamban region on a need-to-know operation. They were deployed six hundred kilometers from Mafani-kio. As they approached their destination, a man was spotted wandering in the mountainous area, heading toward a two-lane highway. Intel conjectured the man was headed for a pickup, so the cruiser hovered at high altitude to avoid detection by the man on the ground. When a vehicle on the highway slowed for the man, the cruiser moved in. Someone inside the vehicle handed the man a weapon then sped away, stranding the man who sprinted back into the hills. When the cruiser pursued the vehicle, its occupants shot a projectile at it. The cruiser evaded the projectile and returned fire with a rocket, destroying the vehicle. Detecting no signs of life in the vehicle, the cruiser landed and the Global Guards tracked the man on foot. The man killed and injured some Global Guards in a firefight, but he was detained by stun weapon and taken to a GSS interrogation site.

"After further questioning my contact," Suron said, "I'm almost positive this happened in the mountains outside the facility right after you left."

"How did they know to look there?"

"That's a question my contact couldn't answer." Suron stood in the middle of the terrace and stared out at the nighttime cityscape, then turned to Mar. "I hate to say it and it's not your fault, but the only logical explanation is they tracked you there somehow and waited for you to leave, then spotted the man."

"How could that be? Could this man have sent out a transmission and the GSS picked it up?"

"It was a high-level GSS operation, and I think the man was just in the wrong place at the wrong time."

"Any identification of the person captured?"

"Closely held. Hopefully, we'll know more soon, but they're mobilizing local forces to search the area where the incident occurred. They're attempting to understand why this man was in such a desolate place and why they received such a violent response from him and the occupants of the vehicle," Suron said. "And maybe why you were there. In the meantime, it goes without saying that the man will be interrogated and tortured."

"And we should probably assume that the individual arrested is this Cerio character who met with Insol. His knowledge is a danger to the facility." Mar stood up and walked over to Suron. "This incident may weaken my negotiating position with Carz. It's unfortunate. I'd like to know how they tracked me to the facility. I have an idea, but I'd rather not speculate. Can you bring Insol to me? She should be locked in her apartment."

"Now?"

"Yes, now!" Mar said, surprised by the harsh tone of her voice. She observed the reaction on Suron's face. "Sorry. It's been a long day and the past three days felt like twelve. But yes, please get her and I'd like you here when I speak with her."

"Got it. Be right back," Suron said and exited the terrace.

Mar stretched from her feet up, then walked over to the terrace railing. She peered out at the view and reflected on what Yorlik had said about being ready for the next crisis. It made her wonder whether that lesson was meant for her.

Mar had planned on coming clean with Carz about the facility, knowing his desire to build more spaceships. She had wanted her confession to be the foundation for them working together for the survival of every Kodan. She hadn't figured he'd discover it before she revealed it, and Mar had to assume that Cerio would've cracked by the time she and Carz had a meeting. Carz wasn't experienced at negotiating, but Mar couldn't afford to take him for granted, either. If he found out about the facility the wrong way, like through Cerio's interrogation, then the facility's existence would come off as a decades-long deception perpetrated to undercut the Global Assembly. She'd have to approach the meeting now in an apologetic stance instead of being the bearer of happy tidings.

Mar went inside the penthouse, grabbed her comm out of her viewer case, and called the Leader's office. It was late, but Kel usually stayed after hours.

Carz answered, "How can I help you, Mar Jeps?"

She was startled. She was unprepared to speak with him.

Carz said, "Are you there?"

"Sorry," Mar said, "I didn't expect you."

"Then why did you comm?"

Mar walked onto the terrace and spotted the Global Assembly building in the distance. "Sorry I didn't get back to you sooner. Things have been crazy over here," Mar said. "I know that's no excuse. I didn't mean to be rude, but we should get together."

"Indeed."

Mar was expecting him to say more, but instead silence ensued while she gathered her thoughts.

Carz said, "You want to call me back when you figure out what else you want to say?"

"No, I..." Mar said, attempting to uncloud her mind. "I was thinking it'd be lovely to meet up at the estate, but I know you've been dealing with your mother's injury and the damage to the mansion."

"It's a big place. We can accommodate you," Carz said. "I'll have Kel comm your office in the morning and we'll set something up."

"Meeting sooner than later would be best."

"I completely agree," Carz said. "Just have some prospective dates in mind before Kel calls."

"Anything you'd like to chat about while we're on the line?"

"Oh, I'll send you a digi-mail about the air circulators, but I think at this juncture anything else should be said in person."

"Sure," Mar said. "If you think that's best."

"I do," Carz said. "You sound tired. Good night." Then the comm was deactivated.

Mar placed her comm in her pocket and focused on the Global Assembly building. She thought she could see the lights of the Leaders' office. The rest of the tower was dark. She could be mistaken, though. Carz could be anywhere on the planet.

Mar heard Insol yell, "Get your hands off me!" She turned to see Insol standing outside the lift's open doors, attempting to punch the guard to her left in the face. He blocked her fist with his arm, then grabbed her arm and twisted it behind her back. Suron stood to Insol's right, observing the altercation unfold.

Mar entered her apartment and approached the scene.

Suron said to the guard, "Why don't you go downstairs? I'll comm if I need you."

The guard released Insol's arm and sneered at her, then he stepped into the open lift, pressed a button and the doors closed.

"Insol," Mar said. "Would you like to sit in here or outside?"

"As my keeper, why don't you decide?"

"You're not a prisoner."

"Then why am I locked in my room?"

"The alternative was leaving you locked in your room at the facility. That's what your mother and Lek wanted," Mar said. "Here, we can get you the help you need."

"I don't need your help."

"So you say."

"Why did you drag me here?"

"We have something to discuss," Mar said. "Please sit down. Would you like something to drink?"

"No, I'm fine. Let's get this over with," Insol said and seated herself on the couch.

Mar sat beside her. Suron took up a position in front of them by the terrace doorway.

Insol said, "What do you want, Mar?"

"I don't understand why you're so combative," Mar said. "I thought we were friends."

"Friends don't lock their friends up or have their goons manhandle them."

Suron said, "Would you rather be put in restraints?"

"Suron, that's not helping," Mar said.

"Yes, Suron," Insol said. "Shut your trap."

"That's not helpful, either, Insol. I called you here on an important matter." Mar modulated the tone of her voice to one of concern. "A matter that could impact the survival of the Kodan people."

Insol cocked her head. She realized Mar was being sincere. "What is it?

"We're in the midst of a crisis." Mar moved closer to Insol and placed her hand on Insol's knee. Insol flinched at first, but she let Mar keep her hand there. "And you can help."

"Me?"

"Yes, you," Mar said. "And to clear things up, you're correct. Our friendship has been damaged by what you perpetrated at the facility. It hurt me. Since Yor met you, I've cared about you and always had the highest regard for you, and since Yor has been gone, I've felt like you were there for me when I needed you."

"I've felt the same way," Insol said. "But the purge changed everything."

"Including our relationship?"

"Yes," Insol said. "I don't know if you can understand this—"

"Try me," Mar said, removing her hand from Insol's knee, scooting closer to her on the couch and looking her in the eyes. "I truly want to understand."

Insol glanced at Suron and then back at Mar. "I'm not comfortable having this conversation in front of him."

"Suron," Mar said. "Head to the terrace and close the door behind you. I'll let you know when we're done here."

Suron exited and the terrace door closed.

Insol sighed and peered off into the corner of the room. "You'd have to experience where I came from—"

"In all the time we've known each other, you've never talked about your childhood. I just assumed since it was spent in Shamba, it couldn't have been happy or uplifting."

"Outsiders like you are usually the enemy, and we survive by not talking about it," Insol said, looking directly at Mar.

"Maybe it's something you need to disclose to a professional who deals with trauma," Mar said. "It might do you some good."

"I don't know. Keeping it suppressed has worked so far."

"Has it?" Mar said. "Look what you did to your brother. He didn't deserve that."

Insol stared into the corner of the room again. "You're right." Her voice shook with emotion. "He didn't deserve it. Seems like the purge has dredged up some old feelings and my brother and you have borne the brunt of it."

"That can be dealt with. I'll set up an appointment for you," Mar said. "Now tell me what your meeting with Cerio was about."

"Oh," Insol said, raising her voice and turning towards Mar. "So all this concern was just a ruse to get me to tell you about what happened at the facility. I thought I made myself clear that I'm not talking about it."

"My concern is genuine," Mar said. "Just like my concern for the Kodan people, and right now, a global crisis is unfolding, and it stems from your meeting with Cerio."

"You've got to be kidding. That's preposterous."

"I wish I was kidding," Mar said. "I wish. But Cerio was captured by the GSS in the mountains outside the facility. I don't have to tell you what will happen next. If the facility is discovered and damaged or destroyed, then decades of preparation to save the Kodan people will be erased. We'll have no way to make up for the potential loss of spaceships, which could mean hundreds of thousands more people dying than in the purge. Now do you understand the implications of what you've set in motion with your meeting?"

"I never intended—"

"Well, those are the consequences regardless of whatever you intended by bringing that man into the facility," Mar said in a stern tone. "I need to know why you brought him there."

"I don't think you have to worry about that," Insol said. "They have no reason to ask him. Your concern about the facility is well founded, though. That's devastating news."

"You're responsible for your actions, but I'm responsible for ensuring the results of your actions aren't disastrous. So I'll ask again, what did you two discuss?"

Insol was silent.

Mar was losing patience. If Insol was truly remorseful, then telling the truth would be easy. "I don't understand why this is so difficult after what I just told you."

"I don't expect you to understand."

"Why? Because I'm not Shamban?"

"Because you've never invested yourself in the Movement like your partner Tetrick did. Yor was involved, but he had his own agenda," Insol said. "I took an oath and I intend to keep it."

"So this meeting had something to do with the Movement?"

"I didn't say that."

"I thought the Movement was about exposing the truth to save the people from extinction."

"That was its roots and that's still the driving force behind it, but since Yor's Breeze Celebration speech twenty years ago, I've been involved in internal debates about making more powerful statements."

"You mean violence?"

"But because of your deal with the previous Leader, those wanting powerful statements were voted down by moderating voices in the Movement," Insol said. "The purge eliminated the majority of those voices."

"So the Movement has become radicalized, and so have you?"

Insol looked directly at Mar. "Correct."

"So why did the meeting need to happen at the facility?"

"It seemed like a good idea. I couldn't go outside the Complex where the GSS was pursuing me, but the Movement can get people into the facility."

"So that's why you took the corporate psych med seriously? That's why you seemed to have an emotional about-face? So you could go to Shamba and have this meeting?"

"I wanted to see my family, too, but yes," Insol said. "If I hadn't lost control outside the facility and got locked up, you never would've known about it."

"So you used me. You manipulated me. I don't know what to say. I'm sorely disappointed in you."

"That's too bad, but our relationship takes second place here."

"I'll remember that," Mar said. "And from what you've said about how the Movement is leaning and what I know of Cerio's background, this conversation at the facility wasn't about a peaceful protest."

Insol stared at the ground. "I've said too much already."

"Insol, I need to know what you talked about with Cerio," Mar said, raising her voice. "For Powers-That-Be sake, look at me—I need that information at my disposal so that when I meet with the Leader, I'm not surprised by news from Cerio's interrogation."

Insol looked up and blurted out, "Cerio was just a go-between for my plan. He gave me a message from the higher-ups in the Movement and I gave him a message for them. From what you've said, he probably never got word to them anyway so you can happily meet with Koda's newest tyrant."

"We don't know what Cerio transmitted from the facility," Mar said. "What was the plan?"

"I'd like to go back to my room now."

"Insol, I need—"

"I'd like to go back to my room now." Insol stood up.

"Suron!" Mar called out.

Suron entered, looking concerned, then assessed the situation and settled down.

"Please escort Insol back to her room, and tomorrow make some inquiries about her safety with your GSS contacts. If she's not on some post-purge list, then it's safe for her to return to her campus apartment, and there's no need to lock her inside her room tonight."

Insol said, "Mar, I—"

"I'll get you the contacts for psych meds in Capitol City. When you want help, when you're ready, you'll know where to find it."

"Mar, I—"

"You can leave now."

When the lift door closed behind Insol and Suron, Mar walked out onto the terrace and collapsed into the antique chair. "Well, Yorlik," she said, patting the armrest of the chair, "I guess my vigilance was lacking, because the next crisis is upon us and I have no idea what comes next."

INSOL

"It's safe for you to leave, but I wouldn't recommend it," Suron said, standing in the doorway of Insol's apartment in the visiting techs building at the Complex.

Insol said, "I have classes to teach and a department to run."

"You're always welcome here. Mar's in meetings this morning otherwise she'd see you off."

"Tell her thanks for the help," Insol said, then waved goodbye to Suron and closed the door.

Insol packed up the clothing she'd accumulated since she was rescued from her office into one bag along with her viewer case. She traveled by rail car from the Complex back to Royal University. On the ride to campus, she manically checked her surroundings—the rail-car station, the interior of the rail car, the streets, the alleys between buildings—for GSS agents following her. She hid her face from surveillance cams.

When she passed through the archway onto campus, she felt less spied on by cams but just as paranoid. She went to her apartment, which had been tossed by the GSS. After she cleaned up, she decided to check out her office. It was after midday and the campus was bustling with students strolling the paths or socializing with friends on the artificial lawn. Others poured out of buildings after class or exited their dorms. She hoped Suron's intel was

Howard Libes

correct, but she assumed GSS agents were impersonating students and Allegiance Program members were lurking to turn a "terrorist" into the authorities.

Insol reached her office and found the door had been replaced by an upgraded Prevor Industries model. When she grabbed the handle, a voice said, "Welcome, Insol," and the locks audibly opened. Inside the office, everything had been replaced, repainted or repaired, including the framed digi-foto of her, Mel, Ador, and Yor. An atmospheric control panel was attached to the wall near the door. A viewing screen mounted above the control panel showed a view of the hallway. On her desk was a memory wafer with an actual blossom in a vase beside it.

She removed her viewer from her case, activated it, inserted the memory wafer, and a vid popped up on screen with a startup image of Mar sitting behind her desk. Insol hit play on the vid.

Mar said, "Hello, Insol. I apologize for not seeing you off. Catching up on everything I missed while we were out of town. I hope you like what I've done to your office. That room was always too hot so the atmospheric control should help. I also added the door cam. I thought it would provide privacy and security. On the wafer is contact info for therapists who deal with post-traumatic stress. They come highly recommended. I'm always here for you, and by the way, the blossom was Ara's idea. She thought it would be a nice thing to find on your desk when you returned. It's real, not artificial. Not much more to say except I love you and I'm here for you. Hope to speak soon." Mar waved and smiled, and the vid ended.

Insol picked up the blossom and inhaled the sweet scent. She felt emotional. She understood that Mar felt disrespected by her, but Mar couldn't understand her attitude toward the Global Assembly. Insol was confident that with time and effort she'd be able to reestablish her relationship with Mar.

Insol worked into the evening when the building was locked and vacant. She was enjoying the peace and quiet and she was startled by a knock at the door. She ignored it. If this were the GSS, they would have announced their presence and she had no desire to engage in conversation with anyone. The knocking continued for a while until the person gave up. She began to read some digi-mail and her comm buzzed. She didn't recognize the contact number and ignored it. It buzzed again and she didn't answer, then it happened one more time and she decided to respond. "Who is this? Take a hint."

A male voice said, "I'm a friend of the Movement. I'm in the hallway. I want to discuss our plans. We need to chat." Then the comm disconnected.

Insol hesitated. Could this truly be a Movement operative? If Cerio had been captured and tortured, then this might be the GSS attempting to entrap her. Then she remembered she had a cam above the door now. She inserted the latest Movement memory wafer into her viewer to access the current password and took note of it.

The door cam showed nobody in the hallway. She pressed the intercom button underneath the viewing screen and said, "Are you out there?"

"Yes," the person said from the other side of the door. "But I'm not stepping in front of the cam and I'm not speaking with you over the intercom. I don't want my image on any feed. I don't want any evidence of this meeting."

"I'm pretty sure nothing is being recorded."

"Pretty sure isn't sure enough."

"All right," Insol said, removing her hand from the intercom. "I'm not opening the door anyway. We can talk like this."

"Fine by me," the person said through the door. "The market for Malrap is always up…"

"…while the Ashtecki have expired so their price goes higher."

"Who writes this crap?"

"I have no idea," Insol said. "Somebody's child murdered in the purge."

"That's dark."

"It's real," Insol said. "State your business."

"I'm the person in the network who responded to your original query for action."

"I assumed we weren't moving forward," Insol said. "After what happened to my contact."

"That person is no longer a danger. His time on this planet has ended with him doing his duty."

So Cerio is dead, Insol thought. *And he didn't give me up or the facility.*

Insol said, "And there are no leaks whatsover."

"None."

"How did you know I was here?"

"My contacts told me you'd returned to Capitol City, and they informed me the minute you arrived back on campus."

"You're eager. You got here quick."

"I fully understand the urgency of the operation," the person said. "After I responded to your initial query and you said you were required to contact the higher-ups, I never heard back from you. I thought the worst. I got back in touch with the network and heard you escaped the purge."

"Barely."

"Barely is better than thousands of others," the person said. "I was informed that the higher-ups liked your plan and they requested direct communication with you, but you were hiding at the Prevor Industries Complex. It was clever to use an intermediary who worked there to establish communication with the higher-ups through a middleman at the Shamban facility."

"You have well-informed contacts."

"I've been involved for a long time," the person said. "Instead of using the drop-off, I thought it'd be more efficient to hand you a wafer with the details the higher-ups requested. I have it here."

"Kind of risky."

"I believe it's worth the reward, and let's say I have an unsuspecting cover and insights into GSS operations."

"It's best to only meet on the day of the operation," Insol said. "Leave the wafer beside the doorway. I'll make sure the higher-ups get it and hopefully they'll approve the operation."

There was no reply.

"Are you there?" She heard the stairwell door at the end of the hallway slam shut. "Are you there?" There was no answer.

Insol opened the door. She peered right, then left down the hall. Nobody was there. A memory wafer lay beside the door. She grabbed the wafer, shut the door, and locked herself in the office.

YOR

Yor was on his back under the control panel, fixing a blown relay that had produced cascading short circuits. During a recent test flight, this problem had caused one of the energy shields to blink out. Yor was tossed around the control room and received a concussion. Had the WAEF been at full throttle, it could've been worse.

Yor was frustrated by the WAEF's never-ending maintenance. He'd begun stripping away the station's metallic walls to create replacement parts with the Industrial Parts Replication Device. He wasn't a metallurgist so he was uncertain whether the materials would meet the necessary standards for the parts to survive the stress of flight. Yor wished more times than he could count that he'd asked Mado specific questions regarding the WAEF's upkeep, but of course his wishes were childish and fruitless. Mado had told him that he had faith in him so Yor did the best he could and hoped for optimum results. That was his only real solace.

The viewing-screen comm buzzed and Yor forgot he was underneath the control panel. He raised his head, banging it hard on one of the horizontal metallic support beams. He saw stars. He lay back down on the floor, took a few deep breaths, and cursed his stupidity. The buzzing continued as he shimmied out from under the panel. When he stood up, he felt like he was going to vomit. He cursed himself again for exacerbating his concussion.

He flipped switches to engage communications, then sat on the floor in front of the viewing screen as a fuzzy image of his mother materialized. Yor leaned forward and hit the side of the screen. The picture came into focus, then he scooted back so his mother could see him.

Yor's mother said, "You don't look well."

"What gave it away?"

"The grime smeared on your face and your pupils are off. Did you take a blow to the head recently?"

"You haven't been a practicing med for years, but you still got it."

"In this case, it's being your mother," she said. "You have to take better care of yourself."

"My living conditions are less than ideal," Yor said. "I don't know how much longer this vessel will be functional. Even though Mado trained me, I'm a scholar not a Space Traveler like him."

"Your experience over the past two decades tells a different story. You've been in space longer than you were scholar."

"How about 'I'm not a spaceship repairman' then?"

Yor's mother chuckled. "Closer to the truth."

"Let's go with that then."

"You do look frayed at the edges."

"Yes, it's just not having contact with…" A wave of dizziness overwhelmed Yor and his head ached.

"I think you have a concussion, dear."

"You think!" Yor could see his mother's reaction to his outburst. She was concerned, and he was being rude. "I'm sorry. Didn't mean it that way."

"No need to apologize. I can relate," Yor's mother said. "You need to take it easy for a few days and put aside the repairs."

"I don't know how Great-grandfather did it. I don't know how he lived by himself for all those years alone on this spaceship. He was made of different stuff from me."

"Your great-grandfather was a unique individual, that's for sure," Yor's mother said. "I don't have a lot of time. I'm calling in reply to your comm."

"Please tell me some good news."

"I don't want to get your hopes up, but I have a few ideas for bringing you home. They aren't fully formulated yet, but I always have you in mind."

"I know," Yor said. "And I'm going on about myself. How are you? You look tired."

"I just returned from the facility and there have been a few concerning complications. I feel like I'm out of practice in dealing with planetary-wide problems, but I'll figure it out."

"You've been dealing with them for the past twenty years, but maybe things are coming to a head," Yor said. "I wish I was there to help."

"You could help me with something."

"Anything."

"Insol is out of control."

"You're going to have to be more specific."

"Insol avoided getting caught in the purge," Yor's mother said. "Then she emotionally abused Ara, beat up Nabo to the point where she broke his nose and put him out of commission for a few days, and her ensuing actions have put the facility at risk. Now she's planning something. It's clear that she's been radicalized."

"She was like that when I met her, but only a few in the Movement agreed with her so she didn't talk about it much."

"I know she was emotionally damaged by the assault before your Breeze Celebration, but something else must have happened to make her like that."

"When we were together, she'd wake up screaming and she never wanted to talk about it, but over the years she told me a few things," Yor said. "Like when she was a young girl in Shamba during the DOME riots. The carpet bombing of the highways was devastating and the authorities in Shamba didn't have the funds to hire the manpower to clear up the roads. Essential goods and medical supplies were blocked from reaching Kuu City. They needed to open the roads as soon as possible or there would've been another disaster—starvation, disease. The authorities knew the Shambans would never volunteer to clean up the Global Assembly's mess so they sent out the military. They rounded up civilians—men, women, children—who were ordered at gunpoint to remove the bodies, dead or barely alive, from the vehicles which were then moved off the road. Insol was forced into a work crew with her family. She was a teenager. I can only imagine the impression that carnage left on her."

"I'd heard about the use of civilian labor to cleanup after the DOME Riots, but since Insol never mentioned it, I assumed she wasn't recruited. I have friends—meds and nurses—who were involved in caring for the survivors of the bombing," Mar said. "I know from what they've told me that as a teenage girl, Insol was exposed to corpses missing limbs or charred to the bone. Innards falling out of body cavities when the corpses were moved. People discovered half-dead who were far beyond saving. They were either put out of their misery or they suffered in screaming agony for days due to lack of pain meds until they passed away."

"Yes," Yor said. "And the workers were forced to load the corpses onto trucks, then unload them into mass graves. She only told me about any of this because when we were discussing the Great Shamban Massacre during the Separatist Revolts, she slipped up and said, 'I've seen that before,' and I pressed her until she told me what happened to her."

"That poor girl," Yor's mother said with tears welling in her eyes. "That explains a lot."

"I'll never forget her telling me how she came across a vehicle where the bodies had been incinerated beyond recognition, but she knew the occupants by the make of the vehicle and its ID tag. She identified her friend burnt to a crisp by a bracelet that Insol had made her. It's been a long while since I last saw her, but before I left, Insol was still wearing the bracelet. Never took it off."

Tears rolled down his mother's face. "How terrible."

"So now you know," Yor said. "We probably shouldn't talk too much longer. We don't want to be detected since I'm still an enemy of the state."

"Yes, we might be pushing it. I meet Carz in nine days and I'll see about changing your status so you can return home."

"How're you going to do that?"

"I plan on discussing us working together to save the Kodan people. Building more ships. Setting the launch dates for the facility spaceships and the Global Assembly ships as a planetary fleet."

"You think that'll go over well? Even after Carz implemented a purge?"

"I have a hunch he wasn't behind it," Yor's mother said. "Anyway, I'll make sure your homecoming is discussed. And you're right, we should probably get off this comm. I love you and hope to hug you soon."

"I love you, too," Yor said, then the screen went dark.

Yor thought about the prospect of returning home. He didn't want to get his hopes up. His head was pounding, and he needed to finish the repairs.

ORN

Orn entered the anteroom at the back of Yor Vander-lord Hall on the Royal University campus, then closed the door behind him, shutting out the buzz of the crowd in the hall. Roneh Rayush was surrounded by four Global Assembly reps dressed in their blue suits with Global Assembly lapel pins. They all stood staring at Orn who smirked at them.

He had tortured—waterboarded, electrocuted, beaten up—all these reps for their vote to support Roneh's Allegiance Watch bill in the Global Assembly Allegiance Committee. When word arrived in the Global Assembly chambers as to why the bill reached the floor for debate after so many years of lying dormant, it passed by a comfortable margin. None of the reps wanted to face what Orn had to offer.

All of them were snide, conniving bullies who used the Assembly to procure what their wealthy constituents desired and a hefty payday for themselves. They had no ethical center and would shift their political position in a heartbeat to stay in power. The average regional Kodan was duped by their broad smiles, their greased-back hair, their warm, soft handshakes, and their lies about obliterating the terrorists lurking in the shadows. Orn despised them. He'd taken pleasure in bringing them pain, but although his actions had fulfilled his deal with Roneh, now he regretted it.

Orn had been blinded by wanting the purge to happen. He'd known unequivocally that his time as the Leader's right-hand man had ended with Vidor's death. He'd also been certain the purge was the way to strengthen the new Leader's position, and that Carz would come around to the idea. So Orn had rushed to team up with Roneh, but she'd played him. She knew Carz would never approve of the purge, and that their subterfuge would ultimately work in her favor.

Orn didn't know how Roneh had done it, but she'd somehow got the new Leader to sign her bill into law. Orn couldn't fathom that Carz didn't understand what he'd introduced into Kodan society with a stroke of his digi-pen. With her new program in place, Roneh became the individual who would lead the Kodan loyalists in their devotion to the Global Assembly. She pulled the strings of their hostility toward the enemies of the state. In this way, Roneh had supplanted the Leader's power.

The reps were still staring at Orn, and they moved closer to Roneh as if they'd be protected by proximity. Orn was filled with rage, catching these reps sucking up to her, so he feigned aggressively moving toward them. A few of them exuded high-pitched shrieks. One chuckled nervously.

Orn burst out laughing, relishing the look of terror on their faces. He said, "I'd like a moment alone with the First Lady."

Roneh grinned and said to the reps, "Why don't you gentlemen take your seats? We'll chat more in the coming days."

Orn opened the door. The noise from the hall filled the room. He scowled at the reps as they made a wide berth around him, scurrying through the doorway into the hall. He slammed the door shut, making sure it hit the last exiting rep in the behind, then said to Roneh, "They're certainly kissing your ass."

"What can I say? You do good work. I don't believe I ever thanked you for your service."

"You've had this planned for a while, haven't you?"

"I don't know what you're talking about."

"You might be able to fool those louts, but I see right through you."

"Maybe, but not soon enough." Roneh turned and peered at herself in the mirror. She lifted a brush off the table in front of the mirror and ran it through her hair, then put it down and applied ultra-red lipstick. She blinked a few times at herself, then searched through the cosmetics bag on the table, removing a small, clear vial and unscrewing the top. She leaned back and held one of her eyelids open with her fingers, releasing a few drops from the vial into her eye. She examined herself in the mirror again and said, "It's awfully dry in this place. Don't you think?"

"Flopsy in the eyeball?"

Roneh observed his reflection in the mirror. "A little pick-me-up. It's been a long day and I deserve it," she said. "It's kind of ironic that I'm giving this speech in Yor Vanderlord Hall, but this was the largest place available on such short notice. If you think about it, it's rather fitting, though."

Orn took a few steps closer to her. He thought about wringing her neck.

Roneh said, "You wanted to discuss something?"

"I already asked you my question."

"And I believe I answered it," Roneh said, then turned to Orn. "How do I look?"

"Like a conniving bitch."

"That wasn't what I was going for, but it'll have to do," Roneh said and chuckled. "I'm glad you're finally up to speed."

"You're not fooling anybody."

"The only fool I see in this room is you," Roneh said, her tone changing to anger. "Vidor Plemso was a fool, too. All those years, he thought he had me under his thumb, allowing me to keep the masses in line for him, but the entire time I was becoming more popular with them. Then he brought me into his family, believing I'd become less of a threat that way, that my followers would attach themselves to his legacy. He grew comfortable in his doddering old age, prepping his son for a job he never wanted and wasn't cut out for. All the while I was working in the wings to consolidate my power. I actually thought you'd figure it out."

"I saw it."

"You say that now, but you had no idea. You were too focused on licking Vidor's boots," Roneh said. "When you came to me about the purge, I couldn't believe my good fortune. It was like everything I'd been planning for years was falling into place. You helped me finish the job. When you were younger, you wouldn't have made the same mistake, but maybe it's time to put you out to pasture."

Orn approached Roneh, reached out with both hands, and wrapped them around her throat. As he tightened his grip, Roneh smiled, lifted up her skirt, then dropped her panties down to her ankles. She leaned back and propped herself up on the table, spreading her legs.

Through her choking, she said, "That's it, baby. That's it. That's how Mama likes it. Now, give it to me." She unzipped Orn's fly and removed his flaccid member. She stared at it for a moment and began laughing.

Orn released his hold, put his limp cock back in his pants, and zipped up his fly.

Roneh lifted her panties back up and examined her neck in the mirror. "Unable to finish the job? I have to say I'm disappointed, but I'm not surprised."

"Now's not the time."

Roneh walked around Orn and opened the door to the hall just enough so she could peek at the crowd.

"You can still join me," Roneh said and shut the door.

"That's not happening,"

"Don't you want to be on the right side of history?"

"We may both be on the wrong side. I have a hunch that the Leader is on to us. He knows what we did."

"Carz? He's as clueless as you, but I'm handling it. I have a patsy in line for the bombing and I've been steering Carz in your direction so he can blame you for the purge."

"I won't let that happen and he won't stand for your impudence much longer."

"You still don't understand the extent of what I've done."

"Your confidence will be your downfall."

"It seems to have been my windfall."

"You don't understand," Orn said. "We need to cover our tracks."

"I'm fine," Roneh said. "Worry about yourself."

"So that's the way it is," Orn said, walking toward the door. "Good to know. You haven't seen the last of me."

"Yes, I look forward to it. Maybe next time you can finish the job. Just make an appointment with my secretary," Roneh said, stepping away from the door. "Now, take a seat, enjoy the pageantry, and don't be such a sore loser. Watch and learn, although you may be too old for new tricks."

Orn wanted to say something in response to this insult, but instead he exited the anteroom and slammed the door behind him. Global Assembly security guards were stationed on either side of the door. They were a visible presence in the hall, protecting the First Lady. The two at the door took note of Orn and one of them said something into his audio implant.

The hall was one of the biggest on campus with a three-thousand-person capacity. Mar Jeps provided the donations that built it. This was a place for daily lectures and visiting speakers. Roneh was a controversial choice for an event, but the Royal University president would never reject a booking by the campus Allegiance Program. The Global Assembly funded the majority of the institution's budget, plus the backlash from the student loyalists would have been disruptive to campus life.

Orn made his way up the staircase, one of two on either side of the seating. Earlier, when Orn arrived, the hall was half-full, but now it was filled to capacity, packed with men, women, and children, and buzzing with conversation.

Many of the spectators wore armbands with "GG" on them and a lightning bolt through the letters. In Allegiance Program parlance, the letters stood for "The Good of the Globe," but the connection with the Global Guard wasn't lost on anybody. When Roneh had originally pitched the armband idea to Vidor Plemso, he was in complete agreement. He'd founded the Global Guard and was thrilled that these citizens saw themselves as the front line against the Global Assembly's foes. At the ceremony unveiling the armband, Vidor had been front and center to give a speech about the armband as a symbol of loyalty to the Global Assembly and how Roneh continued to be a shining example of allegiance to the government.

Halfway up the stairs, Orn observed audience members taking note of him. He had exited the anteroom, so they were wondering who he was in relation to their hero Roneh Rayush. He still valued his anonymity, so he looked away from the crowd and strode faster up the stairs.

Orn thought he would observe the show from the standing-room area at the back of the hall, but it was crowded and he didn't feel comfortable there so he found a place by a viewing-channel cam and its operator along the last row of seats. This event would be broadcast globally in real time. Viewership would be record-breaking. Loyalists were clamoring to hear what Roneh had to say.

Orn felt a tap on his shoulder and a Global Assembly guard told him that he couldn't stand there. Orn showed him his ID and the guard apologized before scurrying away.

Soon, the audience began growing restless. A lectern marked with the Global Assembly symbol stood at center stage. A white banner reading "For the Good of the Globe" in Global-Assembly blue capital letters hung over the back of the stage.

Nine children, around the age of ten, appeared from backstage and lined up in front of the lectern, facing the audience.

A girl in the middle of the lineup who appeared to be the youngest stepped forward in her multicolored Msituan maiden outfit. The crowd quieted. She held up one arm, pointing toward the back of the hall, and yelled at a volume louder than anyone was expecting from such a tiny child, "For the Good of the Globe!" The crowd remained silent, and she yelled out the motto again. Then a few people jumped out of their seats and echoed the sentiment. When she shouted the slogan a third time, half the audience rose and repeated it.

By the fourth time, the entire crowd was on their feet, doing a call-and-response with the child at the top of their lungs. The girl finally curtsied and stepped back. The crowd cheered and roared at the performance, then a boy at the far right wearing a Norian shoreman's outfit took a step forward, cupped his hands around his mouth, and hollered in a booming voice, "For the Good of the Globe!" After three more repetitions of the call-and-response, the boy stepped back and a young girl at the far left in Mlimoan furs repeated the performance, shading her eyes as if she was attempting to see through the glare of the lights. The audience responded the same way. One by one, the young people dressed in the traditional costumes of their regions stepped forward, switching from one end of the line to the other, repeating the routine. The audience was more enthusiastic with each caller. When all the children had their turn, they took a step forward together, rallying the crowd to a feverish chanting of "For the Good of the Globe."

Orn swore the windows on each side of the hall were rattling with the cries of the spectators. An audience member in his twenties wearing a Royal University Allegiance Program T-shirt and a GG armband noticed that Orn wasn't participating. She gave Orn a critical look. Orn glared at her, crossed his hands over his chest to show his scars, and she turned away.

When it felt like the chanting would never end, Roneh stepped out from the anteroom. The audience roared at seeing their idol. She climbed the stairs to the stage and sauntered behind the young girl who had kicked off the event, placing her hands on the girl's shoulders. The audience hushed, waiting for Roneh to speak, then she and the girl and all the other children called, "For the Good of the Globe!" and the entire audience replied at the top of their lungs with ear-piercing volume. At the end of the third rendition of this call-and-response, Roneh held up one hand and waved it with a downward motion. The audience fell silent and sat.

Roneh reached out to the lectern and snatched up the microphone. She kept one hand on the girl's shoulder as four of the children exited stage right and four stage left. "Thank you all for coming," she said into the microphone. "I was only a little older than this wondrous young lady when I first attended Allegiance Camp. How old are you and what's your name?" Roneh placed the mic in front of the girl.

"My name is Ida Fenster. I be seven years old," the girl said in a squeaky voice that hardly matched the clarion cry that had driven the audience to its feet.

"Isn't she incredible? Let's hear it for her."

The audience cheered and Roneh said something into Ida's ear. The girl turned and hugged her. Some in the audience vocalized their awe at this child's show of affection for their high priestess as she ran offstage.

Roneh said, "Children like Ida are the backbone of the Allegiance Program, guaranteeing the good of the globe for the next generation. Am I right?" The crowd cheered while Roneh walked over to the lectern, placed the mic back in its stand, and adjusted it to her height. She wanted to make sure that she would be heard loud and clear by the entire planet.

"In order for us to make it through this crisis, in order for future generations to walk out of the domes into the sunlight and feel the breeze on their faces and breathe the fresh air, we must move toward the future with same goal in mind. How do we attain it? It's simple. We do it by the entire planetary population marching in lockstep, keeping focused on the good of the globe."

The audience called out, "The good of the globe."

"So how do we achieve the population's absolute allegiance to the Global Assembly with unbelievers walking in our midst? That…is your job. You will become part of the new and improved Allegiance Program as members of the Watch. That will begin when you leave this hall.

Your IDs will be scanned, then a digi-pamphlet with instructions on your Watch duties and a special GG armband will be sent to you. A person handpicked by me will contact you via digi-mail. You and this person will go house-to-house, door-to-door, recruiting your neighbors for the Watch by scanning their IDs, and in this manner, create a Watch group in your community, ensuring vigilance in looking out for the good of the Global Assembly.

"Sadly, you'll have neighbors who are uninterested in being loyal to the Global Assembly, or in being part of the Watch. You'll mark these neighbors as dissenters and expert recruiters from the Allegiance Program will be sent to their homes to persuade them to join the Watch and work for the good of the globe."

The audience cried out, "For the good of the globe."

"In this way, we will attain absolute loyalty in all our communities, in all our neighborhoods, among all the citizens in all the domes for the good of the globe."

The audience echoed, "For the good of the globe."

"I have faith that you can do it, and my dear partner, the Leader, believes you can do it, too. He signed off on this project for the good of the globe."

"For the good of the globe," the audience replied.

"Now, unfortunately we've all seen the backlash of the disgruntled disloyal. In the past, the Separatist Revolts brought war and division to this planet. We witnessed the horrors of the DOME riots caused by those who didn't care to follow the righteous path set forth by our dear departed Leader, Vidor Plemso. And we're now living through the repercussions of the catastrophic dome collapses perpetrated by Movement terrorists."

The crowd booed loudly.

"Yes, I'm sure that many of you have lost loved ones in these moments of disloyalty. You've wished bad things upon the people who have committed these hideous acts. Recently, as you may have heard, our Leader took action against the disloyal. It wasn't what any of us would have wished for. I for one had my reservations about…the murder…of men…women…and…children," Roneh said, wiping phony tears from the corners of her eyes. "But the wisdom of the Leader prevails for the good of the globe."

"For the good of the globe."

Roneh sighed and took a deep breath as if she were composing herself. Orn was disgusted by this display. She looked around the audience and spotted Orn. A broad smile spread across her face.

"Sometimes we must do things we regret to make life better for the good of the globe."

"For the good of the globe," the entire crowd responded with enthusiasm.

"I'm confident—and you should be confident, too—that we will persevere through this rough patch in Kodan history for the good of the globe."

"For the good of the globe."

"You will do work that only ordained loyal citizens can do for the good of the globe."

"For the good of the globe."

"You will lead your wayward neighbors down the path of righteousness for the good of the globe."

"For the good of the globe."

"And bring the Kodan people together under the Global Assembly's banner for the good of the globe."

"For the good of the globe."

"You will make the Global Assembly proud for the good of the globe."

"For the good of the globe."

"You will make the Leader proud for the good of the globe."

"For the good of the globe."

"You will make me proud for the good of the globe."

"For the good of the globe."

Then the children walked back onstage and lined up. They began marching in place with Roneh standing behind the young girl again. The entire crowd cheered, rose to their feet, and marched in place while the children led them in chanting, "For the good of the globe…For the good of the globe…For the good of the globe," everyone in the hall voicing their loyalty at the top of their lungs.

Orn pushed his way through the standing and chanting crowd at the back of the hall and exited the building. The door closed behind him and he relished the silence outside like a drowning man filling his lungs with air.

A young woman in her early twenties wearing a GG armband walked up to Orn and asked to scan his ID. Orn smacked the scanner out of her hands and it smashed to the ground. The young woman stared down at the shattered scanner in shock.

Orn strode off. His head was spinning. A coup was unfolding right under his nose. Orn couldn't let it happen. He couldn't let Roneh win. For the good of the globe.

CARZ

"We could mobilize the Global Guard or the Armed Forces and take control of the facility," Tarq Bolonar said as he sat across from Carz on the couch in the Leader's Global Assembly office.

"Let's leave that as an option," Carz said. "I'm meeting with Mar Jeps in a few days. If we're going to build more spaceships, I need her and the workers in that facility. If we infiltrate, we alienate everybody. There will be bloodshed and countless dead and too many people—soldiers, officers, Global Guards, GSS agents—will learn about the place. I don't want knowledge of this facility leaking out. I want its announcement to be a happy one."

"That's wise," Tarq said.

"Can we trust those involved in Cerio Murt's arrest and interrogation to keep quiet?"

"Yes, sir," Tarq said. "Too bad about Murt. Those interrogators were amateur hour and pushed too hard. We should've used Agent Shiv. He's our best interrogator."

"I agree, but I have issues with Orn right now, and I'd like to keep him in the dark about the facility and our current operations."

"Based on the intel I've given you about the bombing and the purge, I understand your concerns. So what's the path forward with him?"

"Let's just say I'm handling it and I'll let you know when I need you."

"I'm curious," Tarq said. "But all right."

Carz said, "Let's focus on security for the Mar Jeps meeting. The press will be there so things can't get out of control."

"I'm on it," Tarq said. "Speaking of things getting out of control, have you heard the disturbing reports about your partner's dome tour? She's recruiting for her Allegiance army and her followers have been terrorizing citizens they deem disloyal."

"Unfortunate," Carz said. "But the new legislation gives her the go-ahead for that circus."

"What made you sign off on it?"

"It's complicated, but I'm handling that as well."

"Sounds like you have a plan in play for Roneh and Orn," Tarq said, moving forward and positioning himself on the edge of the couch's cushion. "But with all due respect, sir, there's a chance that she's becoming more of a threat than you're seeing."

"How so?"

"My sources tell me that she has the ear of the most influential reps in the Global Assembly and the wealthy loyalists. There are GSS agents and officers in the Global Guard who think she understands the way forward better than you do. On top of all that, her popularity in internal polling is twice as high as yours."

"I'm not surprised," Carz said. "She appeals to the lowest common denominators: Hatred and fear."

"Yes, bloodlust is high. I thought your purge would have put it to rest, but it only seems to have fueled it."

"Yes, *my* purge," Carz said bitterly, remembering the corpses stacked in the mine. Since his trip, he dreamed of those people and woke up screaming in cold sweats.

"You all right, sir?"

"No, but I will be," Carz said and straightened himself in his seat. "After this meeting with Mar Jeps, I intend to come clean with the Kodan people about the true state of the domes. I'm hoping to unite them in an effort to leave this wreck of a planet behind."

"We still don't have a destination."

"Let's not get ahead of ourselves," Carz said. "The plan to leave the planet will eliminate Roneh's campaign against the disloyal because it will refocus the people on surviving the crisis instead of terrorizing their neighbors, who will be standing beside them in the same cause. The budget cuts to finance the effort will also defund Roneh's program."

"It's a bold move," Tarq said. "Just let me know how I can help."

"I will, because I'm not sure who I can rely on. After I come clean, Roneh's colleagues will be outraged that I've blown up their agenda, not to mention emptied their coffers."

"Speaking of trust," Tarq said, "how well do you know Glym Atmar? Our security clearance has revealed some red flags."

"He's Davik Atmar's son," Carz said. "I was acquainted with him growing up. He was younger and closer to Minok's age and they were friends. We attended the same military school. I know he had disciplinary issues, and he didn't attend military college or join the forces. I lost touch with him after his father died. Why?"

"Davik Atmar was loyal to your father, but—"

"And put up with my father's abuse for years."

"I wouldn't know about that," Tarq said. "But Glym seems to have been associated with questionable elements in the Movement before he applied for a Global Assembly security job."

"Then how did he get the job?"

"Seems like your father pulled some strings."

"Davik probably asked my father when he was in the right mood."

"That being said, Glym was exemplary in his Global Assembly security job. He received commendations and promotions," Tarq said. "I just thought you should know about his past history."

"Sounds like Glym turned himself around," Carz said. "Since I hired him, he's been doing an outstanding job and my mother and Filo adore him, so I'll vouch for him. Anything else on the agenda?"

"Speaking of which, where's your Chief of Affairs?"

"Minok was rattled by the attack on the estate so he went to Nor to calm his nerves. He was due for a vacation anyway," Carz said. "My father hired him to give him a purpose like getting his dry cleaning and lunch, and I don't really need him around here. Honestly, he has kind of worn out his welcome."

"How so?"

The intercom buzzed. Carz rose from the couch and pressed the button to activate it. "Kel, I told you I didn't want to be disturbed."

"Yes, sir," Kel said, "I know, but Agent Shiv is here and he says it's urgent. You know how he is."

"Yes, I do," Carz said, then deactivated the intercom and turned to Tarq. "You want to be here for this?"

"I'd love to."

Carz reactivated the intercom and said, "Please tell him to come in and continue to hold my calls."

The door slid open. Orn entered and the door closed behind him. He halted when he spotted Tarq.

"You coming in?" Carz said.

"I thought we'd be alone," Orn said. "Your father and I usually spoke alone."

"First, I'm not my father, which seems to be something that I have to keep reminding you of. Second, whatever you have to say to me you can say in front of your superior."

Orn continued walking into the room until he was standing in front of the couches.

Carz said, "What's of such grave importance that you're interrupting me?"

"It's a sensitive subject, sir," Orn said. "I'm not sure if it's appropriate to discuss with others present."

Tarq said, "I can leave."

Even with his father gone, Orn was still feared and considered above the GSS hierarchy. Carz said, "Hum me a few bars."

Orn said, "Excuse me, sir?"

Tarq chuckled.

Orn appeared confused.

Carz said, "Sorry, I forgot you have no sense of humor. I mean, give me an idea of what you want to talk about and I'll decide whether the Head Director needs to leave or not."

Orn said, "It's in regard to your partner's activities. I just attended one of her rallies."

"You mean how she seems to be angling for a power grab," Carz said. "The Head Director and I were just discussing it and I believe I've got it covered."

"Do you sincerely understand the depths of her duplicity?" Orn said. "I have a solution for how to stop her."

Tarq said, "Why don't you file a detailed report on what you think is happening and we'll take it from there?"

Orn said, "File a report?" He was appalled at the request.

Carz said, "With all his years of service, I think we owe it to Agent Shiv to hear him out."

Orn peered at Tarq and crossed his scarred hands over his chest. An awkward moment of silence ensued.

"Yes," Tarq said. "Go right ahead, Agent Shiv."

Orn dropped his arms to his sides and looked at Carz. "Would you care to tell me your plan first?"

Carz wasn't going to show his hand, but it was interesting that Orn wanted to see his cards. "No, you go first."

"All right," Orn said, clearing his throat. "We eliminate her."

Tarq said, "Eliminate her?"

"Disappear her," Orn said. "The best solution would be pushing her out of a dome emergency exit hatch, or her office window would work as well."

Carz chuckled nervously. "You realize that no matter how hideous she might be, she's the mother of my child?"

"Yes, sir," Orn said. "I don't mean to be out of line, but your father created a monster."

Carz thought, *You would know.* "Please elaborate."

"She's power hungry. She doesn't respect you and she wants to fill the vacuum left by your father's death. Her followers worship her, which makes her truly dangerous, and she sees herself as the rightful person to lead the Kodan people."

Carz said, "I won't let that happen. My plan—"

"It's already happening, sir," Orn said. "This program has empowered her. She now has the following of loyalists planetwide who she can call into action at any moment. The coup is in progress."

Tarq said, "He's right, sir. We need to put more resources on watching her. We'd have to find agents who haven't fallen for her act."

Carz said, "Orn, I'm glad you came by, although I notice you still haven't looked into Roneh's involvement in the bombing and those viewing-channel execs."

"I've…been busy."

"Yes," Carz said. "The Shamba thing, but I assigned you the Roneh task a while ago and you haven't scratched the surface."

Tarq said to Orn, "I never asked how you figured out the Shamba thing."

Carz said, "My father kept him around for a reason."

"Thank you, sir."

"Your first priority is keeping an eye on Roneh," Carz said. "Let me know of any further developments. The way you're talking I'm almost positive that she was involved in the attack on the estate. I want you to find out who was working with her inside the GSS. It must've been someone close to my family."

Orn said, "I'd rather lead with my idea, sir."

"I bet you would, but that would erase the knowledge of whoever was working with her. Wouldn't it?"

Tarq said, "That's a good point."

Carz said, "We can keep your idea as fallback. I'll let you know. Dismissed."

Orn saluted, turned, and left the room.

Tarq waited for the door to slide closed and said, "Do you think he knows what's coming?"

"He doesn't have a clue, but I'll make him useful in the meantime."

MAR

The Prevor Industries cruiser landed at the Plemso estate and powered down its engines. Viewing-channel reporters and their cam operators and digi-media correspondents rushed toward the craft and were contained in two roped-off areas on either side of the path that led to the estate's forest.

Suron sat to Mar's right in the cruiser and said, "Look at those vipers."

"Just walk ahead of me and look pretty," Mar said. "I'll deal with them."

"Better you than me."

The Leader had requested a well-publicized meeting with Mar. Although she hated dealing with the media, she had become adept at it over the years. Ara was told by the Leader's receptionist that Mar should stick to the talking point: She and the Leader were discussing the future of technological cooperation between the Global Assembly and Prevor Industries. Mar agreed to the cover story. Carz had digi-mailed her about the air circulators, but she had an idea of the meeting's true points of discussion due to Suron's contacts and her own plan.

Mar said, "I'm good to go."

Suron leaned forward and said to the pilot, "Be prepared to leave at a moment's notice. Keep the comm channels open."

"Yes, sir," the pilot said.

Suron placed a finger behind his ear, activating his audio implant, and said, "Prepare for departure." The guard to Mar's left and the three guards seated behind her prepared to disembark. Unlike the summit with Vidor Plemso two decades ago, these men weren't armed with stun rifles. Instead, they carried the latest Prevor Industries sidearm, which delivered the same wallop as those stun rifles. Like that meeting long ago, the Global Assembly didn't possess these weapons, either.

Suron said, "Let's go."

All the cruiser doors on the side furthest from the media slid open, except for the pilot's, and Suron and his guards exited. Mar admired their disciplined precision. She had argued for less manpower, but she acquiesced to Suron's reasoning that after the bombing, they shouldn't trust estate security.

Suron walked to the front of the cruiser and assessed the people jockeying for position behind the ropes. Two of the guards stood in front of the open door that Suron had exited, and the other guards from the backseat blocked the remaining entry. They all wore green Prevor Industries coveralls with the company logo over their right breast.

Mar awaited Suron's signal. She observed the reporters, salivating for their scoop. All their cams were pointed at the cruiser to catch the instant she stepped out. Suron was taking his time examining the crowd. Over the past few years, he had become more cautious in guarding her. She wondered if he had lost faith in his skills as he was getting older. He made comments about retirement, but she presumed he'd tell her when he felt that a younger man could do his job better.

Finally, Suron turned, peered inside the cruiser, and waved at Mar to come out. Mar slid across her seat and exited the cruiser on the side where Suron was posted, walking up behind him.

"Ready or not," she said to Suron and she headed toward the path between the two roped-off areas. Suron and his guards fanned out around her.

Digi-cams clicked, vidcams whirred, and reporters bunched up behind the ropes, firing questions. Mar had decided beforehand that she'd answer three questions, then proceed to the estate. The reporters were shouting all at once.

Mar called out, "One at a time—you?" She pointed to a well-known viewing-channel reporter. She had blonde hair down to her shoulders and wore a Global-Assembly blue dress with plenty of cleavage showing. She'd recently had plastic surgery on her face and it looked like it might be difficult for her to speak.

"Beb Sween from *Capitol City Edition*. Can you tell us the agenda for your meeting with the Leader?"

"I'm glad you asked that question, Beb. We'll be discussing how the Global Assembly and Prevor Industries can work together so the Kodan people will survive the crisis no matter what the future holds."

Beb said, "What does the future hold? Should the Kodan people be concerned?"

"The future is always uncertain," Mar said. "At Prevor Industries, we attempt to make it manageable for everyone."

Again, the reporters yelled their questions simultaneously.

"You?" Mar said, pointing to a familiar face in the viewing-channel pantheon. He was renowned for his horrible comb-over of dyed red hair. He was wearing a grey suit, a white shirt, and an orange tie with blue polka dots.

"Gat Renzo, *Kodan One News*. There have been reports that the Leader has called this meeting to heal the division between Prevor Industries and the Global Assembly since you and the late Leader had a contentious relationship."

"Is there a question?"

"Is this meeting to produce a reconciliation between your corporation and the planetary government?"

"The well-being of the Kodan people has always been Prevor Industries' first priority. In any relationship, misunderstandings occur, but we've always been able to work for the good of the globe, as some would say. One more question. You there?" Mar pointed to a young male reporter about Yor's age when he left the planet. He wore a white button-down shirt, blue pants, and military boots.

"Milt Marb, G-squared media. Why have you kept the family name of your partner who was a traitor to the Kodan people?"

Mar said, "If you've ever been in love, you'll know why." While she strode between the ropes smiling and waving to the cams, the reporters continued to call out questions. When Mar was well past the cacophony, she stopped with Suron beside her.

"That was weird and infuriating," Mar said to Suron.

"I thought it went well," Suron said.

"Sure, I guess that covers it, too."

Suron chuckled. "You're through that gauntlet. Onward to the next."

A man approached them. He looked familiar, but Mar couldn't place him.

Suron told the guards flanking Mar to fall back. The two guards in front of her repositioned themselves a step behind Mar. The guards in the rear took a few steps back as well.

The man stopped in front of Mar and Suron. He wore the usual outfit for an executive guard: Global-Assembly blue suit jacket, blue pants, white shirt, and blue tie with a Global-Assembly pin designated for executive guards on the lapel. "Greetings, Mar Jeps. I'm Glym Atmar, Head of Security. I'm here to show you to the Leader. It's a pleasure to meet you."

"Atmar. Are you—?"

"Yes, you knew my father."

"I see the resemblance now. I was fond of your father. He was kind to me when I was new to…this world."

"He always had nice things to say about you as well."

"That's good to hear since he couldn't say anything like that in front of Vidor—the Leader, I mean."

"My mother appreciated the blossoms you sent to his funeral."

"I—" Suron said.

"Colonel," Glym said and snapped to attention. "It's an honor to meet you. My father spoke of you and Commander Warver with reverence."

Suron cleared his throat. The old warrior was feeling sentimental. "I was fond of him as well," Suron said, then cleared his throat again and collected himself. "We shouldn't keep the Leader waiting."

"I agree," Glym said. "Shall we?" He turned and began walking ahead of them.

As they moved forward, the guards kept their formation.

Mar said, "You're not using the cart?"

"That thing was crushed and destroyed in the bombing," Glym said, not turning around.

"That's too bad," Mar said. "It was one of the last remnants of the Vanderlord estate. Riding in it brought back fond memories."

"Good riddance," Glym said with disdain in his voice. "I'm glad it's gone."

Mar didn't know what to say to that.

As they passed beneath the estate's forest canopy and silence fell over the procession, Mar listened for the winged creatures overhead squawking at the intrusion into their territory. She breathed in the scent of the blossoms in the underbrush where critters scattered away from their footsteps on the path. She savored the moment since there was nothing like this place left anywhere else on the planet.

Mar had visited the estate many times over the past twenty years as part of her agreement with Vidor to attend executive functions. At the beginning, she hated having to be cordial and stand beside the person who ordered Rajer's death, but as time passed, when she appeared at Vidor's functions, she got over her remorse by reminding herself how she'd bested him.

Emerging from the forest, Mar was stunned by the scene in front of her. She had seen it on viewing channels, but in person, it was shocking. The mansion's terrace was gone. Charred debris jutted out of a dumpster. The restoration had already begun, but only half of the mansion's façade was covered with new siding. The other half was adorned with a tarp and scaffolding. In the middle of the three-story façade was a Global Assembly flag which covered the doorway that once led into the mansion from the terrace. The ceremonial hanging of this flag was considered a mark of defiance against the people who perpetrated the violence.

Bare mounds of dirt encircled where the terrace once stood. They had been flower beds, containing blossoms from around the planet, filling the air with magnificent odors. Now, the air smelled of the terrace's burned rubble.

Glym stopped on the path, halfway between the forest and the mansion. He pointed to his right and said, "This way." A stone-slab trail led off the path to the middle of the estate's lawn where a platform had been built. Flomina was seated there in a wheelchair beside a round table surrounded by chairs. There was a blue tent behind the platform.

Suron ordered two of his men to station themselves where they stood now, then he and the other two followed as Glym led Mar down the path. Carz appeared, stepping up onto the platform from behind it. He stood beside his mother, smiling. He was dressed casually in a light-blue button-down shirt and dark-blue pants. Mar caught the smell of frying meats. Over the years, that was one of the other reasons she hadn't minded coming here. The food was spectacular, and she never ate that way at home.

At the foot of a ramp leading up to the platform, Glym said, "Have a pleasant dinner. It's nice meeting you,

Colonel Suron, and it's an honor, Mar Jeps. I wanted to say that I respect how much you and your corporation have done for the people of this planet."

Carz said, "You're weakening my negotiating position, Glym."

"Sorry, sir."

"I'm kidding, Glym. I'm kidding," Carz said. "Welcome Mar Jeps. Please join us. You can see we're doing some redecorating." He pointed toward the mansion.

"I'm sorry to see it," Mar said. "It's a shame. And I'm sorry to see you've been injured, Flomina."

"I'm mending fine," Flomina said. "Spare me your sanctimonious sympathy."

Carz chuckled nervously. "You know my mother's famous sense of humor. I apologize."

"Carz, don't apologize for me," Flomina said. "Mar knows that I say what I mean."

"I certainly do," Mar said. "I hope you received my condolences for the death of your partner and your father."

"Yes," Carz said, "we received your note and your flowers. That was kind of you."

Flomina guffawed, then said, "You never liked the man. Your note and flowers were a farce."

Glym said, "Would you like anything else before I go, sir?"

"Yes," Carz said. "My mother appears tired. Take her to her room. I'll have dinner brought up to her."

Glym walked up the ramp and behind Flomina, disengaging the wheelchair brake.

Flomina said, "Why are you doing this, Carz?"

"I told you to behave yourself. This meeting is important, but you don't seem capable of self-restraint."

"I didn't know being honest was a lack of self-restraint."

"In your case it is," Carz said. "Glym, please wheel my mother away."

Glym pushed the wheelchair around the table and down the ramp to where Mar was standing.

Mar said, "Good night, Flomina. Always a pleasure."

"If you gained pleasure from my remarks, then I'm losing my touch."

Mar said, "Take it from me, you haven't."

Flomina shot Mar a dirty look before Glym wheeled her down the stone path.

Carz said, "Sorry about that."

"It's all right. We've all known each other a long time, Carz…sorry, I meant Leader."

"You're right," Carz said, "we've known each other since I was a child and I see no reason to stand on ceremony when we're alone."

"Fine by me," Mar said.

"What do you think, Suron?" Carz said.

"Whatever pleases you, sir."

"I see you brought plenty of men with you."

"No disrespect, sir. Protecting Mar Jeps is my primary concern."

"My father always said you were the best strategist he ever met," Carz said. "Of course, he'd only admit it when he had a few Malraps in him. You obviously do your job well. Looking at what happened here, I wish I had more men like you so carry on. Mar, please join me."

Mar climbed the ramp. She could hear sizzling from a grill inside the tent, and the scent of frying meats grew stronger. Suron positioned his men on either side of the platform and stood at the bottom of the ramp.

Mar said, "That's a smell I haven't experienced in quite some time."

"Oh yes, I didn't even notice. I'm spoiled. I hope you like it," Carz said, pulling out a chair for Mar who seated herself. "I had the kitchen brought here. This will be more private. I don't know who to trust these days."

Mar assumed his last sentence referred to Roneh. "Will your partner be joining us?"

"No," Carz said with a hint of disdain in his voice. "She's attending one of her rallies in Mlimoa."

That's when Mar understood they were eating away from the building to keep their distance from Roneh's spies in the household. "That's fine by me…and you, apparently."

"Are my feelings that transparent?" Carz said, seating himself across from Mar. "Let's just say we don't see eye to eye on how I should run the planet, and it's best that she's not here."

"I appreciate your candor," Mar said. "How are your brother and son, by the way?"

"Minok is on an extended holiday in Nor. He went there after the bombing for his nerves," Carz said. "I'll be visiting him soon."

"Say hello to him for me."

"Filo is with his mother. He misses her when she's gone, and she enjoys his company," Carz said. "He is incredible."

Mar said, "They are wondrous at that age."

"Indeed. I don't think I could love anybody more. He is one of the reasons I asked you here," Carz said, then called out toward the tent, "We're ready for beverages now."

A waiter ascended the stairs at the rear of the platform carrying a tray laden with crystal glasses and pitchers of Eglew juice, Malrap, and water. The waiter placed glasses in front of Mar and Carz.

Carz said, "Anything you fancy?"

"Maybe a half-glass of Eglew juice."

"I remembered you liked it."

"Some water, too, please."

The waiter removed another glass from the tray, placed it in front of Mar, and poured her drinks, then served a glass of water for Carz.

"Water?" Mar said. "No Malrap? Your father was partial to it."

"Yes," Carz said. "After I became Leader, I fell down that well for a while."

"It has to be a big change."

"Indeed it is, and I decided if I was going to achieve my goals, then I needed to be clear-headed," Carz said. "And before I forget, thanks for agreeing to regenerate the power in the Capitol City dome. We can't do without those air circulators."

"You're welcome. To a productive meeting," Mar said, raising her glass of Eglew juice and Carz did the same with his glass of water, then they each took a sip. "I was thrust into being responsible for the lives of others so I can relate to your position. My biggest lesson was learning that trouble comes out of nowhere when you least expect it, and it doesn't get any easier."

"I'm beginning to understand that."

"On a planetary scale, the real trick is actually being responsible for everybody, not just one particular group, isn't it?" Mar said, taking another sip. "Your father didn't see it that way, and I'm concerned you may feel the same because of your purge."

As Mar was making her statement, Carz was gulping some water and it went down the wrong pipe. He broke out into a nonstop cough. The waiter and one of the executive guards appeared at the sides of the table. Carz put down his glass of water, then lifted his arms to keep the prospective rescuers at bay and said, "I'm fine. I'm fine."

Both the waiter and guard retreated from the platform.

Carz finally composed himself and said to Mar, "My father always said you were a straight shooter."

"That's one of the things he hated about me."

Carz swallowed the remaining water in the glass. "He despised being challenged, and you certainly kept him on his toes. The purge was the last thing my father signed off on before he died, but I take full responsibility for failing to stop it. I will never forgive myself, but my administration must look forward. Let me be clear. I'm not my father. I brought you here because I know you're aware of the dire condition of the domes."

"How would I know that?" Mar decided to bluff. There was no reason to give up her decades-long advantage.

"Because you have contacts within GACE and you've been reviewing their reports on the domes for years," Carz said. "When GACE's leak was uncovered, people inside the GSS were too scared to tell my father. Turns out Agent Shiv told him. I guess my father wanted to hold off on telling you he knew so you could read about the end coming nearer until his spaceships were ready for launch. And I quote, 'Leaving you behind to die with all the other traitors.'"

"Sounds like him."

"He did have a sadistic side."

Mar finished off her juice and said, "So did you bring me here to continue your father's sadism?" Mar thought she knew the answer, but she wanted to hear it from him.

Carz said, "More juice?"

"Not at the moment," Mar said, raising her full water glass. "This will suffice for now."

"I'll have more water."

The waiter appeared with his tray, poured the drink, then said, "Dinner will be served shortly."

Carz said, "I'll let you know when we're ready." Then he said to Mar, "Where were we?"

"Sadism," Mar said and drank down half her glass of water.

"Right," Carz said. "We both know the domes have maybe ten years before critical failure. Unlike my father, in the years we have left, I want to ensure that I save as many Kodans as possible, loyal or not to the Global Assembly, by building as many spaceships as possible. I want to unify the Kodan people behind saving themselves."

"How do you propose to make that happen?"

"My plan will call on the Global Assembly to minimize all nonessential spending. The wealthy will be taxed on past earnings, and those complicit in the abysmal construction of the domes will be asked to return a large percentage of the trillions they robbed from the Kodan people. The GSS has seized records proving these corporations knew their work was substandard so they could maximize profits," Carz said. "With those funds and your corporation's know-how in space-travel technology, we can mobilize to build spaceships on a massive scale to save every Kodan. The people will be called upon to take part in all aspects of the construction effort to save themselves and their families. I plan on giving a planetary speech that outlines the entire plan to unify the Kodan people behind the effort. Since I didn't give a speech upon my ascension, this will be my keynote to the planet. I also plan on taking responsibility for the purge and I will promise the arrest of the people behind it. I understand the people won't follow my lead unless I clear up this black mark on my record. That's the size of it. What do you think?"

"You realize this will mean telling the Kodan people the truth about the past—that your father lied to them all those years about the environment. Tarnishing his legacy," Mar said. "So why do it? If you leave Koda in the Global Assembly spaceships, then you and your loyal followers can write history the way you see fit."

"That's my father's style," Carz said. "I have to live with myself. I can't look my son in the eye and justify such heinous actions. I'd rather my son be proud of me for being a true leader."

"I have to say, I'm impressed."

"I was hoping to claim your support in the speech," Carz said. "With the global goodwill that Prevor Industries and the Relief Foundation have fostered in making life better for the Kodan people, we can give the effort a legitimacy that will go a long way toward lining people up behind our efforts."

"After the speech, I'd be delighted to make a statement endorsing the course you've laid out, but until then, I find it difficult to back a man whose government murdered hundreds of thousands of innocents," Mar said. "You need to take responsibility for your government's actions."

"As I said, that's my plan."

"Wonderful," Mar said. "Give your speech. Take responsibility without using me as a crutch for your unification plan. That will help gain my trust and that of the people who work with me. Afterward, I'd be happy to go on *The Lure* and give you my endorsement."

"I know my father made it so you'd never trust him or the Global Assembly. I was hoping you wouldn't see my father in me," Carz said. "It's sad, actually."

"I don't see it as sad. I see it as realistic. Your father was a master at cloaking his deceit with a veil of honesty and goodwill, and I don't intend on ever falling for it again."

"You sit there all high and mighty," Carz said. "And it's sad, because my father made you into a dishonest person."

"How's that?"

"While my father had you building his spaceships, you did what you needed to do behind his back and got away with it. I can't blame you. I would've done the same myself."

"I have no idea what you're talking about," Mar said, drinking down the rest of the water in her glass and setting it on the table.

"Come on," Carz said, slamming the palm of his hand on the table, knocking over the empty glasses.

Mar righted her toppled glasses. It seemed like a little of his father was emerging. Suron gave Mar a concerned look.

Carz stared at his glass lying on its side in front of him, then set it upright and said, "Please excuse my outburst. You know...when I found out about your spaceship construction facility in Shamba, I thought, this woman is brilliant. I mean, Mado Prevor set it all up, according to my prisoner, but I admired the fact that you absconded with all those resources, that you constructed spaceships, that you kept it going and kept it secret all these years. I was hoping you'd come clean with me when I told you my plans. I've even kept your secret from the elements in my government who would want your efforts destroyed and you executed for sedition."

Mar looked over at Suron who tilted his head seeking some sort of cue for action. She shook her head at him.

Carz said, "She's fine, Suron. She can leave whenever she wants, but she knows the discussion just got real."

CARZ

Mar said, "Can I get more water? Oh, screw it, I'll have some Malrap." She peered over at Suron again.

Carz said to Mar, "Would you two like to confer on your beverage choice, too?"

Mar chuckled nervously. "Don't be silly. I'll have a half-glass of Malrap and more water."

Carz pushed his chair away from the table and stood. It felt good to stretch his legs. He tended to hold tension there. "I'll be right back, and I'll tell the waiter your order." He descended the stairs into the tent and the strong smell of barbecued meats. He was hungry.

The estate's chef was leaning against the preparation table where trays of entrées, meats and side dishes lay. He threw up his hands in disgust. "My work is getting cold."

"I don't need your temperamental crap right now," Carz said, then felt a twinge of guilt at taking his anger out on the chef. "Please put out an appetizer." He told the waiter to bring a half-glass of Malrap and two glasses of water, then he walked to the back of the tent where his viewer sat on a small table with a guard watching over it. The guard snapped to attention and Carz said, "At ease." He tucked the viewer under his arm and returned to the table.

When Carz climbed the stairs onto the platform, Mar was slugging down the Malrap. Her face scrunched up at the taste, then she put down the empty glass and drank half the full glass of water. A tray of fried tubers filled with pickled vegetables sat on a tray in the middle of the table.

"Would you like more Malrap?" Carz said as he seated himself and pushed in his chair.

"No, thank you," Mar said. "Been awhile since I drank any and now I remember why."

Carz activated his viewer and said, "Nevertheless, I hope it hit the spot."

"It definitely hit something."

"Good to hear. That isn't Yorlik's batch. That was consumed long ago, but it's the best on the planet." On his viewer, Carz opened up a foto of Cerio Murt strapped to a chair during his interrogation. He was naked except for soiled white underwear. Over seventy-five percent of his skin was black-and-blue and his eyes were swollen shut.

Carz turned the screen toward Mar and she gasped.

Carz said, "Horrible, isn't it? He was captured outside of your facility in Shamba. My men attempted to reason with him, but like any person who harbors hate in their heart and has something valuable to hide, he wouldn't tell us the truth without coaxing."

"You call that coaxing? I'm glad you brought out an example of why I can't trust a man like you."

"Three of my agents were killed attempting to appre-hend him and those agents had families. That wasn't a man who deserved to be treated with kid gloves."

Mar sighed and said, "Please close it. I'm not surprised at any of this in a culture where violence is endemic."

Carz reached forward and closed the viewer.

Mar picked up the empty Malrap glass and attempted to obtain whatever drops remained.

"I can get you some more, Mar. No reason to stand on ceremony."

"I shouldn't," Mar said. "Maybe we need to start this conversation from the beginning."

"I agree. I want you to be fully aware of what I know and what I'm willing to do in order to reach my goal… *our* goal."

"I'm all ears."

"I'll try not to repeat myself," Carz said. "To start, I know in the place your people call the 'facility,' you have twenty-seven ships completed and eight approaching functionality."

"More like fifteen."

"All right, fifteen. I know at any one time you have three to five thousand workers and techs laboring around the clock, day and night shifts. I had my people do an audit on the construction of the two Global Assembly spaceships designated XAF-758. They concluded that Prevor Industries—Mado and yourself—overcharged my father on everything from building the base where the construction took place to the screws mounting the toilets to the deck, then it continued with the satellites. My father wanted those projects completed and the budget was coming from a covert fund, so he didn't care about cost. I'm assuming that's how you paid for your facility and its ships. Although the Prevor Relief Foundation has done amazing work to keep outer-Kodans alive, and I thank you for undoing my father's malfeasance and neglect, the prisoner told us that the Foundation was used as cover for smuggling tech into Shamba.

"If you refuse to work with me, you leave me no choice. Once the fact of the facility's existence leaks out to the public—and it will—I'll have to seize it. I assume many of your workers will find the change in ownership distasteful. The facility and ships will be severely damaged in a battle over its control, and many will die on both sides. You know how heavy-handed the military can be. I'd have to arrest you and the people who run the facility. If I didn't take control of the facility and make arrests, there's no way I'd be allowed to keep ruling and save the majority of the people.

"I could attempt to refurbish the facility, but the damage caused by fighting over its control will probably make it impossible to do so. Say I salvage half the ships, I'd still need to build more. In my father's sense of unethical clarity, he had the spaceship blueprints, the science, and the entire construction process for XAF-758 stolen from under your nose."

"I'm not surprised."

"But the XAF site wasn't meant for a planetary endeavor. There's no time to construct a better site so there would be no way to build enough ships to save every Kodan with planetary resources running low and time running out. Therefore, only a portion of the population will survive on the ships available.

"The easier solution is working in concert. I can supplement your efforts and supply resources hoarded for the domes and we can leave Koda sooner than later, saving every Kodan. Now tell me what you're thinking about what I just said."

Mar was looking off into the distance at the forest. She picked up her glass of water and drank down what remained, then said, "Well, you've—"

Crashing and screaming emanated from the tent. Suron and his men drew their weapons. Suron jumped onto the platform and stood between Mar and the tent. There was more banging and yelling, then Karanga leapt onto the platform and onto the table. Carz was startled and pushed back his chair. Karanga scurried up to the edge of the table in front of Carz, stood on his hind legs, and chittered at him. The waiter jumped onto the platform with a meat cleaver in his hand.

Suron pointed his weapon at the waiter and said, "Drop it!"

The waiter released a high-pitched scream and dropped the cleaver, which clanked onto the platform, and threw his hands into the air.

Karanga was alarmed by this racket and raced around the entire circumference of the table, ending up where he started in front of Carz, chittering at him again.

Suron holstered his weapon and said, "Stand down," to his people.

Carz eased himself toward the table, then reached over Karanga who stayed in place and watched Carz's arm as it passed over him. Carz picked up a tuber and held it out to Karanga. "Would you like one, buddy?"

Karanga stood up on his hind legs and extended his front paws.

Carz looked over at Mar who was staring at Karanga in amazement. She said, "Please don't keep your friend waiting."

Almost on cue, Karanga chittered and jogged in place. Mar giggled.

Carz moved the tuber toward Karanga who grasped it and placed it in his mouth, then jumped down to the platform and darted across the lawn into the forest.

Carz said, "That would be our entertainment for the evening."

Mar said, "As you were, Suron."

"That was…odd," Suron said, jumping off the platform to his station.

"That was marvelous," Mar said. "What was that?"

"More like who was that," Carz said. "That's my mother's friend, Karanga."

"Karanga," Mar said. "He is a cute little guy…or girl. I didn't know your mother kept such a diverse group of friends."

"She never ceases to astonish me." Carz turned to the waiter who was still holding up his hands. "Don't tell the chef that I gave some of his culinary masterpiece to the creature, but do tell him that I promise he can serve the main course shortly, and I apologize for the delay."

"Yes, sir." The waiter dropped his hands, picked up the cleaver, and hurried into the tent.

Mar said, "Maybe you are different from your father. Caring about the chef's feelings. The way you dealt with Karanga. No offense, but your father would have squashed him."

"No offense taken," Carz said. "He would have done exactly that and then set traps for Karanga's entire family."

Mar laughed and Carz laughed with her. He noticed Suron chuckling as well.

Suron said, "It's funny because it's true."

Carz said to Mar, "You were going to say something before we were so cutely interrupted."

"Yes," Mar said. "You've laid out a compelling argument for working together and if I'm completely honest, I came here to see if we could make that happen, too."

"Do we have a deal, then?"

"I see now why you called the media here. Very clever," Mar said. "Based on everything you've said and what I've seen here this evening, I believe we can work out an arrangement, but this purge issue is still a big problem for me and it will be for many Kodans."

"I told you—"

"Please listen," Mar said. "I'm pretty convinced that I can work with you now, but in order for us to take the first public steps together, I need to wait until you admit your failure in allowing the purge to happen and outline your investigation strategy. Understand it from my perspective. I can't attempt to convince the workers in the facility to join you before you give the speech. It would be counterproductive because it would look like I've sided with the enemy and they might stop trusting me. If you say we're working together in the speech, they'll feel like I made a deal behind their backs.

"After the speech where you accept responsibility, I can go to them and take the pulse of their reaction, then figure out how we can move forward together. I know it's not much different from what I said before we were interrupted. I know it seems like splitting hairs. I should have explained this earlier, but honestly, I wasn't sure how much you knew about the facility, and I wasn't convinced I could trust you. I'm confident now that we can work toward our common goals for the Kodan people. The speech is just part of the process now. A formality. I'm already onboard.

"In the meantime, let's chat about the details of this arrangement over dinner. I'm famished."

Carz thought, *Thank you, Karanga.*

WHEN HIS MEETING WITH MAR JEPS ENDED, CARZ went directly to the study and locked himself in. Roneh would be home soon, and he didn't want to be disturbed. Carz felt like he was on the way to turning the page from the selfish behavior that had dominated this room and this house for decades.

He sat in an armchair staring at the empty space on the wall where his grandfather's portrait had once hung. He had taken it down and turned it to face the wall by the garbage can. Carz thought about his father growing up in this house with no one to teach him a different way of behaving, and with his current deal in place with Mar Jeps, his mother was indirectly the savior of the Kodan people. Many times during his childhood, she'd stood between Carz and his father's beatings. She'd shown Carz that there were less hostile, more compassionate ways of resolving conflicts. There was a portrait of his mother hanging in his father's trophy room that would be perfect in that space and it only seemed fitting.

There was a flurry of knocks on the door and the person outside tried to open it, but came up against the lock. It could only be Roneh. The knocking continued. He waited, thinking that she'd tire of it, but he was deluding himself.

Roneh said, "Open this door now, Carz. I know you're in there." She began banging on the door again and attempting to open it.

Carz laughed at Roneh's frustration and tenacity. She was a bully like his father. Carz wondered, as he had so many times before, whether his father had foisted this woman on him as a punishment.

"Carz, open up," Roneh said. "You know I can do this all night."

"As much as I'd like to see you do that," Carz said, "go away. We'll speak in the morning."

"I'm sure you'll find a way to avoid me then, too, but you know what?" Roneh said. "Maybe I have you where I want you."

"You mean at the moment or in general?"

"Both," Roneh said and banged on the door once more. "Why would you meet with the mother of that terrorist?"

"Can't you just be happy with your rally tonight and go away?"

"I know what you're planning."

"Really?" Carz didn't want to say any more because that's what she wanted.

"Yes, I do."

"Why don't you tell me?"

"Open the door so we can talk like adults," Roneh said.

"Like adults? That'd be a first."

"Or has this relationship fallen into childishness?"

"I think we've gone lower, but how about this?" Carz said, rising from the armchair and walking toward the door. "You tell me what I'm planning, and if you're right, I'll open the door." The silence from the other side was enough to convince him that she was bluffing. "I'm waiting."

Then Roneh began banging nonstop on the door with her fist.

Carz seated himself in an armchair facing away from the door.

"Ouch," Roneh cried out and the banging stopped. "I hurt myself. Please help me."

"Is that the best you can do?"

"You don't care."

"Comm the executive med to come and look at you."

Roneh groaned, then let out a scream of frustration. "I want to know why Mar Jeps was here."

"Go away," Carz said. "You'll find out soon enough."

There was one more hit to the door and Roneh said, "Why are you being this way?"

"What way?"

"Acting like an ass."

"Is that what I'm doing? I guess I should do it more often because I'm enjoying myself."

"If you're going to be this way, I'll find out on my own."

"Please do."

"This isn't over."

"Knowing you, my dear, of that I have no doubt."

"By the way, I had some information for you about the bombing, but you can't have it now."

Carz was certain this was a ploy, so he said, "Talk about childishness."

Roneh kicked at the door, then there was the sound of her stomping down the hallway into the distance.

Carz slouched in the chair. He was certain he hadn't heard the last of it, but it was clear to him that she had no idea what he was planning, which was exactly how he wanted it. He didn't know how she'd react when the reality of his actions came to bear on her, but he assumed that banging on the door would be nothing compared to the tirade she would unleash.

He noticed Roneh had slid an envelope under the door.

INSOL

Insol was walking across the campus, carrying her viewer case. She had finished teaching a class and was headed for her regular office hours. She had worked here for over twenty years and since the day she arrived, she'd felt like she belonged and that she was blessed to be here.

This was her home. She knew it well and was aware when something was out of the ordinary, like now. She was headed toward a man up ahead standing off the path, observing her. He was dressed like a student, but he held himself like someone with military training. As she approached him, he activated an audio implant and spoke. She decided to leave the path and take a circuitous route to her office, but when she arrived at the back entrance to the building, she found a man stationed there who looked similar to the one she'd encountered earlier.

She decided to run, but when she began to turn, the man said, "Mar Jeps is waiting for you in your office."

The man opened the door, activated his implant with his other hand, and said, "She's on her way up."

Insol wasn't in the mood for one of Mar's lectures on her mental health. Shortly after Insol left the Complex, when she hadn't responded to Mar's digi-mails about making a psych-med appointment, a med had shown up at her office and Insol threw her out. After that, Suron

     Howard Libes

appeared on campus and grilled her about her involvement with the Movement. Insol threw him out of her office, too.

Now, she thought about returning to her campus apartment, but decided against it and entered the building. Mar wouldn't give up so easily. Insol hated to think the worst of Mar, but she assumed that attempting to avoid her would trigger the start of surveillance by Suron's people and this was not the time for anybody to be watching her.

Walking down the hallway, Insol observed another Prevor Industries guard standing in front of her office door. Insol was furious that Mar had occupied her personal sanctum without asking her. She had an image in her head of Mar sitting behind her desk. *How dare she*, Insol thought. The guard activated his implant, said something, and opened the door.

Insol entered her office and Mar was sitting in one of the armchairs, working on a digi-tablet. When the door closed behind her and she and Mar were alone, Insol said, "You have some nerve being here like this."

Mar placed the digi-tablet in her lap, looked up at Insol and said, "Hello to you too."

"What makes you think you can take over my office?"

"Don't be so dramatic," Mar said. "My security said it was the safest place to wait for you."

"You mean Suron."

"Yes, if you need to blame somebody, it was his idea."

"If I want to blame somebody, I'll point a finger at you," Insol said, walking behind her desk and placing her viewer case on top of it. "Why are you here?"

"I wanted to see how you were doing," Mar said. "I hear you rejected that psych med."

"Anything else?"

"I wanted to catch up," Mar said. "Can't we have a civil conversation?"

Insol opened a desk drawer and removed a signal jammer, then placed it on the desk and activated it.

Mar said, "We don't need that thing."

"Humor me," Insol said.

"If it makes you feel comfortable."

"Clearly, the Leader has you brainwashed."

"Brainwashed?"

"Yes, brainwashed," Insol said. "He's cozying up to you, so you don't believe he's listening into your conversations."

"Carz isn't his father."

"Carz?" Insol said, walking around the desk and sitting on the front edge of it. "You and the Leader are on a first-name basis now?"

"Come on, Insol. I've known him since he was a boy."

"Oh, so you two are family now?"

"No," Mar said. "Please sit across from me. Are you that mad at me?"

Insol sighed and sat down in the armchair opposite Mar. "You happy now?"

"I'm getting there," Mar said.

Insol thought Mar was scrutinizing her. "How do I look?" Insol said. "Do I pass the exam?"

"Whoa," Mar said. "I know Shamba put a strain on our relationship. I know when we got back you thought

I was keeping you captive, but I've always had your best interests at heart. I think of you as family."

"Like you and Carz?" Insol said and sneered at Mar. "I have a mother. I believe you've met her."

"Why are you treating me this way? Am I the enemy now?"

"No, certainly not," Insol said. "I just don't understand how you can trust that murderer."

Mar sighed and said, "Trust? First of all, he says that the purge occurred behind his back and—"

"He says? He's the Leader and he let it happen."

"You're right," Mar said. "It was an obstacle in our relationship."

"Listen to yourself." Insol attempted to control her outrage. "Obstacle? It should've been more than a warning sign to not get in bed with him, but he gave a speech, and then you announced your partnership on *The Lure* so it's a done deal. Am I correct?"

"I know this is difficult for you—"

"If you're going to be condescending, then leave."

"Please hear me out." There was sadness in Mar's voice.

Mar was always there for her so Insol felt like she should listen. "These are my office hours so as long as my students don't show up, I'll listen."

"I appreciate it," Mar said. Her voice warbled with emotion. She checked her comm was turned off and set her digi-tablet to the side with the screen facing away from her. "I had a much different upbringing from you and I can't imagine how your experience as a child shaped your feelings toward the Global Assembly. I can't imagine a young person being subjected to that kind of horror."

"You've been speaking to Yor?"

"I have."

"I told him that in confidence."

"I know, but I'm worried about you, and I pried it out of him," Mar said. "As far as the Leader is concerned—"

"You mean Carz."

"Yes, Carz," Mar said. "You have to understand my place in all this. I was happy, helping people as a med. It was my life's calling. Then Mado and Yorlik hijacked my life to finish their plan. At first, I hated them for dropping this responsibility on me, then as time passed and I was CEO of Prevor Industries, with Yor in space and Rajer gone, the work gave my life meaning. I was building a future for the Kodan people."

"Yes, everyone has heard about your first speech at the facility," Insol said in a sarcastic tone.

"That speech was one of the turning points," Mar said. "I know that you're still mourning his loss and I didn't know him as well as you, but when your Uncle Gnivri, who had seen the worst of Koda and still worked to save everyone on the planet, pointed out that I had the stuff to lead, my confidence in my abilities to achieve the necessary goals skyrocketed."

"You've done an amazing job. There's no doubt about that."

"Thank you," Mar said, moving forward in her chair. "I've known for years we've passed the peak of our access to the resources required to produce more spaceships and save everyone. I didn't raise the issue because there was nothing anyone could do about it. I was just waiting for the day when those resources inevitably slowed to a trickle, and we would all need to decide how to proceed without enough spaceships, leaving hundreds of thousands of Kodans behind on this dying planet. The only entity with the reach and power to make a difference was the Global Assembly and there was no talking to Vidor Plemso. Then he died and I had no idea how my meeting with Carz would go. I went into it with the assumption that your friend's arrest—"

"He wasn't my friend."

"Whatever he was to you," Mar said, "I assumed that his arrest had revealed the facility and put me at a disadvantage in my meeting, but Carz told me about his desire to transcend his father's pettiness and be a leader for all Kodans. Maybe my ability to read people was something Yorlik saw in me, and that skill has sharpened over the years. Carz was sincere. I could see in his eyes that he was being truthful.

"He knew about the facility and gave me the choice to join him in saving the Kodan people. He detailed how he was going to make it happen and how he wanted Prevor Industries involved. I didn't give him a pass. I told him that he needed to live up to his end of the bargain and he did. He stood in front of the gathered Global Assembly and governmental department directors in the Hall of Governance in the Global Assembly building with the entire planetary population watching on their viewing channels and came clean. He did everything that he said he'd do. Afterward, the Global Assembly drew up legislation to codify his plan," Mar said. "He did it all. That's why I made the announcement on *The Lure* and that's why Prevor Industries will be working with him. As I said, my intention is to save every Kodan and Carz is the key to making it happen."

"I heard his speech like everyone else, but he's still responsible for the purge," Insol said, hearing the anger in her voice.

"If you heard the speech, then you know he took responsibility," Mar said, softening her tone. "He promised that people would be punished."

"Don't patronize me," Insol said. "By taking responsibility, he admitted he's a monster like his father."

"You're taking his words out of context," Mar said. "Look, I'm not saying the man is particularly bright for letting it happen. Would I rather be building all the spaceships secretly in Shamba and keep the Global Assembly out of it? Of course. Can the Global Assembly extract the resources for the spaceships that we couldn't and mobilize the Kodan people to get it done before the domes critically fail? Absolutely. This is a partnership of convenience. It's the best solution to save everyone and I intend on taking it."

"So hundreds of thousands die and the Leader walks away unscathed?"

"He's going to convict the people who put the purge in motion."

"But he's the one responsible."

"That's arguable," Mar said. "But I need to do what's best for the Kodan people. I wanted to come here and explain myself, and to tell you I love you and I completely understand your point of view."

Insol said sarcastically, "Well, I feel so relieved."

"There's no need for that," Mar said, placing her comm in her pocket, taking hold of her digi-tablet, and standing up. "I also wanted to invite you to the Unification Celebration as my guest. Mel will be there. Yor will land the WAEF in the Arena and he'll be ecstatic to see you."

"Unification," Insol said. "What a joke. All is forgiven. We're one big happy family now. Just kiss the ring of the mass murderer and son of a mass murderer. I can't believe Yor thinks this is a good idea, and he's making a show of it in the place where Rajer saved his life."

"Don't drag Rajer into this."

"How would he feel about what you're doing?"

"I've said my piece," Mar replied. "And for the record, Rajer would see that I'm doing the right thing, and this is the only way to proceed for the good of the Kodan people."

"There it is! For the good of the globe. Do you hear yourself?" Insol said, standing up and stepping toward Mar. "You keep telling yourself whatever helps you sleep at night, but there are some actions you can't forgive. I won't sit idly by and let the dead be disrespected."

Mar pointed her finger at Insol and said, "Don't do anything stupid." She tucked her digi-tablet under her arm and turned to leave.

CARZ

Carz exited the cruiser and walked ten meters through the air-cooled docking portal to the front door of his mother's Norian estate. Much like her Oedor Drive apartment, she maintained this residence as a getaway.

Carz rang the doorbell and a guard answered.

"Is Minok expecting you, sir?"

"That wouldn't be any fun, would it?" Carz said and walked past the guard into the house. Carz's guard, who had been standing behind the Leader, beckoned Minok's guard outside and closed the door behind them.

Carz stopped in the middle of the living room. He'd seen forty-year-old fotos of this room and his mother had preserved every detail.

Carz called out, "Minok…Minok…" He waited for a reply, but there was none.

Then he spotted Minok through the Active-Glass window. He was sunbathing on a chaise lounge by the pool with the Active-Glass canopy programmed to filter out harmful ultraviolet rays, and the rest of the patio was shaded to keep it cool.

Carz opened the door to the pool area and called out, "Minok."

Minok was startled. He sat up and turned around. His hair draped down to his shoulders. He lowered his sunshades to the bridge of his nose and said, "Carz? I wasn't expecting you."

"Yes, I know," Carz said. "Come inside. We need to talk."

"About what?"

"I think you know."

Carz could see fear in Minok's eyes.

Minok stood up. He was wearing a purple bathing suit. He was tanned, but sunburned on his shoulders and face. He looked around the patio with the shades still on the bridge of his nose.

"Your guard isn't here," Carz said. "It's just me and you."

Minok forced a smile, slipped his bare feet into flip-flops, and walked toward Carz. "Great to see you, brother."

"I doubt it," Carz said.

"How's mother? Filo?"

"Mother is on the mend. Filo is great."

"You look like you lost weight," Minok said as he walked past Carz into the house.

Complimenting was Minok's way of endearing himself to a person before they began any interaction. Since they were children, this habit had annoyed Carz because it signaled to him that Minok had no confidence in his ability to get people to like him without greasing the wheels beforehand.

Carz followed Minok into the house, closed the door, and said, "If anything, I've gained weight."

"I don't know what it is," Minok said. "You look good. Can I get you anything?"

"Cut the crap," Carz said, "and sit your ass down."

"Don't talk to me that way."

"I can and I will. Now sit!" Carz strode up to Minok and smacked the shades off the bridge of his nose. They skidded across the floor.

"You can't—"

Carz grasped Minok's neck with both hands and pulled his brother toward him. He said with conviction, "I know it was you, Minok. I know it was you and you broke my heart."

Minok grabbed Carz's arms to free himself, but Carz held his grip. He kissed Minok on the lips, then shoved him away.

Minok lost his balance, backpedaling until he smacked into the couch's armrest and fell onto the cushions. Hurriedly, he realigned himself so he was sitting straight up.

Carz faced Minok with the low table between them. He said, "Settled now?"

Minok leaned back on the couch. He was visibly shaking. "What do you want?"

Carz grabbed the low table, which held a few empty glasses, and flung it aside. The glasses smashed into pieces and the table bounced end-over-end a few times before coming to a stop across the room.

Carz strode up to Minok until they were face-to-face and screamed, "Why, Minok? Why?"

"Why what?"

"You're gonna make me say it?" Carz said. "Why did you help with the bombing?"

Carz could see the moment when Minok began figuring out his path forward. He had seen this move throughout their childhood.

Minok sat straight up again and acted stunned. He crossed his arms and said, "I'm insulted you'd say such a thing."

"Let's not play this game." Carz reached into his pants pocket, removed a folded envelope, and threw it, striking Minok in the chest. "A little souvenir. It shows you were a key player in the bombing."

Minok opened the envelope and read the note inside.

"So?" Carz said.

Minok looked up from the note. He was terrified. "It wasn't my idea. It was Roneh's. She told me the purge needed to happen. That you were blind to the danger of the Movement and if something wasn't done, then you would be toppled from leadership, the government would be overthrown, and the family would lose everything."

"I had a hunch that you...but I didn't want to believe it." Carz took a few steps back. "Why would you listen to Roneh and not come to me?"

Minok threw his hands in the air, the note clutched in one of them, and raised his voice. "She said there was something in it for me!"

"Father took care of you. I would've taken care of you, given you whatever you desired."

"You would've taken care of me? I'm a man, Carz!" Minok said, yelling with spit flying out of his mouth and throwing his arms toward Carz. "I can take care of myself. I'm smart! Nobody else thinks so, but I'm smart. Do you know why Father forced me into the Chief of Affairs job?"

"No," Carz said. "Tell me."

"So he could torture me. He spent every moment of every hour of every workday demeaning me. There were mornings when I woke up and vomited before I got out of bed and I wanted to die rather than go to work for him," Minok said, his voice warbling with emotion.

"Why didn't you come to me?"

"You treat me the same," Minok said. "I'm a man. I wanna be treated like one. The only thing I ever wanted from you or father was respect."

Carz reached into his breast pocket and removed his father's lighter. "I was always told respect needs to be earned, but you can have this. You've earned it by letting the purge go forward. You're more like Father than me," Carz said, tossing the lighter to Minok who caught it. "Now, what did you do? The investigation was baffled. They couldn't figure out who added access codes to the side gate so the attackers could get in. I had my suspicions when you ran off to Nor after the bombing and didn't come back, but I didn't want to believe it. I held out hope. I prayed I was wrong. But when I saw that note, that readout from the estate security system, I knew it was you. Who else would use Davik's birthday as their password to log on to the system? You were the only one in the family who celebrated every year."

"Father made me the keeper of those codes, and it was my task to rotate them. He told me to keep it secret," Minok said. "Roneh had no idea when she asked me to help open the gate."

"Congratulations. Father didn't know you were a terrorist," Carz said sarcastically. "What happened next?"

"I gave the codes to Roneh."

"That was all you did?"

"Yes," Minok said. "It was easy."

"Easy!" Carz said, yelling again. "Easy? My son was there. My child."

"I made sure—"

"Our mother could've died."

"That wasn't—"

"I don't care," Carz said. "I don't care. As far as I'm concerned, you don't exist anymore. You don't live at the estate anymore. Filo will never see you again. If you want to see Mother, you will make an appointment."

"I understand," Minok said. "But tell me, even if it's the last thing you ever say to me, I need to know—who gave you the note?"

"Roneh slipped it to me."

"That bitch."

"She told me the next morning that you were working with Orn and the bombing was all your doing, but I know you're only smart enough to be a pawn," Carz said. "By the way, I'm curious—what did she offer you?"

"She said the bombing would get Tarq fired and I could have his job."

"And you believed her?" Carz said and guffawed. "You're a bigger moron than I ever imagined."

Minok began weeping.

Carz walked off and exited the building. Orn was waiting outside and saluted. Carz didn't look at him or salute back, but as he passed Orn, he said, "Do it." He heard the door close behind him, and as he was climbing into his cruiser, Carz could hear Minok screaming from inside the house.

MAR

As the cruiser flew to the Global Assembly building for the start of the Celebration, Mar couldn't contain herself. She'd been smiling so much recently that her face hurt, and she found herself giggling like a schoolgirl about the day ahead.

The events following her meeting with Carz at the estate went off better than she'd ever imagined. After his Global Assembly speech, Carz had commed her. He was ecstatic. Internal polling revealed the vast majority of the Kodan people embraced Carz's ideas. Even a majority of the Loyalists were on his side, making it easier for the Global Assembly reps to cut nonessential spending and legislate the taxes to build more spaceships.

"So," Carz said to Mar, "are we doing this?"

"Yes," Mar said. "And I have to say you're a Kuvutia."

"Impressive One," Carz said. "I appreciate it."

"You speak Shamban."

"I know all the regional dialects. My father said it was a waste of time, but if I was going to be the Leader of all the people, I knew I needed to learn them."

"Now I'm more impressed, and I've got good news," Mar said. "I've spoken with the community board at the Shamban facility and after hearing your speech, the workers voted to support your unification plan."

"That's fantastic," Carz said. There was relief and joy in his voice.

"It is," Mar said. "But just so you know, you won by a razor-thin margin. I was told my involvement put you over the top, and there's a caveat. The workers want you to proceed with the purge investigation and pass down indictments before expecting the facility to become part of the global effort."

"I'm all right with that," Carz said. "I was saving it as a surprise, but since we're talking about it, I've got the investigation wrapped up. I'll be making arrests at the opportune time."

"Excellent. That'll go a long way toward convincing the workers to embrace our plan."

"I like the sound of 'our plan'," Carz said. "And I agree."

"I do have a favor to ask," Mar said. "In the spirit of reconciliation, I'm wondering if you'd be willing to pardon my son so he can return home."

"There's a few people who won't be pleased with the idea. Most citizens believed my father's propaganda so it'll be like he was raised from the dead, but there's no doubt that Kodans will welcome him with open arms, so let's make it happen. What about Mado Prevor?"

"Unfortunately," Mar said, "he left us years ago." It was a half-truth that made it sound like he was dead, but Mar decided it was best to leave out the fact that Mado was from another planet and looked like an aquatic creature. When she thought about it, she hardly believed it herself.

"That's a great loss for Koda," Carz said with genuine affection in his voice. "He was kind when I was growing up."

"Koda owes him a lot," Mar said. "I have some more good news. Are you sitting down?"

"Yes. I'm at my desk."

"Yor discovered the coordinates to his great-grandfather's habitable planet."

"That's…that's…I don't know what to say," Carz said. "You know what? Let's have a planetwide Unification Celebration upon Yor's arrival and at the same time, we can announce his news. We'll do it at the Arena. Broadcast it to the entire planet. It'll be like Yor has come full circle since the Breeze Celebration where he revealed the Great man's discovery. This is the civilization-saving topper to all our plans and Yor will be a hero to everyone on Koda."

"His great-grandfather gets some credit."

"Yes, of course."

Now, it was the day of the Celebration. When the cruiser obtained clearance to fly into Plaza airspace, Mar asked Suron if they could circle the area. Suron nodded and leaned forward to tell the pilot, who maneuvered the cruiser so it was angled downward on Mar's side.

The Plaza streets were packed with citizens clamoring to enter the Arena. Most of them wouldn't make it inside, but like the Breeze Celebration, massive viewing screens were mounted outside the Arena and on the Plaza buildings. As the cruiser continued to circle, Mar noted that the crowd not only filled the Plaza streets, but also the avenues in the surrounding neighborhoods like the University District, the Royal Quarter, the Old Quarter, and even the newer neighborhoods to the west.

Mar couldn't wait to hear the crowd cheering for her son. It was well deserved and a long time coming.

When Mar made the viewing-screen comm telling Yor that he could return home, his joy had made her smile. The last few times they'd spoken he'd been depressed and lonely so she was happy to see her boy perk back to life again. She asked him how long it would take to travel home for the Celebration. Yor gave her an estimate of a hundred and forty days.

A few days later, Mar commed Yor again and confirmed the Celebration in a hundred and forty-five days. Yor spoke about the maintenance necessary for the journey to Koda and his brow began to furrow. He was concerned about the WAEF's reentry into Koda's atmosphere, too. He said he had to go. There was too much to do, and he'd need to lift off in days to arrive on time.

As the Prevor Industries cruiser circled the Arena a few more times, Mar thought about her appearance on *The Lure*, and how calls had flooded the Global Assembly comm lines from citizens seeking shipbuilding jobs. Carz's speech had met with approval, but the Global Assembly's plea for workers to build spaceships had received a lackluster response. Carz gave Mar credit for this rush of enthusiasm, but Mar knew Mado deserved equal recognition. The public's response to her backing Carz's plan was a continuation of the relationship between Prevor Industries and the Kodan people that Mado had developed. The Kodan people trusted that Prevor Industries was always attempting to make life better for them and had their best interests at heart.

Mar was astounded how the pieces were falling into place for Yorlik and Mado's scheme in a way they'd never foreseen: The Kodan people, Prevor Industries, and the Global Assembly working together to leave the planet.

The cruiser proceeded to the Global Assembly building's landing pad and touched down beside the Leader's executive cruiser. Mar peered out the window to see twelve Armed Forces soldiers lined up at attention shouldering stun rifles, six to a side and facing each other, with a Global-Assembly blue carpet between them. At the end of the carpet were the lift's doors. A vidcam operator was in position, waiting to record Mar's exit from the cruiser and the beginning of the day's historical event.

"Shall we?" Mar said to Suron, who leaned forward and tapped the pilot on the shoulder. Then he activated his audio implant, signaling to his men that Mar was ready to disembark.

The cruiser doors slid open and the Prevor Industries guards took up position, two on each side of Mar's door. She exited with Suron behind her to the right. A Global Armed Forces major had been standing separate from the soldiers, resplendent in a blue dress uniform with gold epaulettes and a chest full of medals. He stepped in front of Mar Jeps and said, "Welcome to the Global Assembly, Mar Jeps. The Kodan people greet you with open arms."

"Thank you," Mar said.

The major's eyes wandered to Suron and the major clicked his heels together, snapped to attention, and held a salute. He called out, "Officer on deck," and all twelve of the soldiers snapped to attention and held a salute as well.

Suron was flustered and said, "Mar, please proceed."

Mar walked down the carpet between the soldiers. The lift doors opened, and Mar entered the lift compartment with her guards.

Suron stopped at the lift entrance and looked back at the soldiers standing at attention, still holding the salute. Suron returned their salute, then entered the compartment. The doors closed and the lift headed downward.

Mar stood at the back with the four guards in front of her. Suron stood to her right, looking straight ahead. He said, "That was odd."

"Things are changing all around us," Mar said, looking above the doors where the readout of the floors descended in number. "I was waiting to surprise you, but those soldiers have obviously been told. You've been reinstated into the military and promoted to general, retiring at the end of today with full pension."

Suron's mouth gaped, then a smile spread across his face. He turned to Mar and said, "Thank you. I never thought I'd see this day."

"That seems to be the overall theme for the day, and you deserve it."

The lift opened and two of Carz's guards awaited them in the hallway. The four Prevor Industries guards closed ranks and formed a wall in front of Mar with their hands on their weapons.

One of Carz's guards said, "We're here to escort Mar Jeps to the Leader's office."

Suron leaned toward Mar and said softly, "Remember, change may be happening, but it's best to play it safe."

"Agreed," Mar said.

"Clear the way for the boss, men."

Two guards stepped to the right and two to the left. Mar exited the lift with Suron walking one step behind to her right, the other guards behind him. They followed Carz's guards down a hallway with a bare Global Assembly-blue wall to the right and a wall of windows on the left looking out on the Plaza.

Before they left the Complex, Suron had told Mar that he had received word from one of his informants about threats on Mar's life. Wealthy loyalists were perturbed at the new taxes, and their military and surveillance industries' investments were taking a hit along with their ongoing profits from the patchwork on the domes. Roneh Rayush was seen as the biggest threat. Irate over her new Allegiance Program being defunded in Carz's unification budget, she had been busily riling up her followers at the injustice of it all.

Mar entered the Leader's waiting room and a middle-aged woman wearing a Global-Assembly blue jacket and skirt rose up from behind her desk. "Mar Jeps," she said, "it's a pleasure to meet you after all these years."

Mar recognized the voice. "Same here, Kel."

Kel reached under the edge of her desk. A click sounded and the door to the Leader's office slid open. Mar could see Carz standing with his back to her staring out a wall of windows.

"He's waiting for you," Kel said, then stepped around her desk and hugged Mar. She whispered in Mar's ear,

"You're my hero. What Vidor did to you was horrific and I never forgave him."

"But you stayed all these years."

Kel continued to embrace Mar and said in her ear, "I knew Suron needed someone with inside information." She released her hold on Mar, took a step back, and winked at her. She peered over at Suron and said, "It's a pleasure to meet you as well, General Suron."

"The pleasure is all mine," Suron said.

Kel said, "Now please, we mustn't keep the Leader waiting."

Mar reached out, squeezed Kel's forearm, and mouthed the words, "Thank you." She put her fist over her heart, pounded it like a Shamban, and proceeded into the Leader's office.

Mar stood inside the office doorway and took in the room. She'd seen fotos, but it was a strange sensation standing in Vidor Plemso's Global Assembly sanctum. Her mind raced through her consequential conversations with Vidor when he was probably sitting behind that desk. The room was smaller than she'd imagined. Her calculation might have revolved around the idea that only an enormous room could contain Vidor's ego.

Carz turned around. "Mar, please join me. Let's take in the view together."

Mar approached Carz who activated his intercom and said, "Kel, please invite General Suron into the office, too."

Mar stood beside Carz as Suron entered the office and stopped halfway to them. The door slid closed. Suron snapped to attention and he and Carz exchanged salutes. Suron seemed to be embracing his return to the military.

"Please join us, General," Carz said. "I wanted to show Mar the view."

"Shouldn't we get to the Arena?" Suron said.

"They can't start without us," Carz said. "Please join us."

Suron stood beside Mar and they looked out the windows.

Carz pointed down at the jam-packed Plaza streets. "Word has it that people have come from every region on the planet. Special cruisers have been chartered with people spending their savings to celebrate the return of your son. Estimates say this will surpass the biggest event in Capitol City history."

Suron said, "That kind of crowd complicates security."

"My guards have it handled. People and their bags are being checked at the Arena entrance. If you're concerned, I'll connect you with my guards when we arrive onsite."

Mar pointed into the distance. "You can see my penthouse from here," she said. "I can imagine your father peering at me disdainfully."

"I wouldn't put it past him," Carz said. "It's too bad Mado won't be here."

"He'll be here in spirit."

"Yes," Carz said. "That's certainly true."

Mar said, "But Suron's correct—we don't want to be late, especially for Yor's entrance. When I left my office, the most recent telemetry from the satellite telescope showed he'll be on time."

"Of course, you're right," Carz said and activated his intercom. "Kel, please inform security we're on our way."

"Yes, sir," Kel said. "I just received word that your mother and son have arrived at the Arena."

Carz deactivated the intercom.

Mar said, "Is Roneh coming?"

"Roneh will not be attending the event."

Mar glanced over at Suron, who appeared more concerned than moments before.

CARZ

Taking the lift down from his office and now walking through the tunnel between the Global Assembly building and the Arena, there was no conversation between Carz, Mar, and Suron. Answering Mar's question about Roneh had brought an ominous pall over the festive mood.

Roneh's lack of attendance at the event clearly meant that she wasn't pleased by it, but Carz's guests didn't know the half of it. Day after day, Roneh had been hounding Carz about the nullification of her precious new program. She was also infuriated about Yor's pardon and perceived the celebration of his return as a personal insult.

Carz continued sleeping in his father's trophy room. He made it a habit to lock the door before he went to sleep. On the nights when Roneh came home late from a rally, she'd pound on the locked door, wanting to argue about Carz's political course of action. Eventually, she would tire and go away, but Mar, Suron, and anybody who had ever dealt with Roneh were aware that she didn't like to lose, and could hold a grudge.

The tunnel ended at the lift to the Arena where two guards snapped to attention at Carz's approach. To the right, the older guard wore a round solid-blue pin. He stared straight ahead, keeping alive Vidor's command that no guard should look the Leader in the eye. Carz had

     Howard Libes

known this guard since his childhood and had chosen him for this event.

"At ease, Theo," Carz said. "How is everything?"

"Running smoothly, sir," Theo said, staring forward. A Global Guard tattoo on his neck peeked out from under his collar. "They're ready for you upstairs."

"Let's get this show on the road, then."

Theo reached behind his ear, activating his audio implant. "Karanga is in the building and headed up," he said, then waited a moment for a reply. "All set, sir."

Carz turned to Suron. "The lift can't carry all our guards at the same time. Why don't half of your men and half of mine head up with us first?" Suron concurred.

Theo pressed the lift button and the doors slid open. Carz entered the compartment, followed by Mar, Suron, and half of the contingent of guards, including Theo. The door closed and the lift headed up.

Standing to Carz's right, Mar said, "Karanga?"

Carz chuckled. "For the event, they wanted a code word for me so any hostile who intercepted the comm wouldn't know they were talking about the Leader. I figured the only people who knew the name were myself, my mother, and you...and I'd get a chuckle out of it."

"Love it. I'm sure Karanga would be honored."

The lift stopped and the doors slid open. In the distance, the roar of the crowd in the Arena was muffled, but they were chanting, "When All Else Fails...When All Else Fails..."

Theo and the guards stepped out, blocking off the entrance to the lift. Mar started to move forward, but

Carz grabbed her elbow and said, "Let's make sure we're all clear before we head out. I'm sure Suron has heard the same chatter I have."

"Yes, sir," Suron said.

Mar said, "It's nice to see you both on the same page."

Theo cupped his ear so he could hear his audio implant over the crowd noise. He said something to the other guards who stepped aside, then said to Carz, "We're good to go, sir."

Before Carz exited the lift, he reached out and took hold of Mar's hand. He understood this was a bold and intrusive move toward the woman who had previously been the Global Assembly's most staunch critic, but he had thought about doing this for the past few days. Solidarity between the Global Assembly and Prevor Industries was the foundation of the plan to unify the Kodan people. With the entire planetary population watching, this event was the best place to hammer this home. Carz assumed Mar understood.

Mar peered down at their joined hands. She gripped his hand tighter, smiled at him, and said, "Let's do this."

The excitement in her voice thrilled him. He smiled back at her, and they stepped out of the lift together. On either side of the Arena's tunnel were viewing-channel cams. Carz had asked for them to be placed there. The cam operators cheered for them. Carz waved with his free hand and so did Mar. Two Msituan girls in the traditional garb of their region handed bouquets of blossoms to Carz and Mar, and they continued down the Arena tunnel toward the ramp leading to the field. Vidcam operators were stationed along the way. Arena workers in Global-Assembly blue coveralls and Global Assembly officials on both sides of the tunnel applauded them.

Carz stopped a few meters before the threshold into the Arena and one of the guards took both bouquets. The sound of the crowd was loud, but they had stopped chanting.

Carz leaned close to Mar's ear and said, "We'll enter from behind the stage and all the cams will be on us. We've been on the Arena's viewing screens since we exited the lift so the crowd knows we're on our way. I assume the lull is them awaiting our arrival. You all set?"

Mar smiled. "How do I look?"

"Ready to go."

"All right, then," Mar said. "Into the foreseeable future."

"Foreseeable future?"

"I'll explain later."

Carz took a deep breath and exhaled. This was the moment when he would move out of his father's shadow and come into his own as Leader. He took another deep breath and exhaled again, then looked over at Mar who was smiling as if she knew what he was thinking.

When he walked out of the tunnel onto the field hand in hand with Mar Jeps, the crowd in the stadium exploded in cheering and applause. Carz took a few more steps, then halted. He was stunned by the ecstatic response. He peered over at Mar who smiled broadly and mouthed the word, "Whoa." Chills shot up Carz's spine.

The outpouring was never-ending. He saw his stunned face on the jumbo viewing screens around the Arena and remembered to smile, then joined Mar in waving to the crowd. He reminded himself that he needed to convey confidence and strength, then he squeezed Mar's hand and they walked together to the space in front of the stage where guards stood in between barriers. Carz scanned the faces of the audience up front, who were mostly Capitol City residents, but a fair number were from other regions. More importantly, they were all jubilant.

Then he felt something grab his leg, and the crowd became louder, screaming in joy. Carz looked down. Filo was hugging his thigh. A guard under the stage appeared horrified at letting Filo get away from him. Things hadn't changed much yet. Everyone still feared whoever was Leader.

Beside the guard, in a wheelchair, was Carz's mother saying something. Carz couldn't hear her over the din of the crowd, but it was easy to read her lips. She was saying, "Pick him up," and gesturing upward with her arms. When Carz looked down, Filo was now standing in front of him, holding his arms straight up.

Carz let go of Mar's hand, lofted Filo above his head, and kissed him on the cheek, then turned his son in his arms so he was facing crowd, which was now chanting his name. Filo waved to them, laughing hysterically. Mar reached out and mussed Filo's hair. Carz placed Filo on his shoulders, then he and Mar continued strolling around the rest of the stage, waving to the thrilled audience.

The stage was an exact replica of the one from the Breeze Celebration where the WAEF had blasted off into outer space. His father would have hated this idea and seen it as an admission of a mistake, which he would never do. Carz thought it appropriate. As Leader, he was embracing the truth that had been told in this place on that day all those years ago. He was about to take Kodan civilization forward from that moment in history instead of denying what had been revealed. Carz didn't think this would be lost on anybody, but just in case, he'd put out a press release to the media saying this replica was a symbol of embracing Yorlik the Great's mission and the SEEDER program as the way forward to survival.

Carz, Filo, and Mar made their way behind the stage. When Carz lowered Filo to the ground, he ran into his grandmother's arms. It made Carz happy to see Filo so attached to his mother.

Carz walked under the stage with Mar beside him.

Suron appeared and said to Mar, "Everything's secure."

Guards were posted around the perimeter of a curtained-off area under the stage. They snapped to attention and saluted as Carz approached. He returned the salute, then passed through the curtain with Mar, Suron, his mother, and Filo.

Immediately, Carz was struck by the pleasant smell of food from the trays laid out on a long table in the middle of the area, catered by the Plemso estate chef. Filo led his grandmother by the hand to sample the cuisine. On the far left, tables had been set up with viewing screens where GSS agents sat, scanning the crowd with surveillance cams, using facial recog software to seek out any troublemakers. To the far right were tables with viewing screens and long-range comm devices where individuals from Carz's newly re-formed Kodan Space Control were tracking Yor's journey home.

A woman rose from one of those stations and headed toward Carz. She had shoulder-length blonde hair and wore a light blue button-down shirt with the top button undone, a dark blue skirt, and sensible shoes. She was the new head administrator of the KSC and a former Prevor Industries employee who Mar had recommended for the job. She stopped in front of Carz and said, "Big day, sir."

"I couldn't agree more."

"Good to see you, Karin," Mar said. "Any news on my son?"

"That's what I came to tell you both," Karin said with excitement in her voice. "The WAEF is in orbit and we just need the Leader's permission for reentry. Yor says— and these are his words—'I'm as ready as I'll ever be.'"

Mar chuckled.

"Tell him to proceed," Carz said, "and that I'm looking forward to meeting him."

"Yes, sir," Karin said.

Carz said, "How long before we open the dome panel?"

"That depends on how smoothly reentry goes," Karin said, looking over at Mar. "I'm not trying to be alarmist, but the WAEF is over a hundred and fifty years old and we have no idea how it will hold up on re-entry. We calculate a thirty percent chance that Yor will need to make an emergency landing outside of the dome."

"Yes, Yor conveyed his concerns to me," Mar said. "His exact words were: 'There's the probability that things could go sideways.'"

"We've done everything we can on our end to mitigate any problems," Karin said. "But we want to be realistic, too."

"We'll just have to pray the Powers-That-Be are on our side," Carz said. "Give him the go-ahead and let us know when we need to deal with the panel."

"Yes, sir," Karin said and hurried back to her station.

Mar said, "I have to say, I may have made light of what Yor told me, but I am concerned."

"I completely understand. You're his mother," Carz said, reaching out and patting her on the arm. "It's going to be a magnificent day and you'll be hugging your boy shortly."

"I'll take your word for it."

"I am the Leader," Carz said and chuckled.

Glym approached and halted in front of Carz, snapping to attention.

Carz said, "Glym, shouldn't you be at the estate?"

"Yes, that's what I thought," Glym said. "But your mother insisted that I come here, saying my father would want it this way. No disrespect, but you know how she can be."

"I do."

Glym said, "I've been checking with my second-in-command at the estate and everything is fine."

"That's good to hear. It's one less worry, knowing you're in charge." Carz glanced over at the catering table where Filo was reaching out with a large spoon, attempting to scoop food from a tray that he couldn't reach, and neither could his mother from her wheelchair. The guard who had been pushing her chair was nowhere in sight.

Carz said to Glym, "Can you please give my mother a hand with Filo? I know you're not a nanny, but..."

Glym spotted the problem and said, "I've got it," then hurried over to the table.

Mar said, "What your mother did for Glym was kind of sweet."

"Sure, but knowing my mother, she wanted Glym around because Filo's nanny got sick at the last minute… although I'm sure on some level she meant what she said."

"Where's your brother?"

"He couldn't make it."

Mar waved to one of the guests.

Carz didn't recognize him. He said, "Someone you invited?"

MAR

Mar waved across the bustling room to Mellick Zonor, who was smiling at her. He looked like he was taking care of himself.

After Yor left the planet, Mel had fallen into a depression about the loss of his family and the inability of the Movement to produce constructive change with their political agenda. His curly mop of hair began falling out. He gained forty kilos. He became unhappy with his life at Royal University and handed over the Chair of the SEEDER-program studies department to Harmin.

So Mar had a sit-down with Mel and suggested a career change. There was an opening as administrator of the Prevor Relief Foundation that would not only allow him to help outer-Kodans like his deceased family, but he would also be ferrying resources to the Shamban facility for the construction of spaceships.

He took the job and his new employment gave his life purpose. Mel lost the forty kilos and worked on his health, becoming muscular and fit. He shaved his head. He met a man and they adopted a baby girl, an outer-Kodan orphan. He was now based out of Shamba and Mar hadn't seen him for a handful of years, but they spoke frequently over the comm, and Mar had invited him here.

Mar turned to Carz and said, "Would you excuse me for a moment?"

"Of course—we have time before your son's entrance."

Mar snaked her way through some of the Leader's wealthy supporters who were pleased with the unification agenda since they would earn a fortune in contracts from the spaceship construction, offsetting any hit on their riches from the proposed taxes. Mar had met them at Vidor's gatherings, so she was polite and greeted them as she passed by.

When she reached Mel, they embraced, then she stepped back and said, "Let me get a proper look at you."

Mel spun in a circle. "What do you think?"

"If I didn't know better, I'd say you've found Rejuv Serum."

"You should talk," Mel said. "You look incredible. How do you do it?"

"Thanks," Mar said, then winked at him. "It's a secret."

"You are the keeper of secrets."

"You don't know the half of it. I'll tell you someday."

"I look forward to it," Mel said, then leaned toward Mar and whispered in her ear, "I heard about the facility's vote to join the Leader's initiative, but how are you getting along with him?"

Mar glanced over her shoulder at Carz who was crouching down, talking to his son while Glym and Flomina observed the interaction. "You mean, do I trust him?" Mar said. "He's done everything he said he'd do, which is far beyond my expectations. It's almost too good to be true. I'm less concerned about him than others in the Global Assembly."

"You mean like that monster there," Mel said, stepping back and gesturing with his head toward somebody behind Mar.

She looked over her shoulder and spotted Orn Shiv on the other side of the room, assessing the people in the crowd.

"He's more of an omnipresent dark cloud and seems feckless and directionless with his master dead and gone," Mar said. "I'm more concerned about political operators like Roneh Rayush."

"Yes, I agree. She is the next generation of monster. Smarter and more cunning in aligning the masses on her side, more dangerous."

Suron appeared by Mar's side. "Did you—"

"Yes, we just saw him," Mar said. "His presence has already darkened my mood, and I don't want him to be one of the first people Yor sees on his arrival."

"He needs to be removed without causing a disturbance," Suron said. "Orn won't listen to me. I'll take this to the Leader."

"Sounds like a plan," Mar said. "Suron, you remember Mel?"

Suron said, "Good to see you, young man. You look great."

"That's the word," Mel said. "For my ego's sake, I need to visit Capitol City more often."

Suron said, "Are we expecting Insol?"

"I was just about to ask the same thing," Mel said. "I haven't spoken to her in over a year—it might even be two."

"That's odd," Mar said. "I asked her recently if she'd spoken to you and she said, 'He's doing his thing.'"

"That's her being truthful but not honestly answering your question," Mel said. "We had a falling-out. Actually, we had a difference of opinion and I've attempted to comm her to work it out, but she's ignored my calls. I've left conciliatory messages. How is she?"

Mar said, "Lately, she's completely out of control."

"Since the purge," Suron said.

"That makes sense," Mel said.

"Can I ask about the point of contention between you two?" Mar said. "You're old friends, and I'm baffled how it could be so bad that she won't talk to you anymore."

Mel hooked his arm with Mar's. "Let's walk away from these people." He led her toward the corner of the under-stage area where they stood with their backs to the crowd. "Sorry. The monster looked like he was reading my lips."

"Good call," Suron said.

Mel said, "Over the years, Insol became incensed by the mounting deaths of outer-Kodans. I told her the Foundation was doing what we could to keep the death count down, but the environmental conditions were worsening and there was no effective way to lobby for outer-Kodans to become dome residents with Vidor Plemso as Leader. She wanted my support for more violent action by radical elements in the Movement. There was a plan to assassinate members of the Global Assembly. I told her that was insane—it would align perfectly with the Leader's misinformation about the Movement being terrorists."

Mar said, "And this started a few years ago?"

"More than a few," Mel said, "From what I've heard, the purge has only made the surviving radicals more intractable. I was thinking this would be a perfect time for them to strike."

Mar said, "An act of violence now against the Global Assembly would be catastrophic to our plans. Suron, maybe you should warn Glym and Carz's security?"

Suron said, "I'll do that right now and say something about getting rid of Orn." He turned on his heels and marched away.

Mel said, "So, you and Suron ever—"

"Our relationship is purely professional."

"That's too bad."

"And he's a partnered man."

Mel turned to face Mar now that the conversation was just about them. "You two have worked together for years and you have a rapport. I just want you to be happy."

"I appreciate it."

"The Leader is headed this way," Mel said, "with what I assume are his guards."

"That was quick." When Mar turned around, Carz was only a few steps away, flanked by his security detail.

Carz halted in front of Mar and said, "My guards have been placed on high alert and I've sent Glym back to the estate to rally his men. Is this Suron's source?" He pointed at Mel who immediately appeared panicked.

"No, not at all. It was one of Suron's informants," Mar said, disturbed by how easily she lied to a man she wanted to be truthful with her.

"Well, you know I respect Suron so I'm not taking it lightly."

"As well you shouldn't," Mar said. "By the way, this is Mellick Zonor."

"Not the Mellick Zonor from your Foundation?"

Mar said, "One and the same."

"It's an honor to meet you," Carz said. "You do great work. We should get together to discuss funding."

Mel peered over at Mar, then said to Carz, "Funding?"

"Absolutely," Carz said. "We need to keep the outer-Kodans alive if we're going to fill our spaceships and save every Kodan. The environment is deteriorating rapidly. I want to build temporary housing inside the domes so we can get the more at-risk outer-Kodans to safety. I've set a considerable amount aside for that in my new budget."

Mel said, "That's wonderful."

"That's what a government should do for its people," Carz said. "I've heard funding has fallen short of building enough shelters to withstand the extreme weather year-round. I figure we can build cheaper inside the domes."

Mel said, "I see you've done your research."

"I find being informed and working out a clear-cut strategy is the best way to get things done, don't you?"

Somebody in the under-stage crowd was yelling, "Where is he? Where's the Leader?" It was Karin. She was frantic, looking around the crowd. "Where's the Leader? Where is he?" Based on Suron's new intel, the guards saw her as a threat and restrained her. The crowd observed. Some were curious, others were frightened.

Carz said to one of his personal guards, "Tell them to ease up on her. Bring her to me." The guard took off toward the ruckus.

Mar thought, *If Yor's descent was going well, she wouldn't be so worked up.*

"You all right, Mar?" Mel said.

"That's the head administrator of Kodan Space Control."

"Oh," Mel said. "Don't worry. Yor has never been late for an engagement, especially one honoring him."

Mar chuckled nervously.

A guard escorted Karin to the Leader, gripping her forearm, but it looked more like she had the guard in tow. When she reached Carz, she said, "Leader, the WAEF has arrived. The panel needs to open immediately."

Mar breathed a sigh of relief. "Isn't that good news?"

Karin said, "Sort of…but Professor Vanderlord never notified us of reentry and we just got word that he's circling Capitol City with bad weather on the way."

"All is well. I've got it." Carz removed his comm from his pocket, activated it, then pressed a few buttons and said, "Open the panel."

Mar was relieved. "That was simple."

Carz said to Karin, "You should probably get back to your station."

"Yes, sir."

Before Karin could depart, Carz took hold of her arm and said to the guard who had brought her to him, "After she's communicated with Professor Vanderlord, make sure she's situated in one of the VIP boxes to witness the WAEF's return."

Karin appeared stunned at this generosity and said, "Thank you, sir. Thank you so much." Then she dashed back to her station.

Mar said to Carz, "That was nice of you."

"People should feel like they're valued rather than live in fear of being punished for the slightest perceived mistake," Carz said. "And this wasn't her fault."

Mel said, "That's refreshing."

"I know my father could be…" Carz said, then lowered his voice, "a bit of a prick, but I'm attempting to move my administration forward with honesty rather than disinformation, with caring rather than by maintaining the status quo for the loyal, with a smile rather than a scowl."

Mar said, "Sounds like you've put some thought into this."

"Pretty much my entire life," Carz said. "And I'm happy to apply it now."

YOR

Yor was sitting in the pilot's chair preparing for reentry. He recalled how a short time before departing in his pod, Mado had explained there was a thirty-nine percent chance that the WAEF's reentry into Koda's atmosphere could lead to catastrophic failure.

Yor had asked Mado, "What does that mean?"

"Cracks in the hull, engine shutdown, and the breaking up of the craft. Loss of life."

"That would be my life, correct?"

"Yes, the assumption is you'll be piloting the ship," Mado said. "The WAEF's hull was never designed to enter atmospheres more than six times, including its return to Koda. On his voyage, your great-grandfather far exceeded that number searching for the habitable planet. That meant the hull's original protective barrier was gone by the time your great-grandfather and I reached the way station, and we still needed to reenter Koda's atmosphere."

"So how did you overcome the problem?"

"For centuries, Prevorians have applied a protective coating to their spacecrafts' hulls for reentry. Later, on Koda, I branded that substance Frezon. I used the chemicals in Yorlik's lab to concoct a batch of Frezon, then we applied it to the WAEF's hull. I calculated an eighty-six percent chance that we'd survive the passage into Koda's atmosphere. That estimate included Yorlik's masterful piloting skills, and as you know, that turned out to be a successful prediction.

"When you made it necessary to rush the WAEF's renovation, there were pressing issues and I didn't have time to apply Frezon. After we came close to the red dwarf and we were at the way station, I tested the hull for temperature variance and calculated the probability I mentioned earlier. That includes your ability as a pilot, which is rudimentary. Since Yorlik's lab is little more than a museum showroom now, I didn't have the chemicals to make more Frezon."

"So you've decided to tell me this now? Why not before?"

"You would've been worrying for the entire journey to Prevor."

"So damn the probability," Yor said, noting the look of dismay on Mado's face at such a statement. "How do you think I survive this dilemma?"

"Practice."

"Practice?"

"I've programmed a HGD simulation. In practicing, you'll need to maximize exposing the part of the hull with the most remaining Frezon to the effects of reentry," Mado said. "The simulation will give you all the information you require to possibly survive."

"Possibly? Will it push my survival closer to a hundred percent?"

"It'll definitely get you closer," Mado said. "You've shown yourself to have the same genetic reflexes as your great-grandfather and an instinctual ability to apply aerodynamic theory. Practicing on the simulation will advance your skills and give you a better chance of the hull failing in a less catastrophic manner."

"Can't I just program the nav computer for your proposed reentry?"

"That's part of the simulation, but if the protected areas of the hull fail faster than I've predicted or if certain systems become inoperable on reentry, you'll need to take control of the ship."

"Sounds complicated."

"You'll have plenty of time to practice on your journey back to Koda."

"Can I ask why you didn't just bring enough Frezon with us when we left Koda?"

"It's embarrassing," Mado said. "With everything that needed to get done…I forgot."

Yor chuckled. "That's a first."

"In all my years of existence, it's not, believe me," Mado said. "In this case, it was a big blunder."

"That statement doesn't fill me with confidence."

"Like I said, you'll have plenty of time to practice. And I believe in you."

After Yor dropped Mado off, he trained on the simulation day after day in earnest. At first, it was frustrating. Alarms went off on every attempt. The WAEF was continuously destroyed, but Mado had built a tutorial into the simulation to point out what Yor had done wrong and how to correct the problem. Yor was so infuriated at one point that he pondered giving up. Maybe he would wait for the spaceships to leave Koda and simply join them on their exodus rather than attempt reentry. But when he was traveling back to the way station, the uncertainty of the timeline ahead and the loneliness that overwhelmed him were motivating factors in continuing to practice.

He doubled his efforts and it paid off. He found himself consistently landing on Koda safely. There were simulations where he made obvious mistakes or where the nav computer completely stopped functioning before reentry and he crashed to his death. The main reason for the nav computer failing was the energy-field generators on the hull. The WAEF wasn't designed with them in mind and the computer detected any maneuverability issues due to the generators as an error in its system and shut down. Yor didn't have the skills to remove the generators so he needed to work with them. The only solution within his grasp was ensuring the nav computer was running in top form before reaching Koda. He tested it obsessively on his journey back from Prevor. At the way station, he rewired the system to guarantee against any breakdowns, and each day of his voyage from the way station to Koda, he tested it and found no problems.

Yor began communicating with Karin at Kodan Space Control when he was halfway to Koda. They worked out course corrections and confirmed the WAEF's speed and distance from Koda to make sure Yor would arrive on time for the Celebration.

When he achieved orbit around Koda, all systems were operational and he spoke with Karin. There was excitement and nervousness in her voice. She was in a room with background noise, and she said she was now stationed under the stage at the Arena which was packed with Kodans looking forward to his arrival. Then she gave Yor clearance from the Leader for reentry.

"Copy that," Yor said.

"The entire planet awaits your return," Karin said. "Just check in before reentry. Kodan Space Control out."

Now, Yor sat in the pilot's chair, observing the planet below with its continents diminished by the expanding oceans and roiling storms sweeping across parts of the globe. His mind went to the Arena full of Kodans anticipating his homecoming, and he became anxious. His heart began racing. He could hardly breathe. He was dizzy. He was having a panic attack. He attempted to calm himself by regulating his breathing, but he kept thinking about all the people down there and their expectations upon his return and whether he could live up to them.

Yor decided the best way to deal with this attack was to get his mind onto something else, so he activated the nav computer and began reentry. He monitored all the temperature gauges and warning lights.

Halfway through reentry, an alarm signaled that the nav computer had gone offline. Yor's first thought was, *How is this happening?* as he smacked the metal cover over the nav computer's circuitry with the palm of his left hand. His second thought was to grab the steering mechanism. Before Yor could adjust the WAEF's angle of entry, temperature warning lights lit up on the control panel in front of him. Yor grasped the steering mechanism with both hands, corrected the angle, and heard the WAEF's hull groan.

As a result of all his practice simulations, Yor had developed an internal clock for the duration of reentry and began counting down from twelve. If he reached zero and the warning lights were still on, he was in serious trouble. Maybe he would never make it to the surface of Koda alive. Maybe he would never see his mother again.

One by one the warning lights went dark and the nav computer reactivated. Yor let go of the steering mechanism and breathed a sigh of relief as the WAEF entered Koda's upper atmosphere. The engines engaged, but before he could take another breath, the nav computer deactivated again, warning lights signaled the engines had gone offline, and the control panel went dark.

The WAEF's power source had shut down. The WAEF was in free fall. Yor grabbed the emergency oxygen mask from under the control panel and placed it over his nose and mouth.

Yor had experienced free fall in simulations, but now, the increasing g-forces surprised him. The WAEF was plummeting fast. The ship's glide ratio—the distance an aircraft can travel forward with power off in relation to the altitude it loses—was nearly one-to-one at hypersonic speeds. That meant for every thousand meters traveled the WAEF would descend a thousand meters. He needed to get the power source and the main engines running or reach a safe location for an emergency landing.

The WAEF was descending into darkness. No lights below. He activated the geo-radar, which would synch with the holo-device to construct a three-dimensional readout of the landscape below. Yor tightened the straps keeping him in the pilot's chair, released the latch holding the chair in place, then spun around one hundred and eighty degrees and locked the chair down. He was facing the holo-device, which had an independent power source and was lit up. It displayed the WAEF as a red dot falling toward the Mlimoan mountain range, possibly the worst place to land on Koda. The peaks below were seven thousand to nine thousand meters high.

The WAEF's altitude was 44,127 meters. Yor spun back around to the control panel and locked himself in place. In his prescience, Mado had built a power-source scenario into the simulation. When Yor experienced it for the first time, he asked the tutorial why the power source might disengage on reentry. It said that the heat from reentry might reach the conduits for the Prevorian power-core, which would trip a breaker and cause a shutdown rather than explode. If this situation arose, Yor had to wait until the conduits cooled while falling through the frigid atmosphere at higher altitudes, then hit the ignition button on the control panel. Yor had no reason to disbelieve Mado's tutorial, and at his current altitude, he didn't have enough time to run down to the engine room, assess the problem, and restart the power source, then make it back up to the helm and reactivate the engines.

So Yor's only option was the big round purple button on the control panel. He had pressed it in the simulation to ignite the power source, but there had never been a reason to do it for real. Even when the WAEF was parked at the way station, the power source ran at a low setting to maintain basic systems like oxygen, gravity, lights, and food replicators. There was one unknown. If there was a circuitry issue with the button, then Yor would be facing disaster with the mountains coming up fast and no clear-cut place to land.

The altimeter read 21,363 meters. Yor made the decision to wait until twelve thousand meters before pressing the button. If the engines started, that would give him enough room to navigate the terrain below.

In the silence of free fall, Yor began to think about his life. He thought about what he'd experienced and how far he'd traveled since he left Koda. It would be ironic to die so close to home.

He flipped off the switches on all main engines and set their thrust so he could start them at full power when they were rebooted. If they didn't start the first time, there was a technique where he could flip them in different sequences to fire them up. He also made sure the nav computer was offline.

The altimeter read 13,482 meters. As the WAEF was jolted by crosswinds, Yor tightened his grip on the steering mechanism to keep the ship level. When the altimeter reached twelve thousand meters, Yor took his left hand off the steering mechanism and pressed the purple button, but the control panel remained dark. Feeling like he might pass out, he took a big gulp of oxygen from the mask, then he balled his left hand into a fist and struck the button. Still no lights on the panel. He asked the Powers-That-Be for help. It had worked once before and what did he have to lose? Then he carefully pressed the button straight down with two fingers and released it. The lights on the panel lit up.

The altimeter read 9,805 meters. The sun was rising, and he could see the jagged mountain peaks directly below. Yor said out loud, "All right, you bucket of bolts. Let's see what you can do." He flipped switches to start four of the main engines at full power, gripping the steering mechanism in both hands. Nothing happened. The proximity alarm began howling. Yor's heart raced. A cliff was dead ahead. He steered the WAEF, barely missing the cliff, and maneuvered into a valley between two peaks. The altimeter read 4,998 meters. He reset the engine switches and flipped them in a different sequence.

The engines engaged.

Yor was pinned to his seat by the force of the engine's thrust. He held tight to the steering mechanism. At 2,211 meters, the WAEF shot across a valley floor. Yor yelled, "Come on, baby! You've got this!" He pulled back on the steering mechanism. The WAEF ascended. The proximity alarm fell silent.

When the altimeter read twelve thousand meters, Yor leveled off again. He checked that the oxygen system was operating, then he removed the mask and placed it back in the holster under the control panel.

Yor took a deep breath and giggled. He glanced over at the foto of his great-grandfather and said, "How was that, old man?" Yor activated the nav computer, unstrapped himself from the pilot's chair, and went to get ready for his entrance at the Celebration.

By the time Yor was back in the control room with his spacesuit on, the WAEF was circling the Capitol City dome. The skies were clear, but Yor could see dark storm clouds headed his way. He went to comm Kodan Space Control to open the dome panel, then realized that he'd forgotten to alert them that he'd left orbit. He activated his comm. "Kodan Space Control. Come in."

There was a click and Karin said, "Professor Vanderlord. Are you ready for reentry?"

"I'm so sorry. This is a first for me and I forgot to check in. I'm already circling the dome."

Karin said, "Circling?"

"Yes," Yor said. "There's extreme weather on the horizon and given the WAEF's current state, I don't know how she'll respond so the sooner the panel opens the better."

"Copy that. I'll contact you again when the panel is opening."

He continued circling, but the storm was getting closer.

"Any word on the panel, Kodan Space Control?" Yor said, then waited for an answer.

When high winds began rocking the WAEF, Yor strapped himself into the pilot's chair, turned off the nav computer, and grabbed the steering mechanism with both hands. If Space Control didn't get back to him soon, then he'd have to move the ship to a higher altitude to avoid the storm, but he decided to wait until the last minute to make that maneuver.

"Any word on the panel, Kodan Space Control?" There was no answer.

When the storm was nearly on him, Yor checked the status lights on the control panel and prepared to move the WAEF. His hand was over the main engine switches when the comm clicked.

Karin said, "Professor Vanderlord, the panel is opening."

"Copy that, Kodan Space Control. Just in time. Descent in progress."

Yor engaged the hovering engines and timed his descent to reach the panel when it was fully open. As he passed inside the dome, he was overwhelmed by emotion.

"We see you entering the dome, When All Else Fails," Karin said. "Welcome home."

"Copy that," Yor said.

He deactivated his comm and began to cry.

MAR

When the WAEF was descending towards the Arena, Mar stood in a VIP box in the midst of the stands facing the stage. The crowd was chanting, "When all else fails…when all else fails…when all else fails." It seemed to be echoing around the Arena, but Mar realized they were chanting in the Plaza streets as well.

Everyone under the stage had been evacuated for safety reasons. Mel stood to the left of Mar. The Leader had invited him here and asked him to join them on stage later as the Prevor Relief Foundation's administrator and Yor's friend. Carz was on Mar's right, with Filo beside him standing on a chair. Flomina was next to Filo in her wheelchair.

Filo pointed up at the WAEF and yelled out, "Papa! You see that?"

Everyone in earshot laughed.

"I do," Carz said. "This is a day you'll always remember."

"Why?"

"I'll explain it to you later, but for now watch closely."

On the WAEF's approach, the roar of the hovering engines filled the stadium. The WAEF's underside appeared charred, and Mar recognized devices mounted on the hull as a version of the energy-shield devices that were installed on the Shamban spaceships.

Then it dawned on Mar that her baby boy was home. She was overcome by emotions and whooped at the top of her lungs. She peered over at Mel and Carz, who stared at her before they both broke out laughing.

Filo said to Carz, "What's wrong with the lady, Papa?"

Everyone else in the VIP box including Flomina, Suron, and all the security guards broke out laughing, too.

"She's happy," Carz said. "She hasn't seen her son since before you were born and he's piloting the WAEF." Carz pointed to the spaceship as it slowed its descent and touched down behind the stage.

Filo said to Mar, "Your son is a spaceman."

"Yes, he is," Mar said.

"I wanna be a spaceman," Filo said. "Can I meet him?"

Carz said, "You're going to see him shortly, but you can't get too close. When the time comes, I'll introduce you."

Filo jumped down from the chair and grabbed his father's hand. "Let's go *now*!"

"All right," Carz said, "if you insist."

AFTER THE WAEF'S LANDING, THE CROWD QUIETED in anticipation of what was coming. Carz walked up the ramp onto the stage. Flomina followed him, being pushed in her wheelchair with Filo in her lap. The crowd cheered for the Leader and his family, but when Mar followed Flomina onto the stage, the crowd yelled even louder. She wondered if Mel was the recipient of this ovation, but he hadn't climbed the ramp yet. This adoration was for her.

Mar was flabbergasted as she waved to the two hundred thousand people in the Arena. She noticed her image on all the giant viewing screens posted around the stadium. She'd never imagined this kind of reception for herself. She saw this day being about her son's return. All those years in that Prevor Industries office, she'd just been doing the job laid out for her by Mado and Yorlik. She never expected the Kodan people to notice.

Carz stood at the podium, extending his arm toward Mar and waving her over to him. When she reached Carz, he took her hand and lofted their arms upward in triumph. Everyone in the stands stood, chanting, "When all else fails…when all else fails…when all else fails."

Carz said in her ear, "This is really something. I couldn't wish for a better partner. I can't tell you how happy I am right now. We're gonna succeed. I know it."

Mar was already overwhelmed by the crowd, but she was rendered speechless by Carz's words. The reality of having the planet's government supporting her efforts after all the years of being scared of them and sneaking behind their backs was something she would never have fathomed. She didn't know what to say. She kissed Carz on the cheek. The crowd stopped chanting and erupted in a cheer. Carz reciprocated and the crowd shouted even louder.

Carz said into Mar's ear, "I should probably introduce your son now."

Mar took a few steps back and waved Mel to her side. Flomina's attendant wheeled her and Filo until they were parallel with Mar and Mel. Flomina said something into Filo's ear. Mar assumed Flomina was telling him what was happening. Mar noticed Suron, his men, and Carz's guards lining the sides of the stage. She stared over her shoulder at the WAEF, looming behind her.

Carz turned on the microphone mounted on the podium. His image was now the only one on the Arena's viewing screens. The onlookers quieted and a smattering of boos emanated from the crowd.

"My dear Kodans," Carz said, his voice ringing out in the Arena. "We have just witnessed a momentous event, marking a new era in our history. Yorlik the Great was silenced upon his return home. My father threatened violence on him and his family if the truth was told about his discovery. Two decades later, Professor Vanderlord attempted to tell us the truth about his great-grandfather's voyage, too. Again, my father's government told you that this was a lie. I am here today with the return of the WAEF to officially tell you the truth. The habitable planet revealed in this Arena at that Breeze Celebration so many years ago does exist and Professor Vanderlord returns to us as a hero, a savior, with the coordinates to our new home planet in hand."

The crowd gasped, then stood in unison, cheering and chanting, "When all else fails…when all else fails… when all else fails."

Carz's mic picked up a loud thud coming from the WAEF. The crowd stopped chanting and erupted in an ear-piercing screech of elation. Carz turned to face the WAEF, then Mar and Mel followed suit. Flomina's attendant directed her chair in that direction, too, and she held Filo around the waist so he stayed put.

The activation of the WAEF's docking-bay walkway had produced the thud and it was now extending toward the stage. The crowd began chanting again. When the walkway reached the stage, the WAEF's door slid open and the crowd went eerily quiet. They didn't want to miss Yor's appearance, but there was no sign of him. Murmurings of confusion arose in the extended silence as the audience wondered what was happening.

Then Yor appeared in the doorway wearing his great-grandfather's silver and orange spacesuit. The crowd erupted in cheers although it sounded like half of them were screaming. Mar observed people on the field fainting. Yor's pause before exiting the ship displayed a dramatic flair, and when he walked deliberately toward the stage, he was doing it again. His image was the only one on the Arena's viewing screens and his sun shield was down. A hand reached up from behind the stage and placed a microphone at the end of the walkway.

Yor picked up the mic, stepped onto the stage, and flipped up the sun shield on his helmet. The image on the viewing screen zoomed in on Yor's face. Since Mar had last spoken with him, Yor had grown a beard laced with grey and the resemblance to his great-grandfather was remarkable. Everyone began chanting, "When all else fails!" at the top of their lungs. Yor peered over at Mar and mouthed the words, "I love you," reminding Mar of the last time she saw Rajer. She began weeping with joy, holding her face in her hands. Mel put his arm around her and waved to Yor who gave him a thumbs-up.

Carz removed the mic from the podium. He said something, but nobody could hear him. The crowd was too loud. Carz signaled to the stage crew to turn up the mic, then spoke into it again. "Welcome home, Professor Vanderlord," Carz said, and this time he could be heard above the cheering. "From all the citizens of Koda."

The crowd quieted.

Yor said into his mic, "Thank you, Leader. Words cannot express my joy at returning home after so long. I've missed my mother. I've missed my friends. I missed Koda. I know we have hard work ahead, but I'm hopeful that the foreseeable future before us is a bright one." Yor winked at Mar.

The crowd began chanting, "When all else fails" until it built into a din like nothing Mar had ever experienced. Her tears had subsided, and she was now overwhelmed at this outpouring of love for her son.

Yor placed the mic on the stage beside him and threw his arms up in triumph with a smile plastered across his face and the crowd cheered in response.

Mar thought, *Yorlik would be proud.*

AFTER THE CEREMONY, MAR HUGGED MEL GOOD-bye and went to meet Carz, who had requested to speak with her under the stage and unveil a surprise.

All the officials and guests had gone home, and Mar was waiting with Suron surrounded by bare tables and empty chairs when Carz passed through the curtain with his guards. Behind him, Orn entered in restraints with guards holding him on either side.

"Mar, I have a gift for you," Carz said. "I'd like you to be the first to know that Orn Shiv is being arrested and charged for the bombing of the estate and conspiring against the Kodan people in connection with the purge."

Mar said, "I can't say I'm surprised."

"Roneh has also been arrested and charged for the bombing of the estate and conspiracy. Both arrests will be broadcast to the entire planet tonight."

Orn said to Carz, "Tell her the best part."

"What does he mean?" Mar said.

"Nothing," Carz said.

Orn said, "Don't be modest. Tell her what you did."

"Take him away," Carz said.

The guards grabbed Orn's arms and attempted to move him toward the curtain, but Orn pulled back and was winning the tug of war. He said, "You should tell her. I couldn't be more pleased."

Carz said to one of his personal guards, "Help get him out of here."

Straining against the strength of the younger men, Orn said, "I always knew you had it in you."

The extra guard pushed Orn from behind and they began to make progress, getting him through the curtain.

Mar was impressed. Orn was nearly forty years older than the guards, but whatever was driving him gave him the vigor to overwhelm them. She said, "I want to hear what he has to say."

"She's going to find out anyway," Orn said. "You shouldn't shirk from your achievement."

Mar said, "What is he talking about, Carz?"

Carz said, "All right. Bring him back."

Orn practically dragged the guards in Mar's direction.

Carz said, "Tell her, Orn."

Orn stood facing Mar and said, "I murdered Minok for our Leader."

Mar gasped. "What? You had your brother killed?"

Carz said, "He conspired with Roneh in the bombing."

"Maybe you are your father's son after all."

"I know. It's wonderful," Orn said.

"I did what I had to do," Carz said. "Maybe this is what ruling dictates. Distasteful decisions are part of the job."

"I'm so proud," Orn said.

"Get him out of here. Now!" Carz barked at the guards who led Orn away.

Mar said, "I don't know what to say."

"This is none of your concern. It's family business," Carz said. "And if it were discovered that my own brother was involved in the bombing, the opposition would think we were weak and take advantage. Now nobody will ever know."

"You're making excuses for murder. You could've just arrested him."

"That wouldn't have been sufficient," Carz said. "I couldn't let my moron brother keep running around, ruining everything. He was a liability, and I say good riddance. I did us a favor."

Mar said, "I might've been wrong about you."

"How so? This doesn't change anything. You got what you wanted. I got what I wanted. We've got our work cut out for us. Let's focus on that."

A guard rushed into the under-stage area, halted in front of Carz, snapped to attention, and said, "An urgent message, Leader."

"What is it?" Carz said in an annoyed tone.

"Two of the four guards who arrested Roneh Rayush turned on the other two, stunned them, and escaped with her."

RONEH

Roneh heard the executive cruiser enter the airspace above the estate and the distinct sound of its hovering engines as it prepared to land. Carz, Filo, and Flomina were returning from the event.

Roneh had been waiting for a few hours in the dark, in silence, sitting on the bed that she'd formerly shared with Carz, alone with her thoughts. She recalled the day when the newest Global Assembly budget had landed on her desk. She'd flipped through the numbers for the Allegiance Program and discovered the Watch would be cancelled. She tried to discuss this decision with Carz, but he wouldn't speak with her, and his unreasonable conduct didn't end there. He formed an alliance with the mother of a traitor and partner of a terrorist so he could build spaceships for the disloyal, then he pardoned the traitor and staged a celebration around the traitor's homecoming, and on top of all that, he had Roneh arrested.

Sitting in the darkness, Roneh was seething mad. Carz had lost his mind. She was ashamed to be partnered with such a turncoat, and she intended to set him straight.

Filo burst through the bedroom door and ran up to Roneh.

"Mama, Mama, you should've been there. You should've seen the spaceship. I wish you'd been there," Filo said, speaking fast and excited. "And Papa said he'd introduce me to the spaceman."

"He did, did he?"

"I missed you." Filo leapt onto the bed beside Roneh and embraced her.

Flomina rolled up to the doorway in her wheelchair.

Roneh said, "Why don't you go with Grandma and get in your jammies? She can tuck you in. I need to speak with your father." Roneh kissed him on the cheek.

Filo jumped off the bed. "Papa said you'd sing me the 'When All Else Fails' nursery rhyme tonight before I go to sleep." Filo grabbed her hand and tugged her toward the doorway. Roneh didn't budge from her perch on the bed.

"Your grandmother can sing to you," Roneh said. "You don't want to keep her waiting."

Filo jumped back onto the bed again and kissed Roneh on the cheek. "I love you, Mama."

"I love you, too," Roneh said, kissing Filo again. "Now run along."

When Filo arrived at Flomina's side, he relayed what his mother had said to him. Flomina gave Roneh a dirty look before she and Filo disappeared down the hallway.

Roneh waited until the sound of Flomina's wheelchair and Filo's steps faded, then she rose from the bed and walked through the mansion to the study. Carz wasn't there. When she turned down the dark hallway toward Carz's current bedroom, no guard was standing by the entrance, which was odd, but there was light emanating from under the closed door.

She tried to open the door, but it was locked so she knocked. There was no answer, so she knocked harder and said, "Open up, Carz."

Carz said from behind the door, "You have some nerve coming here. I have nothing to say to you, but I'm alerting the GSS so they can arrest you properly."

"That's all right, but let me say my piece before they get here."

Carz groaned. "Actually, that's not a bad idea, because from this point forward you'll be out of my way."

The door lock disengaged. Roneh entered the room, closed the door behind her, and relocked it. She headed straight for the bed and sat down.

Carz was standing on the other side of the room, talking on his comm. When he deactivated his comm and placed it in his pocket, he pulled a cushioned chair toward the middle of the room and seated himself facing Roneh. "The GSS is on the way so say what you need to say," Carz said. "By the way, I've had a wonderful day and wanted to thank you for not attending. Your son loved it. He talked all the way home about how he wanted to be like Yor Vanderlord. I promised to take him to see Yor tomorrow in quarantine."

"Yes, he already told me."

Carz was smirking.

"You think you're so clever," Roneh said. "Anything else you want to gloat about?"

Carz paused, grasping his chin between the thumb and fingers of one hand, pretending that he was thinking. "No. That's it. You can speak now, but make it brief."

Roneh stood up and stepped towards Carz until she was directly in front of him. "I've been trying to talk with you for days."

"Yes, I've been avoiding you. I was hoping you'd be smart enough to notice, but hoping hardly ever gets you anywhere. Strange, isn't it? People are always hoping things will get better, that someone will appear, or something will happen out of the blue and grant their wish for them. People just need to take matters into their own hands. Don't you—"

Roneh slapped Carz across the face and yelled, "Will you shut up!"

"That's a good example," Carz said and felt his face with his hand where Roneh had hit him. "Although I thought you were stronger. Did you hold back?"

"You're a failure as Leader," Roneh said. "You're pathetic, encouraging the worst elements into believing they're relevant to Kodan society."

"The worst elements, as you call them, do seem happy with me."

"For now, but they're not loyal to you."

"As my father and you fail to realize, political discourse is a good thing."

"Ha! You think any of those fools will act for the good of the globe?" Roneh said. "This unification nonsense is a waste of time. You just need to pack the Global Assembly spaceships with loyalists. The Watch program has allowed me to compile a list. Then we can escape this planet and leave the disloyal behind."

"How can you think one life is more valuable than another based on their political beliefs?" Carz said. "You'd blithely commit another genocide. It's mind-boggling."

"You're weak and you're a disgrace to the memory of your father."

"My father," Carz said. "Maybe you should have part-nered with him. You have no respect for me. You never loved me. I think it's time we parted ways, which will be easy once you're arrested and executed."

"You need me."

"You obviously didn't catch the Celebration today," Carz said, rising from the chair. "I don't need *you*!" Carz raised his voice and jabbed a finger in her direction.

"You do," Roneh said. "You're just too stupid to realize it."

"I'm done talking," Carz said. "You're starting to ruin my day."

"I'm not finished."

"Yes, you are," Carz said. "I'm calling the guards, and they'll hand you over to the GSS when they arrive."

Carz took his comm from his pocket, activated it, and turned it toward Roneh so she could see him press the autodial for security. Roneh shoved Carz with both hands. He backpedaled, tripped over his own feet, and fell, hitting his head on the armrest of the chair.

Roneh gasped and rushed to Carz. No matter how she felt about him, he was still the Leader. Carz lay on the floor, groaning and cradling his head. His comm had flown from his hand and across the floor, his call to security was beeping on its speaker. Somewhere in the vicinity, a comm was buzzing like an echo of Carz's.

Then a window slid open and Glym climbed through it into the room. He said, "Perfect timing." From his pocket, he removed his comm, which was buzzing from Carz's call and deactivated it.

Roneh said, "What were you doing out there?"

Glym said, "I was climbing the scaffolding with some friends who'd like to meet with the Leader."

Three men dressed in black emerged through the window into the room, holstering sidearms. Insol Renta entered behind them, also clothed in black and carrying a weapon.

Carz got to his feet and said to Glym, "What's going on? Who are these people?" He winced and grabbed the back of his head.

Glym said, "A small group from the Movement who are going to end the Plemso dynasty."

"That's ludicrous," Roneh said.

"Not at all, and we have you to thank for setting it in motion."

"I would never."

"You know, you might be right. Minok should get the credit. He encouraged me to apply for a position here some time ago because he wanted a friend around and it was an opportunity to plant a Movement operative inside the Leader's home. When I heard through a member of our faction about the plan to bomb the estate, we made sure the attack produced an opening in security."

Carz said, "The guard who stopped coming to work and ended up in a dumpster."

"Minok didn't know about that," Glym said, "but he was involved in Roneh's scheme and was happy to help me. He was confident you would be traumatized by the bombing and if you ran into me on the rooftop, my presence would make you feel nostalgic and safe, and you'd hire me."

Carz said, "Minok wasn't that smart."

"Obviously you underestimated him, although becoming Head of Security was pure luck," Glym said, brandishing his sidearm. "As far as ending the dynasty, we all came prepared." Glym pointed his weapon at Carz.

Carz said, "Why are you doing this, Glym? We're family."

Glym cackled. "Family? You're more deluded than I thought. Until recently, you hadn't seen me in years. You weren't even at my father's funeral."

"My father was there."

"Yes, and he gave a hilarious eulogy, making fun of my father," Glym said with sarcasm. "My father ran himself ragged his entire life, serving the Leader's every whim and being abused by him. When my father was sick and dying, your father threatened incessantly to revoke his pension if he didn't get back to work right away. I'm surprised my father didn't get sick and die sooner putting up with your old man."

Roneh said in a defiant tone, "He was the Leader."

"That didn't give him the right to treat my father or anyone else that way." Glym returned his attention to Carz. "Your father was an abomination, and for all your grandstanding about unifying the people, you've already proven yourself as bad as him with the purge and—"

Carz said, "The purge wasn't my idea, and I'm not my father."

"Really?" Glym said. "How about having your own brother killed?"

"You killed Minok?" Roneh said.

One of the men dressed in black said, "Glym, they're stalling. We don't have much time. You distracted the guard, but he'll be back soon." The man broke off the door lock with the butt of his weapon so it couldn't be opened, then said to one of the other men, "Restrain the Leader."

The man grasped Carz's arm to put restraints on him, but Carz kicked him in the kneecap. As the man screamed and bent over in pain, Carz hit him with an uppercut, knocking him to the ground.

One of the other men approached Carz from behind and put him in a choke hold while another placed restraints on Carz's wrists and held him in place. Glym picked up Carz's comm from the floor and deactivated it.

Roneh reached into her pocket and activated her comm. Insol knocked it out of Roneh's hand, then punched her in the face. Roneh fell back onto the bed.

Insol stood over her and said, "That felt good."

Roneh sat up. "You can't do this."

Glym said, "Why not? He ended the lives of tens of thousands and now we're returning the favor by ending his family's tyranny." He pointed at Roneh and said to Insol, "Keep your weapon on her, and if she moves a millimeter, shoot her." Insol aimed her sidearm at Roneh.

The black-clad men put on black masks with only holes for their eyes. The one holding Carz moved him against the wall, then joined the other two. They all stood in line, unholstered their weapons, and pointed them at Carz.

Everyone on Koda was aware that two simultaneous shots from a civilian-grade stun weapon would incapacitate a person for days or put them in a coma, but three would guarantee death.

Glym removed a mobile vidcam from his pocket and began filming the scene. He said, "On this day, the Movement executes the Leader Carz Plemso for high crimes against the Kodan people. Do you have any last words?"

"You can eliminate me and satisfy your desire for revenge, but no matter what you think of me, I'm sincere in my attempt to save every Kodan citizen from the crisis," Carz said, his voice shaking. "You can take my life, but the person who fills the void will be far worse than me."

Insol said, "That won't happen, because the next person will be a President chosen by the people."

"Good luck with that," Carz said, then he peered over at Roneh. "Take care of Filo."

Roneh got to her feet and dashed toward the door, but Insol stiff-armed her. Roneh fell back on the bed again, then hollered, "Help! Help! Guards!"

Glym yelled, "Fire!"

There was a burst of weapons discharging. All three shots struck Carz at once, producing the smell of burning flesh.

Roneh vomited.

Carz stood frozen in place, then his legs buckled and his body collapsed to the floor.

"No!" Roneh screamed.

Somebody tried the door from the other side, then a guard in the hallway called out, "Leader! Stand back. I'm going to blow the lock."

"Hurry," Roneh shouted. "There are five intruders including Glym."

"Let's get out of here," one of the men in black said, heading toward the window with the others following. Glym was behind them.

Insol stood in the middle of the room, glaring at Roneh. "What about her? We can't leave an eyewitness."

Two of the men were already through the window. Another was climbing out.

Glym returned from the window and grabbed Insol's arm. He said, "Forget about her. We have to go." Glym pulled Insol toward the window.

The lock on the door exploded. A guard rushed into the room with his weapon drawn. He fired at Glym who crumpled to the floor, the mobile vidcam falling out of his pocket.

Insol fired at the guard and he collapsed.

More guards were running down the hallway toward the room.

Halfway out the window, Insol paused and said, "I hope this hurts, bitch." Then she aimed her weapon at Roneh and fired.

Roneh felt her midsection go numb, then the rest of her body, and she was losing consciousness while she watched Insol climbing out the window as a contingent of guards entered the room.

MAR

"I'm meeting up with Insol, then heading over to see you," Yor said. "In the meantime, you can watch me move the WAEF. You have the best seat in the house."

"I'm looking forward to hugging you. Quarantine was far too long," Mar said.

"You're telling me."

"Also, we need to make some decisions on how everything is going to proceed now that everything has changed."

"It's hard to believe."

"I know," Mar said. " We were so close to making something great happen."

"After finding out about Minok's murder, you have to think Carz may not have been who you thought he was."

"Sure, maybe Insol was right and the man really was a monster like his father, but that wasn't going to stop me from constructing more spaceships with the Global Assembly's assistance. Saving lives is my priority, and I would've dealt with the consequences of Carz's personality defects later."

"Killing your brother is a bit more than a defect."

"Look, Yor, I had to think about the millions I could save first."

"Sure. I get it."

"I do keep thinking about Flomina losing both her babies," Mar said. "Makes me feel lucky to have mine back home. Now, go do what you need to do. See you soon."

Mar deactivated her comm and walked out to the terrace railing, observing the twinkling of the city's lights and the bright beacon of the Plaza in the distance. She sat down in the antique chair, picked up a glass of Eglew juice from the low table beside the chair, and took a sip.

Fifteen days had passed since Carz's assassination. Vidor had left no formal path for succession and Minok was gone so Roneh had declared herself Leader. The majority of the Global Assembly reps had no desire to contest her claim. They were loyalists or stooges for the wealthy. There was no advantage in electing a President by the will of the people. Roneh was their best option, especially with her army of followers.

In her ascendance speech to the Kodan people, Roneh said she and Carz had decided that if he died, she would become Leader. Carz's assassin Glym Atmar was in custody and would be executed. She wove a tale about how Carz's unification idea was forced upon him by the Movement terrorists who bombed the estate. If Carz didn't follow their wishes, they had threatened to murder his family, including Roneh.

Mar chuckled at this fiction. She was one of the few people on the planet who were aware of Carz's honest intentions. In the days following Roneh's speech, the viewing channels spun a tall tale, showing footage of Glym doing his job, walking beside Carz, with a narrator describing Glym as a harbinger of doom. At the Arena celebration, Carz had wanted out of the blackmail and Glym murdered him. Roneh's followers and the Global Assembly loyalists bought it. There were even non-loyalists who wondered why Carz was acting so differently from his father, so they believed what the viewing channels were selling, too.

Mar was disgusted by the disinformation campaign. Even though Carz had shown a darker side of himself in his confession about Minok, she'd never had second thoughts about moving forward with their plans and was devastated about Carz's death. She knew it probably marked the end of working with the government to save the Kodan people, but she had attempted to contact Roneh and convince her otherwise. Kel had been fired, and Mar was rebuffed by Roneh's receptionist day after day.

Four days ago, Mar received word from the Prevor Industries techs who maintained the Global Assembly spaceships. They told her that Roneh planned on launching the ships as soon as possible. Vidor had inserted a fail-safe into his shipbuilding agreement with Prevor Industries. In the event that the domes began failing sooner than expected or the satellite telescopes found a viable planet, trained and loyal engineers, pilots, mechanics, and scientists housed at the launch site along with Prevor Industries techs would ensure the spaceships were ready for lift-off at a moment's notice. The techs said that Global Guards were keeping an eye on them so they couldn't leave without finishing their job. Roneh wanted the countdown close to launch when she arrived on site.

Suron's GSS contact also confirmed that Global Assembly reps, the wealthiest Kodans, and citizens registered under the Watch program had been sent digi-mails notifying them to get their families ready to leave the planet. They'd been given instructions on what they could bring on the spaceships. They had eighty-seven hours to board a ship or be left behind. Special cruisers at specific locations in each dome had been assigned to ferry them to the launch site.

Roneh and the loyalists were leaving, and Mar would need to fill the vacuum. She'd find someone who was sympathetic to her efforts and have them form a government. The new government would mobilize the Kodan people to leave the planet before the domes failed.

Powers-That-Be help me, Mar thought, then she slugged down the remaining juice in her glass. A bright light radiated from the Arena and the WAEF appeared above it. She stood and walked over to the railing. The dome above the Arena reflected back the incandescence of the engines. The WAEF hovered above the Arena for a few moments, then moved away from the Plaza toward the field on the edge of the dome where the WAEF had been placed on wheels for the Breeze Celebration parade all those years ago.

After Carz's assassination, for Yor's protection, Suron had posted guards around the clock outside the WAEF and the quarantine pod. Even so, Yor didn't feel safe in the midst of the Plaza and wanted the WAEF moved as soon as possible.

Mar didn't think he should worry. If Roneh cared to arrest Yor or destroy the WAEF, then she would've done it already. Mar also argued that wherever he landed the WAEF, Roneh could strike at will, but Yor thought if the WAEF were parked in the field it would have greater maneuverability for escape from any threat.

As the WAEF flew off into the distance, Mar noted an ominous stillness in Capitol City. Roneh had lengthened the curfews so fewer rail cars were running at this early evening hour, and other than the WAEF, there were no cruisers flying overhead.

Maybe Roneh was just focused on getting ready to leave, but Mar was concerned by her silence. In Roneh's speech, she threatened to wipe the Movement off the face of the planet in retaliation for the assassination, but she hadn't taken any sort of retribution. She hadn't gone after Yor, either. Roneh was playing at something, and Mar needed to figure out her game.

She was also troubled about the habitable planet's coordinates. When Yor was heading to Koda, he had presented the coordinates to Carz at a private viewing-screen meeting. That had been part of the pardon agreement. Roneh had the coordinates now and Mar was concerned about the ramifications. If Roneh and her loyalists arrived at the habitable world first, then how would they greet the rest of Koda's population upon their arrival? Mar couldn't stop thinking about it, but that was a problem for the future. She needed to grapple with the present and figure out how to get as many Kodans as possible off the planet.

The WAEF was now a speck of light in the distance.

Then there came Suron's familiar knock on the terrace door. Mar's heart raced. The only news these days was bad news.

Without turning around, Mar said, "What is it now, Suron?"

"Disconcerting reports."

"Has the proverbial shoe dropped?"

"Not yet. You might want to sit down," Suron said, walking to join Mar at the railing. "The Global Assembly spaceships are—"

Mar's comm buzzed.

RONEH

Roneh waited at the end of the ramp in the hangar, examining the Global Assembly spaceship stationed in front of her. Even though it'd been built by Prevor Industries, she had to admit that it was an astounding feat of engineering. The other ship was docked in a hangar nearby in the same facility in the Mauan mountains.

Above her, the hangar roof began opening to reveal clear skies. Originally, she thought Carz's exodus scheme was born out of fear that the Kodan people would never love him and that by placating them, he could bring them into his fold. With access to the latest GACE report showing the fallibility of the domes, Roneh thought Carz's sense of immediacy to leave the planet and Vidor's spaceships made complete sense. For the good of the globe, Vidor had prepared for the possibility of the domes' failure, for the day when these magnificent spaceships could be launched and a new Koda could spring forth on a new planet populated with his true followers. His foresight and wisdom were clear. Now, as Leader, she would complete Vidor Plemso's plan.

In the distance, a hangar doorway slid open. The Supreme Commander of Global Assembly Forces entered and was heading her way.

A voice came over a speaker. "Eighteen minutes to launch."

The Supreme Commander snapped to attention a few meters from Roneh and saluted.

Roneh returned the gesture and said, "Status report?"

"Spaceship Leen's hatches are secured. All passengers are in cryo and the crew is ready for lift-off. Spaceship Rayush is securing all hatches and waiting for you to board while prepping for launch. All passengers, including your son and Agent Shiv, have been placed in cryo."

"Are Phases One and Two in place?"

"Yes, ma'am," he said. "Ready for implementation on your order."

"Very good. Do you have a comm for me?"

The Supreme Commander removed a comm from his breast pocket and handed it to her. "The number is already programmed in."

"Wait here until I'm finished."

"Yes, ma'am," he replied. "We need to board at twelve minutes to launch."

"This won't take long, and they won't leave without us." Roneh turned away from the Supreme Commander and walked a few steps up the ramp. This was her moment. She wanted it all to herself and she couldn't help but smile. She pressed autodial.

Mar Jeps answered the call. "Hello?"

"Hello, Mar."

"Roneh?"

Roneh's smile broadened as she heard panic in Mar's voice. "Yes, it's me."

"I've been trying to comm you for days."

"Yes, well, I've been busy," Roneh said, glancing over at the Supreme Commander who looked impatient and concerned. "First of all, I want you to know that Glym has been pushed out a dome exit. Unfortunately, I don't have time for theatrics. Is Suron there with you?"

"Yes, he just walked in."

"Did he tell you anything yet?" Roneh said, turning away from the Supreme Commander again.

"No."

"Fantastic. First, tell Suron that his spy Tarq is dead. And I wanted you to hear directly from me that I'm about to bomb your Shamban base out of existence and destroy all your terrorist spaceships," Roneh said with glee in her voice.

There was silence. Roneh could almost feel Mar's shock through the phone.

Roneh said, "Are you there?"

"I beg you, Roneh. Please don't. There's no reason."

"See, that's where you're wrong. There are so many reasons that I don't have time to explain right now, but the best reason is the sound of despair in your voice and the joy it brings me."

"Why would you condemn so many to death?"

The distress in Mar's voice made Roneh laugh out loud. She couldn't contain herself. It felt so good. "Oh, yes, and Insol Renta won't be around much longer, either. She helped murder Carz."

"What do you mean?"

Roneh deactivated the comm, tossed it onto the ramp, ground it under her heel until she heard it crack, then waved the Supreme Commander over. He approached and halted in front of her. Roneh was exhilarated by the call. She wanted to bask in the moment, but there was no time. She said, "Alert the cruisers in Shamba to begin Phase One and give Phase Two the go-ahead."

"Yes, ma'am," he said. "You should board now."

"I will do nothing of the sort until I hear you make the comm."

The Supreme Commander stood staring at Roneh, unmoving.

Roneh said, "Is there a problem?"

"Are you sure you want to do this? And what about the loyal battle-cruiser pilots you're leaving behind? They have no idea."

"I won't ask a second time," Roneh said, reaching behind her for the stun weapon tucked in her waistband under her blouse. She pulled the weapon out and pointed it at the commander. "And I won't regret shooting you and leaving you here so you can perish with the other disloyal morons on this dying planet. Do I make myself clear?"

"Yes, ma'am." The Supreme Commander removed a comm from his pocket and activated it, then pressed a button. "Yes, it's me—"

Roneh snatched the comm from the commander with her free hand. "Is this the officer in charge of operations? This is your Leader."

The voice over the comm said, "Yes, Leader. It's an honor."

"Yes," Roneh said. "I want you to enact Phases One and Two and I want to listen while you do it."

The Supreme Commander grabbed at the comm and Roneh kicked him in the balls. He doubled over groaning, then Roneh shot him, and he collapsed on the ramp.

Roneh said into the comm, "Do it now! If you disobey, I will have you thrown off Spaceship Rayush."

Roneh heard the officer say, "Phase One Commander, you are a go." Then a voice coming from a comm speaker at the operations station responded, "Copy that. Phase One is go."

"Now, Phase Two."

Roneh heard the same dialog with the Phase Two Commander, then she said, "Thank you for your service. Now go to cryo."

"It's been a pleasure to serve, Leader," the officer said.

Roneh deactivated the comm, then threw it in the distance. She peered down at the Supreme Commander's unconscious body and kicked it. "Such a disappointment."

As Roneh strode toward the spaceship, she recalled the ramp where she had attempted to shoot Yor Vanderlord and Rajer Jeps had tackled her. "You've come a long way, baby," she hollered out loud, her voice echoing in the hangar. She cackled as the spaceship door slid open at her approach.

She would lead the true Kodan people to populate the habitable planet and leave the unworthy to die. Her destiny had been fulfilled and she'd had the last laugh.

YOR

Earlier in the day, Yor's mother had a Prevor Industries employee leave a cruiser in the field where Yor would land the WAEF, and now he flew it to visit Insol at Royal University.

First, he went to Insol's campus apartment. At this time of night, he assumed she'd be there, but after knocking on the door countless times and calling out her name, Insol's neighbor emerged. She told him that she hadn't seen Insol in days.

Yor decided to check Insol's office where he noted the brand-new Prevor Industries door and the security cam posted over it, then knocked. He'd seen light in Insol's office windows before he entered the building so he knew she was here.

Yor knocked again, waved to the cam, and called out, "Insol, I know you're in there and I'm not leaving until you speak with me."

Insol said, "What makes you think I want to?"

"Because you're talking to me now."

Insol groaned, then the door lock disengaged. When the door slid open, Insol was standing in front of him. The voluptuous young woman in her late twenties from Yor's past had just turned fifty, and she was still gorgeous with streaks of grey in her hair. If his mother hadn't told him about providing Insol with the prosthetic eye, Yor wouldn't have known it.

     Howard Libes

Yor said, "You look—"

"Like crap."

Yor chuckled. She still had her sense of humor. "No, I was going to say incredible, as beautiful as ever."

"You were always the flatterer, but I'm not going to sleep with you," Insol said. "You might as well come in. The door needs to be shut."

Yor stepped into the office and past Insol. A mat with a sleeping bag and pillow on top of it lay in the corner of the room furthest from the windows and door. The armchairs had been moved aside, and the emergency shelter was open.

Insol closed the door and the locks engaged.

Yor said, "Expecting somebody?" He walked to the windows overlooking the campus's serpentine paths lit by lampposts.

Yor said, "I missed this view."

"When you abandoned the people of this planet, you obviously found one more to your liking."

"Abandoned?" Yor said, turning toward Insol.

"Yes, when you ran away and hid for twenty-two years."

"Ran away and hid? You know what would've happened if I'd returned sooner."

"You would've faced what everyone in the Movement faces every day."

"My coming back early wouldn't have done any good," Yor said. "I learned more about space travel, about things that'll be important to the Kodan people in the future, than if I'd been hiding in a hole." Yor pointed to the shelter.

"Many in the Movement see you as a coward."

"Do you?"

"Yes," Insol said without hesitation. "I do."

Yor went cold. He'd been so happy to see Insol when he entered the room and now he was filled with anger and a sense of betrayal. "I'm sure your life hasn't been so tough sitting in this office."

Insol strode up to Yor and got in his face. "I've gone through a lot in the name of the Movement," she said, poking her forefinger into Yor's chest.

Yor swatted Insol's hand away. "Don't do that."

"I was assaulted and raped. I was in a coma. I lost an eye. I went through rehab to walk again," Insol said. "In the purge, my uncle and brother were killed, and friends I've known for thirty years were wiped out of existence along with their families by the new Leader."

"You don't have to worry about him anymore. Now there's an even worse person running the Global Assembly."

"Yes, that's unfortunate," Insol said. "I thought the Kodan people would rise up and take control of the government, but the assassination didn't go as I planned."

"Wait," Yor said. "You planned it?"

"Is that so hard to believe?"

"It was you and not Atmar?"

"Glym was there."

"Do you know what you've done?"

"What needed to be done."

"Your actions have undermined everyone's chance of survival."

"You live in a fantasy, Yor. Not everyone survives. You should return to outer space where you belong. A vacuum. This is reality," Insol said, turning and heading toward the door. "You should leave now."

"Is this your reality? Living behind a barricaded door and surveillance cams, ready to jump into your shelter?" Yor said, walking toward Insol who was unlocking the door.

"Yes."

"You call this living?" Yor said. "How long can you do this?"

"However long it takes."

"Why not stay at the Complex?"

"And be your mother's prisoner? No thank you."

"From what I've heard, she was protecting others from you."

Insol slid open the door. "Perception is reality," she said. "Now leave." She pointed into the hallway.

Yor exited, then turned to Insol. He saw anger in her face, but also sadness in her eyes. "If you'd like to get hold of me, you can call me," he said, removing a comm from his pocket. "I can give you my number."

"Goodbye, Yor." Insol slammed the door shut and the locks engaged.

Yor walked along the hallway, then down the stairwell. He was stunned by Insol's hostility, but he couldn't blame her. She was the product of her personal experience, which had been full of violence and death. Rage had consumed her and now controlled her. She had become a monster of a different stripe.

When he was outside, Yor sighed and activated his comm. His mother had been calling and she'd left a handful of messages.

Yor sat down on a bench facing Insol's building and peered up at the lit windows. His comm buzzed. Sadness swept over him. Since he'd found out that he was returning home, he'd been looking forward to seeing Insol. He still loved and cared for her, but that relationship only existed twenty years ago. It had died on the vine. He wondered if there was anything he could do to revive it. His comm buzzed again. Insol's office light turned off. Yor answered the call.

Before he could say anything, his mother said in a panic, "Why haven't you been picking up? Are you all right?"

"What's wrong?"

"Roneh called and threatened Insol, and you were planning to see her. I thought you might've gotten caught up in it."

"And Roneh isn't one for empty threats."

"Exactly," Yor's mother said. "She claimed she was about to destroy the Shamban facility, then hung up. I've attempted to call Rika, Lek, anybody there and all their comms are down. Suron is looking into it."

"That would be tragic."

"I haven't said anything to you, but the Global Assembly spaceships are launching shortly," Yor's mother said. "And Roneh has the habitable planet's coordinates. Even if we get there, she'll never let us live there, too, and you have to imagine she'll bring the military with her so—"

Yor broke out laughing.

"I don't see what's so funny."

Yor couldn't help himself. It felt good to laugh after his meeting with Insol. "Those coordinates won't work."

"What do you mean?"

"I wasn't sure whether we could trust Carz so I gave him the coordinates for the habitable planet with Prevor as the point of origin. He trusted you and didn't have time to verify them, and obviously, Roneh hasn't checked," Yor said. "When she arrives at the coordinates, thinking Koda was their point of origin, there will be nothing but more outer space." Yor realized his comm had gone dead. He didn't know what his mother heard him say.

Then he heard the sound of an air-battle cruiser's engines getting louder and closer. He spotted the cruiser descending in his direction. He stood up from the bench and was about to run when a missile zipped overhead and an explosion knocked him off his feet.

MADO

Mado walked along the shoreline. Clo skipped ahead of him, snaking in and out of the receding and incoming surf. He looked over his shoulder at the ramshackle shack that was his family's current home. It was barely big enough for all of them to lie down on the floor and sleep. Mado had spent last night staring up at the sky through the gaping hole in the roof, wondering about the future.

Fifty-three days ago, the doctor had told Mado that the Prevorian Protectorate had been notified about Clo. Subsequently, Mado found out that the Protectorate had decided to use Clo's case as a way to distract the public and hold on to power.

It seemed the prosperity that had blessed Prevor for centuries was coming to an end. Space Travelers had been journeying further than ever and returning home without detecting the vital resources that could replenish Prevor's.

Household items considered staples were now more difficult to purchase, and Prevorians were unhappy with this turn of events. They questioned why Space Travelers were failing in their primary mission when the Space Agency received a preponderance of the Protectorate's funding. The public wanted answers, and they'd threatened to vote out the current members of the Protectorate.

In the midst of this controversy, the authorities were informed by the Protectorate Medical Council that one of their most famous Space Travelers had a child who might be a telepath. They jumped on this as a way of diverting the public's attention from them. They held a press conference about their ongoing investigation into why Mado and Alba hadn't reported the birth of a possible telepath and whether the Space Agency was covering it up. Shortly thereafter, Mado and Alba received notice that they'd been suspended from their jobs while the Protectorate looked into their behavior.

A future date was set for Clo along with her brother and sister to be taken to Triniti, the Prevorian capital, for examination by the Protectorate's top physicians. Mado discovered that by order of the Protectorate, the physicians were concentrating their attention on the two brain scans indicating telepathic ability and were disregarding the falsified negative one.

If Clo or her siblings were found to possess telepathic abilities, then the Protectorate would not only have the fodder to save their positions of power by blaming the Space Agency for negligence, but would also proceed with the sterilization and exile of Mado and Alba's extended family.

As soon as the doctor told Mado how the results of the brain scan had gotten away from him, Mado began planning for the worst. He wasn't going to allow his family to be ruined by this foolishness. He and Alba were in agreement that the time was coming to relocate on Prevor where the Protectorate couldn't find their family. The next step would be leaving the planet, so they'd require a reliable mode of transportation for space travel.

Assuming that he and Alba would soon lose their jobs, Mado had stolen a power source for a spacecraft, and he had researched the Agency's database for a spacecraft that was decommissioned for age instead of bad condition, and which hadn't been parted out yet. While he still had the clearance, he visited the spacecraft graveyard to guarantee that the one he wanted was space-worthy. When he'd decided his choice fit the bill, he removed the spacecraft's tracker.

After being suspended, Mado and Alba made an arrangement. Alba still wanted to persuade the authorities that if Clo was raised properly by her parents, she wouldn't be a threat to Prevorian society and could live a normal life under Protectorate supervision. Mado wouldn't abscond with the craft until she felt that her efforts had hit a dead end. She began at the lowest level of Prevorian governance, but jurisdictions from local to district explained that Protectorate law existed for a reason, no matter how archaic, and they meant to apply it. There was no room for compromise. Of course, the lower-level bureaucrats didn't dare counter the authorities above them about adherence to doctrine because they feared losing their cushy jobs. Alba was told this off the record more than a few times.

Stymied in her efforts, Alba gave Mado the go-ahead to move forward with procuring the spacecraft, but she thought it was too dangerous for him to do it alone. She offered to assist him, but Mado balked at the idea. Alba was in the latter stages of pregnancy. She wasn't physically agile and there was no reason to endanger the unborn child. Also, if things didn't go well, the children would be without a parent. Mado agreed help was required and believed Pino was the best candidate.

Pino was a prankster at heart, and Mado thought he could use this attribute to their advantage. They had twenty-seven days before the authorities would come for Pino and his sisters. They hadn't been taken into custody because Mado's subterfuge was inconceivable in a society based on the Prevorian code of honor and the Protectorate wanted to prolong their preliminary investigation to showcase their distress over the Space Agency's negligence. Mado explained the seriousness of the task ahead to Pino and began training him.

Alba worked with Clo and Jana to get the household packed for a quick escape. Pino and Jana attended school as usual so there would be no hints of what the family was planning. Clo had been banned from close proximity with other children, so Alba homeschooled her.

The night of the heist the entire family ate dinner together and performed the traditional sharing of their feelings. Jana broke down crying, which caused everyone around the table to be enveloped in feelings of sadness, anger, and confusion.

Mado refused to allow his family to wallow in these emotions. He said, "I won't stand for it. Tonight, I refuse to live by the dictates of our feelings. We need to see beyond them. We need to understand that the consequences of our actions tonight will shape our future. I have confidence in the strength of each individual here, no matter how small, no matter how young, to do their part, so tomorrow at supper we'll be basking in how each member of this family has supported one another. That's who we are. That's our strength. Am I right?"

There was a moment of silence as the entire family looked around the table at one another.

Mado repeated, "Am I right?"

Alba said, "Yes, of course."

The children said in unison, "Yes, Father, you're right."

"Now, let's enjoy our dinner and the company."

The spacecraft graveyard was a half-evening's swim from the shore near their former home. Pino was a strong swimmer, so Mado wasn't concerned about him making the distance or having any problems with the current. In fact, Mado assumed Pino would beat him there, because Mado had the power source on his back. Pino proved him right.

When Mado emerged from the water within walking distance of the graveyard, Pino was already sitting on the beach smiling at him.

Pino said, "What took you so long?"

Mado chuckled. "I would've told you to conserve your strength, but I know better."

Pino stood as Mado approached. "That swim was exhilarating."

"Glad you enjoyed it," Mado said. "Now comes the serious part of the plan."

"No problem," Pino said, bouncing up and down on his heels. "I've got it covered."

Mado placed his hands on Pino's shoulders and recalled the focus it had taken to piece together the shattered engine of the WAEF.

Pino stopped bouncing up and down.

"Remember that feeling," Mado said. "I know your role involves something you do well and enjoy, but it's imperative that you visualize the details in working toward the end result."

"Yes, Father."

"All right," Mado said, patting Pino on the shoulder. "Let's go!"

The graveyard had one guard. He was an ex-pupil of Mado's who washed out of the Corps and was offered this job as a reward for his incompetence. The position was meant to afford him time to study, and after working as a guard for a while, he would be given the opportunity to rejoin the Corps and become a Space Traveler. Mado knew the young man well. He was friends with his father and had watched him grow up, but Mado didn't believe he had the ability to become a Space Traveler. He wasn't inquisitive or intelligent. He was easily distracted, out of shape, and a hostage to the pleasures of eating and drinking.

He was in the guardhouse when Pino knocked on the window. Pino and the guard had socialized at functions where their families commingled for a meal, and they got along well. Mado thought the young man would be surprised but pleased to see Pino. Guard duty was tedious and Pino was known to be fun, and that's where Mado used Pino's skills to their advantage. Pino was carrying two things: A drink that Mado had concocted at home and a set of juggling sticks.

Mado would find out later the guard said to Pino, "What're you doing here?"

"I was bored and there's no school tomorrow. I remembered that you worked here so I snuck out and swam over. I stole something tasty from my father, too. Are you thirsty?" He reached into his pack and removed the jug containing the drink. He uncorked it and handed it to the guard through the open guardhouse window.

"What's this?" the guard said, examining the jug.

"Have a sip. It's Dawa that my father makes," Pino said, pulling the juggling sticks from his pack. "It'll take the edge off your horrible job."

As Pino began juggling, the guard sipped from the jug, then took a few gulps. Dawa was a cherished Prevorian libation that was only broken out on special occasions. The guard was excited at the treat and took another gulp. Mado had also laced it with a fast-acting hallucinogen.

Pino's juggling became a hypnotic streak of colorful trails, and the guard was mesmerized while continuing to sip from the jug.

Mado watched this interaction from a distance. When he was satisfied the guard was preoccupied, he snuck through the fence. During his earlier inspection of the spacecraft, Mado had buried a manual crank nearby. He unearthed the crank and used it to open the main hatch, then sealed himself inside the craft. The mobile utility light housed near the hatch assisted him in finding his way to the engine room where he installed the power source.

Mado was running up the spacecraft's systems when he noted the craft had received a transmission. He thought it might be an old message that had been saved before the craft was shut down. He activated the communication system to erase it.

A voice said, "Mado, stand down. We see the energy signature. We know that you illegally hacked the Agency's security system to abscond with the decommissioned spacecraft and suspected you stole a power source. We told the security guard to notify us if there was any suspicious activity."

Mado thought he'd hidden his tracks better, but somehow the authorities managed to detect him. Undaunted, he continued prepping the spacecraft for launch.

The voice said, "Mado, stand down. This is your final warning."

Mado said, "I don't think I will." Then he turned off the communication system.

Out of the control-room window, Mado observed a Protectorate Security craft hovering by the guardhouse where Pino was still keeping the guard busy, aiming a spotlight on the scene. Another spotlight shone into Mado's control room from a Security craft above him.

In the distance, Mado watched Pino climb atop a graveyard spacecraft, then begin leaping from one junked craft to another, headed in Mado's direction. The security vehicle followed, hovering behind Pino with the spotlight on him.

Mado removed the emergency escape ladder from a utility closet, then ran to the main hatch and opened it. He attached one end of the ladder to plugs in the floor directly inside the hatch, then threw the ladder out the hatch and ran back to the control room. It had always been part of the plan to pick up Pino with the ladder. Mado jumped into the pilot's chair, pushed it closer to the control panel, and powered-up for lift-off.

Mado took the steering mechanism in hand and launched vertically. He was aware that the Security craft was still above him, but he hoped its pilot was smart and fast enough to avoid a collision. Mado's spacecraft was bigger and sturdier with more powerful engines and could seriously damage the Security craft. When there was no impact, Mado noted the vehicle careening starboard out of control.

Mado pushed the throttle on the impulse engines, pinning himself to his seat, and headed on a collision course with the craft following Pino. Mado was taking a calculated risk. The pilot of the Security craft had already seen Mado's recklessness with his companion and he had two choices: Move out of the way or stand his ground and bet that Mado wouldn't collide with him.

As Mado passed over Pino and closed in on the Security craft, he could see fear in the pilot's eyes and at the last moment, the Security vehicle veered off to port.

Mado passed over the graveyard's fence line and slowed down, then steered one-hundred-eighty degrees and flew back. The guard was sitting against the guardhouse, drinking from the jug. The Security vehicle pursuing Pino had crashed and was wedged between two decommissioned spacecraft. The pilot was climbing out of the top hatch.

Mado didn't spot Pino and began to worry, then he noticed a light on the control panel indicating that the main hatch had been closed. Mado heard Pino's footsteps behind him.

Pino said, "I'm here, Father. I caught the ladder and climbed up like we planned. It was fun."

Mado breathed a sigh of relief and said, "Great job, son. Now hang on."

The craft previously above Mado's had regained control and was now in pursuit. Mado went to full impulse power and headed for a nearly orbital altitude. The Security craft wasn't built for that kind of speed and didn't have orbital capability, so Mado easily lost him.

Mado embraced Pino. They'd done it. Since Mado had removed the spacecraft's tracker, nobody on Prevor would be able to find him.

When they reached the beach by the family home, it was low tide, so Mado landed the spacecraft on the shore. Alba had already piled their baggage outside the house and they quickly loaded up. It was logical to believe that the authorities were on their way. They flew off to a remote island that Mado had chosen for its small, isolated population, and on his scouting mission there, he'd discovered the abandoned ramshackle hut.

Mado didn't sleep much that night, staring through the hole in the roof, thinking about the multitude of Prevorian laws he had violated by stealing the spacecraft. He plotted what was next for his family. They couldn't stay on Prevor. They'd always be on the run. He had thoughts on planets to explore, but he had no idea about their final destination.

Thinking about the past fifty-three days leading to this moment, walking along the shoreline with Clo skipping ahead of him, Mado realized that he'd put Koda behind him for good. His family had his full devotion. He loved them more than anything in his existence and like last night, he would do anything for them.

Then out of nowhere, one of the alien spacecraft appeared and landed about fifteen meters ahead of Clo who began running toward it. A doorway appeared in the craft's smooth metallic dome and a ramp extended from the doorway to the beach. Clo was almost at the ramp when Mado hollered for her to stop, but she ran up the ramp and entered the spacecraft.

Mado stopped at the foot of the ramp and heard a voice in his head say, "Come, Mado. We have much to discuss."

Mado walked backwards up the ramp, seeing Alba by the shack in the distance calling to him, but he couldn't hear what she was saying.

He shouted, "I need to retrieve Clo. Be right back."

She held her hand up to her ear. She couldn't hear him, either.

The voice said, "She'll be all right, Mado, and you'll want to hear what we have to say."

Mado waved to her, then turned and headed up the ramp. As he approached the spacecraft's doorway, it dawned on him that the saying "Make of it what you will" had ancient Prevorian origins. He wondered why he hadn't thought of it before. He walked into the craft, and the inner chamber was exactly the same as the one he'd experienced at the way station. He approached Clo who was standing still in the middle of the room with her head tilted back and both sets of eyelids closed as if she were dreaming.

"What are you doing to her?" Mado said out loud.

"She's being welcomed by her people," the voice in his head said.

"Her people?"

"You've already realized that she is one of us. We were exiled from Prevor a hundred millennia ago," the voice said. "We are ecstatic to greet her. She will be an important leader in the future, and she completes us."

"Completes you?"

"Yes. As a collective, every consciousness completes us."

"Is that why you're here?"

"A consequence, but we're also here to help."

"*Now* you're here to help? You're a little late."

"From our perspective, we're early," the voice said. "Please tell Alba and your children that you're all coming with us. Load your belongings onto our ship."

"Not until you explain where we're going."

"We'll explain on the way. You can trust that we'll treat you with respect and honor your wishes."

Clo opened her eyelids, turned to Mado, and said, "They're telling the truth, Father."

YOR

Yor had been unconscious. He didn't know for how long. When he'd struggled to his feet, he was shocked by the scene in front of him. Fire poured from the blown out windows of Insol's office and had begun consuming the rest of the building. Students wearing sleeping attire had gathered, watching the spectacle from a distance.

Yor presumed the missile was some sort of incendiary device. Even if Insol was in the shelter, Yor doubted she'd survived. Fire vehicles had begun to pull up outside the building and volunteers readied the equipment to spray fire retardant.

Yor remembered his mother's call and Insol telling him about Carz's assassination. Like the Shamban facility, this was part of Roneh's revenge. Yor thought about the WAEF and began to run. When he reached his cruiser, he engaged its engines and took off, speeding back toward the WAEF.

As the city passed below, he thought about all the Kodans who had no idea how their future had been altered. He wanted to go faster, but the cruiser was already at full throttle. He checked his comm and it was still dead. He thought about his mother and whether Roneh had attacked her, too. He contemplated turning around and going to Prevor Industries, but Suron would keep his mother safe in the tunnels under the Complex. She was probably calling from there when they last spoke.

     Howard Libes

Yor landed in the field at the edge of the dome and dashed out of the cruiser without shutting the door and sprinted toward the WAEF, which couldn't have been more than fifteen meters away. Due to not running hard for years except on the spaceship's treadmill, he was winded by the time he reached the WAEF. He removed a remote device from his pocket and activated it, and the loading bay ramp began to descend. He didn't wait for it to open all the way, just enough for him to dive through the open space and rolled into the WAEF. As he stood, he hit the button on the wall to close the ramp, then ran upstairs to the control room where he darted around activating the necessary systems.

Yor commed his mother again using the WAEF's transmitter, but the line was dead. He commed Suron and the line was dead. Mel had given Yor his comm information, but his line was dead, too. Yor wondered if in another spiteful act, Roneh had destroyed the planetary communication array.

The proximity alarm went off. Yor's heart raced as he turned on the radar scope. Multiple objects were headed toward the WAEF from all sides. Yor turned off the alarm. He couldn't tell the size of the objects from the scope, but he assumed they were missiles fired from an air-battle cruiser at a distance.

Yor leapt into the pilot's chair and secured his harness, then flipped the switches for lift-off. He engaged the main engines with as much power as he thought was safe inside the dome. He decided it'd be best to fly out through the collapsed section of the dome. If he did it fast enough, he could break through the temporary covering, which was nothing more than an enormous extreme-weather-proof tarp.

The missiles were getting closer.

In the distance, he could see that Prevor Industries wasn't burning. He caught sight of the objects headed toward the WAEF. They were larger than any missiles he'd ever seen, moving faster than he would have imagined possible and still closing in on him.

He decided to throw caution to the wind and increased the engines' power, but the missiles seemed to be gaining speed and were coming at him from every angle. He wouldn't reach the breach in time, and he saw no way of evading the missiles inside the dome.

Yor thought, *Is this how I die?*

A voice over his comm said, "No reason to rush off, Yor."

At first, Yor thought he was hysterical, because the voice was Mado's. And that's when the objects speeding toward the WAEF were close enough for him to see that they weren't missiles at all, but a fleet of the alien spacecraft.

"Mado?"

"Yes, it's me," Mado said. "Slow down, will you?"

Yor throttled back on the engines.

"And we're fine," Mar said.

"Mother?"

Mado said, "Have you hit your head? You seem to be asking obvious questions."

Yor chuckled. "I have, but…how? I'm surprised to hear from both of you and see these spacecraft."

"Join the club," Yor's mother said.

Yor cut the main engines to minimum power and engaged the hovering engines. The fleet of spacecraft encircled him.

Noticing motion out of the corner of his eye, he released the latch keeping the pilot's chair in place, then spun around to see holographic images of his mother and Mado. "Where are you both?"

Mado said, "I'm on the fleet's command ship."

Yor's mother said, "I'm at the Complex being conferenced into…I guess this is some sort of comm."

"Strange," Yor said. "I have lots of questions, but the one that comes to mind first is what's going on here?"

Mado said, "The Vorians—that's what the aliens call themselves—have come to help your people leave this planet."

"What happened to the Shamban facility?"

"The facility was badly damaged in Roneh's attack," Yor's mother said. "We've lost almost half the ships, but casualties have been minimal. Lek and Rika are fine."

Mado said, "The Vorians are going to help in rebuilding your spaceships and ensure you get to where you want to go safely, but there's a catch."

"There always is," Yor stated sarcastically. "I thought you said they didn't want to be involved in affecting the course of history?"

"They say, 'The present is history,' whatever that means. They know how you tricked Roneh. They say that'll cause the loss of all the lives on the Global Assembly spaceships and they can't abide that," Mado said. "But they have a solution to the animosity between Roneh and her loyalists and the rest of the Kodan population."

Yor said, "I'm listening."

"There's another habitable planet in the solar system where Yorlik discovered his world. The Vorians are giving you the choice of whichever you prefer and they will guide Roneh's spaceships to the other. When all Roneh's passengers have disembarked, the Vorians will take away the ships and the Kodan technology so Roneh can never reach out and harm you. The Vorians will erase all the passengers' memories of Koda, and they will keep watch over their descendants," Mado said. "You'll have a choice between the third planet from the sun in the system, which is your great-grandfather's discovery, or the fourth."

Yor said, "How do we choose?

Mado said, "The Vorians will leave it up to your mother and I think its best if I stay out of it."

Yor said to his mother, "What do you think?"

"I'm not sure," she replied and threw up her hands. "From the information they've given me, I'm leaning toward the fourth."

"I was telling her," Mado said, "we should call the planet Mars."

Acknowledgements

A PROJECT LIKE THE SEEDER SERIES DOESN'T COME to fruition without the assistance of other people. First of all, I'd like to thank David Weddle who told me to write this series for the joy of it, without any other expectations, and his words resonated with me many times over the past eight years. Around the fourth draft of each book in this series, my critical readers—Elise Crum, Jeff Forester, Kathleen Kaser, David Weddle, Jim Berg—gave me invaluable feedback which greatly improved the final product, and my proofreaders Cheryl Krauss and Dustin Lanker were key to the final polish of Books Two and Three.

Dave Snider graced me with his singular talent in creating the stunning covers for *Foreseeable Future* and *What You Will.* Those books without those covers are unimaginable. I'd also like to thank the people behind the *When All Else Fails* cover design, Tony Figoli and Claire Flint Last, who laid the foundation for the graphic imagery that's symbolic of the entire series.

I have many wonderful family and friends who supported me in this process, but in particular, I'd like to express my gratitude to Adam Wendt, Tom Matott and Bennett Libes. Finally, more than anyone else, my sister—Marcia Libes Simon—deserves my gratitude for reminding me in the final months of her life that this existence is brief and tenuous and I should follow my bliss.

HOWARD LIBES has been a writer for more than thirty years and is a graduate of the University of Oregon Writing Program. He edited the 2,300-page manuscript of *If They Move…Kill'em: The Life and Times of Sam Peckinpah* by David Weddle (Atlantic/Grove Press) and worked as a collaborator—writer and interviewer—on *Among the Mansions of Eden: Tales of Love, Lust, and Land in Beverly Hills* by David Weddle (William Morrow/HarperCollins). He has been a freelance writer for many publications, including *Los Angeles Times Magazine*.

Currently, he is tapping into his lifelong obsession with science fiction. *When All Else Fails* (Happy Mistake Publishing) and *Foreseeable Future* (Happy Mistake Publishing) are the first two books in The SEEDER series.